Laura is a writer, editor and actor. As well as writing novels, she has penned several film and television projects for her production company Sibylline Films. Laura is also co-founder of Three Fates Theatre Company, and has performed across theatre, film and television. She lives in Naarm, Melbourne.

@lauramccluskey__

Also by Laura McCluskey

The Wolf Tree

Laura McCluskey

THE CURSED ROAD

HEMLOCK PRESS

Hemlock Press
An imprint of HarperCollins*Publishers*
1 London Bridge Street,
London SE1 9GF

www.harpercollins.co.uk

HarperCollins*Publishers*
Macken House, 39/40 Mayor Street Upper
Dublin 1, D01 C9W8, Ireland

Published by HarperCollins*Publishers* Ltd 2026

1

Copyright © Laura McCluskey 2026

Laura McCluskey asserts the moral right to be identified as the author of this work.

A catalogue copy of this book is available from the British Library.

ISBN: 9780008681517 (HB)

This novel is entirely a work of fiction. The names, characters and incidents portrayed in it are the work of the author's imagination. Any resemblance to actual persons, living or dead, events or localities is entirely coincidental.

Printed and bound in the UK using 100% Renewable
Electricity at CPI Group (UK) Ltd

All rights reserved. No part of this publication may be reproduced, stored in a retrieval system, or transmitted, in any form or by any means, electronic, mechanical, photocopying, recording or otherwise, without the prior written permission of the publishers.

Without limiting the exclusive rights of any author, contributor or the publisher of this publication, any unauthorised use of this publication to train generative artificial intelligence (AI) technologies is expressly prohibited. HarperCollins also exercise their rights under Article 4(3) of the Digital Single Market Directive 2019/790 and expressly reserve this publication from the text and data mining exception.

*To the people who notice when you're not there —
even when you're right in front of them.*

THE DOE

The first breath of freedom feels like being born again.

Not because it's joyful, or because it carries a sense of arrival, or of being received into warm and welcoming arms. Newborns don't scream because they're happy to have made it out – they scream because they're scared of what comes next.

That's what this first breath feels like: fear, as if she's been dropped from a great height into a place where everything is strange and unknown and full of shapeless threats and bared teeth. Though she wears jeans and a stolen jacket that protects her upper body from the breath-snatching chill, she feels completely naked right now, running for her life through the suffocating darkness that precedes the dawn.

And the worst thing is, this was the plan – knowing that cold air would burn her nose and throat, that frost would soak the hem of her trousers, that her head would pound and chest ache and legs feel like jelly. Because she got out – she's *outside* – and now, instead of restraints and doors, there's only grass and rocks between her and her destination.

The road.

It's been weeks since she was last out here – she *thinks*. Time is blurry and she can't remember when she last ate or drank anything that didn't make her head spin. Her toes are already numb, ankles and shins soon to follow, but after grabbing the boots there wasn't time to find socks as well as the jacket, and the jacket was far more necessary, considering what she has sealed up inside it. What she intends – if she makes it out of here – to show the world.

Her ragged breaths almost drown out the thud of her pounding heart, but she both hears and feels a splash when she plunges to her ankles in boggy water. One of her boots is immediately swallowed in grasping mud, and she wastes precious seconds trying to free it before she's forced to continue on with one foot bare. Somewhere close by, she thinks she hears an echo of her escape, a phantom set of feet, but she can't risk looking back now – not when the road is only yards away, down a short but steep embankment, and when her hunter knows this land as intimately as a lover. They are master of its peaks and divots, its traps and shadows, and she knows that – factors it into every desperate step across this unfriendly ground.

But she didn't factor in that the moon is under the hunter's dominion, too – suddenly, the clouds part and light floods the hills, as bright as midday sun. The shock of it makes her falter, one misstep turning into a stumble.

And that's when she hears the *crack*.

She doesn't feel the impact right away. What she does feel is confusion when her legs suddenly stop communicating with her brain, when her knees plant into the earth, when she slumps onto her side just an arm's length from the edge of the embankment.

But when she finally realises what's happened, and a man's boots skid to a halt beside her head and harsh hands rip at the buttons of her jacket, the next thing she feels is *rage*.

It wasn't meant to go like this; not just the plan tonight, but every moment of her life that led to this one – her blood watering the grass of a foreign land, her eyes gazing up at unfeeling stars. This plan was just one of hundreds she made in her short life, plotted out and pursued with a singular desire to make the world better for those who can't do it for themselves.

She's always been a sucker for a good cause.

But rage is a magician's fire – it flares and fades, and is just as quickly replaced with the original fear: *what comes next?* As she feels the heat leave her chest, her jacket empty of everything now except ribs and flesh and a failing heart, she is struck yet again with the sensation of being a newborn.

And, like a baby who has just been delivered into this big, wide and terribly cruel world, she opens her mouth to scream.

CHAPTER 1

It takes less than six hours for the press to start calling her Bambi.

The moniker is as cruel as it is inaccurate; in the story, Bambi survives. What they really should have called this woman, her body found in a remote area of the Scottish Highlands just before dawn this morning, is 'Bambi's Mother' – especially after the pathologist dug out the bullet, a .270 Winchester, from between her third and fourth ribs.

'A perfect shot,' one local police constable was quoted admitting, 'if you thought you were bringing down a deer.'

But just as effective in bringing down a person, George thinks as she thumbs through the article on her phone. According to this tiny piece, barely two paragraphs long, a .270 is a popular calibre among deer stalkers. Both fallow and roe deer are in season right now, which means amateur and professional hunters from all around the world will be descending on Scotland with the intention of bagging a buck – or a doe.

The journalist has clearly had a great time with that play on words, too, labelling the unknown woman 'Scotland's newest Jane Doe' – despite the term rarely being used in any official capacity here. They must be gambling on their readers being fans of American crime shows in order to understand the poor-taste pun.

Despite the constable's hedging, the tone of the article hints at foul play rather than an accident – but if the author has evidence to support that theory, they haven't deigned to share it in this piece. It wouldn't be the first time a journalist has opted for sensationalism over fact.

She inhales deeply and closes her eyes.

I can think, I can move, I'm all right, she reminds herself.

'George?'

Nowadays, those words feel less like a mantra and more like a curse.

'*Inspector Lennox.*'

Her phone hits the floor with a thud.

Dr Kassab smiles as George scrambles to pick it up. Luckily for her screen, his office is cushioned with plush carpet and other soft textures in shades of grey and white that are probably meant to encourage introspection and sharing, or at least make you feel safe enough to crack open your rib cage and let the muck pour out.

She sits in her usual spot, on the right-hand side of the couch, slightly curled into the arm. He's in the boxy armchair, long legs crossed at the knee.

'You seem distracted today, George.'

She tries to mirror his relaxed posture. 'I'm fine.'

'Mm. And the last two weeks?'

'Yeah, all right. Nothing to report.'

Dr Kassab just smiles again. He has always accepted her small lies in exchange for harder truths.

But then he nods towards her phone. 'Something going on?'

'Oh, it's nothing. Just work stuff.'

'I see. Do you need to reschedule—'

'No, no, it's nothing to do with me. I'm not assigned to anything that ... important at the moment.'

'I see,' he says again, one of his favourite responses, and George swallows around the discomfort of knowing that when he says that, he means it.

She was anxious and on edge during their first session – still nervous being out in public with news segments continuing to spit out her name, and struggling to articulate the mess in her mind – and spent most of their time together devising reasons to not come back, as she'd done very successfully with the three therapists she'd tried *before* finding Dr Kassab. Left feeling patronised and misunderstood after each of those experiences, she didn't have high hopes for this latest attempt. But there was something about his demeanour, his endless patience and the melodic rhythm of his accent that brought her back for a second session ... and then every fortnight since.

'Any progress with your colleagues?'

She makes a *so-so* gesture. 'It's back to normal, for the most part. Some people are still a bit ... awkward around me. But like I've said, I don't blame them. Besides,' she adds with an indifferent shrug, 'no one's ever accused me of being Miss Congeniality.'

He tilts his head, ignoring the diversion. 'You don't think you deserve a bit of grace? You served your time. Pun intended.'

She acknowledges his joke with a twitch of her lips. To the public, her month-long administrative leave in February was explained away as a Police Scotland policy, designed to protect the mental health of officers involved in serious incidents. But everyone within Police Scotland knows what a punishment looks like, no matter how you dress it up.

'I still have a job,' she explains. 'That bothers some of the less ... understanding ones.'

Dr Kassab nods, but he also makes a note on his pad. 'How are the headaches?'

Relieved by the change of topic – if only to a slightly less difficult one – George rushes to answer. 'Less frequent. And gone within a few hours if I turn off all the lights and drink a couple of litres of water.'

'You're still not using painkillers?'

'Not worth the risk.'

'And you're not using any other medications?'

'Not unless you count the heroin I swiped from the evidence room.'

He laughs, and she allows herself a smug smile. Humour may be a crutch, but it's one she can wield like a weapon.

The headaches he's referring to are a lingering consequence of a case George worked a couple of years ago. Entering the house of a murder victim named Margaret Villo, she was attacked by the killer and fell from a balcony. An extended hospital stay was followed by crippling paranoia and an addiction to prescription medication.

The memory makes her smile wilt, and it has no reason to return after his next question.

'Any progress with the nightmares?'

She looks down at her phone, surreptitiously checking the time. Eighteen minutes out of their allotted forty-five have passed – it's moving slowly today. She knows there's a clock positioned strategically behind the couch, angled in such a way that Dr Kassab's eyes can slide to it from his patient and back without them noticing.

But George notices everything nowadays. The deep lines around Dr Kassab's mouth. The new leaf sprouting from the monstera in the corner. The lingering sweetness of an aerosol room spray. The rumble of cars on the busy street below. The twitch in her left eye, which she smothers under heavy blinks.

'George?'

'Er,' she stalls, rubbing the offending eye, 'only a couple of nights a week now.'

'Mm. The same one?'

She looks down at her fingers, flexing them inwards. 'I'm still being dragged across the ground. And then … the, er. The grave. And there's a push. And I'm …' She inhales sharply, gaze flicking to the door, the windows. 'Sorry, is it warm in here or am I …?'

Dr Kassab immediately leans forward to retrieve a remote from the low table between them. A quiet beep precedes a whirring, and a few seconds later George feels cool air against her hot cheeks. She runs a hand through her hair and looks down at the phone screen.

Twenty-one minutes.

'Is that better?'

She swallows. *I can think, I can move, I'm all right.*

'Better,' she says truthfully. But then her forehead falls into her shaking hands. 'Why is this still happening to me?'

'What do you mean?'

'This ... *panic*. I know where I am, I know I'm not in danger here.'

'Anxiety attacks don't care about logic. And there's a difference between what you know, and what you *know*.'

She looks at him through her fingers. His expression is compassionate.

'This won't last forever, George. I've worked with many people in very similar situations to yours. You've already made incredible strides – you might not see it, but I do.'

She nods, but an argumentative voice in her head protests. *Many people?* As far as she's aware, there's only one other person on Earth who can relate to how she feels after arriving on the lonely Hebridean island of Eadar for the sole purpose of investigating an alleged suicide, only to end up uncovering a century of bloody secrets. But she doesn't say that, because Dr Kassab leaps at any opportunity to discuss the other detective who worked that case with her; and though she might have made strides in some areas, George is nowhere near ready to let him prod that particular bruise. So she just smiles tightly and glances at her phone. Twenty-five minutes.

The rest of the session drags, and when Dr Kassab's eyes flick to the clock behind her, George is already rocking to her feet.

'Sure, sounds good,' she says, though she can't remember what he suggested or what she is agreeing to.

'Heading into work now?'

'Yes.'

'Well, I hope you have an uneventful day, DI Lennox.' He crosses to the door and opens it for her. 'I'll see you in two weeks.'

CHAPTER 2

It's almost an hour's walk from Dr Kassab's office to the station across the River Clyde, but she prefers the crisp November air to the claustrophobia of a train or bus, so after ducking into a café for a giant latte, she pulls on her gloves and sets off towards the South Portland Street Suspension Bridge. Her heart rate is still a little high after that episode, so as she steps onto the bridge, she focuses on her breathing.

In-in-in, out-out-out.

This technique didn't come from therapy; it's something her dad taught her when she was a kid, maybe eight or nine, and training for her school's cross-country race. Even now, twenty years later, George remembers the jarring thud of her feet pounding the asphalt path around their local park, her dad's voice as he effortlessly kept pace beside her.

'Steady breaths, Georgie. Three beats in, three beats out,' he said, reaching out to tap her chin, 'and keep your head up. Set little targets. The next big tree. That lady with her dog. The footbridge. When you pass them, set the next target.' He tapped her chin again, a reminder. 'Little wins until the big win.'

And she *had* won a few races over the years, came top three in most, and her dad beamed when she showed him the ribbons, regardless of whether they were blue, red or green. It was an early and informative lesson: for better or worse, she's built for endurance.

She's halfway across the bridge – where the concrete ripples and bunches underfoot like someone grabbed the end just before it set and tugged – when she raises the takeaway cup to her lips for a sip and the bottom drops out.

'*Fuck*,' she hisses, leaping back as coffee spills down her wrist, over her stomach and thighs. 'Fuck,' she says again, more quietly, examining the angry red patch blooming on the strip of skin between her sleeve and glove. There's no point even inspecting the damage to her jacket and trousers – she just hopes nobody will see the wet patches on the navy fabric. Despite the afternoon sun, there's a sharp wind coming off the Clyde today. True winter is still weeks away, but the days are growing shorter and the temperature drags its feet after the sun. The cold air presses against her wet thighs uncomfortably as she hurries on, grumbling to herself. Unlike her mental health, this streak of bad luck – ranging from vexing to life-threatening – that has been dogging her steps for the last couple of years has not improved with time.

Glasgow's city centre is busy today. There is the usual swell of people getting their Christmas shopping done early, tourists being overcharged for hot chocolates at Winterfest, and city workers like herself who have to fight the crowds simply to get from A to B. And George knows that as the temperature drops over the next few weeks, the holiday season will coat the streets: twinkling lights wound around poles and statues and trees, thick green garlands lining the eaves of department stores, and the dazzling projection on the City Chambers building.

She rounds the final bend, the police station ahead. A figure leans casually – or at least has made the effort of looking casual – against a wall between her and the front doors. He's holding a coffee cup and reading something on his phone.

She groans. 'This had better be a terrible coincidence, Shaw.'

Hendry Shaw looks up, his full lips already tugging into a wide grin at the sound of her voice. 'You're early! I thought

I'd be waiting another five minutes to see your gorgeous, surly face.' His eyes flick down to her trousers. 'Have you wet yourself?'

She picks up her pace, walking right past him. 'Have you forgotten what I said last time, about the sentence for a stalking conviction?'

He jogs to catch up, holding his cup carefully. 'Up to five years in prison,' he says, licking a drop of coffee from the lid, 'but it really only applies if I've caused you fear or distress. And I don't know about you, Georgie, but over these last few months I've come to think of us as friends.'

'Friends don't follow each other around all day with a voice recorder, and they definitely don't keep publishing bullshit stories. And it's Detective Inspector Lennox to you.'

'Oh, come on. Surely we can drop the formalities. Like *I* said last time – and the twenty times before *that* – you can call me Hendry.'

'I'll be calling you by your prisoner number in just a few months' time if you don't leave me alone.'

He has the gall to laugh, which isn't that surprising; nothing she says ever seems to faze Hendry Shaw, even when it's far more laden with expletives. Actually, today's dialogue is the most civil it's been in a while.

George appraises Hendry from the corner of her eye, the tail end of the laugh still curving his lips as he slips his phone into a pocket of his navy pea coat. She recognises it; it's the same one he was wearing the first time they met, back in January.

As soon as the sliding doors of the hospital's front entrance slid open, she was assaulted by the flash of cameras. The raised voices of the assembled journalists and onlookers blended into one another, a wall of sound that felt as hard to push through as the jostling bodies. A constable had one arm thrown around her shoulders, using his other to force a path, but for a few seconds she was worried that she'd get swallowed by the pack.

But then a new arm looped around her waist, and a loud voice joined the constable's in ordering people to move aside. And when they finally reached the police car, the constable pushed George and her new companion into the back seat without a second glance. The flashes continued, lenses pressed to her window.

'Here,' the man beside her said quietly as he draped a navy pea coat over her head and shoulders. He was around her age, with brown skin, short curls and pretty brown eyes. Based on his simple suit, she guessed he was either another detective or someone from the legal department.

'I'm not a criminal,' she said, even as she tugged the coat tighter around her face.

'If you don't get ahead of the narrative,' he murmured, '*they* get to decide for you.'

Sound rushed in with the opening of the passenger door as the constable climbed in, then cut off again with a slam. 'Fucking morons,' the constable muttered as the car pulled away from the kerb. He twisted to look at her. 'All right?'

'I've been in a crowd like that before,' she said, letting the coat drop around her shoulders. 'Just not used to being the one they're taking photos of.'

He laughed – but his smile disappeared when his eyes slid from George to her companion, who was now staring out the window with a strained expression.

'Who the fuck are *you*?'

The man sucked in a quick breath, then swivelled to face George. '*You* can control the narrative, Inspector Lennox. And I can help you do that.'

The last thing her companion said before being hauled bodily from the car was, 'My name is Hendry Shaw – my card is in the top pocket!'

She didn't call him, of course; though he managed to get her private phone number and call her at least eight times that first week. Her dad ended up answering, telling Hendry he could collect his coat at any time – though he may want to hurry, as 'it's currently sitting in a rubbish bin at the entrance to Queen's Park'.

Hendry must really be attached to that coat to have made the effort to fish it out, clean off the rubbish, and *still* wear it to bother her today.

'What do you want?' she asks bluntly. 'I've already told you, I'm not interested in a profile piece.'

Hendry clucks his tongue. 'The ego on you, Georgie. You're not the only woman in Scotland the public want to read about.' In response to her confused frown, he continues. 'The dead woman found up north early this morning. Gunshot wound to the side? I have a piece in the *Guardian* with what little I've been able to sniff out, but they won't give me front page unless I can prove it wasn't an accident.'

The description sparks recognition; this must be the article she read this morning. She didn't check the byline, but she's not surprised that Hendry broke the story. As frustrating as her own experience has been as the subject of his focus, she has to admit that his ability to find information is impressive. And troubling.

'Go fish somewhere else, Shaw. I'm not talking about an active investigation.'

'I won't put your name to it, golden girl. It'll be "a Police Scotland source".'

'Don't call me that.'

'Can't call you Georgie, can't call you "golden girl". How about we split the diff and go with GG?'

She grits her teeth, vehemently hoping that Hendry's boot catches a crack in the footpath. She'd enjoy leaving him sprawled across the ground as she walked away. 'Even if I wanted to help you, I don't know anything.'

He seems genuinely surprised. 'Aren't you their go-to murder girl now?'

'Fuck off.'

'I'm serious. I figured they'd be stamping your name on every dead body within a fifteen-mile radius. I mean, you single-handedly both discovered and cracked Scotland's biggest murder case of the last decade. Century, probably.'

George already feels like an exposed wire after dredging through these memories with Dr Kassab, and Hendry's words hit her like a wave you don't see coming: bone-chilling and breath-snatching – especially because they're not entirely true. She *didn't* solve the case single-handedly.

When she and her partner, Richie Stewart, were sent out to Eadar to investigate the death of eighteen-year-old Alan Ferguson, neither of them could have predicted the horrors they would uncover hidden behind the polite smiles of the secretive locals. George very nearly became their latest victim; at one point she was literally standing in a grave.

It doesn't help that her dogged actions on the island – though they resulted in Eadar's shadowy crimes being thrust into the national spotlight and similarly forced her onto the front pages – were also reckless enough to earn the censure of senior Police Scotland staff and drove a wedge between herself and many of her colleagues.

Before Eadar, Richie was one of her best friends. But now …

Hendry doesn't seem to realise that George is drowning in memories; when she doesn't reply right away, his tone becomes insistent. 'It could be worse, you know. I didn't have to kick off the hero cop angle; that was a choice I made because it was the more interesting story. And it worked – we were both the talk of the town for January, February and most of March.'

'And every few weeks since then,' she growls. It's only a slight exaggeration – whenever Hendry or one of the countless other reporters following the Eadar story unearths some new detail, George inevitably receives another fifteen torturous minutes of fame.

'Exactly! We're scratching each other's back.'

This brings her to a lurching stop. 'Do you actually think you've *helped* me?'

'I told you, I made the more interesting choice. And it shows – people read my coverage because I give them a reason to be justifiably angry with the police, but keep rooting for the amazing DI Georgina Lennox.' He grins. 'People love the underdog.'

For a second, she's breathless with anger. 'You made my life *hell*, Shaw. Your lot were crawling all over me, all over my family. I could barely leave the house—'

'Hero cop suspended because she broke protocol,' Hendry says, sweeping his hand through the air like a newspaper headline. 'Yeah, *total* hell.'

'I wasn't suspended,' she snaps. 'It was administrative leave.'

'I know that, *obviously*. My editor is responsible for the clickbait headlines – but still, it only makes you look good. And you're going to need all this goodwill when the inquiry starts.'

Her heated blood runs cold. 'What does that mean?'

'Come on, you know how these things go. They'll be combing through the Eadar reports looking for mistakes everywhere, even from you. *Especially* from you, if the Crown is still trying to figure out how to press charges. The investigators, the prosecution, the *defence* – they'll all be digging right in to find all the ways you might have fucked up.'

Her hands are starting to shake – she shoves them deep into her pockets. The smooth plastic of her phone case acts like a balm.

He incorrectly interprets her silence as a weakening of resolve; he steps closer, his expression earnest. 'Talk to *me*,' he urges in a low voice, 'tell me how it really went down out there. If it turns out that, yeah, maybe you didn't *quite* follow the rulebook – so what? I can make you a victim. I can make you a saint. I can make you untouchable.'

She bites her lip, looking up and down the street warily. 'You want the real story?'

'Yes.'

'Off the record, for now?'

He hesitates, then nods.

She closes the distance between them until her mouth is level with his ear.

'I'm *already* untouchable, Shaw,' she whispers. 'Remember that the next time you try to blackmail information out of me.'

She pulls away, enjoying the new slackness to his jaw.

'I read your article, by the way,' she continues, walking backwards so that he can see the derision on her face. 'Was it your idea to call her Bambi, or are you going to blame your editor for that one, too?'

He swallows, but strives for nonchalance when he shrugs. 'Got your attention, didn't it?'

'Because getting attention is all that matters to you, right?' She clicks her tongue. 'Classy. Can't *wait* to let you write my story.' Before he can protest, she adds, 'If you follow me to work, Shaw, I will slap a stalking charge on you so fast that the only thing you'll be remembered for is the self-destruction of your promising career.'

It would be such an easy blow for him to say that she's just about done the same thing; he's smart enough to see the irony. But he doesn't, and she realises that his silence is a far graver insult because it means that, beneath his flirty façade, Hendry pities her.

CHAPTER 3

Despite the repartee with Hendry, she's still early for her afternoon shift, though it's unlikely that anyone at the neighbouring desks is watching her closely enough to notice. And it's not like she's doing it for the brownie points, though her ledger is definitely still in the red on those.

She told Dr Kassab the truth earlier – the atmosphere at work is mostly back to normal. The majority of her colleagues offered her a polite 'welcome back' after she returned from leave, but she knows there are a few who are struggling to understand why she wasn't kicked to the kerb as soon as it was revealed that she was nursing a drug dependency for the entirety of the Eadar investigation. These holdouts don't make a secret of their displeasure that they're still rubbing shoulders with a colleague who was using while on duty. And, like she said to Dr Kassab, she can't really blame them – she's more surprised than anyone that she wasn't thrown to the wolves.

The first couple of weeks after stepping back onto the mainland were – are still – a blur. Her parents tried to take her home to Edinburgh, but she knew that once they sealed her into her childhood bedroom, they might never let her out again. Instead, they camped out on her living room floor for a month, cooked and cleaned and played music to fill the moments when she trailed off midsentence to clutch at her head or stomach. They even hired a specialist to monitor her withdrawal from the tramadol and zolpidem, when the nausea and hot flushes turned into intense stomach cramps and vomiting. During these moments, they gave her the additional gift of going onto the tiny balcony to cry.

Her sister, Jane, flew in from Dubai for a few days; friends dropped in with flowers and packed her fridge with food. But there was a notable absentee in the line-up of visitors.

Before Richie became her unofficial mentor a few years ago, George had acquired a reputation for being somewhat ... *prickly*, a response to the snubs, rejections and outright insults young women weather while rising through the ranks of male-dominated workplaces. In George's case, she opted for an offensive stance: strike *first*, and strike *hard* – a stance that she was battle-ready to deploy when she was introduced to Detective Inspector Richard Stewart, until she discovered that not only was he an excellent police officer, generous with his knowledge and gentle in his guidance, but he was also a kind, warm and funny person. He observed her icy exterior, understood it, and enthusiastically signed up for the painstaking process of thawing her out. She never lost her sharp edges, or the instinct to throw the first punch, but George can't deny that she was invited to way more social events after she and Richie were paired up.

She shifts in her chair, her wet trousers scraping uncomfortably against her thighs. Spilling her coffee was both the latest entry in her logbook of bad luck and a reminder – something all of her therapists agreed on was that she shouldn't aggravate her freshly diagnosed anxiety with caffeine. But she figured that after going off the tramadol and zolpidem cold turkey, and being encouraged by the withdrawal specialist to give up alcohol as well, she should be allowed to keep this *one* vice. It's something she can control, when every other part of her life often feels so wildly, terrifyingly out of her shaky hands.

And she figures twenty-nine is too old to take up smoking.

A message box pops up on her computer.

She wants to see you.

Then again, a smoke break would be very handy right now.

Superintendent Kylie Cole holds up a finger, her desk phone wedged between her bony shoulder and ear. 'We'll need to get the team leads in a room for that,' she says, pointing George towards a chair. 'No, I don't think Adrian is back yet. Might be worth trying to get him on the phone, though.'

A window behind Cole shows the overcast sky, the light peeking between plastic blinds. There aren't any personal adornments on the walls; even the nameplate at the front of the desk is standard issue, and the desktop monitor and clunky black phone are the same ones that sit on George's desk downstairs. It always feels a little chaotic in here – papers are spread out everywhere, pens and Post-It notes tossed around. A phone charger is tangled up in the mouse cord, and Cole has a real cup-collecting problem.

Cole hangs up. 'What a fucking day,' she groans, pushing her glasses up into her short blonde hair. 'Right, Lennox – how are you doing?'

George dips her chin. 'Yep. Fine.'

'Managing the work all right?'

She works to keep the grimace from her face. 'There's nothing too taxing on my plate, ma'am.'

There's a knock at the door and, without waiting for a response, DI Adam Farley strides into the room, eyes on a file in his hand. George fights the instinct to shrink; Farley is one of those officers who have made their opinion of her continued employment with the force evident.

'I'm looking at these satellite images again, boss, and I'm thinking we should take a few uniforms along to cover all that ground—'

He breaks off when his beady eyes land on George. She wonders if Cole sees the way his lips curl, how his narrow shoulders tighten. 'Oh. Pardon the interruption.'

'It's fine,' Cole says briskly. 'You were saying?'

But Farley is already backtracking to the door. 'I've actually – er, there's something I've left at my desk. Back in a mo.'

He closes the door behind him. There's a beat of silence, then George speaks.

'Yeah ... I've been doing really good.'

Cole purses her lips disapprovingly, and George braces for further interrogation – but the superintendent's next question surprises her.

'Have you spoken to Richie lately?'

George starts to answer in the negative, then hesitates. Technically, they spoke to each other just a few days ago – she held a door open for him, and he murmured a thanks.

When she and Richie returned from Eadar, there were a few days when they were still a united front, marching in lockstep into countless meetings with senior police staff and legal advisors. Together they answered questions for hours on end: *who was where, who were you with, who saw what, and when, and why?* It was a gruelling process made even more painful by the ominous tick of the truth bomb that Richie held in his hands – more accurately, the ominous rattle of pill bottles. And the day she showed up to a meeting room and Richie wasn't there, she knew that he'd finally dropped it.

Since then, they've been ... cordial. Polite greetings, a stiff nod across the room. For the most part they're like ships in the night, she and her old partner glancing off each other like the negative ends of two magnets.

'Not really,' George says, a little defensively. 'We're working different cases. Not a lot of time to chat.'

Cole *tsks*. 'You aren't just colleagues, Lennox. I know you're good friends.' Suspicion sparks in her eyes. 'You're not angry that he informed us about the drugs?'

'Of course not,' she replies quickly. 'He did the right thing. I only wish I'd had the guts to tell you about it before he had to.' Then she takes a breath and smiles tightly. 'Will that be all, ma'am?'

Though disapproval still tugs at her lips, Cole nods.

Back at her desk, George slides down in her chair until her head is level with its back, ignoring the curious look from her desk mate, and raises her trembling hands to cover her eyes. *In-in-in, out-out-out.*

No, she's not angry with Richie about what he did. He's a police officer first, her friend second. She's always known this ... and yet it didn't stop her from hoping, back when they were on the island, two drops of blood in a shark tank, that he'd grant her a little more time to prepare for the fallout.

In-in-in, out-out-out.

Gripping the armrests, she focuses on the air moving in through her nostrils, out through her rounded lips.

She's not angry with Richie.

She just really, really misses him.

CHAPTER 4

There are two locks on her front door – her dad installed the second one the afternoon they got back from the hospital. He found it hard to believe that she could work in Major Crimes and feel safe with just a standard lock: didn't she know, more than *anyone*, how dangerous the world can be?

She doesn't turn on the overhead lights when she enters her flat but navigates the short hallway through to the open kitchen and living area in total darkness until she can find the switch for the lamp. It casts a yellow glow across the small, neat space. There's a two-seater couch against one wall, a television mounted opposite. The narrow balcony is obscured by thick block-out curtains that her parents have instructed her to draw back every day – but after falling off one, she still doesn't feel too comfortable on balconies.

There are some framed pictures and a pot plant on a ladder shelf; a limp peace lily, an attempt by her mam to bring a better energy into the space. It flourished under her mam's care, but now that George is its sole provider, its yellowing leaves droop miserably. She's sure she could be doing something to help bring it back from the brink, but that would require more investment in its wellbeing than she has capacity for.

In her tiny bathroom she sheds her clothes, kicking them into the corner to be dealt with later, then releases her hair from its clip. Running her fingers through the oily strands to loosen it, she feels a little repulsed at the sensation it leaves on her skin. Thankfully, the water heats up quickly and she steps straight under it, saturating her hair then reaching for the shampoo.

It's on the second round of scrubbing her scalp that she pauses, her fingers lingering on the raised scar behind her ear – another souvenir from the Villo case.

Was that a knock at the door?

She's lived in this building for a few years now, and the rent is fairly reasonable for the area. A lot of young professionals are in this building, and it's mostly quiet save for some thumping music every other Friday. Her next-door neighbour must have just had a baby – George can sometimes hear it at night, wailing through the thin walls, a distressing sound that makes her skin crawl when it goes on too long and sometimes seeps into her dreams. But that's not what she heard just now.

She shuts off the shower and flings a towel around her body before pressing herself against the bathroom door. Her heart is beating so fast that she can almost feel the wood pulse with it – there's less padding between her rib cage and the outside world lately. When she can't hear anything, she cracks the door slightly and peers out. The open-plan space is actually very handy for someone with her strain of paranoia – she can see every potential hiding spot, and whether there are any knives missing from the magnetic strip on the wall beside the stovetop. Her bedroom door is open, too, and she kneels to check under her bed and then in her closet.

It's only after she's returned to the living room that she notices the broken pot.

'How the fuck …?' she mutters as she carefully makes her way to the ladder shelf, dodging shattered pieces of ceramic and spattered dirt. The lily itself has survived the tumble, standing upright with a good amount of soil still clumped around its roots. The top shelf has collapsed, knocking over a few pictures on its way down.

'My bad luck continues,' she mutters, taking in the damage. Thankfully the glass within the frames didn't shatter.

She retrieves a bowl from the kitchen and scoops the lily into it, pressing the soil down around the stem, her fingertips sinking into the earth—

She jerks her hand back, almost dropping the bowl.

Think, she tells herself quickly, *remember what Dr Kassab said about being present*. It takes concentration, discipline, a hand pressed over her hummingbird heart – she breathes in the familiar smell of her flat, hears the throb of electronic music from the upstairs neighbours, sees the glow of her lamp in the corner, touches the edge of the rug beneath the couch. *In-in-in … out-out-out.*

Leaving the lily and the mess on the floor, she beelines for the bedroom again. Her hair is still wet and a little sudsy; she lays the towel across the pillow and pulls the blanket up over her damp, bare skin.

The mess can wait for the morning.

The ground is cold, and smells of disturbed earth, brine and the unmistakable odour of rot. She can hardly see – the lamp is broken, or off, or it simply doesn't exist here, and the moonlight is subdued behind thick clouds. Part of the fear is the not knowing who or what is around her, even though this dream – this recurring nightmare – is rooted in real memories.

So she still jolts when the stubby fingers clamp onto her head, hook into her hair and start dragging her backwards across the ground. A deep, quavering voice chants, 'Sorry, sorry, sorry,' and she tries to fight back but her arms are rubber, her legs are lead, and her scream is pathetic, a breathy, frustrating whimper that barely passes her lips.

Then the hand releases her, and at the same time the ground beneath her disappears. Stomach flipping, she falls.

Down, down, down.

The sound of something vibrating yanks her from the breath-stealing freefall. When she wakes, her palms slap the mattress on either side of her hips as if to catch onto a ledge. It takes a second to orient herself; she pants, looking around in confusion.

She left her bedroom door ajar last night, and a slice of warm light from the living room lamp falls over her bed. As soon as she recognises the source of the buzz, she's up on her feet and dashing to the kitchen.

She barely registers the station phone number before she accepts the call.

'Lennox.'

'Can you come in early?' It's not Cole – maybe her new assistant? George has forgotten his name on multiple occasions and felt guilty every time.

She brings the phone away from her ear to check the time. 'It's half-five in the morning, and I'm not meant to be in until the afternoon.'

'I know, but you're needed. When can you get here?'

Despite her tiredness, something sharpens in George's brain – there's a note of urgency in his tone that he's trying to hide. 'What's going on?'

'When can you get here?' he repeats.

She rubs at her eyes, already heading towards the bathroom. 'Er … thirty minutes.'

'I'll let them know.'

He disconnects before George can press him for more information, and it's only when she's sitting in the too-warm interior of a taxi ten minutes later that she starts to wonder who he meant when he said *them*.

She isn't sure what she'd been expecting – some kind of uproar, people running in and out of offices, phones ringing off the hook. But the station is relatively quiet, the day shift having just taken over from the overnight crew. A few eye her curiously as she makes her way towards the stairs – but then Cole's assistant is there, waving her towards the lifts.

They don't speak on the way up, and he strides quickly towards Cole's closed door. He raps twice then swings it open.

Seated behind her desk, looking like she hasn't moved since their brief conversation yesterday afternoon, Cole nods a greeting. 'Thanks, Lachlan,' she says, beckoning George in. 'Put Maxwell straight through when he calls. And grab me a coffee, please, when you can. You need one, Lennox?'

She stifles a yawn. 'Please.'

Lachlan nods and departs.

'Thanks for coming in early,' Cole says, rolling her chair across the room to retrieve a stack of papers and a tablet from a side table. She unlocks the tablet and thrusts it towards George. 'This is what we've got.'

At first, the photos are confronting. George sucks in a quick breath, then steels herself to lean forward. If she's totally honest, she has seen worse – grislier, bloodier, more violent scenes of death. But there's something about the way this woman – late teens, maybe, though perhaps her unlined face is just good genes – is sprawled across the ground that makes George's throat feel thick. There's a graze on her left cheekbone, the one that's turned towards the sky, which hasn't bled much but sits atop a nasty bruise. Her dark eyes are wide, staring off to the side of the lens. Her lips are pale, slightly parted. Bleached hair that has started to go coppery fans out around her, the overgrown roots almost black in comparison.

George pauses on the next photo. It's another close-up – but this time, the camera is focused on the woman's torso. Blood has soaked through her quilted blue jacket, the stain concentrated underneath her armpit. And when George zooms in even closer, she can just make out the puncture in the fabric.

'Oh,' George breathes. 'Is this Ba— er, the woman from the papers?' Luckily, she caught herself in time – *Bambi* was on the tip of her tongue. 'She was shot, right? A calibre typically used in deer hunting?'

Cole grunts. 'When I find the bastard who leaked that detail, there are about twelve people waiting in line behind me to tan their hide.'

George assumes that threat is likely why the informant – *Hendry's* informant, she realises – is remaining deep in anonymity. She wonders if they went to Hendry with the information, perhaps as part of an existing relationship of information trading, or if Hendry sniffed out the story and charmed his way to the details. He really is annoyingly good at his job.

Having her suspicions confirmed has only left her more confused. 'Boss,' George begins tentatively, 'can I ask why you called me in early?'

The door opens; Lachlan enters with a mug in either hand. He deposits them silently, then exits again. Cole reaches for her mug and takes a long sip.

'We suspect she may have been tied up before her death,' she says, 'and that she was shot elsewhere.'

'Why do you think that?'

Cole gestures for George to keep swiping through the images. 'Not as much blood as there should be.'

At the first wide photo, George whistles through her teeth. In terms of final resting places, the killer didn't choose the location for its looks. Aside from the bright slashes of crime scene tape, the colour palette is grim, with patchy brown hills to the right, a grey, rocky outcrop to the left. If the photo were to be taken two weeks from now, she speculates that a thin layer of snow would transform this area into something more postcard-worthy; as it is, the seasonal rain has turned the land into a mire. The dirt road that cuts through the middle of the photo is riddled with dips and marshy holes; it would be an absolute nightmare to drive on in anything other than a four-wheel drive.

'See the cone?'

George spots the flash of yellow to the left, the small patch of rust-coloured grass beneath it – the body must have been collected before they took this photo.

'That's all there was, and no rain to blame. Not enough for the gunshot, says the pathologist, but even the first responders knew that.'

'Okay ... so she was shot somewhere and then dumped at that location?'

'Possibly. We've got people checking whether any petrol stations or residences in the vicinity have security cameras, but it doesn't seem to be standard practice in such a rural area.' Her lips thin with disappointment.

George peers at the outcrop, the hills beyond. 'Where is this, exactly?'

'Up in the Highlands. This road starts about half an hour south of Aviemore, at the top of a village called Kirkcree. It's a small place, but it's one of the Highland Gateways to Cairngorms National Park, so it sees its fair share of tourists.' Cole leans forward, pointing at the screen. 'This road winds east, then south for about twelve miles before it peters off into nothing.'

'Anything along that road? Farms, residences?'

'A deer-stalking company took over an old country house a few miles in, about sixteen years ago.'

George raises her eyebrows. 'I assume we're not treating the fact that she was killed with a bullet used for hunting as a coincidence.'

'They're currently sitting at the top of our persons of interest list, certainly. Two constables spoke with the owners of Fiadhain Lodge yesterday morning, but nothing fruitful came of it. The website says they offer "exclusive experiences",' she says, rolling her eyes, 'which means the constables walked away with nothing more than the phone number for their lawyers. They've thrown up quite a few roadblocks already which, if it were up to me, I would have bulldozed through and brought the whole company in for questioning. But,' she says, pasting a saccharine smile on her face, 'the owners are blessed with friends in high places, so we've been instructed to keep our distance until we have *approval* to approach them again.' Her disgust is evident.

Lawyering up isn't always an indication of guilt, but with all roads pointing to a likely culprit ... 'Who found her?' George asks.

'A couple of tourists. According to their statement, they thought they'd discovered a shortcut into the national park.'

A memory from yesterday resurfaces. 'Is Farley on this? Is that why he was asking about extra hands?'

'He was,' Cole says, her mug paused halfway to her lips. 'I called him about an hour ago to let him know it had been reassigned.'

'Oh. To who?'

Cole smiles. It's strained. And very pointed.

George groans. 'Why?'

'Well, from what I read in the papers, you're the only employee of Police Scotland who's actually doing your job.' Cole's delivery is dry, a sparkle of humour in her tired eyes.

George glowers, ignoring the bait. 'Why *this* case?'

'Isn't it enough that a young woman has died, and we need to know why?'

Leaning back in her seat, George waits.

After a moment, Cole's lips quirk up approvingly. She motions for George to hand her the tablet and swipes a few times before handing it back. 'Tell me what you see.'

The woman now lies on a sterile table, her clothes replaced with a plain sheet, her skin dull under the harsh lights. There are bruises that George hadn't noticed earlier; a shadow across the left side of her jaw, a fist-sized patch above her breast, polka dots in varying states of healing speckled across her arms. And George can now see the marks around her wrists, evidence of being recently restrained.

But these observations take a back seat to the mess of blood and flesh on her right forearm.

'Jesus,' she mutters, feeling a crackle run down her spine. 'What the hell happened there?'

Cole doesn't answer, and suddenly George feels nervous – is this a test? Despite the circumstances, if she's finally being put back on a major crime, then she's going to give it her best shot.

'Something sliced up her arm,' she says. 'Maybe a fall? Or an animal attack?' But these don't look like wounds made by claws or teeth. And it doesn't look like anything's been torn away, although it's hard to tell with all the blood and swelling.

Cole rubs her eyes. 'The pathologist estimates the wounds occurred approximately an hour before her death, and the time of death is estimated to be within a few hours of the body being discovered.'

George finds a photo taken from a new angle; in this, most of the dried blood has been sponged away, but there's still some crusted in the jagged lines and curves. And the longer George analyses the woman's thin arm, the more her fingers start to tingle.

'You know,' she says, aware that Cole is watching her intently now, 'it's a mess, but it almost looks …'

'Mm?'

Her eyes dart up to Cole's. 'Like writing.'

Something shifts in her boss's face. 'Go on.'

She returns to the picture. 'I can't really … a C, maybe? And an A, K – no, R … another R, maybe an O? And an F?' She winces, imagining how painful this must have been to endure. She hopes this poor woman wasn't conscious for it. 'Do we have any pictures of the wound after it was cleaned up?'

The door to Cole's office opens again. George ignores Lachlan's return, trying to see through the screen, through the layers of dried blood, to read the message beneath.

'There's no need,' Cole says, her eyes flicking over George's shoulder. 'We know what it says.'

George looks up. 'And?'

'It's a name,' a new voice answers. Not Lachlan's, but still familiar. George twists in her seat, her lower back protesting against the urgency with a crack.

There's a beat of silence in which George and Richie stare at each other; George has no idea what her expression looks like, but Richie's jaw is tight, lips thin.

'Cara Reid,' he continues, nodding towards the tablet. 'The letters spell out Cara Reid.'

Her voice gets trapped somewhere behind her tongue; she swallows, then croaks, 'Who is Cara Reid?'

It's Cole who answers this; George gratefully turns away from Richie's hard face. 'She's been listed as a missing person for a decade, and her case has been cold almost since day one.'

George gestures to the tablet, to the images it contains. 'Is this Cara, then? She's been found after all this time?'

'I wish that was the case,' Cole says, then points at the current photo – a close-up of the woman's face, her eyes open and unseeing. 'But despite knowing that the carvings in this woman's arm say Cara Reid, the only other thing we know for certain is that this woman is *not* her.'

CHAPTER 5

As soon as Richie steps out to make a call, George rounds on Cole. 'We can't work this together.'

Cole raises an eyebrow. 'Can't?'

'He doesn't want to work with me,' she rephrases.

'Good Lord,' Cole scoffs, 'am I running a police department or a primary school?' But then her expression becomes stern. 'Are you refusing this assignment, DI Lennox?'

George bites the inside of her cheek. There is something about a case so lacking in upfront information that beckons to her like a siren. This is what she used to be good at – is *still* good at, hopefully.

'No,' she finally says. 'No, of course not.'

'Smart choice,' Cole says. Then her eyes dart to the door. 'Because this is why I called you in early – why I swapped you in for Farley. I need you to do something for me.'

Apprehension stirs within her. 'What?'

'Keep an eye on Richie.'

George isn't sure what she expected Cole to ask, but this was not on the cards. 'Why?'

'Because he's been … a little off. For a while now. There have been complaints from other officers, but also a couple from members of the public.'

George's jaw drops. *Complaints about Richie?* Not possible – the man's favourite pastime is small talk, for Christ's sake. 'What are they saying?'

'The same things, really – that he's abrasive, insensitive, impatient. He walked out of an interview three weeks ago, no explanation, left a DS alone with a suspect in a burglary. The DS said the suspect was getting lippy, and there was a moment when he thought Richie was going to hit him.' Cole heaves a sigh. 'I have moved small mountains to get these complaints handled discreetly, but he is not making it easy. I tried to convince him to hand this assignment to someone else. But Cara means a lot to him, and he's … stubborn.' Cole smiles reluctantly. 'Your behaviour must have rubbed off on him.'

George can't appreciate the joke; her thoughts are reeling. She can't reconcile this information with who she knows Richie to be – he was going to *hit* someone?

Her shock must be clear on her face; Cole nods gravely.

'Something's going on with him, Lennox, and despite what you told me earlier, you still know him better than anyone here. And I'm running out of ways to keep him afloat on my own.' Cole's expression softens a little. 'I understand that things are strained between the pair of you, and I may seem unsympathetic. But you might be the only one who can help him keep his head straight enough to get the answers we need.'

George suppresses a snort; she's barely keeping herself above water these days – how is she supposed to make sure Richie floats, too?

'And what will you do if I fail? If he can't keep his head straight?'

Draining the last of her coffee, Cole slumps back in her chair. 'That'll be all, Lennox.'

It's a dismissal that brooks no further argument. Silently, George exits.

Richie is waiting for her in the lobby, his car keys in hand. 'Have you got your bag?' he asks tersely.

'My bag?'

He seems confused by her confusion. 'Cole didn't tell you? We'll be staying near the scene tonight.'

This new information concerns her for several reasons, but she's distracted by the fact that this is the most Richie has said to her in months. It's a little overwhelming to suddenly have his full attention.

'Oh, right. Well, I'll need to head back to my place to pack.' She shuffles around him and heads for the front doors. 'Meet you back here?'

'Did you drive in?'

She stops at the exit, turning to face him. 'Taxi.'

He walks towards her. 'I'll drive you.'

A warm current swirls through the chilly ocean in her chest. 'Oh, it's fine, you don't have to do that.'

He shakes his head. 'I'm already packed. We'll leave straight from your flat.'

He passes her, and though he holds the door open, his expression is hard again.

The current dissolves into the depths.

They don't speak on the drive; he's been to her flat enough times that he doesn't need to ask for her address. And since she can't think of anything worthwhile to say, the silence is a breeding ground for her anxiety. As she watches the dashboard clock turn from 6.29 to 6.30, it occurs to her that there might be another reason she's being put on this case.

To *support* Richie, first and foremost – which is how she's chosen to frame Cole's assignment, instead of *supervise* or, worse, *surveil*. And obviously to get an outcome for both cases: ideally, this woman's killer caught, justice served, and the connection to Cara Reid discovered.

But on this point George realises that, for the force, there are advantages to her failure: the media will latch onto the story and the public will see that DI Georgina Lennox is no more talented or skilled than any other detective in Scotland.

Maybe this is what Hendry meant when he said he chose the more interesting route. He's spent the last ten months putting her on a pedestal – what could be more interesting than documenting her spectacular fall?

Richie says he will wait in the car while she goes upstairs, so she's surprised when there's a knock on her front door only ten minutes later. Her overnight bag is on her bed, packed aside from the toiletries she's currently throwing together. Toothbrush in hand, she checks the peephole before opening the door, wincing at the audible clunk of both locks. He now has a black puffer jacket zipped over his customary suit and tie.

'I was just about to come down,' she says, getting ahead of his criticism.

'It was getting cold in the car,' he says quietly.

She stares at him for a moment, then opens the door wider.

In the past, he used to head straight for the kettle, chattering away while he made them both a cup of tea or a coffee to go. Now he just stands in the middle of her living room, hands tucked into his pockets.

It's been a while since she's had a chance to really look at him. The same blue eyes, the same silvery hair – though a little longer now, almost brushing his collar. But he looks … smaller than she remembers. George has always been a little taller than him, but he's significantly thinner; around his middle, across his shoulders. And is she imagining the new depths to the lines around his eyes and mouth, the hollows under his cheekbones that weren't there back in January?

More importantly, is this change in his appearance linked to the reported shift in his personality?

Her appraisal goes unnoticed by Richie; he's looking around with dull curiosity, taking in the new additions. There aren't many, but she suddenly feels anxious about what he might be gleaning. Maybe he can feel the bad energy in here.

His gaze lands on the shattered remains of the pot, the soil still scattered across the floor.

'It fell,' she says quickly.

He just nods, briefly meeting her eye before glancing away.

'Er ... you can turn the TV on, if you want. Or make yourself a cuppa ... You know where the kettle is. I'll be quick.'

In the bathroom, she spends ten seconds silently ordering herself to get it together. Then she throws a few more items into a toiletry bag, hurries to her bedroom to grab the overnight bag, and returns to the living area.

'We can make a hot drink for the— Oh.'

Richie straightens from where he's bent over her rubbish bin, a dustpan in hand. The floor has been swept clean, the lily now sitting on the bench.

'I would have cleaned it when I got home,' she says.

'Well, now you don't have to.'

She feels a flash of annoyance. 'I wasn't fishing for you to do it.'

'For God's sake,' he grumbles, sliding the dustpan onto the counter. 'How could I forget that you prefer to suffer in silence?'

Without allowing her a chance to snap back, he heads to the door. 'Let's go. We've got a long drive.'

Their victim was initially taken to a small hospital near the site where she was found, but after the leak she was moved to Raigmore Hospital in Inverness. They're on their way to see her body in person; more specifically so that they can confirm the gory writing with their own eyes.

Looking at the photos on her phone now, zooming in on the swollen letters, George figures it's probably the right call.

'What do you think they used to write on her arm?' she asks. 'Wasn't a knife or a scalpel, that's for sure. That would have been far easier to read.'

'I don't know. I've never seen this done to someone before.'

'Yeah. Neither.'

It starts to rain just before eight am. Richie keeps the headlights on as they leave the city behind; it doesn't get heavier than a consistent drizzle, but the sun has barely made it into the sky yet. Yet, despite the gloom outside, George observes the shifting landscape with a quiet sense of awe.

She's been a city girl for most of her life – born and raised in Edinburgh before transferring to Glasgow. Outside of the odd school excursion or family holiday, she hasn't spent much time in the Highlands, but it's easy to understand why so many people from around the world have this region on their bucket list.

There's an undeniable romanticism to the untamed countryside unfurling outside the windows as the car winds north towards Inverness. They pass dense woodlands of stunning autumn foliage, deep reds and rich oranges, buttery yellows and warm browns. Breaks in the trees reveal sweeping glens of lush green grasses, hardy sheep and cattle meandering through sloping paddocks; occasionally the land gives way to water, glistening lochs shivering under the light rain, small rowboats moored along tilted docks built long before George was born. And in the distance, in every direction, are mountains, the highest peaks dusted with the first snows of the season.

She snaps a few pictures to send to her family, then thumbs across to her emails. The latest is from Richie. He must have sent it while he was waiting in the car.

She opens the first attachment in the email, which turns out to be Cara Reid's initial missing person report. Richie already informed her that they have someone monitoring incoming missing persons reports; there's a slim but not negligible chance that this woman is also called Cara Reid, a terrible coincidence that could be confirmed by a new report. But until that happens, they have to assume this bloody inscription refers to the woman who disappeared a decade ago; and George's gut is telling her that the latter scenario is more likely.

'I looked Cara up when we were leaving the city,' she says. 'I could only find a couple of articles back from when she first went missing, but they weren't very detailed. Just her name, age, a picture. It's terrible quality, looks like a photo of a photo of a photo. And she has a brother?'

'Younger. Benjamin. He reported her missing after a couple of weeks with no contact. She was on the move a lot, but would normally check in with him every few days.'

'Parents around?'

'Mum was an addict, crashed her car into a tree when the kids were eight and three. The kids were somehow fine, but she didn't survive. And Dad left when Ben was a few months old. Never heard from him again.'

'What a shitty start to life. Any other family?'

'It's just the two of them. Though Ben's married now, to a nice woman called Dani. Two little ones of his own, two girls.'

George looks at him curiously, and notes with surprise that there's a few days' worth of stubble across his jaw. The only time she's ever seen Richie with facial hair is when he and his wife, Jenny, went to Italy for three weeks, and he returned with a beard so horrendous that George participated in a Stewart family intervention about it. 'You know a lot about them.'

'Those articles didn't tell you who the lead investigator was?'

'No, there wasn't even an official statement. To be honest, it looked like a pretty lacklustre effort from everyone involved,' she says, only for the realisation to drop into her stomach like an anvil. *Cara means a lot to him*, Cole said in her office this morning. 'Oh, fuck. It was you, right?'

'It still *is* me,' Richie says in a low voice. 'Until I find her, or I leave the force. And after ten years without a single lead, I always thought it would be the latter.'

Until now, she hears him silently add, and George hurries to pull up the grainy image of Cara again. She might be fifteen or sixteen in this, expressionless as she looks into the lens.

Her make-up is typical of the early 2010s: filled-in eyebrows and lips overdrawn with a shade of pink gloss that stands out brightly against her brown skin. She might have a piercing in one eyebrow, but the quality of the photo is so awful that it's impossible to know if it's a metal hoop or a water spot. The image is also cropped in a strange way, cutting off the person who is standing beside her – a male's hand is on her shoulder, thick fingers just visible under her black shoulder-length curls.

'She was – what, twenty-one? Twenty-two when she disappeared? Why wasn't the press all over this?'

Richie laughs harshly. 'You hadn't heard of Cara, but I'm guessing you're familiar with Amy Buchanan.'

'I am. Why am I?' She opens the search engine on her phone. 'She's got that foundation, right? The consent campaigner.'

'That's her. She's also Terrence Buchanan's daughter.'

'The neurosurgeon? *Oh.*'

Seeing Amy's picture pop up on her screen – her rosy cheeks, long blonde waves, braces-straightened teeth – brings it all flooding back.

George was nineteen when Amy's story hit the headlines. The stunning daughter of Scotland's pre-eminent neurosurgeon had been sexually assaulted while she and her friends were on a meandering road trip from the east coast to the west coast. Despite the vicious assault, she managed to escape her attacker and has dedicated herself to lobbying politicians for new laws, harsher sentencing, and nationwide consent education in secondary schools.

'I do remember her – God, her picture was *everywhere*.'

'Oh, yes. She was young and pretty, and very well connected, all of which is great for front pages. I'm not saying that Amy's assault shouldn't have received the attention it did,' he says quickly. 'She survived something terrible, and she channelled public outrage into very important work. But there's no denying that covering her story meant that Cara's never had a chance.'

'Because Amy's dad is famous?'

'Because Cara wasn't the right candidate.'

She could keep reading through the email attachments, but Richie is clearly the better resource. 'What does *that* mean?'

He shrugs, adjusting the wiper speed as the raindrops intensify. 'Even if Amy's attack didn't happen at the same time as Cara went missing, they never would have run stories about her.' He lifts a finger. 'Troubled upbringing.' Another finger. 'History of drug use and sex work.' And a third. 'A person of colour.'

'Jesus.'

'You know I'm not wrong.'

'I know it's not *right*,' she mutters. 'So – what? Nobody reported on it because she wasn't pretty enough, or white enough? Because she'd had a harder go of things?'

'Nobody would ever say that outright, but I have no other theories. She and Amy were the same age. Cara was last seen shortly before the attack on Amy. The only differences are what they looked like, who raised them, and what they did for work. Hell, the media could have run wild with a serial killer angle and I would have let them, if it meant Cara would get her moment in the spotlight.'

'*Could* it be linked to Amy's attacker?' George taps on an article and scans the paragraphs. 'Robert McAllister, twenty-five, sentenced to twelve years in jail. Two years to go, Robert,' she adds in a mutter, and then gasps. 'Oh, *shit* – he's from Kirkcree.'

Richie nods grimly. 'He attacked Amy at a camping ground just south of the village. According to the prosecution, he followed her there after seeing her group pick up groceries in Kirkcree.'

'Do we know where Cara was last seen?'

'About thirty minutes north of the village at a petrol station. The CCTV is blurry, but it's her. That was the day before Amy was assaulted.'

'Was she staying in the area?'

'I checked nearby hotels, caravan parks and camping areas, but her brother said that sometimes she stayed in places under different names and paid in cash. Had a nasty ex, but he was in London when she disappeared. Could have been something he set up, but he seemed genuinely surprised to hear she was missing when I spoke to him.'

'And you have no idea where she went after she left the petrol station?'

'In the video, you see her walk out the front doors and turn right. Don't know if she got a taxi, hitched, was picked up by someone she knew, hopped on a bike … no clues whatsoever.'

George hears the decade of frustration in his voice. He's had a very long time to turn over these dead ends in his head.

'Could she have made it to Kirkcree?'

'I thought it might be possible. I spoke to the officers handling Amy's case, and they said they'd ask Robert about Cara. I don't know if they did; I never heard back either way. I tried to push the Crown prosecutors on it too, but they told me they didn't want to dilute their case by throwing speculation about Cara into the mix.'

'That's … incredibly lazy.'

Richie lifts a shoulder half-heartedly. 'I would have done the same thing in their position. If I knew I had a hole-in-one lined up, I wouldn't start digging extra holes.'

She muses on this for a moment. 'Well, the force certainly seems to care about her now.'

'When they're in the middle of a media shitstorm, aye,' he says bitterly. 'And now that violence against women is being spoken about more publicly, when it's easier to whip up the right amount of outrage.' Richie shakes his head, then glances at her. 'You know all this, Lennox. Ten years ago, it was exceedingly difficult to get the press to put stories like this on the front page. Now … well, Cole says they're getting ready to play defence in anticipation of the public finding out that we let Cara's case – and too many other missing women's cases – get this cold.'

Considering that there's already been a leak about the details of this woman's death, George wonders just how long they can realistically keep the link to Cara contained. But she doesn't raise her doubts as she pivots back to researching Cara. She finds a missing person notice that was posted on the Facebook page of a women's support group a few months after her disappearance, then reposted a year later. But other than that, there's just *nothing*. She is beginning to understand Richie's frustration; there's already a knot in her chest that keeps twisting tighter with every dead end.

Finally, she searches 'dead woman Kirkcree'. Four more pieces have popped up overnight under different mastheads, but they all seem to be a regurgitation of the information Hendry already shared. She reads the handful of comments that have been posted beneath one of the articles. The tone is heated, one predicting 'another one the pigs will just fumble'.

It doesn't occur to her until a little while later, when the rain has stopped and the landscape is once again rolling glens and gentle hills on the turn from green to yellow, that seeing both her and Richie's names side by side might evoke an even stronger response. He was mentioned in most of the articles that came out about Eadar, but, as far as she can recall, none were specifically singing the praises of Detective Inspector Richard Stewart; her conversation with Hendry yesterday wasn't the first time she's heard someone say she was solely responsible for solving that case.

It's not fair to him, really. The breakdown of the trust between them lands squarely on her shoulders; after all, she went to great lengths to hide her addiction. Remembering some of the situations she got herself into back in January – and, if she's honest, in the months before that – shocks her now, and makes her wonder again who people think she *helped*. Certainly not herself; nor the man beside her, who over the past few months seems to have lost his warmth, his softness; and certainly not the families separated forevermore by death and the bars of a cell.

So, considering how much this case means to Richie, she wonders if the only way she can be of any help to these two women is to not help at all.

CHAPTER 6

George has been in a lot of mortuaries during her career, and they all follow roughly the same blueprint. White walls broken up by evenly spaced cabinets, trolleys on well-oiled wheels. This one smells faintly like cleaning chemicals, though she can feel crisp, fresh air pumping out from ceiling vents. Since sounds echo in here, noise is kept to a minimum, as demonstrated perfectly by the softly spoken man who approaches them now.

'DI Stewart,' he says, reaching out to shake Richie's hand, then George's. 'And you must be DI Lennox. I'm Dr Bùi – please, come through.'

He leads them to an autopsy table in the back of the room. A slim figure rests atop it, draped in a white linen sheet.

Dr Bùi retrieves a pair of gloves from a dispenser mounted on the wall, then glances at George and Richie. 'Ready?' When they nod, he draws back the sheet, folding it neatly just below the woman's collarbone. Her skin is bloodless, her closed eyes sinking into their darkened sockets. Her lips are dry and losing colour around the edges. Her collarbones stick out all the way across her chest. Someone has brushed her hair back from her face. The dark regrowth is more evident in person; George estimates that it's been at least a couple of months since she last had it bleached.

Richie bows his head, and his lips move with what George knows is a silent prayer. His faith has always been an important part of his life, one that has never appealed to George – especially after discovering the disturbing traditions practised by Eilean Eadar's zealously religious community. Still, it's a relief to see that Richie hasn't lost this core tenet along with whatever else seems to have shifted in his personality.

When he finishes, he asks, 'How old are these bruises?'

'They range. These ones here,' Dr Bùi says, indicating the discolouration across her chest, 'are fairly fresh, within the past five days. This one under her jaw, I estimate at closer to ten days, perhaps a little longer. You see the yellowish patch there? The haematoma was in the process of healing when she was killed. This blow to her cheekbone occurred at or just before the time of death. The ones down her arms are a mix of old and new,' he continues, leaning over the body to fold back the sheet covering her right arm, 'which of course, leads to *this*.'

Richie's intake of breath is especially audible in this room of polished metal surfaces. But George can't blame him – her next inhalation is a little shaky as she leans in for a closer look.

'It's so clear,' Richie mumbles, sounding a little awed.

The woman's forearm is still a mess, the skin swollen and bruised, but with the blood cleaned away, the letters are easy to make out.

C A R A R E I D

And below it, in line with the C:

F

'I took the liberty of looking up Cara Reid's missing person report,' Dr Bùi says. 'She was a different ethnicity to this woman, a different body type. Ms Reid was five foot seven, this woman is five foot two. Ms Reid was twenty-two when she disappeared, and though she looks young, this woman is perhaps twenty-five ...' He trails off, looking between them curiously. 'I'm wondering what you think the connection might be.'

'I don't think it would be helpful for us to speculate this early in the investigation,' George says firmly, thinking about Hendry and his secret sources.

The pathologist nods, seemingly unbothered. 'Of course. Well, I'm still trying to narrow down the tool used to make the cuts,' he says, drawing his pointer finger across his forearm. 'It had a pointed tip, but it didn't have a smooth cutting edge; something *dragged* through the skin instead of making a clean slice. Whatever it was, it was perhaps one to two millimetres thick. I've also collected DNA samples from her hands and fingernails, taken swabs for any evidence of recent sexual intercourse. But again, you'll have to wait.'

'How long?' Richie presses, his tone sharp enough to draw George's eye.

Dr Bùi's lips thin. 'Hopefully, within the next few days. You understand that this isn't the only dead body in Inverness, yes?'

'But this case is a high priority,' Richie insists. 'You understand *that*, yes? Or do I need to have someone more senior remind you?'

George's mouth pops open. *Is he threatening the pathologist?*

Dr Bùi seems equally as shocked – his expression twists with outrage. George steps forward, putting herself between them before Richie can rack up another complaint.

'What can you tell us about the cause of death?' she asks quickly. 'Anything additional to the previous pathologist's determination?'

Eyeing Richie darkly, Dr Bùi turns to her. 'Loose lips aside, their initial findings were sound.' He carefully folds back a section of the sheet to show the bullet wound in the woman's side, keeping her breasts covered.

'A .270 Winchester was removed from between the third and fourth ribs on her left side,' he continues, fingertip circling the entry wound in her torso. 'It took a little digging to get it; the bullet hit her back ribs and was deflected back towards her sternum. She would have bled out quickly.'

Thinking about the proximity of the hunting lodge, George asks, 'Can you tell how far away the shooter was?'

'The previous pathologist tested for gunshot residue on her clothes and skin, but there was nothing to find. Bit of a pointless test, in my opinion.'

'Why?' Richie demands.

Dr Bùi's tone is tart when he replies. 'I can't give you a *precise* distance, but if she'd been shot at close range with a high-powered hunting rifle, the bullet would have gone straight through her, ribs or not.'

'So, her killer has good aim,' George surmises, thoughts drifting back to Fiadhain Lodge and the owners' refusal to speak to police. 'Have you still got her clothes?'

On an empty table, Dr Bùi lays out each item carefully. 'These have already been examined,' he explains. 'We found some hairs, fibres, dirt, of course, and blood.'

George bends to examine the jacket, the hole that the bullet punched through.

'This has seen better days,' she notes, indicating a missing button, the sweat stains at the armpits and around the collar. Then she points to a white tank top, the fabric also punctured and stained with blood and sweat. 'And she was only wearing this under the jacket? And no underwear or socks?'

'Everything she was wearing is here.'

'She would have been freezing,' Richie murmurs.

George looks at the jacket, the top and mud-encrusted jeans, then the boot. 'That's a man's jacket. And a man's boot.'

'Maybe that was her style?' Richie suggests.

'Perhaps, but they're both about four sizes too large for her,' Dr Bùi says, moving to the end of the table. 'And on that note …' He lifts the sheet, folding it at her calves.

Her feet are small, a few flecks of black polish still stuck to the tips of her toenails. Her leg hair has grown out, dark against her marble skin, and on the outside of her right ankle is a red ink tattoo of a cartoon pig. But Dr Bùi directs their attention towards the soles of her feet. George and Richie move closer, and she sees what the doctor is getting at – both are dark with encrusted dirt.

'At some point quite recently,' he says, 'she wasn't wearing any shoes at all.'

George looks up at the woman's face; her upturned nose, sharply angled brows, hollow cheeks. A face George will never see in animation, creasing in a smile or a frown, unless they're able to discover her identity – maybe then there will be photos of her, videos from better times. She hopes that this woman has loved ones who are looking at those images right now, sharing them online, broadcasting this woman's identity far and wide. It's a terrible thing for a person to be reduced to their shell.

It's during this observation that George realises that Hendry, or Hendry's editor, strangely hit the mark when they branded this woman as Bambi. There is something about her – perhaps the innocence of her youthful face, the coppery tint to her brassy hair – that brings a baby deer to mind. Maybe it's also the knowledge that she spent her final moments lost and stumbling around on skinny legs across that rugged land.

Though she'll never admit it to Hendry or say it aloud, thinking of the woman as 'Bambi' feels more personal than 'the woman' – and far kinder than 'the body'.

Taking a deep breath, wincing at the sterile smell that permeates the room, George raises an eyebrow at Richie, their usual signal to wrap things up. He doesn't look happy, but he nods.

'Call me as soon as those drug results are in,' he says to Dr Bùi stiffly, then adds, 'please.'

'Of course,' the pathologist replies in a clipped voice.

Without further comment, Richie turns on his heel and leaves. George follows, but pauses at the door. She doesn't want to apologise for Richie, but she feels like she ought to offer some explanation for his behaviour – and hopefully get ahead of a new complaint.

'Cara's case is close to his heart. He's been waiting for answers for a long time.'

'I have a lot of people waiting for answers, Inspector. It's not the best idea to bite the head off the person who's trying to get them for you.'

'I know, I know.' She laughs weakly. 'He's, er, normally the one telling me to cool it.'

'Then hopefully he can take his own advice.' His irritation holds for another few seconds, then he looks down at the covered body. A worried crease appears between his eyebrows. 'Inspector?'

'Yes?'

'I know it's not my job to speculate. And of course, I understand you can't possibly know this early on …' He gently pats Bambi's shoulder, then looks at George. 'If this poor woman is connected to Cara Reid by the same killer … what message are they trying to send? And who are they sending it to?'

CHAPTER 7

Their next stop is a row of identical semi-detached red brick townhouses, with tiny front yards enclosed by a low wall of the same red brick. Richie has parked in front of number eight. The double driveway is neat, the lawn is a little overgrown and littered with children's toys – dolls in various states of dress, a tricycle, a plastic playhouse in primary colours.

'You've kept a relationship with him?' she asks as Richie rings the doorbell.

He looks strangely nervous. 'Tried to.'

The door opens. George is staring into empty space at first; she lowers her gaze and sees a small girl standing in the gap, her hair floating around her head in wispy curls.

'What do you want?' she demands in a high voice.

Richie squats. 'Hello, Miss Mia. Is your mammy or daddy home?'

'Mammy is doing a poo. Daddy is in the shed.'

Richie frowns. 'I don't think you're meant to be opening the door without them, are you?'

'Mammy said I could.'

A reprimanding voice calls from inside. 'No, I bloody didn't. And I'm *changing* a poo, not *doing* one.'

The door opens wider to reveal a blonde woman in her twenties dressed in jeans and a baggy hoodie, a snotty toddler on her hip. She bears the evidence of several sleepless nights beneath her eyes, but she smiles when she sees Richie.

'He mentioned you might be popping in,' she says, using her leg to nudge Mia to the side. 'You've brought a friend?'

Richie introduces George, and the woman nods a greeting. 'Come through. I'll pop the kettle on.'

Wariness forgotten, Mia explodes with excitement when Richie and George step inside. George allows Mia to take her hand and tow her to the kitchen, where the woman has already placed the toddler in a high chair. George's eyes flick around the space, taking in the sliding glass door, the windows, the knife block on the counter.

'Just let me throw some lunch at Mia and Lily,' the woman says, already dropping two slices of bread into a toaster. 'Then I'll get you a cuppa.'

Richie waves her off, walking around the counter. 'I can get those going, Dani.'

'Yeah, go on.'

Mia pushes George towards a seat at the dining table, and as the little girl gives her a tour of her colouring set, George's attention keeps getting drawn back to the kitchen. Richie and Dani chat easily, questions about work and their families bouncing back and forth between them. He reaches for a cupboard above the stovetop and Dani clucks, then points to one beside the fridge.

'You keep rearranging things,' he complains lightly, retrieving four mugs from the lower cupboard.

'I'm never satisfied,' she says. The smell of the toast reminds George that she hasn't eaten anything since lunchtime yesterday – her stomach rumbles, a dog sniffing the air. She presses her palm against it, a warning to behave.

Mia taps on George's cheek with the end of a pencil. 'Are you looking?'

'Sorry, yes.'

'Pencils down, lovie,' Dani says, coming over to the table with a hard plastic plate. 'Eat this.'

'I want yoghurt.'

Dani pushes the plate towards Mia, the toast cut into triangles and arranged into the shape of butterflies. 'This first, then some fruit, then yoghurt.'

Mia grumbles, but obediently begins to chew. Dani tears the other slice of toast into small pieces and drops a few onto the high chair's attached table. Lily launches in immediately, smearing jam all over her pudgy hands as she brings the pieces clumsily to her mouth.

'Piglet,' Dani says affectionately, going to wash her hands at the sink.

Richie hands Dani a steaming mug, and slides another across the bench that George assumes is for her; she rises to claim it. The movement makes her stomach growl again, and she takes a hasty sip in an attempt to smother the sound.

But Dani quirks an eyebrow. 'Can I make you some lunch, too?'

'I'm fine, thanks.'

Dani chuckles. 'They not paying you enough to eat?'

Richie laughs, too. George quietly soaks up the sound as she sips her tea again.

'We drove up from the city just this morning,' he explains. 'DI Lennox and I have barely had a moment to think.'

Dani's eyebrows rise again, and she looks between them enquiringly. 'Something's going on, then?'

Richie hesitates. 'Will he come in, if I ask?'

She shrugs. 'You can try, but you know how he gets.'

Richie picks up the remaining mug and exits through the sliding glass door to the backyard. It's a small space, filled with almost the same amount of toys and play equipment as the front yard. A shed is in the back corner – before Richie closes the sliding door behind him, George hears rock music playing from within it.

Both she and Dani watch him approach the shed and use the toe of his boot to knock twice. The door opens, but George can't see inside. After a moment, Richie enters.

Dani sighs. 'This can't be good news.' She looks at George, her round face nervous. 'I'm guessing you found Cara?'

'No, I'm sorry.'

'Oh. Just a check-in, then?' She frowns. 'But Richie was here a few months ago.'

George is surprised. 'How often does he come?'

'Every year since Cara went missing, according to Ben, but I've only been around for six years.'

She drops another slice of bread into the toaster, then looks at George over her shoulder, a little suspicious now. 'Why *are* you here, then?'

George nods towards the backyard. 'We should wait for them.'

Dani studies her for a moment, and George wonders what she's reading on her face, hearing in her non-answer. George suspects that nothing much escapes Dani's notice – a point that is proven correct when Dani takes the freshly popped toast, smears a thick layer of butter and jam onto it, then thrusts it on a plate towards George.

'Eat,' she orders. 'I can't eavesdrop on what's happening out there with your stomach performing a solo.'

She accepts the plate with a guilty thanks. 'You and Ben have been together for six years? How'd you meet?'

Dani snorts. 'Ah. It's not a cute story.'

'Sometimes those are better.'

'You can decide after you hear it,' she says with another laugh. 'We met at rehab. He wasn't doing well – Cara had been gone for four years at that point, and there hadn't been any new information for a long time. And he hadn't kept in contact with any of his foster families, so he was just out on his own, trying to make himself feel better in whatever way he could. He was lucky that he had a doctor who knew him as a kid, who still gave a shite. The doctor pulled some strings and got him a spot in a good clinic.'

'And you were there?'

'Yep. Third cycle, but third time's a charm, right?'

'I thought you weren't meant to …'

Dani smirks knowingly. 'Hook up with fellow addicts? Yeah, *strongly* advised against. I get it – you're emotional, you're vulnerable, and it's easy to replace one addiction with another.' She shrugs and sucks a bit of jam off her thumb. 'But we finished our treatment, moved into a shitty flat, I went back to school and he got a job, and then we got this place and married and pregnant all at once. Bang-bang-bang. Literally.'

'Sounds like it worked out for the best.'

Dani smiles, tired but warm. 'He deserves to have something work out for him. It's not been an easy road, for either of us, but especially for him. Cara meant everything to him.' She goes quiet, looking out at the shed again. 'You swear you haven't found her?'

'I swear.'

Dani hums contemplatively. 'It's the not knowing that's killing him now. He'd almost feel better if she was found. A full stop at the end of the story, you know? But this ongoing *thing*, this constant wondering where she went, what happened. And did she go by choice? Is she sitting on a beach in Mexico, or guiding fat tourists up a mountain in New Zealand? That might be worse for him, if that's what happened. If she chose to leave him behind. And I know how guilty he feels about that – that he'd rather she was dead in a ditch somewhere than alive and living without him. But he's still a kid in there,' she says, tapping her temple, 'when it comes to Cara, anyway. Everything he's learnt since then – in his career, being a husband, a dad – all of that falls away when he thinks about her. He's a kid again. He's a little kid, and his big sister is gone.'

Dani takes a deep breath, then glances at George – and does a double-take. 'Are you *crying*?'

George blanches, then hastily pats her cheeks. They're mortifyingly damp. 'Oh my God, I am so sorry.'

Dani plucks two tissues from a box and thrusts them towards her. 'No, *I'm* sorry.'

George presses the tissues to her eyes. 'This is incredibly unprofessional.'

Dani snorts. 'That's stupid. I told you something sad, and you're a human being.'

'I'm a police officer.'

'Well, half a human being then.' She grins, but George can't even muster up something false to send back. Luckily, Lily abruptly and loudly decides that she is done with being seated – her scream makes George jump. Dani shoots an *Are you kidding me?* look at her daughter.

'Is she all right?' a new voice asks.

A man she assumes is Ben steps into the kitchen, Richie on his heels. He's tall and skinny, and like his sister, he has a long face framed by curly dark hair. On his jumper is the logo of an Inverness car-detailing clinic.

'She's just been fed, watered and waited on hand and foot,' Dani says, passing Lily to her husband, 'so obviously she's miserable.'

Ben bounces her with an expert hand, then gives George a shy nod of greeting. 'Let's put the girls in the playpen for a few minutes, Dani. They have something to show us.'

Dani straightens up from wiping the high chair. 'Sure,' she says lightly. 'Mia, follow your daddy.'

But Mia won't go unless Dani carries her, and for a few seconds George and Richie are left alone in the kitchen. The sudden absence of sound – no more baby babble, chatter from Mia, or banging of fists and feet on hard surfaces – makes George realise how tense she'd become in its presence.

When Dani and Ben return, Dani pulls out a chair and drops into it.

'We've got about seven minutes before those two start beating the shite out of each other,' she says. 'And Lily might be a baby, but she's built like a cement truck.'

Ben takes the seat beside her and grasps her hand. She smiles at him, squeezing his fingers reassuringly, before she turns to Richie. 'So talk fast.'

CHAPTER 8

As expected, the photos of Bambi's lifeless face make Ben and Dani recoil.

'Sorry,' Richie says again, the fifth time in as many minutes. He's curated a gallery of photos for the pair to examine – some of the location after her body had been removed, the least grisly looking close-up of Cara's name – but there's no avoiding the confronting images of her lifeless face, and Richie continues, 'But do you recognise her?'

Dani immediately shakes her head; a beat later, Ben murmurs, 'No.'

George can sense Richie's disappointment; he brings up another photo, taken from a different angle. 'Are you sure? Look at this one.'

'I don't need to see her from all sides, Richie,' Dani says, 'I don't know her. Christ.' She looks at George, her lower lip starting to tremble. 'What kind of fucked-up guy does that to someone?'

'We don't know who did this,' George says quickly. 'Male or female.'

Dani pulls a face. 'Of course it was a man. It's always a man doing shit like this to women. Do you think he killed Cara, too? Wrote her name just to fuck with us all? And that next letter, it's an F?' Dani looks at Richie now. 'Could there be others? More dead women out there, and this fella's just snatching new ones off the street?'

George glances at Richie. Letting family members speculate and work themselves up rarely aids an investigation – something Richie knows very well.

So she's shocked when he says, 'We'll be investigating that line of enquiry, of course. And if that's the case, I promise you that I'm going to find out who is behind it. And,' he continues, pushing the phone towards Ben, 'it's why I need you to look at this picture again and *really* try to think if you've seen her before.'

George has been observing Ben, watching his expressions, his body language. When the writing was brought up, it seemed like Dani's hand was the only thing keeping him at the table; as each photo was shown, he withdrew further and further into himself. So she's not surprised when he doesn't look at the phone again; instead he looks at Dani, then down at their linked hands.

'Richie ... I know that you care about Cara,' he begins, eyes still on their hands. 'Even when the rest of your lot fucked us around, you never did. And it's hard for me, still. To talk about her. To not know what happened. And I know that you want to find her, almost as much as I do. But ...'

As if she knows what's coming next, Dani presses a soft kiss to Ben's temple, then leaves for the living room, where Mia's voice and Lily's squeals are both rapidly rising in volume.

Ben gestures to Richie's phone. 'I'm not saying this isn't something. It's something in almost ten years of nothing. I hope it goes somewhere, I really do.'

'It will,' Richie says immediately.

'But if it doesn't—'

'There's something here, Ben, I really think—'

'Richie.' Ben's voice is still low, but very firm. 'If this is just another dead end, then I don't want you coming round anymore.'

Richie flinches, eyes wide.

'I appreciate everything you've done for me, for my sister. But I can't be the best da to my kids when I've got half my mind on their auntie. And I can't keep making Dani suffer for it, having to manage the emotions of everyone in this house. She deserves all of me, *here*. And I can't give her that if I'm always waiting for you to call.'

Richie appears to be totally lost for words. The moment stretches on too long, so it's George who breaks the silence.

'We understand,' she says softly, and without waiting for Richie's go-ahead, she stands. Ben rises, too; Richie a few seconds later, his expression a little dazed.

'If anything comes from this, we'll call,' she says, holding out her hand for Ben to shake. 'Either way, we'll let you know. And then that'll be the last of it.'

'Thanks.' He releases her hand and looks to Richie. 'I mean it. Thank you.'

Richie just stares at him, and it's only George's prodding that gets him following Ben towards the front door. In the living room, Dani is helping Mia choose a cartoon to watch, and Lily is babbling as she scoots around the playpen. Dani calls a goodbye and encourages Mia to wave.

It's when the door is about to close behind them that Richie snaps out of his stupor, turning quickly. 'I really do feel there's something about this lead, Ben.'

A flicker of irritation crosses Ben's face, but he just nods and says, 'Okay, good luck with it.'

Then the door is closed, and George presses her hand between Richie's sharp shoulder blades, urging him towards the car. After a few steps he shakes her off, wrenching open the driver's door and climbing in.

She enjoys the peace, the fresh air, the quiet of the street for a few more seconds, before stepping into the storm.

'What was that?' he snaps.

'I was about to ask you the same thing,' she retorts, twisting to reach for her seatbelt. 'Letting Dani speculate about a serial murderer in the Highlands? The most likely scenario is a careless hunter from that wanky lodge is doing a terrible job of covering up a misfire. Manslaughter, not murder, Rich.'

Richie's seatbelt is stuck; he tugs on it fruitlessly. 'I said *if* – and even if it was an accident, why would she be tied up? And why write Cara's name on her?'

'I don't know – *and neither do you*. So why let Dani think something that we're not sure of ourselves? Unless that's your plan? Get people riled up and afraid just so Cara's case finally gets some attention from the public?' She jerks her thumb back towards the Reids' house. 'Were you just planting the seed in there for when a journalist comes knocking at their door?'

A red flush is spreading upwards from below Richie's collar, colouring his cheeks. 'Enough, Lennox. That's an order.'

'An order?' She laughs without humour. 'We have the same rank.'

Richie glowers, an expression she's rarely on the receiving end of from him. 'This is my case—'

'*Our* case—'

'So I'll be deciding how we approach the investigation,' he continues, his volume rising, 'and all you need to do is keep your mouth shut and look busy if someone does show up and decides to take your picture!'

She rocks back as if he's hit her; he may as well have, considering the way her eyes immediately start to prickle with tears. But a jab to the nose would have hurt less than this.

'Jesus, Richie,' she says, her voice higher than normal. *In-in-in.*

He swallows thickly. 'I … I didn't mean that.'

Out-out-out.

Richie looks at her, eyes roaming across her face. She wants to turn away, to hide her wounded expression until she can haul a mask of indifference back into place, but then he opens his mouth and she braces for something more painful.

Perhaps it's that subtle flinch that makes him snap his mouth shut and face forward, hands limp in his lap. Then the keys find the ignition, the next destination is typed into his phone, and they pull away from the Reid home, Richie likely leaving for the final time.

Heading south now, the landscape shifts again as they drive past wide, grassy pastures, swathes of purple and green winter-flowering heather, and vast forests. As beautiful as the sights are, George notes the distances between buildings growing with a corresponding sense of trepidation; soon there's a mile between villages, then two, then five. If it weren't for the stream of other vehicles on the road, George would feel as if the two of them have accidentally passed through some kind of portal to a remote and uninhabited planet.

She gazes up at the massive trees on either side of the road, previously a distant blur of green and brown, now close enough that she can see they're clustered patches of pines and evergreens. The road narrows to two tight lanes as it winds around another vast loch, its steely grey water flanked by steep slopes on three sides. A low metal barrier and thin white trees are clearly meant to prevent cars plunging into the loch, though George suspects they'd be as effective as toothpicks if one actually did veer off the road.

An unexpected shaft of sunlight breaks through the low cloud to bounce off the shimmering water; Richie scrambles in the glove compartment for a pair of sunglasses, and George resolves herself to squint against the glare. A road sign ahead warns of deer crossing, and George wonders just how much damage would be done – to both the car and the deer – if one was to leap out from the treeline and Richie was too slow to react.

They take an exit that angles south-east. There's no mention of Kirkcree on any of the road signs yet, despite Cole describing it as one of the gateway villages to Cairngorms National Park. George recalls a high school geography teacher trumpeting the fact that the park is larger than the country of Luxembourg, and that almost half the land has been declared 'wild'. She wonders if the title of 'gateway village' is a self-appointed honour; almost every village they pass claims to be *The Gateway to Somewhere* or *The Home of Something*, and considering the almost exorbitant number of hotels, inns and B&Bs in each place, they've clearly convinced tourists that they're telling the truth.

The Cairngorms are part of the vast Grampian mountain range, their cratered grey faces like the rough surface of the moon. The higher peaks are dusted with pearly snow, giving way quickly to muddy green and grey lichen and moss, or whatever other flora is hardy enough to survive the altitude and temperature. Even down at road level, George can feel the temperature dropping; she presses her hand against the window, and the glass is chilly against her skin.

The climate inside the car is just as frosty. Richie put music on right after they left Ben's house, and the rumbling voices of Marty Robbins, Neil Diamond and Johnny Cash have served as a buffer between them for the past hour. Cole calls for an update, and George tells her about the pathologist's findings, but when she asks, 'Anything *else* to report?' George bites her lip. With Richie right beside her, she can't exactly go into detail – besides, she's not sure if Richie's outburst is the exact behaviour Cole is looking for. And even though his comment still smarts, she doesn't think it's worth mentioning.

After she hangs up from Cole, she checks her phone battery. This was something else her prior therapists had pointed out, in varying degrees of bluntness – her attachment to her phone. She didn't understand their expressions of concern: a working phone means she can call for help. When she explained that to Dr Kassab, he just nodded and told her that was very reasonable, then moved on.

The road they're travelling along thins, roughens and climbs over the next hour. There aren't any crofts or farmhouses as far as George can see out either window, but crumbles of stone and mortar appear infrequently – the corpses of great towers and clan strongholds. She wonders what the landowners are meant to do about these ruins, whether they're protected by the National Trust – the former homes of lairds and ladies now as aged and crooked as a hunched great-aunt or -uncle who sits in the corner at family events.

The last of the ruins are a speck in their rear-view mirror by the time they finally come to a fork in the road. A large sign on the median strip between the two roads encourages them to continue on the asphalt road to the right; to the left, a malnourished dirt track angles sharply upwards before disappearing into an enormous thicket of dark green shrubs.

'*Welcome to Kirkcree*,' George reads as Richie accelerates to the right, '*Gateway to the Cairngorms*.' And given the proximity to the mountains, now towering overhead, she actually believes this title.

They arrive in the heart of Kirkcree five minutes later. It's a neat little place, about five or six narrow streets of houses and a high street of shops that bisects the village. There's a uniformity to the design of the buildings here: spare, utilitarian architecture, double-storey, and painted cream or white with red trim along the windowsills and doors. Though there's enough room for each house to sit independently on its own block of land, like the farmhouses and crofts George and Richie passed on the way here, Kirkcree's buildings huddle like pack animals – shoulder to shoulder as if for warmth, or safety. A battered car idles outside one of the houses, a sooty cloud puffing from the exhaust pipe; a few doors down, two elderly neighbours chat over the low, chain-link fence between their properties.

The high street is where they find Kirkcree's heartbeat. The road is wider here, with enough space for two-way traffic and a faded pedestrian crossing right at the mid-point. A few cars are parked on the side of the road, a couple more in a small carpark to the left. On a patch of grass just beyond that is an old caravan mounted on concrete blocks.

The shopfronts stick to the same design as the houses: white walls, pops of dull red, and all crowded together, and along the rooftops, smoke or steam chuffs from tarnished chimney pipes. There's a steady trickle of people going in and out of a little supermarket with faded images of tomatoes and artificially pink ham slices peeling from the windows, and a few others wait outside a Chinese takeaway; a little further down, some teenagers lounge across a metal table and benches that have been drilled into the footpath outside a café.

A street sign directs tourists towards the Kirkcree Information Centre, a low timber building standing alone on a block of yellowing grass. A couple stand beside a blocky timber noticeboard, both wearing bulky hiking backpacks, and one is folding a large paper map back into a neat rectangle. A large information stand shows a map of the national park, with walking trails marked in coloured lines.

Despite it only being late afternoon, the height of the surrounding mountains is already starting to block the sun; the dimming light casts a certain sleepiness over the street that makes George stifle a yawn.

Around the first bend is what seems to be the accommodation sector of Kirkcree. There are a few modest bed and breakfasts with roughcast exteriors in whites and creams and baby blues, but there are a couple of older, grander houses that have been given a hotel makeover, promising tourists a taste of old-world glamour – as long as they ignore the sagging eaves and flaking paint. And it's into the driveway of one of these houses that Richie turns the car.

The sign for Ivy House is a glossy white piece of plywood bolted to long steel legs. There's only one other car out front, a muddy Land Rover with rental plates and three expensive-looking mountain bikes strapped to the roof, and Richie pulls into the space beside it. Stepping out, George rocks up onto her toes and pushes her hands up over her head as far as they can go until she feels a few satisfying pops. The temperature of the air feels especially crisp against her cheeks after being in the warm car. It smells clean out here, and a little damp; the showers from this morning are lingering as mist in the air.

She retrieves her duffel bag from the back seat; Richie pulls a surprisingly large rolling suitcase from the boot.

'We're just staying tonight, right? Looks like you're moving in.'

He glances at her bag, then down at his own. 'I brought everything I need,' he says, a little defensively.

'Including your mattress?'

He tuts, irritated now, then drags the case with difficulty over the gravel path. She suppresses a sigh. He would have laughed at a joke like that once – even if grudgingly.

Ivy House is a neat three-storey building with a sepia-toned palette of rust-brown stone and beige roughcasting. It looks very old, even to George's untrained eye, though she suspects the upper floors were not part of the original blueprints; she hopes she's only imagining the way the ground-floor roof seems to be bowing under the weight. A shallow porch with ornate wooden trim is a far more recent addition, probably tacked onto the front of the house sometime in the last twenty years; the posts and trim, as well as all the window and doorframes, have been recently slapped with the same glossy white paint as the sign beside the road. A knee-high hedge forbids guests from trampling into the neat garden beds that abut the porch, and it quickly becomes clear where Ivy House got its name; thick arteries of vines creep up the face and sides, finding purchase in cracks and curling around drainpipes.

The reception area is a small space made smaller by a low ceiling, layered carpets and claustrophobic wallpaper. In the centre of the room, a woman is hunched over a low writing desk, lazily twisting from side to side in a creaking office chair. She doesn't look up as they enter, and George sees that she's reading a thick book propped on the lid of a silver laptop. Behind her, a flight of carpeted stairs leads up to the first and second floors.

To the left is a sitting room lit by warm yellow lamps, with a few patterned armchairs placed in pairs around the squashy space; to the right is a dining area with a long table in the centre. The air smells artificially floral, the scent floating over old wood smoke. A dormant fireplace in the sitting room seems to be the source; there's a stack of wood waiting beside the grate.

It's all very homey, cosy and welcoming, despite the fact that the woman still hasn't noticed their presence. Her dark hair is pulled back into a flicky ponytail, and her ears have been swallowed by a chunky pair of headphones. She flips a page, humming along to a song.

'No situational awareness,' Richie mutters, then steps forward and raps his knuckle on the desk.

The woman jerks back.

'Fuck me,' she yelps, knocking her headphones around her neck, 'where did you come from?'

George tries not to laugh – the woman is young, maybe in her mid-twenties, and either has been naturally gifted with enormous eyes, or their appearance has *really* startled her. A mild odour of cigarettes wafts from her side of the desk. There's a nametag drooping off the lapel of her chunky green cardigan: *ZOE*.

'The front door,' Richie says incredulously.

Zoe glares at the door accusingly, as if it should have announced their presence, then adopts a pleasant customer-service expression. 'So sorry about that. How can I help you?'

'We have a reservation.'

She looks between the two of them with confusion – then her expression clears. '*Oh*,' she says, drawing the sound out, 'of course you do.'

She opens the laptop and wakes it up with impatient clicks, then tugs a pair of round glasses from her pocket.

'Okey dokey,' Zoe says after a minute, her eyes flicking across the screen. 'We've got you booked into the deluxe double for two nights, full breakfast, and I've already put the extra blanket out at the foot of your bed, as requested.' She turns a bright, practised smile on them. 'And on behalf of Ivy House, we'd like to congratulate you with a complimentary bottle of champagne.'

Richie looks at Zoe blankly. 'Congratulations for what?'

'Er ... your marriage? To each other? To your *wife*?' Zoe adds in a louder voice, pointing at George.

'Oh, God,' George breathes, as Richie's cheeks redden. 'No, no—'

Zoe's brow furrows, and she looks down at the screen again. 'You're the Dunnetts, yeah? Nigel and Faye?'

'No,' Richie says firmly, and George swallows a hysterical laugh. 'My name is Richard *Stewart*. This is Georgina *Lennox*. We're in standard rooms. *Separate* ones.'

Zoe's mouth falls open – George expects another round of apologies – but laughter bursts forth instead.

'I was going to say,' she giggles breathlessly, waving a hand towards them, '*this* wasn't making sense. Not that you're not a silver fox,' she says earnestly, nodding at Richie, 'but the vibes were way off for newlyweds. No *heat*, you know?'

Ironically, Richie looks as if he's about to detonate. Zoe continues, oblivious to his rising temperature. 'Well, I don't have you in the system, so I'm guessing Dean took the booking.' She sighs. 'He owns the place, but we're six months into this new system and he still refuses to learn it. I told him to leave the bookings to me or Harris, or literally *anyone* under the age of seventy, but does he listen?'

Still grumbling, she opens the desk drawer. 'Ah-*ha*.' She reaches in and retrieves a purple notepad.

'*Two standard rooms, one night, Stewart and Lennox, coming sometime today,*' she reads. Her frustration melts into a grudging chuckle, and she goes to toss the pad down – then pauses, her eye catching on something. She stiffens. 'This says you're police?'

'Detectives,' George says.

'Oh, *shit*.' Zoe straightens up, her humour vanishing. 'Is this about that girl? Someone from the lodge shot her, right?'

'We can't comment on that,' George says quickly, before Richie can repeat his antics from Dani and Ben Reid's house. 'It wouldn't be wise for *anyone* to jump to any conclusions at this early stage.'

Zoe only looks slightly abashed as she turns back to the laptop. 'Sure. Just chalk it up to the curse of *An Rathad Damainte*.'

George glances at Richie, who shakes his head – he doesn't understand much more Gaelic than she does. '*An Rathad* ... sorry?'

'The Cursed Road. Where the girl was found.'

The skin at the back of George's neck prickles.

'We were told that it was a disused road,' Richie says, still sounding a little disgruntled. 'I wasn't aware that it had a name.'

'It's not, like, an official thing. It's just what people here call it. Did you see the Kirkcree sign on your way in?' When Richie affirms, she says, 'Did you see the skinny dirt road off to the left?'

George recalls the fork in the road, the track that disappeared into a thicket. 'That's the ... Cursed Road? Is it boobytrapped, or something?'

'That's not why it's called that – at least, not according to the stories.'

'What kind of stories?'

'About the road and the land around it.' She lowers her voice. 'And about the people who used to live there.'

As George opens her mouth to interrogate further, Richie clears his throat. 'How about we save the ghost stories for around the fireplace, DI Lennox?' To Zoe, he says, 'So, have you got a couple of rooms for us?'

Zoe gestures towards the empty dining and sitting rooms. 'We're fully booked – can't you tell?'

She plucks two keys from a row of hooks on the wall and returns to the desk.

'I'll put you next to each other on the first floor,' she says, pushing the keys towards them. 'Just in case you need to be close. And give me a shout if you need anything.'

She clears her throat, her customer-service façade returning. 'I'm Zoe, this is Ivy House, and you're in the stunning village of Kirkcree.' She flashes another bright smile. 'I hope you enjoy your stay.'

CHAPTER 9

There are only three rooms on the first-floor landing. Richie rolls his case to Room Three, the wheels leaving deep grooves in the carpet.

'We'll head out in ten minutes,' he says, stepping into his room.

'Roger that,' she says under her breath, before entering Room Two.

It's exactly what she expected: a double bed with a tartan coverlet, lacy curtains, dark wall panelling, an antique desk, and a spindly chair that she knows just by sight will creak with panic under any stress. There's an electric heater in front of a bricked-up fireplace, and one of the two narrow windows is slightly ajar, which could be considered strange considering the cool temperature outside, but there's a faintly musty smell lingering in the air that George suspects Zoe is trying to chase out. She dumps her bag on the end of the bed and gives the blanket an apprehensive sniff. Detergent, maybe a spritz of something floral – lavender or hyacinth; the smell of time passing must be coming from the walls themselves.

There's a guest book on the desk beside a well-stocked tea station. She gives the kettle an experimental shake. It's half full, and the hollow slosh reminds her that she hasn't eaten anything since lunchtime yesterday except that one piece of toast at the Reids' house. A cup of tea – or one of these home-brand instant coffee sachets – will have to do until Richie gives her leave to get something to eat.

As the kettle boils, she connects her phone to the Wi-Fi and pulls her laptop from her duffel bag to connect that, too. Having so much technology at her fingertips reminds George just how much of an outlier her experience on Eadar was – the total lack of connection to the outside world that was, in fact, the reason why the crimes went unchecked for so long. And yet, even as she logs in to the Police Scotland portal, and shoots a quick text to her parents to let them know she's arrived safely, she can't fully shake the anxious feeling of isolation.

She knows it's because they're staying the night here, in another remote place; she hasn't worked on any cases outside the Glasgow city limits since January, and the low thrum of anxiety from being even a few hours from home is making her wish she'd argued to just drive back late tonight.

Just as the kettle clicks, there's a knock on the door. She looks through the peephole before opening it.

'Are you ready?' Richie asks. He's got a windbreaker on now, and has swapped his shoes for a pair better suited for walking.

George looks at her phone. 'It's only been six minutes.' She steps back, propping her door open wider. 'Kettle's just boiled … I can make you a cuppa?'

He looks past her, his eyes darting around, taking in the bed, the desk, the windows. 'Same as mine. That's good.' Then he steps back, clearing his throat. 'I'll just, er, meet you downstairs.'

She watches him go, her eyebrows furrowed, then steps back into her room.

With her rushed packing this morning, her choices are pretty limited – and she certainly hadn't planned for the same conditions Richie seems to expect. Her leather boots and jeans will have to do, but after eyeing the overcast sky she does put another long-sleeved shirt on. Then with a regretful look at the kettle, she slides into her jacket, grabs her room key and phone, and hurries out.

There's only one way in and out of Kirkcree, so navigating back to the fork is simple enough. Richie brings the car to a stop beside the *Welcome to Kirkcree* sign, and for a few moments they both stare at the mouth of the dirt road – the mouth of *An Rathad Damainte*, apparently.

It certainly doesn't look like a proper road – in fact, if it weren't for the fresh tyre impressions pressed into the mud, George would think that the last vehicle to pass that way was probably pulled by a horse. Her gaze snags on an unexpected flash of colour among the shrubs.

'Pretty flowers,' she observes, pointing to a few bright pink blooms peeking out between the thick, glossy leaves.

But after Richie follows her gesture, he makes a disgusted sound. 'That's rhododendron.'

She isn't surprised that Richie knows the name; he has an almost encyclopaedic knowledge of Scottish flora. 'Why did you say it like a rhododendron killed your mother?'

Richie shifts the car back into drive and they roll forward. 'It's Scotland's most invasive plant. Spreads like wildfire across the land and strangles the natives, blocks them from getting any sun. There are teams of people who go around destroying infestations like this.'

The rhododendron is so overgrown that the thick stems scrape against their doors; the light squeal against the metal makes George shiver, her shoulders pulling up around her neck. A pink blossom caresses her window, looking completely – deceptively – harmless.

Beyond the choking tangles of rhododendron, old forests stretch outwards on either side of the road; behind them, massive hills rise like false suns, stained a watered-down yellow – like tea made with a single dunk of the bag – and there are more vast patches of dark green and purple heather, the mottled shade a creeping necrosis across the landscape.

Suddenly, the layer of glass and steel between George and the wilderness surrounding *An Rathad Damainte* feels as thin as a sheet of paper, their car as insignificant as a tiny beetle scurrying across the floor of the ancient forests surrounding them. She feels even smaller; she wedges her phone more securely beneath her thigh on the fraying seat, and starts mentally listing everything she can see, feel, touch and smell before the bud of anxiety in her stomach can bloom into something more poisonous.

She's glad Richie swapped his compact, city-friendly car for the four-wheel drive – they probably would have had to tackle this road on foot if he hadn't. It's still not a comfortable ride – they both pitch and jolt around in their seats as the tyres drop into unavoidable depressions, or slide on slick patches. According to the team who worked the crime scene yesterday, Bambi was found roughly six miles from the mouth of the road. It's probably for the best that neither of them is attempting conversation right now – she's trying not to accidentally bite her tongue off, and Richie is white-knuckling the wheel.

Eventually, there's a break in the trees on both sides of the road, the forests temporarily giving way to the sickly hills and rust-coloured peat hags. A rocky outcrop erupts from the earth on the left-hand side of the road; the tape and cones are gone, but it's a landmark that George recognises from the photos. Even if she hadn't, there's another indication that they're in the right place. A mud-splattered police vehicle is parked on the shoulder just ahead, directly under a precarious overhang of rock and shrubbery.

As they park on the other side and get out of the car, George wonders at the sense of that parking spot, considering how loose some of those rocks look, but as soon as the officer opens his mouth, she realises that sense is a department he seems to be lacking in.

'What a shite piece of real estate this is, eh? Uglier than my mother in the morning, and she's been dead three years.'

With that preamble, the man leaning against the car sticks out his hand. 'PC Merrick Bear.' He looks over her shoulder, back towards Kirkcree. 'Just the two of you, then?'

PC Bear's palm is fleshy and damp against hers, just like the rest of him; even with a breeze ruffling his fluffy moustache, his forehead remains shiny. A yellow high-vis vest strains across his chest.

'Who else were you expecting?' she asks, retracting her hand with a suppressed grimace.

'No, no, I just thought … you're Lennox, aye? Busted that island of savages? Been all over the news.' He glances over her shoulder again, and George thinks he looks a little disappointed. 'Figured the cameras would follow you everywhere.'

George smiles blandly. 'This is DI Richard Stewart,' she says, happily stepping aside. 'He's running lead on this.'

'Call me Merrick,' the man says, grasping Richie's hand. 'Not much for the formal stuff, myself.'

'I wasn't aware someone was going to meet us,' Richie says, surreptitiously wiping his hand on his trousers.

'Aye, well, I heard you'd be coming out this afternoon, and considering I responded to the initial call' – Bear pauses, as if waiting for canned applause – 'I volunteered to meet you.'

'You were first on scene?' Richie clarifies.

'Aye,' Bear says proudly, 'after the folks who found her. They were blubbering all over me when I pulled up, even the bloke! I put his wife in the back of my car and told him to pull himself together. He got all huffy after that, said he wanted to give his statement to someone else.' His lower lip juts out at the memory. 'Anyway, I'll run you through it.'

He swaggers towards the front of his car. 'The call came in around ten past six in the morning,' Bear booms over his shoulder. 'I was the closest and it still took me about an hour to get here. Only stopped once for a breakfast sandwich from Costa on the way. I pulled up just over there, and their car was a bit further up. We all had our headlights on, as it was still basically night at that time. They said that's why they thought it was a mannequin.' Bear chuckles. 'Nobody's throwing good mannequins out the window, though, eh?'

'Just good women,' George says coolly. 'What were they doing out here?'

'Hikers, they said, and they were driving a big bastard of a car and had all the right gear, so I believed them. Wondered for a minute if they might have actually hit her themselves, until I got a good look at her and saw the wound.'

'So they pulled over and realised it was a person, and then called it in?' Richie prompts.

'Aye. I knew this was going to be important, even before we started getting calls from the bigwigs in Glasgow. And I was right, eh? Look who's come – the one from the papers, and her sidekick.' He throws an elbow towards George's ribs, which she neatly sidesteps.

Ignoring him, Richie crouches to examine the ground in front of Bear's vehicle. 'Has it rained here since she was found?'

Bear lowers himself down beside Richie. He presses one fat finger into the ground, pulling back to rub the grains of dirt against his thumb in a caricature of a seasoned tracker. 'Overnight,' he says. 'Less than an inch.'

Richie glances up at George. 'Blood's gone.'

'This is the right spot, though,' she says, ignoring the way Bear is looking between them, desperate to be included. 'I remember this overhang from the pictures. She was in line with this grassy bit.'

He nods, then turns to Bear. 'The area was thoroughly searched?'

'We combed every inch of the road.'

'She was missing a shoe.'

He shrugs, a huge movement of his shoulders. 'Probably still at the lodge. I mean' – he chuckles – 'that's what we're all thinking, right?'

As Bear continues detailing his initial observations, George steps back onto the road. The recent tyre tracks continue past their cars, rainwater collected in the treads, until the road curves around to the left and into some woodlands. To be fair to the couple, from this angle, it does look like the road should end up right at the base of the mountains.

'How far is it to Fiadhain Lodge?' she asks, interrupting whatever Bear had been saying.

The PC blinks at her, then squints into the distance. 'The entrance is a few miles up from here, on the other side of those trees. Takes another half-hour to drive, though, 'cause of all the bloody holes in the road.' He holds out a closed fist in front of him like he's grasping a set of reins and makes a rocking motion with his hips. 'Feels like you're riding a bull, eh?'

She ignores this. 'And this is all their land?'

Unclenching his fist, he sweeps his hand towards the outcrop, then wider to encompass the entire left-hand side of the road. 'Everything on this side, as far as you can see – from the highway to the mountain. Everything on the other side is Crown land, untouched woodlands all the way down into Kirkcree. Apparently, there are plans to carve it into lots and bribe people to settle out here with some funding scheme. Not sure how much luck they'll have.' He jerks his thumb towards the lodge side of the road. 'You wouldn't believe how much these folks paid. I've been on a couple of calls up here over the past year, usually cars knocking heads on narrow roads, people not used to driving this far up in the hills.' He looks around, and his nose wrinkles. 'It might be good for deer stalking, but the land itself is crap.'

Leaving Richie to handle Bear, she drifts off to the other side of the road. She keeps one ear on the conversation, though, and hears Richie redirect Bear back to the point multiple times with thinning patience, as she starts circling the area. Based on what she's heard and seen from PC Bear thus far, she almost expects to find the missing shoe, the gun and a signed confession.

But as she prowls the road, a light breeze ripples through the brown grass and curls like a finger beneath her chin, drawing her gaze upwards – towards the outcrop. Her fingertips tingle.

Up here.

'Were you one of the constables who visited Fiadhain Lodge?' Richie asks.

'Aye. Waste of time. We barely got a word out of them before they ran us off.'

'I can't imagine why,' Richie mutters, then gestures towards the side of the road that Bambi was found on, beyond the jutting rock of the outcrop. As he asks about land boundaries, George examines the outcrop thoughtfully. After identifying a path along the most convenient cracks and footholds in the stone, she takes off her gloves and stuffs them into her pocket.

She's halfway up the rock face before Richie's shout comes.

'Oh my— George!'

'It's fine, I've got a good grip.'

Footsteps approach at a jog, and then his voice is directly below her. 'What on earth are you doing?'

She pauses, taking a few restorative breaths. Once upon a time, even just looking at something this high up used to send her spinning with vertigo – another outcome of the Villo incident – but Dr Kassab gave her tips to manage that panicky sense of imbalance when it threatens to strike. Now, heights don't bother her so much, even if balconies still do.

'Just following a hunch,' she says.

There's a beat of silence, then—

'Be careful.'

Heaving herself over the top is the hardest part; when she does, she flops very ungracefully onto her back. A variety of hard things poke into her – rocks mostly, but also some broken branches that must have washed down the slope in past rainfalls. She raises her head carefully, then sits up. No vertigo.

'I'm all good,' she shouts, getting slowly to her hands and knees.

'Want me to come up?'

She laughs quietly at the image of him trying to recreate her climb up here. 'I'll have a look around first.'

'Stay away from the edge, okay? Lennox?'

She notes the return to her surname and sighs. 'Copy.'

The rock doesn't extend as far back as she expected; it gives way to that pale grass within a few yards. And beyond that is ... nothing, and *everything* – up here, she can properly take in how vast the land is, with no structures or signs of habitation in sight. She wonders how far back the lodge sits on the property; it could easily be hidden in a dip between hills, over that grassy ridge, or even within the trees. The breeze returns, sending the overgrown grasses swaying, and cooling her flushed cheeks. She can smell something malodorous in the otherwise fresh mountain air, earthy and overripe.

Still on her hands and knees, she visually sweeps the ground around her. She's not exactly sure what she's looking for, but she felt that tingling in her fingers – a weak echo of the uncanny magnetic *tug* she used to get, a crackle of electricity through her veins that used to tell her when she was on the right track. Dr Kassab theorises that this ability was rattled as hard as her skull when she went over that balcony and, like her brain, will take time to heal.

After a minute of flipping leaves and pushing aside rocks, a glint of light bouncing off metal catches her eye.

'When you come down, I'll spot you,' Bear calls. 'I've got my hands ready.'

She ignores him, brushing aside a clod of dirt to get a better look at the item – and her whole damn hand starts to buzz.

As promised, Bear has his hands up in the air when she begins her descent – and keeps them up until she has to firmly ask him to step back for her final drop to the ground.

'Just trying to help,' he says sulkily, shoving his hands into his pockets.

Richie doesn't look much happier. 'Was that worth giving me palpitations?'

'You tell me.'

Withdrawing one of her gloves from a pocket, she carefully unrolls it and holds her palm out to him. Resting atop the wool is a circular campaign badge, the kind people might attach to their shirts or tote bags. The plastic face has popped off somewhere else, leaving only the metal backing and no indication of who or what the badge was promoting.

But it's the thick safety pin on the backing that Richie's eyes zero in on.

'Oh my,' he breathes. 'That looks like—'

'Blood? I think so, too.'

'You think it could have been used to write—?'

'Could have been.'

Richie looks up at her, and there's the ghost of a smile on his lips. 'Good work, George.'

For a terrifying moment, she feels a prickling sensation behind her eyes. She ducks her head, offering a nonchalant 'Thanks'.

The moment is interrupted by a pointed cough.

'I don't get it,' Bear says, frowning down at her outstretched hand. 'Why are you two so worked up over a grubby old badge?'

CHAPTER 10

Understandably, Richie is reluctant to let PC Bear transport the badge for testing.

But George eventually convinces him that they have too much to do in Kirkcree, and he acquiesces after they both take photos of the badge from all angles before sealing it in a plastic evidence bag, and sending PC Bear speeding off towards Inverness.

Richie calls the pathologist as soon as they're back in the car, absently tossing George the keys. Dr Bùi sounds a little disgruntled to hear Richie's voice so soon after the strained meeting this morning, but he does agree that the writing on Bambi's arm could have been done with a thick safety pin. He tells them he'll take a look as soon as Bear drops the badge off, but reiterates that he has 'a queue of pressing issues to attend to'.

Richie fumes over that last part. 'A queue,' he echoes bitterly after the pathologist ends the call. 'Has nobody up the chain stressed the importance of this case? Or is he just lazy?'

George frowns. Richie has always been the antithesis of her; he's usually warm and charismatic and kind, and leads with an empathy that coaxes honesty from witnesses and suspects alike. Based on what she's seen over these past few hours, she's starting to understand Cole's concern – and feel it herself.

Something PC Bear said floats back to her. *Lennox, aye? Busted that island of savages? Been all over the news.* She takes her eyes from the road for just a second to look at Richie, now scowling down at his phone. Could the stark change in his personality be tied to *jealousy*? That he's been relegated to the foil or forgotten entirely in every version of their story that's been broadcast to the public?

She would never have picked this reaction from him – perhaps he didn't know he was capable of it, either. But if it's true, if he resents the fact that the headlines read LENNOX not STEWART, she'll be more than happy to explain to him the long-term side effects of being thrust into the spotlight.

Richie makes a few more phone calls during the drive back to Ivy House; it isn't until she has parked the car and is about to get out that he speaks to her.

'Do you still get vertigo?'

'Er. Not really.' She hesitates, then squares her shoulders. 'It's one of the things I've been working on with my therapist.'

'Right ... and how's that going?'

'Therapy? It's, er, good.'

'Good?' he echoes, as if he's never heard the word.

'Yeah,' she says, unsure of the direction of his questions. 'It's been ... helpful.'

Richie glances at her, then away. 'That's ... that's good.'

Then he sniffs in a topic-changing way, and says, 'I'm waiting on the go-ahead from Cole for us to take another run at Fiadhain Lodge. In the meantime, let's talk to the locals.'

But he doesn't get out. George waits, and after a few seconds her patience pays off.

'I tried it. Therapy.' He looks down at his left hand, flexing his fingers around the door handle until his knuckles turn white. 'Didn't help.'

She's not sure what she's meant to say, but she can't leave something like that unanswered.

'I went through a few therapists before I found this latest one, so I didn't think it would either ... but it does. Eventually.' *If you let it*, she wants to add, but she's uncertain of the boundaries of this small pocket of vulnerability.

He hums, a sound that reveals nothing more, and gets out. With a sigh, she follows.

'We'll do the hotels by foot,' Richie says, 'then take the car into the village.'

She looks across the lawns to the hotels and B&Bs on either side of Ivy House, and those across the street. 'There's a fair few to cover. Should we split up?'

'No.'

She glances at him. 'Why?'

He angles sharply across the lawn of the next hotel. 'Because I said so.'

This conversation sets the tone for the next forty minutes as they tour Kirkcree's accommodation options: Richie shows Bambi's and Cara's photos to every staff member, guest and passer-by, and when nobody recognises either of them, he stomps out with a muttered 'Thanks.' George only lingers long enough to smile apologetically and leave Richie's phone number at the front desk before hurrying after him.

She can feel his mood growing fouler as the minutes pass; he's crackling like a thunderstorm by the time they arrive at the final hotel. And after the receptionist shakes her head at both photos, George worries that lightning is about to strike. It's easier to attribute his mood now to the long, break-less day they've had – she's tired, and her stomach is growling loud enough that she's given up trying to hide it. And if she hasn't eaten in hours, then Richie hasn't for far longer.

They walk back to the car in silence. Ivy House's porch light has been turned on against the darkening sky.

'Can you believe that?' Richie mutters as they get in.

George turns the ignition on. Though it is cold outside, her body has grown uncomfortably warm under her layers; she unzips her jacket and starts shimmying it off. 'Well, I mean …

we're not exactly making it easy for them.' She eases the car out of the driveway and turns for the village centre. 'We don't even know if our victim came to Kirkcree or, if she was here, *when* that might have been. It could have been days, weeks or months ago – in Cara's case, *years*. And we both know that even recent memories aren't always reliable – even if someone thinks they remember seeing Cara a decade ago, I wouldn't stake my case on their evidence.'

He stares out the window, and George can see the line of his jaw is tight. 'I trust *my* memory. This is exactly how I remember it being ten years ago – all questions, no answers. A decade on, and nothing has changed.' He makes an irritated sound, but she can tell tiredness is bleeding into his attitude. He probably got less sleep last night than she did, too.

But her sympathy doesn't stop her from taking the opportunity.

'One thing *has* changed since then,' she says gently, turning onto the high street.

'Mm?'

She shoots him a kind smile. 'You've got loads of wrinkles now.'

There are a few beats of silence.

His irritated snort is quiet, but she hears it. And he seems slightly less miserable when he directs her to pull in at the small carpark opposite the supermarket.

It's busier now than it was earlier – the pre-dinner rush has begun, and there's a stream of people heading in and out of the shops, many with kids hanging off their arms, or with grocery bags looped over their shoulders. It's not an ideal time to be asking questions, but she can guess how Richie would respond to a suggestion that they delay this until the morning.

Eyeing the crowd, he says, 'We should be okay to split up here. Don't go further than the shops, though. And don't waste time in each place – in and out.'

'Understood.'

His eyes flicker to her for a moment. 'I saw a decent-looking restaurant just back there. Red and black sign. Let's meet there when we're done.'

Watching him walk away, she notes the way his jacket hangs off his shoulders, the lack of bounce in his step, and it occurs to her that this feeling she has, this gnawing worry in the pit of her stomach, is exactly what Richie must have felt last year every time he looked at her.

CHAPTER 11

Ironically, The Kirk Hotel is not, in fact, a hotel.

It is a fairly large, bistro-style restaurant, with blocky tables and loud classic rock music and the scents of spilt beer and frying meat. The waitress, who greets George with a large smile, directs her to a table big enough to seat four and drops two laminated menus in front of her.

'Back in a few,' the woman says, before hurrying away to a table where a man sits with his hand raised, gesticulating at her impatiently.

A baby girl at the next table stares at George over her dad's shoulder, his hand patting rhythmically against her little back. George smiles, scrunching her eyes a little, and the baby smiles back – then the smile trembles, and an air-raid siren starts to build from her chest.

The dad has whisked the baby off to a quiet corner by the time Richie arrives a few minutes later, slinging his coat across the back of the seat. His hair is glistening under the yellow lights.

'Is it raining?'

'Just started,' he says, dropping into his seat with a groan. 'What's wrong? You look upset.'

She presses her forefingers along her browbone – there's an ache forming, but nothing like the debilitating migraines she used to get. 'Oh, nothing. Crying babies just make me edgy.'

He makes a sound of agreement. 'Poppy was a crier. Drove Jenny and me up the tree. And she was our first, so we had no clue what to do. People kept offering to drop off food. We just wanted some sleep.' He rubs a hand over his face and stares down at the menu blankly. 'I'm starving,' he announces, as if it's news to him, too. 'Have you ordered?'

'Only just got here. The waitress will be back in a minute.'

He nods again, then looks around. She observes him silently, wondering if he's mapping the room for the same reasons that she does.

'If she comes back,' he says suddenly, rising, 'ask what the biggest pasta is, and get me that.' Without waiting for her response, he beelines for the bathrooms in the back corner.

The waitress comes just as the door closes behind him, and, with their orders placed, George leans back in her chair to wait. There's a couple up at the bar, the woman perched on a high stool, her partner standing close beside her. She can't see the man's face from here, but she can tell that he's speaking. His partner seems to be listening closely.

George cocks her head. On closer inspection, the woman is actually leaning *away* from the man, and there's a rigidity to her shoulders and neck. George had incorrectly guessed her stillness as attentiveness; she supposes it is, in a sense – the way a deer freezes in a car's headlights.

George is about to stand, wondering how to subtly ask the woman if she needs rescuing, when a phone starts ringing nearby. The sound makes her jump – she grasps her jacket pocket but doesn't feel the vibration; it's not her phone, and nobody else in the vicinity is diving for theirs. Then her eyes land on Richie's side of the table, to where his phone is buzzing against a fork. Wondering if it might be Cole, she turns it around to check the caller ID.

Her stomach drops a little.

JENNY

She glances over her shoulder towards the toilets. Richie will be back soon — and she's not his secretary.

The woman at the bar is gone, but the man is still there, hunched over his pint glass. He's not that tall, perhaps only a little more so than Richie, but solid — she can't tell if it's muscle or fat, but either way he looks strong. And when he turns around to lean back against the bar, she doesn't blame the woman for wanting to get away.

It's not that he's horrific to look at — there might even be something appealing in the angle of his sharp cheekbones, emphasised by his buzzed head. He's wearing a long-sleeved sweatshirt with a graphic design splashed across the front, and a pair of fraying jeans that ruck up over workman's boots.

But it's the eyes, especially when they fix on George, that make her want to pull back. Even from this far away, she feels the piercing chill of them, an ice pick pressed to warm flesh. Precise. Focused. Knowing.

And then, as if he has no idea of how his gaze is affecting her — or as if he knows *exactly* how it is — the man raises his glass towards her and smiles.

Richie's phone, which had fallen silent again, buzzes. It's a text message this time, and George is grateful for the excuse to turn away from the creep at the bar, even if it is to invade Richie's privacy yet again.

IF YOU DON'T ANSWER THE NEXT ONE I'M CALLING KYLIE

'Oh, shit,' George mutters, and that's all she has time to do before the phone lights up again with another incoming call. With Jenny's threat fresh in mind, she answers.

'What the hell are you playing at?' Jenny's voice cracks down the line like thunder. 'What did I say, Richard? Answer. Every. Call. Respond to *every* text. No excuses!'

George looks for Richie again, a little desperate now.

'Well? Rich?' Jenny sounds less sure now; it's the tremor of fear in her voice when she says Richie's name again that spurs George to respond.

'He's in the bathroom,' she blurts out.

'George? Is that you?'

'Yeah,' George replies weakly, bracing. When Jenny Stewart is mad, her wrath can bring giants to their knees.

'Oh. Oh, *love*.'

A lump forms in George's throat. *Not anger. Something worse.*

'H-how are you?' Jenny continues, her words coming fast now. 'Are you all right?'

George clears her throat once. 'Yeah, I-I'm fine.'

'I'm sorry I haven't reached out, love. I've just been so focused on getting Richie through the day—'

'You don't have to explain,' George says, looking around nervously. Still no Richie, and the creep has disappeared too. 'I wouldn't have wanted to talk to me either, after the way I treated him.'

'What? No, George, that's not—'

'It's fine,' George says, sharper than she means to.

Jenny groans. 'Lord, you're as bad as each other. Is he eating, at least?'

'We're about to. But I'll get him to call you right after.'

'Thanks, George.'

She's about to hang up when she hears Jenny say her name again. 'What was that?'

'Keep an eye on him, please.'

A laugh escapes before she can cut it off – if only Jenny knew how closely she's watching Richie. 'Of course.'

'And be kind to yourself.'

She digs the heel of her palm into her prickling eyes one at a time. *Don't you dare*, she orders herself. 'I will.'

The line disconnects. George puts the phone down on the

table and, just to be safe, presses her palms against her eyes until she can be sure no tears are going to spill out.

'You all right?'

She jolts. 'Jesus, Richie.'

He slides into his seat. 'Sorry. Your eyes are red.'

'I was just ...' Oh, what the hell. 'Crying.'

He freezes. 'Why? What happened?'

She waves towards his phone. She watches him scroll through the missed call notifications and the texts, sees his confusion twist into strain. 'You spoke to her?'

'She was getting worried.'

'I'm sure she was,' he mutters, tapping out a message before slipping his phone in his pocket.

The waitress arrives with their meals.

'My parents are the same way,' she says through a mouthful of pasta. 'And Jane, but the time zones help keep her messages to only ... five per day.' Richie stares at his own plate, his thoughts clearly elsewhere. George remembers Jenny's question. 'Don't let that get cold.'

He picks up his fork but doesn't move to take a bite. 'I can't believe nobody knows her.'

'Our victim?'

'She's young, she's fit, she's attractive. She has a tattoo, which means she sat beside a tattoo artist for a length of time. Someone looked this woman in the eye, spoke to her, handed her things, said hello and goodbye.' He jabs the fork into the pasta, the prongs squealing against the ceramic. 'Where the hell are those people? Why aren't they missing her?'

'Cole still has people looking for cameras in the area, right? Maybe they'll find something, and we'll be able to go from there. And someone will be missing her, Rich. It's just a matter of time until we find something.' As soon as she says it, she regrets it – who is she to preach the concept of patience to someone who's been stuck on a cold case for a decade?

She sees it in his face, the exasperation, and rushes to fix it. 'I know you're disappointed—'

'*Disappointed* doesn't begin to cover it, Lennox.'

'But it's okay if you are. My therapist says—'

Richie laughs, a harsh noise that sounds wrong coming from his mouth. 'Oh, *this* should be good.'

Her next breath catches in her chest, squeezed by something Richie has never made her feel in all their years working together – small. And he seems to know it, too – he leans back in his chair, and scrubs a hand along his jaw roughly. But he doesn't take it back, doesn't elaborate or excuse himself.

She stares down at her food, heat blooming across her cheeks. *In-in-in.*

He still doesn't speak when she drops the car key in front of his plate and heads for the door. It's only when she's jogging down the stairs into the crisp air that she realises she didn't pay for her meal.

Fuck him, she thinks viciously, sparks of embarrassment and anger catching on tinder in her gut. *He can cough up £15 as an apology.*

A breeze stirs the loose hairs around her temples and neck and the corners of a flyer taped to a nearby streetlamp. It's advertising a street market happening in a couple of nights' time; the text promises food, mulled wine, crafts and live music. She looks around – identical posters have been taped to bins and tacked inside windows – and wonders if it's an annual thing or something designed to lure visitors into Kirkcree for an evening. Only half the tables in The Kirk were occupied; perhaps tourism slows down here over winter.

A waft of cigarette smoke precedes a voice. 'Inspector?'

George startles, then spots the speaker approaching her. 'Oh, Zoe. Sorry, I didn't see you.'

Zoe chuckles. 'Story of my life.' She raises a lit cigarette to her lips but pauses before inhaling. 'How did you go this afternoon? You went out to *An Rathad Damainte*?'

George wraps her arms around her chest, remembering the painful squeal of the rhododendrons against the car door. 'We went out there, yeah.'

Zoe observes the movement and smiles knowingly. 'It's strange, isn't it?'

'You mentioned stories.'

'*Stories* probably wasn't the right word,' Zoe says, tapping the cigarette; the ash disintegrates on its journey to the ground. 'It's just ... history, I guess. *An Rathad Damainte* got its name in 1800 – before then, all that land from the road to the mountains was owned by two rich families: the Fairgrieves and the Grants.' She clucks her tongue. 'Safe to say, they did not get along.'

This is news to George. 'Land disputes?'

'That was part of it, but I think they were just mean old bastards. Started accusing each other of raiding their supplies, messing with their water. Things just got nastier and nastier over time until ... well, only the Fairgrieves were left.'

'The Grants moved?'

'Er, technically.' At George's questioning look, Zoe adds, 'They went as far as the cemetery, I guess. The Selbys up at Fiadhain Lodge own that land now – the old Grant house was falling to pieces until they took over and did it all up.'

But George is stuck on the first half of her answer. 'What do you—? Are you suggesting that the Fairgrieves *killed* them?'

'Suggesting, stating,' she says, tilting her head, 'depends who you ask. There was going to be a wedding between the two families, to try and mend fences, I guess, but it all went tits-up on the day. All the Grants were dead before the cake was cut.' She laughs. 'Talk about toxic in-laws, am I right?'

'Were the Fairgrieves punished?'

'According to them, the Grants started it – and there weren't any Grants left to tell a different tale.' She takes a final puff of her cigarette before stamping it out against the top of a nearby bin. 'But everyone in Kirkcree knew they were guilty. Some of the village leaders wanted to confront them, but their house is a *literal* castle – one of those old fortified mansions with turrets and a million rooms. There's even a crypt, which I'm *dying* to see. Not literally,' she adds with a grin. 'So with the Fairgrieves barricaded inside their fortress, the locals did the only thing they could think of: pretended they didn't exist. Shunned them from gatherings, refused to do business with them, marriage proposals were rejected—'

'And the only road in and out of their land got a new name.' George frowns. 'Why *cursed*, though?'

'Well, cursed is only one definition of *damainte*; it also means damned, condemned. But all of them are accurate, considering what the villagers intended.'

'Which was?'

'For the Fairgrieves to die out. And for nobody to ever forget that that road is a one-way trip to damnation.' She lifts a shoulder in a casual shrug, the gravity of that statement no match for youth's invincibility.

A shriek makes them both turn sharply. Across the street, two black Range Rovers are idling in a No Parking zone. The occupants are exiting in a tumble, laughing raucously – the one who shrieked almost fell in a tangle of legs – and all are weaving as they cross the street. George steps closer to Zoe to get out of their way.

The youngest is a willowy blonde woman with huge glossy lips, a few years younger than Zoe, and the oldest is a square-jawed man wearing a close-cut wool jumper. His voice is the loudest – American, as is the young woman's – but George can hear other accents among the group: Spanish, maybe, and a polished English. They're all dressed similarly, in tailored jeans and fur-trimmed jackets, fingers and wrists and ears sparkling. And though George has moved all the way to the left on the footpath, the American is so off-balance that he still manages to clip her shoulder with his own.

'Hey, watch out,' she says.

'You watch out,' he slurs, barely sparing her a glance. 'This is fucking Burberry.'

This gets another chorus of laughter from the group, and George is relieved when the sound cuts off as they enter The Kirk.

'Arrogant pricks,' Zoe mutters. 'They were like that last night, too.'

'Are they staying in the village?'

'Mr Burberry? No way.' She mimes pumping a shotgun, then aims the imaginary muzzle directly at George's chest. 'They're guests at Fiadhain Lodge,' she says, letting the gun dissolve through her fingers. 'But apparently luxury gets boring – they've come into the village a couple of times to splash their cash and rub shoulders with us commoners.'

There's a muffled vibration, and Zoe pulls her phone out. Looking at the screen, her expression softens into something a little goofy. 'I'd better go,' she says, heading for The Kirk. 'Harris wants a burger – a bloody chef who never wants to cook for himself. Oh,' she adds, stopping midway up the stairs, 'you didn't *see* anyone out on the road, did you?'

George frowns. 'Like who? Tourists?'

Zoe just cocks her head, staring at George for a beat. Then she grins. 'Never mind. See you back at Ivy, Inspector Lennox.'

As the doors close behind Zoe, George starts off for Ivy House, but after only a few steps the skin on the back of her neck starts to prickle. She glances at the circles of light thrown by the streetlamps and the deep pools of shadow between them. With a start, she realises that she's alone on the street – a brief moment when nobody is coming in or out of the supermarket, or exiting a takeaway cradling heavy bags of steaming containers.

Her chin on a swivel, George steps onto the road, looking both ways. A fallen poster is snagged by a gust of wind, the paper skittering across the ground towards her in a tumbleweed of dead leaves and empty food wrappers. With everything else so quiet, even these sounds – the breeze rustling through the nearby trees, catching in the shell of her ear like a wave – make the prickle travel down from her neck to the base of her spine, as if something is dragging a pastry-cutting wheel along her skin.

The most difficult part of her anxiety, in her opinion, is struggling to differentiate between paranoia and reality – does she just *think* she's being watched, or is she ignoring her body's innate cues to check for danger? Fear used to motivate her, force her into action, regardless of how risky the outcome could be. But now, just like that woman at the bar earlier, her body locks up under the pressure.

There.

A narrow lane between two buildings, the orange flare of a cigarette on the inhale. And then footsteps, a scuff of a boot against the pavement.

The man from the bar, the man with the hunter's eyes, steps into the white light spilling from the supermarket. He drops the cigarette to the ground and raises one foot to hover over the smoking butt.

And then he looks right at her. Traps her in his gaze. And presses the toe of his boot onto the butt and slowly, purposefully, grinds it to a pulp.

CHAPTER 12

George thought that all those months of physical and mental recovery after her head injury last year had taught her everything she needed to know about patience.

That was until her parents insisted on twice-weekly family phone calls.

As George anticipated, today's call kicks off with a barrage of questions.

'Do you have phone reception?'

'Have you eaten? When? How much?'

'Where's the closest police station? Hospital?'

'Exactly how far away is your car parked? And you said you're on the first floor? Go look out the window, tell me how far you are from the ground.'

'She's not going to be shimmying down drainpipes,' Jane says. 'She's not Lara fucking Croft.'

'She might need to get out of a tight spot again,' her dad argues. 'Just remember, Georgie, bend your knees when you land.'

'She's not leaping out of windows,' Mam cuts in with a hiss. 'She's got her head on straight now, and she's got Richie with her. He'll be looking out for her.'

'Like he looked out for her last time?' Dad mutters darkly.

George wraps up the call pretty quickly after that, and her phone pings with a message from Jane a few seconds later – an eye-roll emoji, followed by: *But seriously, bend your knees xo*

She draws back the light coverlet on the bed, ready to sink into the soft mattress with her laptop, planning to throw herself into the latest missing persons reports, when there's a knock at her door. She knows who it's going to be, so she doesn't bother throwing a jacket over her mismatched pyjamas.

Richie is still in the clothes he's been wearing all day, and the pink in his cheeks suggests he's just come in from the cold.

'Just wanted to check you got in all right,' he says quietly, not quite meeting her eye, 'and to say that Cole gave us the go-ahead to take another run at Fiadhain Lodge in the morning.'

'Great. Night.' As she goes to close the door, Richie extends a foot to block it.

'I spoke to Jenny,' he says. 'She was upset.'

'Because of me?'

'No. I mean, yes, because of you – but she's not upset *with* you.' He looks down at his hands, twisting his wedding ring. 'I'm sorry that this ... that just because you and I ... I'm sorry that I made you think *she* didn't care. Of course she does. She loves you.'

'Oh. Well, that's ...' George clears her throat twice, trying not to wince at his distinction of *she*. 'Thanks for telling me.'

'She's asked if she can see you, when we get back.'

George nods, not trusting her voice.

'Okay. Good. Well, goodnight.'

For a beat, she's stuck at the door. Then her muscles loosen again and she takes a running leap towards the bed, squirms down until the blanket covers her head, and hopes Richie can't hear her hitched breaths through the shared wall.

If he heard, he apologises for causing her tears by not mentioning them – in fact, he greets her with tentative warmth when they meet in the foyer early the following morning, his suitcase already beside the front door.

'How'd you sleep?' he asks, scanning her face.

Her regular nightmare played again last night, her nose filled with the scent of damp earth and sea spray and concluding with a terrifying fall – a horrible combination of two of her most disturbing memories. Last night she *swears* she also felt the scuttle of spider legs running up her arms and across her face before she was thrown over the edge. She woke once, breathing hard, and dragged the lamp closer to check the blankets for critters before she felt brave enough to lie back down.

'Not great,' she admits. 'But it's better than the last place we were sent.'

The corner of his lip twitches. 'I think so, too.'

The reception area is vacant, but there's an elderly man stacking more wood beside the fire in the sitting room.

'Excuse me, sir,' Richie calls. 'Do you work here?'

The man straightens in slow motion, then turns to peer at them owlishly. His face is round, the skin almost translucent with advanced age, and deeply lined across his forehead and around his mouth. When he speaks, his sagging jowls quiver. 'Eh?'

'Do you work here?' Richie repeats, enunciating.

'Eh?' he says again, shuffling forward a few steps. 'What did you say, lad?'

A suspicion occurs to George. 'Are you Dean?'

His pale lips split in a smile. 'Oh, aye. You must be the police officers. And married, Zoe said?'

George turns a laugh into a cough; Richie shoots her a dark look.

'We're checking out now, sir,' he says.

'You're leaving already?' Dean's soft Highland accent is tinted with confusion. 'You know what happened, then?'

'Not yet, but I can assure you, we're looking far and wide for answers.'

'Far and wide? Oh, no,' he says earnestly, shaking his head, 'no, you won't be needing to go too far. *An Rathad Damainte* has the answers you need.'

Richie scratches his head contemplatively, then pulls out his phone. 'Can I show you a couple of photos, sir?'

'Oh? Well, aye.' Dean pats the pockets of his brown trousers searchingly. 'Now, where did I put my …?'

'On your head, sir,' George calls from the door.

He stares at her as she gestures towards her own head, then chortles when his fingers brush the wire frames digging into his bald, liver-spotted scalp. Blinking a few times as if to adjust to the sharper visuals, he beckons Richie closer.

'This first woman was found a couple of days ago along *An Rathad Damainte*,' Richie explains, 'and this is Cara Reid. She went missing a decade ago. Do you recognise either of them?'

Dean hums. 'Oh, aye.'

For a second, George thinks she misheard him – then she sees the shock on Richie's face, as if he's questioning his hearing, too.

'You *have*?' Richie chokes out. 'Which one?'

'Both of them.'

George feels like her eyes are about to fall out of her head. 'When?'

'Last week, I'd say.'

For a second, George feels a flood of elation. This is *not* how she thought this case was going to go, considering the disappointing results from their interviews yesterday; Richie is almost trembling with anticipation.

But then—

'And I saw her a month ago, and twenty years ago, and tomorrow, and next week,' Dean continues, plucking his glasses from his nose. 'Same faces, same fates.'

That elation rushes out of her like breath after a gut-punch. 'What do you mean?'

He looks at George with a serious expression. 'It's the same story, you understand? Young women like them go off on their own and the night swallows them whole. You see it on the news every day. Always the same story.'

He repeats those final words a few times, then looks down at his glasses. 'Oh, there they are,' he chortles, holding the glasses aloft. 'They were in my hand.'

Richie can't even muster a farewell; he runs a hand over his face, then heads for the front doors, only pausing to toss their room keys onto the reception desk. She starts after him.

'Lass?'

She turns back. 'Yes, sir?'

Dean's fingers play with the arms of his glasses. 'Be careful, aye? It's dark out – don't get swallowed up.'

He sounds genuinely concerned, so she nods. 'I'll be careful, sir.'

She doesn't look back again, but she feels Dean's eyes follow her all the way out the door.

Despite his meandering mind, Dean wasn't wrong – it *is* dark out here. The sun is yet to rise, though there's a faint glow over the top of the distant hills. A gauzy fog hugs the tarmac; Richie navigates the road out of Kirkcree with extra care, and the yellow wash from the car headlights creates an eerie, dream-like glow ahead.

The fog seems heavier at the base of *An Rathad Damainte*. After hearing Zoe's story about how the road got its name, George wonders if the unsettling feeling she gets as they pass the reaching rhododendrons is actually coming from the ground itself. She doesn't bother relaying the information to Richie; she already knows how he feels about ghost stories.

The road was difficult enough to traverse in daylight; with the sun still trapped behind the mountains, and the fog lingering, they're forced to drive at a crawl. Turning on her phone torch, George pulls out her notebook and recaps. 'So, Fiadhain Lodge is an exclusive deer-stalking operation owned by a couple, Francina and Patrick Selby. The property includes a fortified house, a loch, numerous outbuildings … spans a hundred square kilometres. They also have a private helipad – guests are flown in from Inverness.'

'I wish we'd put in a request,' Richie mutters, wincing as the car plunges into an especially deep divot.

She can't picture Cole approving that invoice. 'Fiadhain Lodge has been in operation for sixteen years and they've won a bunch of luxury travel awards, hosted a few members of the royal family – a handful of second cousins, but they still bragged about it. I found an article from a few years ago that said three people were caught tampering with one of the lodge's vehicles. Fiadhain Lodge's legal team claimed they were members of an animal activist group that's been waging an "ongoing guerrilla campaign" against them and other hunting organisations around the country, accusing them of causing millions of dollars of damage to equipment and property over the years.'

In a move that proved unhelpful to the defendants, around twenty members of the activist group Fearless for Fauna showed up at the courthouse to protest against the guilty verdict. A photo that accompanied the article showed them standing in a row, a wall of white shirts with a red logo on their chests, and all were wearing surgical masks and sunglasses to conceal their identities. According to the article, the group held up posters showing mutilated animals that they claimed had been recovered from lodges all over Scotland, and handed out pamphlets accusing lodges of tranquillising animals to make them easier to hunt, as well as FFF-branded badges and wristbands to pedestrians passing the courthouse.

'Mm. Cole told me that the lodge's legal team are a nightmare to deal with. We've been instructed to treat them with kid gloves,' he adds with a derisive snort.

Based on what she's read, and Cole's mention of the Selbys' 'friends in high places', George isn't surprised by the instruction. She's just worried about Richie deciding to rip the gloves off halfway through the interview.

She turns the torch off, stowing her phone again. It reminds her of a question she wrote down last night. 'Did Cara have a mobile?'

'She did, but seemed to only use it to communicate with Ben, or sometimes to move money around in her bank accounts. And to answer your next question,' he adds, 'she had no more than a thousand pounds to her name at any given time, and none of it has been touched since she disappeared.'

She swears. 'Okay ... any social media, online presence?'

'Social media requires the *social* part, and from everything I've learnt about her, Cara only cared about Ben.'

'Nobody is that one dimensional.'

'I know, but it's the only side of her I've been able to verify. There're snippets from other parts of her life, but they're like ... just *bits* of her. That photo, a hairclip, an old coat. Parts, important parts, but not as important as the whole.'

'She had an ex.'

'A string of them. They ended fast – usually after violence, but none of that is officially documented. Just Ben's word that she often showed up to see him with bruises.'

These answers are giving George a strange, panicky kind of sadness. 'Friends? Co-workers, neighbours, hairdresser, a regular dealer?'

'Believe me,' he says, acknowledging her tone with a grim smile, 'I've asked all these questions.'

'But she had to have been doing *something* with her time. She wasn't just sitting around, twiddling her thumbs in between calls to Ben.' George chews her lip, wondering again how Cara could possibly be connected to Bambi, or to the wealthy Selbys of Fiadhain Lodge. 'Could she have owed someone money?'

'Possibly. She seemed to be getting herself straight. Ben said last time he spoke to Cara, she was three weeks sober. Which might not sound like a lot, but—'

'When you're using every day, it's huge,' George finishes, and when Richie glances at her, she answers his silent question. 'Ten months last week. Do you know that they don't actually hand out those little sobriety coins, like they do in the films? My therapist said I should buy and eat a whole cake for milestones instead. I think he forgot that I have to chase people for a living.'

'What was it like?'

'What?'

'Getting ... sober.' His expression is carefully neutral. 'You don't have to tell me if you don't want to.'

Why not? They've still got a long way to go until they reach Fiadhain Lodge, and the confessional atmosphere of the darkened car, with dawn light about to break over the eastern peaks, is making conversation easier than it's been this whole trip.

'It was the hardest thing I've ever done. Not just because of the physical pain, the withdrawals,' she says, recoiling from the memory of her sweat-slicked skin sliding over the cold tiles of the bathroom floor, the cramping, the bile burning the back of her throat. 'But there was so much *mental* work I needed to do. I didn't realise it when I first started seeing therapists – I think it's why I kept quitting them and looking for new ones. I just thought they were meant to tell me how to fix my head and move forward. I wasn't ready, or willing, at the time, to look *back*.'

She swallows, fixing her gaze on a spot through the windscreen. They're among trees now, the road curving around to the left.

'I lied to so many people to hide what was happening to me, what I was doing. And because there were lies, there was shame, and defensiveness, and so ... God, just *so* much self-loathing. And all of it stemmed from fear – that I wouldn't get better, that people would think I was weak. That I'd lose my job, my reputation, and any and all respect I've ever earnt.' She takes a quick breath for courage. 'And that I'd disappoint you, Rich. I was really, *really* fucking scared to let you down.'

She laughs sardonically. 'And all of those things came true, in their own way. Officially hit rock bottom. Spent most of this year climbing out.'

Richie is silent for a while; she's not even sure what she wants him to say. What does she need? His forgiveness, certainly, but she hopes he doesn't feel like she is begging him for it with a sob story. She'd also be fine with him simply acknowledging that, despite what Hendry and his cohort have been writing, Detective Inspector Georgina Lennox hasn't exactly been having a dream run this year.

Somehow, his eventual response is better than she could have hoped for.

'I thought you were looking a little haggard.'

A surprised laugh bubbles up from her chest. 'Jesus. Looked in a mirror lately, old man?'

He snorts a short laugh, and the glacier between them starts to thaw as the sun slowly rises. They've long since passed the spot where Bambi was found, and, as the fog clears, George has to acknowledge that there's a harsh beauty to this landscape, and a challenge – it's hard to imagine how a luxury lodge built for blue-blooded guests can exist out here.

A low granite wall is the first sign of civility taming the wilderness. Rounding a bend, they see it rises to a tall arch over a crushed-rock driveway, the wall picking up again on the other side. At the exact peak of the arch is mounted the clean, bleached skull of a mature stag, its full set of antlers like dark lightning against the sky.

It takes another ten minutes along a far smoother path to arrive at the main house. The gardens wrapping around the exterior of the building are visually jarring in contrast to the untamed hills beyond, the browns and dark greens and purples; here, under the watchful eye of a hardworking groundskeeper, the lawn is a vibrant, almost faux green, lined by tall hedges trimmed to either ninety-degree angles or into soft, stacked spheres that remind George of snowmen. A hulking SUV is parked in front of a white four-car aluminium garage, one of the pair she saw the loud group falling out of last night, and about thirty yards away, on a meticulously rolled circle of that same plasticky-looking grass, is a glossy black helicopter. George can't help chuckling; it's all so incredibly ostentatious.

And then they come upon Fiadhain Lodge itself – according to Zoe, the former home of the slain Grant family.

Richie whistles.

Somehow, the pictures George saw online of the fortified house pale in comparison to seeing the place in person. The building looks like something out of a fairy tale: a white three-storey stone structure that seems to glitter in the rising sunlight, as if the stone contains crushed diamonds. The trim along the windowsills and doors is a soft cream colour, the paint continuing up along the crow-stepped gables and ending at the dark slate roof, at the end of which—

'Is that a fucking *turret?*'

'Language, Lennox.'

'That house has *turrets*,' George says, undeterred. 'Jesus, no wonder they're so popular with royals – they must feel right at home.'

Several chimneys smoke lazily in the morning air, but other than that sign of life, the house and its occupants seem to be rising as slowly as the sun.

'I think they were hitting the whisky before rolling into town last night,' she tells Richie as he brings the car to a stop. 'I don't think they'll be happy about a pre-dawn door-knock.'

'As it happens, their happiness is not my top concern.'

She waits for him to exit the car before she rolls her eyes. Once upon a time, Richie pompously informed her that 'you attract more flies with honey' – a suggestion for her to work on her people skills, especially when trying to gain the confidence of witnesses, victims and suspects. Clearly, he doesn't believe in that approach anymore, but she's encouraged by the slow return of his humour.

Despite the apparent lack of activity within the house, the double front doors are wide open; so, after a confirming glance, George and Richie enter the reception hall.

Inside, the colours and textures are a rich contrast to the minimalist exterior palette. Every light is on, illuminating buttery yellow walls and mahogany side tables topped with linen runners, tall windows open to the dawn framed with powder-blue drapes. An elegant staircase with a glossy banister is to the left, and a hallway breaks off to the right. There's a mix of antique and contemporary chairs, in the French Provincial style, that George suspects nobody actually sits on.

And, where in any other stately manor you might find oil paintings or tapestries, there are decapitated heads.

At least ten of them in the front hall alone, and more lining the hallway; the taxidermised heads of red stags and fallow and roe bucks with antlers of varying sizes, glass eyes polished and fur clean and shiny. Regardless of their kempt appearance, George's nose wrinkles with distaste; she understands that killing animals for resources is ingrained in rural life, but that understanding stops well short of trophy hunting.

Richie calls out, but when nobody comes running they follow another hallway past a sitting room, where George sees more taxidermy – this time trophies from around the world, including the heads of a snarling mountain lion, a brown bear, and a bison – then through to a formal dining room. It looks like a *Country Living* spread, complete with a large timber table already set for a meal, props she would think were just for show if not for the lingering smell of roast meat and rosemary, melted butter and warm bread. There's a set of French doors at the far end of the room that open to a large deck; the view is of the loch, the water a deep blue in the pre-dawn light. Zoe mentioned that the Grant house was in bad shape before the

Selbys took over, but it's hard to imagine this place as anything less than picturesque.

'For an organisation that likes to hide behind lawyers, their security is strangely lax,' Richie says, looking around in confusion as they make their way to the doors. 'I can't believe we're this far into the house and haven't seen a single person.'

'Probably don't need locks when you're this removed from reality.'

He hums, then his gaze catches on something outside. Without a word, he pushes through the doors, George on his heels.

They were wrong before: the house and its occupants have clearly been awake for a while. The back of the house is a hive of activity – figures moving around in the weak dawn light, calling out instructions, and somewhere close is the sound of an engine idling. The group George saw in the village last night are huddled in a loose semicircle on the lawn beside another white garage. The roller door is up, flooding the area with harsh white light. The engine rumble, as well as a strong petrol smell, is coming from within.

As she and Richie cross the grass, still damp with morning dew, George hears a deep male voice.

'... east for an hour, to a lovely spot where we'll break for breakfast. Finlay is going to zip ahead on the quad bike to set everything up, so you'll have a hot meal waiting for you at the first rest stop. And you'll need it – the forecast says we're in for a bit of drizzle later on.'

The voice belongs to a tall, broad-shouldered man. He has his back to the garage, and he's too far from the house for the interior lights to illuminate his features. All George can see is his breath fogging in the air when he speaks.

'It's going to rain?' someone whines.

'The only thing we can't control is the weather,' the man says, tugging at the straps of his bulky backpack, 'and we're working on that. Hopefully, we'll have it sorted by your next visit.' He seems to be waiting for a laugh; when it doesn't come, he forces a laugh of his own, then claps his hands. 'Right, let's get going. Liam, Belle?'

Two figures peel away from the shadows of the garage, and a young woman's cheery voice calls, 'Okay, team! Let's get your packs on.'

As if that was a cue, the engine revs loudly and a beast of a quad bike rolls out, driven by a lanky young man who looks barely old enough to have a licence. At the same time, another woman jogs out of the house with a couple of stuffed canvas bags slung over her shoulders, a large cooler in her hands. She helps the boy strap these onto the back of the bike with bungee ropes, and barks orders to someone moving around further back in the garage.

The group chat as the staff help them thread their arms through straps, settling backpacks — all of which have the butt of a rifle jutting from the top — between their shoulder blades. George's stomach tightens; very few members of the police force carry firearms, so it's unusual to be around so many at once, and being carried by civilians, no less. Her hand slips into her pocket to rest over her phone.

'Who are you?'

The woman who brought the bags out is approaching, her striking features arranged in distinct displeasure. She's in her mid-forties, very tall, with long blonde hair pulled back into a tight ponytail, a fleece jumper zipped up over a powerful body. George recognises her from pictures online — this is Francina Selby, one of the owners of Fiadhain Lodge.

'This is private land,' Francina continues in a thick South African accent. She stops in front of them, slightly too close for comfort, and folds her arms over her chest.

'I'm Detective Inspector Richard Stewart, this is DI Georgina Lennox,' Richie says flatly, clearly unimpressed by her show of intimidation. 'We're here to ask you about the dead woman found on your *private* land.'

Francina doesn't bat an eye; in fact, her expression barely flickers as she stares Richie down, only glancing at George once before she turns her head and barks, 'Pat!'

The man who was addressing the group jogs over. Up close, George sees that he's as striking as Francina is, with high cheekbones and deep-set eyes. It's Patrick Selby, the other owner – and Francina's husband. Standing side by side, they're an intimidating pair. George wonders if people with their kind of alien beauty just naturally gravitate together.

Assisted by his equally impressive height, Patrick looks down his nose at them. 'You're the detectives, I assume.'

'Stewart and Lennox,' Richie repeats, but before he can continue, Francina holds up a finger to silence him.

'First of all, the girl wasn't found *on* our land. She was on the road *beside it* – the publicly accessible road, open to anybody and their mother and their dog to wander along. So before you start tossing around accusations, you'd better have the correct information. Understood?'

'We're speaking with you as a show of goodwill,' Patrick adds, the glower he turns on them far less effective than Francina's. 'We haven't done anything wrong, so we're happy to cooperate – as long as things stay pleasant.'

George mentally begs Richie to follow that request. 'That works just fine for us,' she says, plastering an easy smile on her face. 'We're only here to see if you can help us fill in some blanks.'

Francina stares at her for a few more seconds, then rolls her eyes. 'At least you didn't bring that buffoon from the other day. One of your bumbling constables all but accused us of murder.'

'So as long as you're not going to repeat his mistakes, you can ask your questions,' Patrick says with an impatient gesture. 'And quickly. We're on a tight schedule.'

Richie doesn't waste time – he holds up his phone, the photo of Bambi already on the screen. 'Do you recognise her?'

'No,' they say in unison, seemingly unaffected by the post-mortem photo; they answer similarly to the photo of Cara.

Richie swaps his phone for his notepad. 'You haven't seen her around the area recently?'

'No,' they say.

'Not walking along the road, not in Kirkcree?'

'No, and no.'

Their synchronised replies are off-putting ... and sound very rehearsed. But then Patrick continues solo.

'We don't have any reason to go into the village,' he says with a sneer. 'We get everything we need through more ... high-end suppliers.'

'So you have delivery trucks coming down the road?' Richie asks, perking up. She understands why – deliveries mean GPS tracking, a paper trail, maybe even dashcam.

But Patrick turns a patronising look on him. 'We fly our supplies in. I'm sure you saw the helicopter.'

'Couldn't miss it,' Richie mutters, crossing something out in his notepad.

'How long have these guests been here?' George asks, her cheeks starting to feel the strain of her forced smile.

Francina tilts her head. 'Is that relevant?'

'She asked,' Richie interjects, his eyes flashing as he meets her gaze, 'so yes, it's relevant.'

George tries to subtly kick his foot but misses. *Kid gloves kid gloves kid gloves*, she thinks in his direction.

Francina grits her teeth. 'Four days.'

George calculates timelines; it might come down to only a matter of hours, but these guests would have been here when Bambi was shot. Could the Selbys be covering a misfire from one of their rich guests?

'And do you ever track deer out to the road?' she asks, striving for nonchalance.

'Never,' Patrick says, seeing straight through her. 'Our protocols are in strict accordance with the best practices outlined by the Scottish Gamekeepers Association. We *never* shoot near roads or in areas where there's public access.'

'That's good to hear,' she says, throwing in an earnest nod. 'And are you out every day?'

'Our guests come here to hunt,' Francina says. 'It's what they pay a *lot* of money to do. It's our job to provide the experience they expect.'

George nods mildly, but she caught the tension in Francina's voice – beneath the arrogance and regardless of the manor behind them, Francina is ultimately working in customer service. And her customers have deep pockets, loud voices, and move in elite circles. Her theory is bolstered when she appraises the group again. Compared with the staff, who are all wearing practical hunting gear, the members of the stalking party look like they've stepped from the pages of a Ralph Lauren catalogue – tweed pants and calf boots and leather gloves that creak in the cold morning air.

As she observes them, she feels eyes staring back – the man who bumped into her in the village last night keeps looking in their direction, a slight frown on his face. And he's not the only one – a few of the others are glancing over, twisting to whisper in one another's ears as the lodge staff check their packs. But then the square-jawed man says something in a low voice, and there's a collective stiffening of spines and dropped conversations.

'Are your guests experienced hunters?' Richie asks, and George wonders if he's caught her train of thought.

Patrick rubs a hand along his sharp jaw. 'Er, I think …'

Francina fixes him with a look; in a firmer voice, he continues. 'Yes, several of them have been doing it for years.'

Richie twists to scrutinise the guests. 'And the others?'

'Are less experienced,' Patrick admits reluctantly.

Francina takes over. 'We assist our guests *every* step of the way. We also have a professional stalker leading the hunt, assisted by a ghillie, and nobody pulls a trigger unless a shot has been authorised by one of our staff.'

'And you stay together at all times?' Richie asks. 'Or are the more experienced guests allowed to go off on their own?'

'Never,' Patrick says emphatically. 'Nothing happens on our land that we're not fully aware of.'

Richie looks at him hard. 'But you're apparently blind to things happening just beside it.'

'I read that you've had people sneaking onto the property in the past,' George says quickly, drawing their attention to her. 'Has that activist group hassled you since the court case?'

Francina barks a laugh. 'They're too cowardly to try. They know that when it comes to protecting ourselves, we don't show mercy.'

After a pause, Patrick adds, 'Legally speaking, of course.'

'Of course,' George says, agreeing easily, and she maintains that levity when she asks, 'Can you tell me about your guns?'

Patrick blinks at the abrupt topic change, side-eyeing Francina. 'Well, we ... we use a range of rifles. Rugers, Mausers, Tikkas, a couple of Bergaras.'

Richie's pen flies across the page. 'In what calibres?'

'Oh, for Christ's sake,' Francina says. She looks at Pat and jerks her thumb towards the detectives. 'You can see where they're going with this, can't you?'

To Richie, she says, 'We read the article. We know she was killed with a .270 Winchester, which several of our rifles take – and do you know why? Because it's one of the most popular calibres for deer stalking. Go ask any hunter, any farmer, and I guarantee they'll have at least one .270. In fact, I hope you *are* planning to ask other people, because our lawyers will tear you to shreds if you're ignoring real suspects in favour of pursuing us.'

'We're just asking questions at this stage,' Richie says, his tone icy in contrast to her heat. 'But there may come a time when we'll want your rifles for forensic testing.'

Francina bares her teeth, leaning into Richie's space. 'Good luck getting a warrant.'

Patrick makes a nervous sound; he disguises it by gesturing towards the eastern sky – now streaked with gold and pink. 'Look, we really do need to get going. The family of fallow deer we're tracking has been elusive for the past few days, and our guests are very keen to bring one down today.'

As if the rising sun is a full stop in their conversation, Francina turns on her heel and strides away.

'What are you waiting for?' George hears her call sharply to the staff. 'Finlay, start the engine. And has Rab loaded the chairs?'

The rev of the engine and the spin of wheels drown out any further instructions. As the quad bike tears off across the hillside, the group begin to move in the direction of the loch. As the roar of the bike fades, George hears cupboards opening and closing in the garage, and footsteps scuffing across concrete. The artificial light flickers every few seconds; she can almost feel the crackle of electricity along her arms, making her shiver even though she is swaddled in three layers of clothing.

'I should apologise,' Patrick says, a phrase that sounds unnatural on his tongue but gets her attention nonetheless. 'Francina is a fifth-generation hunter; her family operates hunting lodges all over the world. Preserving that reputation means everything to her – to both of us.'

George glances at Richie; he's already writing it down.

Patrick looks over his shoulder at the departing group, then rubs a hand across his jaw – a nervous habit, George notes. 'Look, our day is split in half – we're breaking for the afternoon, then heading back out in the evening. I think you should come back tonight and join us for a stalk. Then you'll be able to see the operation up close, see how impossible it would be for someone to … for something bad to happen.'

George glances at Richie, expecting his immediate refusal. But he just says, 'Thank you for the offer. And for answering our questions.'

Patrick flashes a catalogue-worthy grin. 'Oh, our pleasure,' he says, lying through his perfect teeth. 'I assume you're planning to speak with the Fairgrieves next?'

George's eyebrows fly up. 'I didn't realise they were still around.'

Richie looks at her curiously, and she remembers she hasn't told him Zoe's story.

'What's left of them, yes,' Patrick says. 'We bought this estate off some distant relatives of the Grant family sixteen years ago, and we've been gradually acquiring Fairgrieve land ever since – but what remains of that foul family retains some of their original holding.' After a pause, he adds, 'For the moment, at least.'

'Were you made aware of the … history when you bought this place?' George asks, feeling Richie's eyes on her.

Patrick scowls. 'After the sale went through. But the land is perfect for our needs, and the story isn't too widely known. We certainly don't advertise it, nor do we share it with our guests when they get here.' He shakes his head. 'At least the murders didn't happen on our land.'

George can't resist. 'Just beside it,' she says, echoing Francina's words from earlier. Patrick's only response is a slight narrowing of his eyes.

Catching on fast, Richie asks, 'Where can we find the Fairgrieves?'

Patrick points to the west, back towards Kirkcree. He seems far more amenable when Francina isn't around – or perhaps less guarded. 'See that ridge over there, a few miles out?'

George follows his finger. The ridge he's indicating is the one she saw from the top of the outcrop, though from the other side. It's a long, low rise in the earth, less than half the height of the surrounding mountains; mostly pale green grass and shelves of mottled rock, but even from here George can see a wide dirt track winding down from the crest and disappearing in the tree-lined base.

'That's Murtair Beag, the current edge of their property,' Patrick says, stressing the word *current*. 'Just over that is the house.'

His lips curl in a sneer. 'That's where you'll find the Fairgrieves.'

CHAPTER 13

Patrick instructed them to head back along the road towards Kirkcree, and to keep their eyes out for a break in the trees.

'The driveway is overgrown, but you won't miss the gate,' he said darkly. 'It's an eyesore.'

Now back in the car, George is keeping watch out her window. They've been driving for ten minutes and the only landmark of note is a sagging barbed-wire fence running through the first layer of trees along both sides of the road. The sun has cleared the mountains and weak light is filtering through woodlands; enough for Richie to drive a little faster, but she still has to squint into the shadows, searching for the gate they apparently missed the first time they passed this way.

'Do you want to go tonight?' she asks Richie. 'On the stalk?'

'I don't *want* to, but it would be interesting to see how they operate.' He glances at her. 'It will mean staying another night.'

Her jaw clenches before she forcibly relaxes it. 'Yeah, I figured. We'll need to run that by Cole.'

'I'll call her after we speak to the Fairgrieves. Have you ever hunted before?'

She shoots him a revolted look. 'Have you?'

'Jenny's uncle owns a farm, and he calls us up whenever the rabbits or foxes start helping themselves to his crops or hens. But never deer.'

She thinks of the skulls back at Fiadhain Lodge – specifically of one with a bullet hole between its eyes, her mind automatically linking it to the bloody hole between Bambi's ribs. 'You know they'll be on their best behaviour if we're there tonight,' she says. 'I don't know what we'll get out of it other than watching rich people doing rich things.'

'We'll be watching for lapses in proper hunting protocol that might have resulted in a woman being shot,' Richie says firmly, 'and using the opportunity to question the rest of the staff and the guests about our victim and potential connections to Cara, ideally out of earshot of the Selbys and without their legal team breathing down our necks.'

Well, there's no arguing with that. She looks back out the window to resume her silent watch for the Fairgrieves' gate, and catches a flash of something among the trees.

She whips around in her seat, peering out the back windscreen.

'What?' Richie asks urgently. 'Was it the gate?'

'No, I ... I thought I saw someone back there.'

Richie twists around, trying to follow her gaze. 'Someone from the lodge? A tourist?'

Though the person's light-coloured clothes were stark against the dark woods, she can't see anything now. 'I couldn't tell,' she says, settling back into her seat. 'They were tempting fate wearing an outfit like that in such a muddy— Rich!'

He turns around in time to see the danger ahead and stomps on the brakes. They both lurch forward as the car skids to a stop; George throws her hands onto the dashboard to absorb some of the seatbelt's tug against her chest and shoulder. They sit in shocked silence for a moment, staring out through the windscreen.

There are three of them; the first two deer have already made the dangerous dash across the road and disappeared into the trees on the right. But the third is still on the left side of the road, and it takes George a second to understand its erratic movements, the way its hind legs thrash without forward momentum.

'It's stuck,' she breathes, hand already reaching for her door. 'Fuck – I think it's stuck on that fence.'

'Lennox, don't—'

But she's already out and moving cautiously towards the deer. She hears Richie curse before his door opens, too. The ground slopes sharply as she picks her way up into the first line of trees – she uses the spindly trunks to support her weight. It's a slow process, and every time she moves, the deer oscillates between wild bucking and trembling stillness.

She was right – the fence's rusty prongs are embedded in the soft flesh of the deer's belly. There's blood oozing from the wounds, staining its tawny, white-speckled fur. Its eyes are bright when they roll towards her, flanks heaving.

'Calm down,' she says in a low voice, 'we'll get you out.'

The fence posts are old and rotten; when the deer thrashes again, the earth at the base of the posts heaves. 'I think I can kick one of those down,' she calls to Richie.

'And get kicked in the head in the process? Come on, we can call a wildlife rescue, or even the lodge.'

'So those rich bastards can have an easy shot?' When Richie doesn't answer, she looks at him. He's at the base of the slope, looking up at her anxiously. 'I can do this, Rich.'

'I …' He swallows. 'Get up higher so you can kick it downhill, towards the road.'

It's good advice, and she finds a point in the fence that sags enough for her to swing a leg over, then makes her way to the post closest to the deer. She prods it experimentally with the toe of her boot then, after nodding at Richie, delivers a hard kick right to the base.

The post rips from the ground, the weight of the wire tugging the barbs free, and the deer streaks across the road in a spray of dirt and leaves. A tuft of bloodied fur remains on one of the barbs; she grimaces as she jimmies the post back into the earth, pressing the toe of her boot into the soil to pack it around the base.

'You all right?' Richie asks as she climbs down to the road.

'Yeah, course.' She pauses, eyeing him. 'You?'

He laughs – a high, wispy sound. 'Just enjoying the reminder of what it's like to work with you.'

She's not sure what to take from that comment – it didn't exactly feel like a compliment – so she slips back into the car without responding.

Understandably, Richie drives very slowly until George points out a subtle break in the trees again. He turns the car into the mouth of a very overgrown driveway.

'Well,' he says, 'that's certainly a gate.'

Ten feet high, dark iron bars, twisting up into sharp peaks – the gate to *Fairgrieve Castle*, as a tarnished plaque reads, is as horrible as Patrick described. The gate seems a bit redundant considering that the crumbling stone pillars on either side look one strong breeze away from collapsing entirely; a section of wall further down to the right already has, leaving a gap large enough for people to stroll in and out.

Richie keeps the car running as George gets out.

Upon closer inspection, the metal looks ancient, probably handmade by some medieval smithy, rust and dirt encrusted in all the hinges. The stone pillars and walls on either side are mottled grey and plagued with some kind of blue-green lichen that gives the overall impression of mould. She can smell it, too, a sickly sweetness that makes her nose wrinkle.

A thick chain is keeping the two halves closed; when she gives it an experimental shake, flakes of rust and dirt float down to the ground. There's no padlock, the weight of the links apparently enough to keep it from swinging open. She gets as close as she dares to the moss-covered bars to peer down the driveway. It continues straight for about eighty feet before curving to the right and disappearing behind trees. No buildings in sight, no sound beyond that of leaves rustling overhead.

Richie winds down his window. 'Well?'

'The chain isn't locked, but it doesn't scream "Welcome".' She looks down the road. 'Maybe there's another entrance?'

'Patrick only mentioned one gate.'

They look at each other for a moment longer. Then she jogs back to the gate, unwinds the heavy chain, and drags both halves open.

For the next five minutes the driveway snakes through copses and open, muddy pastures that are empty of livestock, though collapsed fences and rusted troughs indicate that animals were once corralled there. Back among the trees, they come across their first sign of habitation – a bridge, less than fifty feet from end to end, blanketed in a layer of fallen leaves in browns and muddy oranges with black spots and curling edges. There's a small stone guardhouse on the other side, its windows dark, where the driveway picks up.

Peering through the windscreen as the car rolls towards the bridge, George frowns, then taps the dashboard. 'Pull up here for a second.'

Richie brings the car to a stop. 'What's wrong?'

'Checking something.'

Approaching the bridge on foot, her suspicions are confirmed. Through gaps in the thick leaves she can see that there are many missing stones along the base, the bonds weakened by time or weather or heavy use, leaving holes large enough for a toddler to slip through.

Richie joins her as she approaches the edge of the steep gully that the bridge spans. It isn't too deep, perhaps twice George's height, with uneven sides that twist with bulging tree roots and half-buried rocks. The ground is wet from recent rain, covered in leaves and branches and loose stones that bear an ominous resemblance to the ones making up the bridge, but it's clear that water hasn't run through here in a very long time. Things are growing down there – dark green, creeping tendrils working their way towards the surface. An image appears in her mind, of those clinging fingers wrapping around her ankle and pulling her down, down, down.

She skips back a step. 'There's no way that's safe to cross.'

Richie stretches a foot onto the bridge and shifts his weight experimentally. When he's not immediately sent plummeting to the gully floor, he places both feet together and rocks onto his toes. George's heart skips a beat – but Richie seems satisfied with the test.

'It'll be fine,' he says, turning for the car – but he glances back at her loud scoff.

'We are not *driving* across this bridge, Richie. I'm afraid to even look at it too long – it'll collapse under the weight of my gaze.'

He rolls his eyes, but seems to think it's not worth an argument; he sets off with alarming confidence across the bridge. She follows with far more tentative steps, and her stomach unclenches gratefully when they arrive on the far side. There's mud at the foot of the bridge, and Richie points out a set of fresh-looking tyre tracks. 'We would have been fine,' he says smugly.

'Since when are you the risk-taker?' she mutters, walking over to inspect the tiny guardhouse. Thick cobwebs drape across the windows, the timber splintered and warped. George cups her hands over her eyes so she can look through the glass. It's too dark to see much; she makes out a wood stove in the corner, a table, an empty gun rack mounted on the wall. A cobweb sways in a light breeze and tickles her forehead. She brushes it aside absently … yet the tickling sensation continues. Swiping at her face again, she pulls her hand back – and yelps.

Several baby spiders scuttle across her palm, moving too quickly for her to count, frantically weaving between her fingers in their search for the web they just fell from.

George makes a sound of disgust and smacks her hand against her trousers until they drop to the ground and scatter in all directions. *The bad luck continues*, she thinks darkly, patting her face and hair for strays.

'You okay?' Richie calls, having already started up the driveway.

'Living the dream,' she mumbles, jogging to join him.

The trees thin on this side of the gully, and to the right undulating hills stretch all the way to the ridge that demarcates the Fairgrieve property from Fiadhain Lodge's land. The air smells musky, sweet with decay, thick and unshifting – even when a breeze skims the hills and snares loose strands of George's hair.

For the next few minutes they walk in silence, only speaking to point out buildings along the way – the shell of what was once a two-storey croft, then an open stone shed that might once have been stables but is now empty and sagging to the right. Ironically, it's as Richie is in the middle of pointing out the eerie quiet that they hear the gunshot.

'Bloody hell,' Richie yelps, ducking on instinct; George follows suit, dropping into a crouch. A few seconds later, another shot rings out; George hears the shift of air first, the slicing of the bullet through space, before the *crack* follows – the way sound travels across this wild landscape creating a strange error in the sequence of events. She scans the hills, adrenaline making her limbs buzz.

Based on the distorted sound, she can only guess that the shot was fired within a mile of where they're standing now. The lodge guests were heading out in the opposite direction this morning – could they have circled back towards the dividing line of Murtair Beag in pursuit of a deer? Or is someone else stalking these wild lands?

After a stretch of quiet broken only by the distant shriek of disturbed birds, George stands. Holding out her hands, she observes the way her fingers tremble slightly. She flexes them, pulling them into a tight fist.

In-in-in, out-out—

A pained sound makes her spin.

Richie is still bent in an awkward half-crouch, his arms up over his head.

'Richie?'

He doesn't look at her, doesn't even seem to hear her. His eyes are darting wildly, chest heaving fast; it reminds her of the trapped deer.

Oh, fuck.

'Rich?' She steps into his line of vision. 'Rich, it-it's okay. I don't think it was near us.' She reaches out a hand – steady now, her anxiety dwarfed by whatever is happening to him. 'It's okay. You're okay.'

'What?' he pants. 'Where did it … I don't …' He looks up at her finally, his eyes wide. 'Are we okay?'

She nods, her throat too tight to speak.

'We're okay?' He swallows, nodding rapidly. 'We're okay, we're …' He looks around again, then his gaze returns to her, looking her over head to toe. When he refocuses on her face, he freezes. 'Why are you looking at me like that?'

'It's okay,' she says stupidly, her mind blanking on anything more articulate. Her hand is still reaching for him, and he looks at it as if he's never seen a hand before. 'You're safe, you're—'

His expression twists; George pulls her hand back.

'I'm fine,' he says roughly. 'Just … just back off, Lennox. Give me a-a bloody moment to—' He cuts himself off abruptly, sucking in a breath. Then he storms off, continuing up the driveway.

She drifts after him slowly, her heart still skittish from the gunshots – but Richie's reaction has troubled her far more. The expression on his face, the look in his eyes … it's a feeling she knows all too well, a primal fear she never imagined Richie – warm, stable, unflappable Richie – could feel. Observing the tension in his too-narrow shoulders and the clenched fists swiping through the air with every stride he takes ahead of her confirms, with a sinking feeling of guilt, that she was entirely selfish in thinking that the terrifying events on Eadar only affected her.

A low wall rises from the ground to guide their way, curving around to the left past another large shed, covered in brambles and empty save for some tools and a flat tyre rolled into a corner. She stays a half-step behind him as they walk, saving him from having to look her in the eye, and saving herself the pressure of thinking of something to say.

Then Richie, shoulders still stiff, points up in the sky above the bramble shed. 'There.'

A plume of smoke is rising from somewhere nearby. Using it as a guide, they walk down a grassy embankment and over a series of low stone walls, passing a large rectangle of freshly turned earth with an overturned wheelbarrow beside it, then through a gap in a tangled hedgerow.

'Jesus,' George breathes as they look up at the house. Unlike Fiadhain Lodge, this place has not stolen her breath because of its beauty.

Fairgrieve Castle really is … well, *a castle* – a miniature version, anyway. An imposing fortified house, three storeys of brown-grey stone that might once have been grand but have long since been allowed to languish. The huge L-shaped structure has a pitched roof with four blunt chimneys, pockmarked walls, and medieval features that suggest the weight of the centuries that have passed since the first stone was laid: there are corbelled bartizans on each corner, triple arrow slits set into the stone, and a curtain wall that closes the L into a defensive rectangle.

The windowsills are grimy, the glass caked with dirt on one side and dust on the other, and the roof slate is an even more despairing shade of grey. Sections of it have completely caved in, so much that she can see daylight streaming through the top-floor windows, threadbare curtains fluttering in the breeze. A crow flutters through the ceiling in a blur of black wings.

'People live here?' she wonders aloud. 'It looks condemned.' Remembering Zoe's story, she supposes it is.

They pass beneath a wide arch cut into the curtain wall and enter a stone-flagged courtyard. The garden beds in here are overgrown with weeds and thistles so dense that you'd need a chainsaw to hack through them. There's an alcove set into the stone to the right, a nondescript door beyond.

The path ends at a short flight of steps that leads to the double front doors, the wood scuffed at the base from the careless boots of generations of Fairgrieves. There's a heavy iron door knocker set up high; Richie gives it two solid goes before stepping back and flexing his fingers. They're kept waiting for a while, but then one of the doors is dragged inwards with a painful scrape of timber.

George is a little taken aback by the contrast between the derelict house and the beautiful young man standing in the doorway. He's in his late teens or early twenties, half a head shorter than her, with a mop of curly brown hair. Deep dimples crease his rosy, peach-fuzzed cheeks when he smiles, confused but polite.

'Can I help you?' he asks, looking between the two of them with pretty hazel eyes.

'I'm Detective Inspector Stewart, this is DI Lennox. We're with Police Scotland. Are you a member of the Fairgrieve family?'

His eyes widen with alarm, and he nods rapidly. 'I'm Rory.'

'And are your parents around, Rory?'

'Just my father. We lost our mother a while back – sorry, what's going on?'

'We have a few questions about an incident that occurred just down the road from here. May we speak with you and your father together?' Richie asks.

'Er ... hang on.' Rory calls out for his father, then waits a few seconds with his ear trained towards the back of the house. When no response comes, he beckons them inside. 'Please, come in – we'll go to him.'

Unlike its ancient counterpart on the other side of Murtair Beag, Fairgrieve Castle has fallen victim to the years. The grimy windows let little light into the foyer; what does come through only highlights the deterioration: carpets worn so thin that the floor peeks through; brown water stains that start from the high ceilings and end halfway down the walls; cobwebs suspended between the prongs of the wrought-iron chandelier. A layer of dust covers any surface capable of catching it and the rest clogs the air, tickling George's nose enough to bring on two sudden sneezes.

A wide staircase begins directly in front of the doors, but the stairs disappear into shadow about two-thirds of the way up; to the right, open double doors lead into a similarly darkened sitting room. Taking a tentative breath – wary of triggering more sneezing – George notes that the entire space smells musty, with a tang of mildew and damp, and she wonders when they last opened any windows.

'Sorry about the dust. It's not normally this, er …' Rory pulls one of his sleeves down over his hand and swipes a line through the dust. 'We've been working on some outdoor projects for the last few weeks. Haven't had a chance to run the vacuum over the place.'

George guesses *weeks* is actually *months*, but Rory already seems embarrassed about the state of things, so she just waves away his apology and tries not to let it show on her face that she's desperately holding in another sneeze. She also notes a distinct lack of power outlets that one might plug a vacuum into, and wonders again how it could be possible that the Fairgrieves really live here permanently.

Jarringly, what the foyer lacks in furniture, it more than makes up for in artwork. There are countless paintings of varying sizes stacked atop each other on the walls: of the Cairngorms and countryside, horses captured mid-hunt, battle scenes, portraits of austere-looking people throughout time. Some have been painted straight onto pieces of wood that have faded over centuries; more are canvas, the edges curling away from the confines of their frames. One face among them catches George's eye: a portrait of a young woman in a pale yellow dress, the low neckline richly embroidered and lined with white lace. Blonde ringlets frame her face, and she has mournful eyes the colour of dark honey and thin, downturned lips.

Rory notices her preoccupation. 'That's Edith, my great-great-great …' He trails off. 'I'm not even sure how many greats, actually, but they have *grandmother* at the end of them. She painted that herself, and most of the others.'

'She was very talented.'

'She had a lot of time to get good. Became a bit of a shut-in sometime after she married my great-whatever-grandfather.'

He leads them down a long hallway lit by a single naked bulb overhead.

'Who else is home?' Richie asks, eyeing the stained walls with trepidation.

'My brothers are around somewhere.' Rory throws an awkward smile over his shoulder. 'I can't keep track of them, even with half the house closed off.'

'How many of you are there?' George asks.

'Three. I'm the youngest.'

'We'd like to speak with them as well,' Richie says.

'I'll find them.'

He turns down another hallway and knocks on the first door. Even though a response doesn't come, Rory pushes it open.

They enter a long room with a large fireplace to the right, two low armchairs before it. A low fire burns in the hearth, smoking enough to make George's eyes water – the chimney must not have been cleaned out in a while – and making the space uncomfortably warm. There's a bulky desk at the far end, an elegant but fraying wingback chair behind it.

'You can wait here,' Rory says as he crosses to another door at the end of the room. He pauses before exiting. 'Can I get you a cup of tea?'

'No, thanks,' George says quickly. After Rory leaves, she says, 'Didn't think you'd mind me answering for us both.'

Richie turns in a slow circle, taking in the room. 'I've toured a few historic houses across Scotland and England before, a few as old and big as this one, but they were all maintained by the National Trust. People buy tickets to visit them. This place—'

'Definitely isn't tourist-friendly.' She uses the toe of her boot to flip the corner of a thin, patterned rug back, exposing the stone floor. 'Zoe told me this place has a crypt – want to ask for a tour of that?'

He seems briefly interested in the idea. 'I have visited several crypts. They can be surprisingly extensive – some have long tunnel systems and multiple entrances located around the property.' But then he peers towards the filthy windows, and his expression pinches. 'However, considering the residence is barely habitable, I suggest we stay above ground.'

There's no argument from her. 'What's keeping them here if they can't manage the place?'

'Pride, I suspect. If they're an old Highland family, and whatever wealth they once had has been lost over the centuries, perhaps this house is the only thing this latest generation of Fairgrieves has left to their name.'

And it's falling down around them, George observes, feeling a pang of pity for Rory and his family. Even if it is pride keeping them here, an obligation like that – one they were born into – is a heavy burden to bear.

Footsteps approach, and then the door opens.

'Found him,' Rory announces. 'Inspectors, this is my father, Gerald.'

George expected an aged version of Rory to walk through the door, handsome and grey-streaked, but at first glance the only thing the pair seem to share are those hazel eyes. Gerald Fairgrieve's brown-grey hair falls in limp waves to his sternum, and he has a waxy complexion and a broad nose that's been broken at least once. His shoulders are narrow beneath his bottle-green knitted jumper, and a curve in his spine keeps him slightly hunched. After Rory introduces the detectives he smiles politely. The action produces dimples in his cheeks, another link to his youngest son.

'Well, it's not every day we get a visit from police,' he says as he lowers himself into the wingback. 'Did you not offer them a cup of tea, son?'

'I did. They said no.'

He *tsks* quietly. 'Run and put the kettle on. We don't let guests have empty hands in our home. And when you come back, drag those chairs over from by the fire – we won't keep them on their feet.'

Before George can protest, Rory exits. Then Gerald leans back, and his smile fades. 'I imagine you're here about that poor lass on the road?'

'That's correct, sir,' Richie says. 'We're speaking to everyone who lives in the area.'

Gerald shakes his head, his expression troubled. 'It broke my heart to hear of it.' He gestures towards the door Rory just left through. 'She was around his age, aye? Lord, I don't know what I'd do if I lost any of my boys. Children are gifts from above, and ought to be treated as such.'

His voice is thick; after clearing his throat roughly – in a way that reminds George of her own father – he asks, 'Do you know her name? Her family?'

'Unfortunately not,' Richie says, reaching for his phone, 'but that's partly why we're here today. Would you mind taking a look at this photo?'

Rory returns, his hands conspicuously empty, and he comes to look over his father's shoulder at Richie's phone. He gasps.

'Oh, oh my God,' he says, rocking back on his heels. 'That's ... she's ...'

Gerald grasps his forearm. 'It's all right, son. Take a breath.' Then he frowns at Richie. 'You couldn't have warned the boy?'

'Do you know her?' Richie presses, looking at Rory hopefully. 'She might have been around the village in the last week or so.'

'No,' he says, his face wan, 'but we don't really go into Kirkcree much. You think she might be a tourist?'

'We asked at all the hotels in the village,' George says. 'Nobody recognised her.'

'And there's nothing out here to see,' Gerald says, then smiles sheepishly. 'You'll have noticed that we're a bit off the beaten track. We don't see many strangers wandering around, unless they've got themselves terribly lost.' He purses his lips thoughtfully. 'Or they belong over at the lodge. Perhaps she was a guest?'

'We're exploring all possibilities,' Richie says, withdrawing his notepad. 'Did you notice anything out of the ordinary on Tuesday morning, or the night prior?'

Gerald shakes his head. 'None of us—'

He breaks off suddenly with a rattling cough. His expression twists with discomfort as he reaches one hand into the sleeve of his opposite arm and withdraws a pale blue handkerchief, pressing it to his lips. Rory pats him on the back.

'Are you all right, Mr Fairgrieve?' Richie asks, seemingly unsure about whether to get closer or stay well back. George agrees – that cough sounds nasty, possibly infectious.

Gerald holds up a finger, and when he finally draws in a full breath, he gives them a pained smile. 'Oh, aye. Nothing to worry about, lass. Fairgrieve men have always suffered. I had an uncle who passed young, and both my brothers died as children. As I was saying,' he continues, the rattle still audible in his voice, 'none of us noticed anything strange that night. Have you spoken to those bastards over the ridge?'

Since she's unaware of any other neighbours, George assumes he means the Selbys. 'We have, and they said they don't know her,' she says. 'We understand they've been buying land from you over the past few years?'

Gerald barks a bitter laugh. 'Aye, and they gave us less than half of what it's worth. Absolute thieves, taking advantage of our misfortune, completely ignorant of our history. There's been a Fairgrieve on this land for five hundred years – my family's blood is in these hills, our ancestors worked this land, and I've a room full of treasures to prove it. The Selbys,' he spits, his lips twisting on the name, 'after taking bites out of our property for years, came to me to say they wanted all of it – including this castle. An invasion dressed up as a paycheque. I rejected it, of course, but they've got friends in the Forestry and Land service, and they've put pressure on us to move along. But we'll never give up – not even if we have to sell all our other possessions and eat nothing but broth and bread until the day we return this castle and land to its former glory. Until children fill these halls, and the land is fertile again, and our name isn't uttered in the village like a *curse*—' Words fail him; when Rory clasps his shoulder, Gerald covers his son's hand with his own.

Richie's theory was right, then; Gerald burns with a fierce familial pride that George finds kind of moving. Stubborn, maybe, stuck on some dated values and ultimately doomed to fail, but she can't help having a soft spot for an underdog. And having seen Fiadhain Lodge with her own eyes, and met the people who run it, she can believe that Francina and Patrick are used to wielding money and influence to get their way – they must be furious with the Fairgrieves' ongoing refusals.

Richie's thoughts seem to align with hers. 'It certainly doesn't sound like a fair fight.'

'They don't care about fair,' Rory says glumly, releasing his father's shoulder. 'We have to patrol our borders because the staff and guests trespass on our land all the time … or just shoot straight across it.' He points towards the windows, to the wilderness beyond. 'We've found bullets lodged in tree trunks right up beside the house.'

Gerald grunts. 'But God forbid we even *think* about hunting on their side of the boundary.'

'You hunt, as well?' Richie asks.

'Only small game, rabbits and foxes,' Rory qualifies. 'We made a deal with the Selbys three years ago to leave the deer for the guests. I guess if you're paying that much money, you'd want to be taking down something worthwhile.'

'Do they trespass onto your land often?' George asks.

'At least twice in the last couple of months.'

'For which they apologised with their chequebook,' a soft voice says, 'and we graciously accepted.'

A very thin man has entered the room, clutching a silver serving tray laden with a delicate tea set between his pale hands. He's wearing a long-sleeved shirt tucked into jeans; the belt around his waist is wrapped almost twice over, the tail folded back in on itself through one of the loops.

'This is my eldest brother, Hamish,' Rory says to George and Richie. 'Hame, this is DIs Stewart and Lennox.'

Hamish's gait is unsteady as he approaches the desk, as if his feet aren't following his brain's instructions. When he lays the tray down before his father, the dainty teacups and saucers rattle. Rory starts to pour immediately, placing the first cup in front of his father. Hamish retreats a step, gripping the back of the wingback, and straightens – not fully, and it's with a wince. He has the same waxy skin as his father; perhaps he's also a victim of the mysterious Fairgrieve 'suffering'. He looks to be in his late thirties, and from the way Richie glances between the eldest and youngest Fairgrieve sons standing side by side, George knows he's also noting the age gap. She wonders where the middle brother falls between them.

'I wondered if we'd get a visit from you,' Hamish says in a librarian's whisper. He hasn't looked George in the eyes yet, or Richie – his gaze drifts from her collar to Richie's shoulder. It doesn't feel rude, more shy; George gets the sense that Hamish is similar to Gerald in his aversion to enduring people's pity.

His reaction is as muted as his voice when Richie shows him the picture of Bambi. 'Pretty girl,' he murmurs, 'I wish there was something we could have done.' His eyes rise to George's collar again. 'Did the Selbys send you here?'

'We were already planning to speak with you,' George lies. 'But we understand there's some tension between you and the Selbys.'

Hamish smiles ruefully at her shoulder. 'I wouldn't be surprised if they pointed you in our direction. They do like to take advantage.'

'Opportunists,' Gerald grunts.

'Bullies,' Rory finishes.

'Hey,' an irritable voice shouts from the hallway George and Richie entered through, 'there's no hot water *again*!'

The Fairgrieves all look up. Rory takes two quick steps around the desk, heading for the door.

'Angus is checking the boiler,' he calls.

'He didn't fucking fix it last time, did he?' the voice volleys back, getting closer. 'Hasn't got two brain cells to rub together, let alone—'

It's hard to know which of the three of them – George, Richie or the woman who lurches to a stop in the doorway – is more taken aback by the others' presence. But the woman, her dark blonde hair piled up on her head in a knotted heap, one sinewy shoulder poking out from the stretched collar of her T-shirt, is the first to break the silence.

'Who,' she says, looking past them to Hamish, 'the *fuck* are they?'

Hamish ducks his head. 'They're … they're—'

'They're, they're,' she repeats mockingly. 'Spit it out.'

'Detective Inspectors Stewart and Lennox,' Richie interjects. 'And you are?'

The woman's thin eyebrows fly up. She looks to be around thirty, with a permanent frown line between her brows. 'Police? Like actual, real police? Badge and radios and guns?'

'Just the badge,' Richie says. 'No radio, and Scottish police don't carry guns.'

She raises her chin. 'So what are you meant to do when someone points a gun at you?'

Gerald laughs, an unexpected boom. He extends his hand towards the woman, and she approaches his side with a scowl.

'No need to bite their heads off, love,' he says, wrapping his arm around her waist.

'Why are they here?' she persists. 'Do they have a warrant?'

Gerald jostles her arm like an incorrigible child. 'They're just here to talk to us.'

'About *what*?'

Richie glances sideways at George; she offers him a minute shrug, similarly nonplussed by this woman's attitude. 'What is your name?' he asks her.

'Emma,' she grunts.

'Fairgrieve,' Hamish finishes.

Richie frowns at Rory. 'You didn't mention a sister.'

'She was brought into the family by my middle son, Angus,' Gerald says, smiling fondly up at Emma. 'When she's not hissing and spitting like a wildcat, she's a delight to have around.'

Emma glowers. The hems of her baggy jeans bunch up on the floor, spilling over her bare feet.

After staring at Emma for a beat longer, Richie holds out his phone again. 'Do you recognise this woman?'

Emma stares at the screen, then tilts her head. 'I might.'

George starts. 'Really?'

Gerald also looks shocked – but when he cranes his neck to see the screen, a crease appears between his brows. 'That's a different woman from the one you showed us before.'

'This is Cara Reid,' Richie says, tilting the screen towards Rory and Hamish. Rory flinches – probably expecting another post-mortem photo.

'Cara Reid?' Gerald echoes. 'Who's she?'

'A missing woman,' Richie says briefly, still staring at Emma. 'Hasn't been seen in ten years. But you *might* know her?'

Emma chews her lower lip, looking at the photo of Cara. Then she laughs. 'God, that lippy doesn't suit her at all.'

Richie exhales sharply; George can tell his patience is paper-thin. She shifts her weight, unsure if she should step in. 'Is that a yes or a no?' he asks tersely.

'It's a maybe,' she snaps, and Gerald *tsks* again. 'It's a shit photo – I can't tell.'

A muscle in Richie's jaw jumps as he swipes to Bambi's photo. 'What about this woman?'

There's no laughter this time. Emma shrieks and staggers out of Gerald's hold. 'What the fuck?' she gasps when she gets her breath back, pressing a hand to her throat.

Gerald starts to rise, his knees cracking, and Hamish clasps his hands anxiously. 'Em, it's all right,' he murmurs.

'All right?' she repeats faintly.

Rory looks stricken, but Emma is apparently oblivious to the distress of her family – despite the fact that it's drawing them all towards her like a magnet.

'She's a-a real person,' Emma stutters, 'with a mother w-who loves her, probably … and you just put her dead face in *my* face like it's a fucking holiday snap?'

Her distress is plucking at George's own anxiety. *Three windows, two doors*, she thinks, eyes flicking around the room. *In-in-in. Out-out-out.*

Emma looks like she could benefit from that mantra, too – but just as quickly as it came, her shock transforms into a sizzling anger. 'Is that how the police deal with murders now?' she snarls. 'No wonder you can't figure anything out.'

'Emma, love. That's enough,' Gerald says, reaching for her again.

'We never said it was a murder,' Richie says, taken aback by the force of her tirade.

'You're coming round here asking questions, showing her picture – you aren't doing that if she had a fucking heart attack!'

'I said that's *enough*.'

Gerald's voice rings out; everyone, including George, freezes. He rises to his full height with difficulty, and crosses to Emma. Placing his hands on her upper arms, he waits for her to meet his eye; when she does, angry tears brimming, he chucks her under the chin gently. Then he turns to Richie.

'That's twice now that you've upset a member of my family,' he says, all warmth drained from his voice. 'I warn you against doing it a third time.'

Richie opens his mouth to reply; George doesn't give him a chance.

'We've taken up enough of your morning,' she says, sensing Richie bristle beside her. *Too fucking bad*, she thinks savagely, her heart still racing from the rush of anxiety. 'We'll be on our way.'

As if her words flick a switch, Gerald's expression shifts; he suddenly looks mortified. 'Now, now, there's no need to run off. You haven't even drunk your tea – what kind of a host would I be if I let you go out into the cold without something warm in your bellies?'

Reminded by his father's words, Rory pushes two cups across the desk towards them. It sloshes up towards the cracked rims, almost spilling over. There's no milk or sugar, and the tea itself is weak.

'Thank you,' George says patiently, backing up a step and trying to telepathically order Richie to move with her, 'but we really ought to be going.'

'But I wanted to show you my treasures,' Gerald protests, wringing his hands. 'We get so few visitors – please, let me play host for five more minutes.'

George hesitates. From the tightness in Richie's lips and jaw, she knows that what she *should* do is get him out of this house and away from people as soon as possible. But she's also aware of Emma's stiff shoulders, the waves of anger still rolling off her as she slopes out of the room; of Rory gnawing on his lower lip.

She sighs internally. Richie is already racking up complaints from members of the public – if she has to *ooh* and *aah* over some antiques for a few minutes so that Gerald won't pick up the phone and add another strike to Richie's name, it's a trade she's willing to make.

She forces a smile. 'Lead the way.'

CHAPTER 14

Gerald takes them through the rear door into another short hallway, and then through an identical door to the right. Heavy curtains block the windows; however, a shaft of muted daylight slices through a hole in the ceiling. When George passes underneath it, she can see all the way to the ceiling of the room directly above. The air is musty, thick and unrelenting, and there's a layer of something else, something plasticky – like rubber, or dried glue.

Gerald moves around the room, flicking lamps on as he goes. The yellow glow illuminates the dust motes that swirl with his passing; it also lights up the glass cabinets that line the walls. They're overflowing with trinkets: delicate ceramics with chipped rims, tarnished jewellery, a music box with a moth-eaten silk trim, and – to George's dismay – more taxidermy. But these haven't been maintained like the ones at Fiadhain Lodge. Loose feathers dust the shelf below the crows and pigeons, there's a fox with a missing back foot, and thick wire sticks out of the crooked backbone of an otter posed on a log. Her stomach turns at the sight of the curled body of a tiny lamb, eyelids grotesquely stretched over glass eyes that are too large for the sockets.

But it's the rows upon rows of deer heads that send a full shiver down George's spine. At least forty by her reluctant count, mounted on the walls above the cabinets. Some are so old that time has worn away the muzzles, taken the gloss from the fur;

others look more recent, though George can still see a layer of dust on the boards they're mounted on. George doesn't like the feeling she gets from looking at any of them directly; and perhaps she's not the only one who's felt that way – someone at some point in time has tried to balance the depressing effect of the display by adorning the busts with random accessories: a silver necklace, a length of pink ribbon, a knitted scarf, a pair of round vintage glasses, a single white silk glove. She can't decide if it eases her discomfort or makes it worse.

Beside her, Richie is also staring up at the deer heads, his forehead furrowed.

'I brought that one down myself, the day after I brought my new wife home,' Gerald says, pointing to one of the busts with a worn muzzle and a ribbon tied in a bow around one ear. 'It's a tradition in our family to begin marriages with a successful hunt. Tracked her for miles, all the way to the base of the Cairngorms, but she accepted her fate eventually. That's Emma,' he says, pointing to a bust below the one representing his wife, then looks at Rory. 'We'll have to get *permission* from the Selbys for you to hunt when you're married,' he says resentfully.

Rory makes a noncommittal sound, and George is diverted from coming up with a way to keep the unpleasant conversation going when she notices the veritable *armoury* of weapons displayed in the rest of the cabinets.

Swords, bows, axes – some as short as her forearm, others she wonders if she'd even be able to lift. Beside these are a rack of pikes with rusty tips, two round targes – one propped up in two halves, a crooked split running right down the centre – and, most alarmingly, four antique muskets.

'Jesus,' she breathes. 'Where did you get all of these?'

Richie seems equally astonished – and perturbed – as he bends down to examine a neat row of dirks with chipped blades.

'They're ours,' Gerald says proudly, 'our family's. Passed down from Fairgrieve fathers to sons for hundreds of years.

Some were given away, sold, *stolen*,' he adds, bitterness clouding the pride, 'but over the years, I've bought them all back.'

He points at one of the longer swords, scuffed but shining. 'See that? Hundreds of years old. That's *real* silver in the grip, worth a fortune for that alone. But the history attached makes it priceless.'

'Or worthless,' Rory mumbles. He's leaning against the doorframe. Hamish stands behind him, looking at the floor.

Gerald *tsks*. 'We've no reason to be ashamed, son. Clyde Fairgrieve was trying to make peace when he proposed the marriage – it was the bastard Douglas Grant who betrayed our hospitality by drawing his blade.'

George's ears perk up; this is the story Zoe started last night. 'I heard about this in the village.'

'If you heard it in the village, then you've been fed lies. None of them were here when it happened – none knows the truth of the matter.'

Resisting the urge to point out that the current Fairgrieves *also* weren't there when it happened, George simply asks, 'What's the truth, then?'

Gerald beams. She supposes he doesn't have many opportunities to tell his side of the story to people who weren't born into the prejudice.

'The Fairgrieves and the Grants were once allies. Two great families, respected by the people of Kirkcree as beacons of strength and custodians of the Highland way of life. We hunted these lands together, ate together, fought enemies side by side, strengthened our ties through marriages. For two hundred years we shared the fruits of our labours with the villagers who worked for us, and offered the protection of our warriors in return for rent – which we split evenly between us.' His expression sours. 'Until around 1700, when the Grants suddenly decided that they deserved more than their fair share.'

He leads her to the sword he pointed out earlier and gazes up at it. 'It started with thefts – tools, weapons, sheep. Then it was poisoning wells, spoiling crops, and skirmishes along the border. It became clear that the Grants were determined to see us ruined and drive us off our land. What choice did we have but to fight back?'

Without waiting for an answer, he continues. 'The feud went on for decades – not only hurting our families, but the people of Kirkcree, too. Under the Grants' relentless attacks, it got to the point where we had so little that we had no choice but to turn workers from our door and increase rent in order to keep a roof over our own heads. The villagers were soon up in arms … and, as your history classes would have taught you, lass, it was a torrid time right across our country.'

'The Jacobite Risings,' Richie supplies, saving her from having to bluff her way through a response. 'Many clans were divided between those throwing their support behind the former Catholic monarchs of Britain, the House of Stuart, and those loyal to their replacements, the Protestant Hanoverians.'

'Aye,' Gerald says approvingly, 'and in the years after the Jacobites were defeated at Culloden in 1746, the Highland way of life was being destroyed – people were being evicted from their ancestral lands; traditional clothing, music and language were banned – and yet the Grants continued their assaults. So, in 1800, our ancestor Clyde Fairgrieve decided that it was nothing short of foolish for two strong Highland families to continue feuding when our people were suffering so much. He knew that, despite the animosity, one of his sons had his eye on one of Douglas Grant's daughters, so he proposed that a marriage could be a fresh start for the two families. To his surprise, Douglas accepted, on the condition that the event remain a private affair – just the two families. The announcement was met with joy in the village; people saw it as a sign that Highland culture was returning to the region, not to mention that peace between the families would mean that fewer villagers would have to leave Kirkcree to find work. The wedding was set to take place a fortnight later.'

'That fast?' George asks. 'Did Douglas's daughter get a say in this?'

Gerald blinks, like he's never considered that. 'There's no record of Edith's feelings on the matter, but I'm sure she would've been proud to help heal the rift between the two families, and to better the lives of the villagers.'

When he says the bride's name, George glances at Rory. He nods once in confirmation to her unspoken question – Edith is the woman from the painting in the hall, the artist with the sad eyes.

'On the day of the wedding, the Grant family arrived at Fairgrieve Castle – but what began as a promise of new beginnings turned to violence once the vows were spoken. The Grants never wanted peace – they wanted a chance to strike while our defences were down, and with no villagers there to witness the cowardly attack.' To George's surprise, he grins. 'But we Fairgrieves are survivors. Dirks were drawn, and by sunset, all the Grants – except for young Edith, who was by then a Fairgrieve – were dead.'

'Jesus,' George mutters. No wonder Edith looks so miserable in the portrait – her entire family was murdered at her wedding, and she was forced to live with the perpetrators. 'It sounds like the Red Wedding. *Game of Thrones*?' she adds when she's met with blank expressions. It occurs to her that she hasn't seen a television in any of the rooms they've passed through.

'An entire family slain in one night?' Richie asks, blowing past her tangent. 'And happened just over two hundred years ago? How have I never heard of this?'

'Word travelled, of course,' Gerald replies, 'but it was a handful of deaths among thousands in a wounded nation, and people were just trying to stop the bleeding. The story was lost in the turmoil.'

'But the villagers remembered,' George points out. 'They didn't accept Clyde's version.'

'They refused to accept the *truth*,' he says, emphasising the last word by punching a fist into the palm of his other hand. 'They didn't care that we had spent centuries protecting them, providing for them. They didn't want to believe that the Grants had started the fight, and they blamed our ancestors for how they'd ended it. So they cursed our family with tragedy and misfortune …' He lingers on this, his chin trembling. 'And, like fruit on a poisoned vine, our numbers have withered ever since.'

He gestures at the cabinets, the only remaining evidence of his family's former glory. 'So Clyde renounced the villagers in turn, though he never gave up hope that we would restore our family's name – a mission he entrusted to his son, who passed it on to his son, and so on. A standing order to rebuild our legacy. To fill these halls with Fairgrieves again.' His eyes shift to his sons, still lingering at the door. 'Maybe not in my lifetime, but perhaps in theirs.'

He looks at George now, his face sagging with the weight of his ancestral mission. 'Until then, we only want what's been denied us – what's *owed* to us.'

A door slams somewhere within the house. Rory, who's been staring pointedly at the wall as Gerald told their tale, seems grateful to head towards the sound, and Hamish steps into the gap he leaves.

The movement seems to jerk Gerald out of his melancholy; he smiles sheepishly at George. 'I'm sorry, lass. I promise I didn't bring you in here for a pity party.' He turns his gaze on Richie and, with visible effort, brightens his smile. 'Come, have a look at these,' he says, beckoning Richie towards a cabinet of modern-looking hunting rifles.

Richie's eyebrows rise at the sight; George's interest is piqued, too – perhaps they'll find out if the .270 Winchester is as common as Francina claims.

'What kind of rifles are these?' Richie asks, following Gerald towards the back of the room. George moves to join them – but stops when she hears a creak from above. She peers up at the hole in the ceiling. The beam of sunlight flickers, followed by another creak.

'Birds.'

For the first time, Hamish is looking directly at George.

'What?'

He points up. 'The birds get in through the roof. Can hear them up there crying to one another all night.' His eyes drop back to the ground. 'We're saving up to get the roof fixed, but it's just one of many things needing our attention.'

Rory returns. 'Angus needs help with the boiler.'

Richie perks up at this. 'I'd like him to see the photos.'

'He's a bit, er, tied up right now,' Rory says, before looking guiltily at Hamish. 'He broke a pipe.'

Hamish groans – adding yet another costly item to the to-do list, George imagines.

'Show the inspectors out, Rory,' Gerald says gruffly, striding to the door. 'And best of luck with your investigation. I hope someone can finally bring those bastards to justice.'

Hamish trails after his father, and Rory watches them go with a worried expression. But when he turns back to George and Richie, he plasters a smile on his face. 'This way.'

Rory leads George and Richie back to the front hall, hurrying ahead to push open the doors. A breeze sends a handful of dead leaves skittering across the grimy floor, and flutters the curling edges of the pictures. The painting of Edith catches George's eye again. At this angle, she seems to be looking right at her.

They're crossing the threshold when a sound reaches George's ears. She pauses, cocking her head.

Richie looks back at her. 'Lennox?'

She listens for a few seconds. 'I thought I heard ...' Then she remembers Hamish's comments about the birds, how their cries travel down from the menagerie on the top floor. She waves him on. 'Never mind. Let's go.'

But then a voice calls out behind them. 'I didn't answer.'

Emma stands halfway up the grand staircase, her face shadowed. She descends, stepping into the weak light spilling in from the front doors. 'You didn't wait to hear if I knew her,' she continues. 'The dead one.'

'Do you know her?' Richie asks.

She shakes her head. 'She doesn't look like she's from around here.'

'What do you mean?' Rory asks, confused.

She directs her scowl at him. 'It means they're barking up the wrong tree. But they didn't wait for my answer. That's their fucking job. We shouldn't have to remind them how to do it.'

George takes a deep breath, trying to temper a rush of annoyance. This woman clearly has an issue with police – or maybe she's just naturally inclined for combat.

'Right,' she says, striving for patience – and conscious of Richie's short fuse. 'Well, get in touch if you remember anything. And thanks,' she adds, one final attempt to smooth things over, 'for your feedback.'

A snide 'You're welcome' follows them down the front steps.

They're silent as they exit the courtyard. Richie strides ahead, and George senses he needs a few minutes alone to process yet another disappointing interview. But Rory stays by George's side, and he breaks the quiet as they pass the patch of dirt George noticed on the way in.

'We're trying to grow our own food,' he explains, nodding towards the raked dirt. 'Be self-sufficient, maybe save a little money, you know?' He pauses, then in a more sombre tone adds, 'This will be our fifth try. We've cleared a few different spots across the property, but the seeds just don't take.'

'Why not? Is something wrong with the soil?'

'Depends who you ask. My father wasn't being dramatic when he said the villagers cursed us as punishment for the massacre … but I think the Grants just poured salt over everything. And with the lodge buying up so much of our property, we're running out of places to dig.'

Considering the villagers renamed the path to Fairgrieve Castle 'The Cursed Road', she supposes that Gerald has *some* evidence to support his claim. 'You seem less convinced by Clyde's version of events.'

Rory laughs bitterly. 'Well, it's a bit convenient, isn't it? Nobody knows for sure who started the feud, just like we'll never know who actually started the fight at the wedding – but there's no way that our ancestors weren't giving as good as they got. And the worst part is, I think my father *knows* – he's just too proud to admit that there are holes in the story. I've told him that people in Kirkcree don't feel the same way now that they did all that time ago, but he refuses to believe it. And since he rarely goes into the village, he hasn't seen it for himself. The world's moved on, but he's stuck in the past.'

George recalls the way Gerald gazed around his room of grisly treasures, tarnished and broken symbols of the once great Fairgrieve family. 'What do your brothers think?'

He glances back at the house looming behind them. 'Hamish and Angus have the same doubts as me, I think, but they haven't spent much time in the village either.'

George frowns. 'Didn't they go to school?'

He shakes his head. 'Our mother taught them at home. She taught me, too, but after she died I had to go to the village school. I was the first person in our family to use the internet – can you believe that? My father still never has, and my brothers have only used it at the library – and that was with me showing them how it works. And even so, they treat me like I'm just a kid. Like what I want doesn't matter.' His jaw is tight now, eyes fixed on the muddy path ahead.

George feels a rush of sympathy for Rory; out here on this poisoned land, the youngest member of a dying line, he seems so very lonely. 'What did your father mean when he said' – she trails off, trying to remember the specific wording – '"our numbers have withered"?'

'Well, a lot of Fairgrieves left to settle elsewhere because of the feud, so there were already fewer of us by the time the wedding came around. And after that ... well, our reputation was ruined. The people who weren't forced to leave Kirkcree for work didn't want anything to do with our family, let alone marry into it. And fewer marriages meant fewer new Fairgrieves being born.' He clears his throat, his cheeks burning. 'My father talks about *that* all the time. He's obsessed with our legacy, has always badgered Emma and – and Angus to ... you know.'

She laughs, trying to alleviate his discomfort. 'I do. My mum has finally given up trying to squeeze a grandchild out of me. Then again, there are plenty of Lennoxes in the world.' She pauses. 'Does he pester Hamish about finding a partner so he can get cracking on rebuilding Clan Fairgrieve?'

Rory keeps his eyes averted. 'No. Not anymore.'

George chides herself for her thoughtlessness. Clearly Hamish is suffering with some kind of health issue – finding a wife might not be his top priority right now.

'Well, what about you?'

He looks at her sideways, his eyes wide – too wide, a façade of innocence. 'What about me?'

'You said you don't go into the village much, but that can't be true. You're young, and friendly – surely you've got a social life.'

'I mean, I do the grocery shopping,' he says limply. Then he speaks in a rush, like he's making a terrible confession. 'I have a few ... well, I wasn't great at making friends at school, but some of the lads from my year invite me to play rugby whenever I'm in the village. As for girls ...' He trails off, shaking his head in apparent mortification — either at the general thought of girls, or because he's realised that he's discussing his love life with a police officer.

George chuckles. 'Get down there more, make proper friends. Maybe you can encourage your brothers to do the same — even if your dad disapproves.'

He makes a noncommittal sound, and is quiet for a moment. 'That woman. The second one your partner showed us.'

'Cara?'

'Right. How long has she been missing for?'

'About ten years.'

Rory glances at her, his rosy face scrunched with confusion. 'Do you think she's still around? Alive, I mean.'

George hesitates, eyeing Richie. He's well ahead of them, already stepping onto the bridge.

'I don't think it's likely,' she finally says. 'But we're still very interested in finding out what happened to her.'

'But if she died ages ago, what's she got to do with this one now?' He cocks his head. 'You think the Selbys might have killed her, too?'

'George!' Halfway across the bridge, Richie has sunk down into an awkward crouch. 'George!' he shouts again, his voice high.

'Shit.' She takes off towards him at a sprint. 'Coming!'

'Careful — my foot's gone through!'

She hits the brakes, slowing to a walk as she approaches the middle; if stones are giving out beneath their feet, she's going to treat it like she's walking across a thin layer of ice.

'Do you need help?' Rory calls, waiting back at the edge.

'Not sure yet,' she replies, conscious of the extra weight — and of protecting Richie's pride. She can see the back of his neck is already burning up.

She makes it to Richie and takes stock of the situation. Richie's left leg has plunged through a small hole, the circumference tight enough that his weight has him wedged just above his knee. His other leg is crumpled in front of him, so he's supporting most of his weight on his hands. It must be painful; she can't see his face, but his shoulders are rising with quick, strained breaths.

'Any wiggle room?'

'A little,' he pants, pressing his palms into the ground. 'Just can't – *argh* – raise myself high enough.'

She clicks her tongue, thinking fast. The longer his leg is trapped, the more damage it could be doing to the soft tissue. And she'd rather not stand on unstable ground for more time than she needs to.

Decision made, she stoops and slides her arms under his, threading her fingers together over his sternum. 'Push up with your other leg on three.'

He adjusts with another pained groan. 'Count it.'

She shifts her weight, pressing down into her heels. 'One, two, *three*.'

He doesn't budge for the first few seconds, and she grunts with the effort of supporting his weight. But then she feels the stone give, and with another pull he's free. He staggers to the right, leaning heavily against the parapet wall – but she doesn't want to hang around in this spot; she wraps her arm around his waist and starts towing him to the other side where, thankfully, their car still awaits.

'All good?' Rory shouts.

George flicks him a thumbs up. 'Bye, Rory.'

She doesn't release Richie until they're at the car, setting him against the passenger side so she can open the door. He slides in, gritting his teeth.

She crouches beside him. 'How bad?'

'It's fine. It'll just bruise.'

She purses her lips, looking at the dirt and crumbs of stone circling his thigh. 'Could have caused a bit more damage than that.'

'I'll look properly when we get back to the hotel.'

Her stomach tenses. 'So, we are staying another night, then?'

He cocks his head. 'The Fairgrieves said that the Selbys and their guests frequently trespass and recklessly fire guns – two things the Selbys swore *never* happen on their watch. And the suggestion that they've been weaponising a government body to pressure the Fairgrieves into leaving?' He grins, but it's nothing like his usual smile. 'That's more than enough for Cole to let us dig deeper.'

Before she can argue, he lifts his phone to his ear – effectively cutting her off. 'Lachlan, it's Richie Stewart. Is she free?'

George doesn't need to hear this part; she wanders away, back to the edge of the bridge. Rory has disappeared, probably on his way back to the house.

From here, she can't even see the roof of the castle. Despite the fact that they've lost so much land to the lodge, the Fairgrieves have retained a decent slice of the Scottish Highlands. Thinking of the square footage of her own flat, and the one potted plant she's sure will be dead by the time she gets home tomorrow, George wonders if she could get used to living out here, despite it being such a strange place.

'Lennox.'

Richie is leaning out of the car, the phone extended towards her. She takes it.

'Hello?'

Cole doesn't bother with greetings. 'Do you think you'll gain anything valuable from another night?'

She makes sure she's well out of earshot of the car before answering. 'There *is* a possibility that guests or staff at Fiadhain Lodge are engaging in unsafe, possibly illegal practices, but there's no hard evidence – just an accusation from a neighbour they're already on shaky ground with.'

Cole hums thoughtfully. 'Questions are trickling in from the media. It's clear they suspect that we're suppressing something. I've promised pain of death to whoever leaks the Cara Reid connection, but it's only a matter of time before someone slips up.'

'And you want something solid to give them when word gets out.'

'Ideally. The most frustrating thing about this is that none of them actually care about Cara – but as soon as this comes out, she'll be the lost daughter of Scotland.'

'Isn't that a good thing?'

'Not when they make it entirely our fault that she hasn't been found.' Cole's voice gets distant – she's leant away from the mouthpiece to speak to someone in the background. Then she returns, sounding harried. 'Your call, Lennox. Yes or no?'

George takes a deep breath, and regrets it immediately – that sickly odour of decay fills her lungs, and she shudders at the thought of mouldy spores latching onto crucial pieces inside her.

'Just one more night,' she relents, despite the heavy feeling of unease those words give her.

'All right. And Lennox – how goes your other task?'

She looks back at the car. Through the rear window, she can just make out Richie's silhouette, slumped in the passenger seat.

'Nothing to report, boss.'

There's a pause. 'Keep me updated.'

Cole hangs up, but George keeps the phone to her ear for a few moments longer. If Richie looks into the rear-view mirror right now, it will look like they're still talking. And by the time George walks back to the car, her breathing is calm, her face serene.

She has no qualms about lying for him; and she can repress her anxiety about being away from home for one more night. She owes him this much – one last chance to close the case that's been haunting him for a decade.

CHAPTER 15

Zoe is surprised by their reappearance at the reception desk, but she happily hands their room keys back. Richie keeps pace with George up the stairs, although she suspects it's out of stubbornness rather than ease – she noticed him wince as he got out of the car, and he's definitely favouring his left leg as he stops outside his door.

'Let's meet back out here in an hour, okay?' she says. 'If you're not going to get that checked out, at least put your leg up for a bit.'

'Fine,' he grumbles, 'and that's the last I want to hear of it.'

'No more outward shows of concern welcome,' she says pithily. 'Got it.'

He pauses, his shoulder wedged in the gap of his open door. 'That's not what I meant.'

She tilts her head back, suddenly feeling exhausted. 'I know.'

The silence stretches as they look at each other, heavy with tiredness and hurt and frustration that neither seems to have the words to lighten. It never used to be this hard.

'One hour,' he says, and steps into his room.

She's about to enter her own room when Zoe appears at the top of the stairs, a bundled blue towel in her hands.

'I brought Inspector Stewart an ice pack,' she says. 'He was limping, right?'

George isn't sure if Richie will accept the help, but she nods anyway. 'Thanks, Zoe.'

Zoe beams. 'Do *you* need anything, Inspector? Any injuries to report?'

'None that ice can fix.'

An impish smile creeps onto her face. 'That married couple didn't want the free bubbly. Would that fix whatever's got you down?'

Despite her flat mood, George laughs. 'No, thanks. But good initiative.'

Zoe winks and raises her fist to Richie's door. 'I'm around if you need anything.'

George is already in her room by the time she hears Richie open his door to Zoe's knock. She can't hear whether he accepts the ice pack or not, but she hears his door close a few seconds later.

After she half-heartedly unpacks, she makes a couple of calls: a disappointing one to the officer who is checking local CCTV for footage of Bambi, and then to Dr Bùi's office to check on progress with the pin. He doesn't come to the phone, but his assistant politely – yet firmly – informs George that 'he's working as quickly as he can through an incredibly high volume of requests'. Frustrated, she tosses up whether she should do some digging into the Selbys; perhaps there are whispers of a less-than-ethical relationship between them and government agencies, but she's not quite sure where to begin on that. Annoyingly, Hendry Shaw comes to mind: no doubt he has a connection or a source who would point her in the right direction.

But then it occurs to her that she doesn't need to sink as low as asking Hendry – not when she has her own source just downstairs.

A trail of soil and ripped-up plants leads her to Zoe, bent over the garden bed beside the front steps, hands swallowed in gloves far too big for her. George doesn't consider herself an expert gardener, but she's been subject to enough of Richie's lectures on plants to know that only sixty per cent of the ones scattered here are weeds.

Oblivious to her mistake, Zoe smiles a greeting. 'Changed your mind about the champagne?' She drops her voice to a conspiratorial whisper. 'It's actually sparkling wine, but we can pretend.'

'Unfortunately, I'm on the clock.' *And on the wagon.* 'I was actually hoping we could chat.' George settles on the bottom step, stretching out her legs. 'Did my partner take the ice?'

'He did – after he asked if you'd told me to bring it.' Zoe hesitates before adding, 'He's a bit … snippy, that one. Nothing like you.'

If George didn't already know things were bad, that assessment proves it – in what world is *she* the friendly one?

'He had a little mishap at the Fairgrieve property,' she explains. 'But I actually wanted to ask you about the Selbys up at Fiadhain Lodge. What do you know about them?'

'Aside from the fact that they're total snobs?' Zoe taps her chin thoughtfully, leaving a smudge of dirt behind. 'I mean, I was just a kid when they bought the Grant place. I remember a lot of people were excited about all the new tourism it would bring to Kirkcree. Francina and Patrick went around to all the local businesses to introduce themselves and talk about their big plans – they said they wanted to put Kirkcree on the map, that they'd be bringing in VIP clients with lots of money to spend, and they'd be encouraging them to spend it in the village. My mum used to work front of house at The Kirk and remembers Patrick coming in to suggest that if they wanted those customers, they should transition from pub fare to fine dining. The owner laughed him out of the place.'

'They're a bit out of touch, then?'

'They're just liars,' Zoe says simply. 'None of what they promised came true – guests only occasionally come into the village, the hotels are still pretty much empty outside peak seasons and special events, and I only ever see the housekeeping staff at the supermarket buying the basics.'

'Are any locals employed there?'

'A few, mostly just for cleaning and maintaining the place, but they flew the rest of the staff over from other Selby lodges in the UK. Guess they wanted people who already knew how they liked things done.'

And who were already loyal, George muses. She pulls out her notepad and makes a note to ask for the full staff list of Fiadhain Lodge. 'Have you heard anything about what the Selbys are like as bosses? Are they good to work for?'

'My older brother did some groundskeeping work for them a few years back. He said they were pretty awful to be around, and weirdly strict – he wasn't allowed in the main house when the guests were around, and he only had access to the gardening sheds. Said they didn't like the staff talking to one another during shifts, wanted everyone to keep their heads down and work. The pay was decent, but after just a few weeks out there he quit.'

George perks up at this. 'Why? Did the Selbys do something?'

Zoe hesitates. 'Remember when I asked if you saw anything along *An Rathad Damainte?*'

This is not the direction she expected Zoe to go in. 'Yes?'

'Well, my brother was driving out to the lodge for a morning shift and he … saw something.'

The back of George's neck prickles. 'Something?'

'A person,' Zoe says reluctantly, as if expecting George to mock her, 'at least, he thinks so. He never got a good look – just a glimpse.' She bites her lip, then clearly decides she may as well spill it all. 'Standing right at the spot where the Grant and Fairgrieve lands used to be divided back in the olden days.'

The prickles are now travelling down her spine – George recalls seeing *someone* among the trees, gone by the time she looked out the rear window of Richie's car. 'It was probably someone from the lodge,' she says, echoing Richie's earlier words, 'or a tourist.'

Zoe shakes her head. 'It was Edith Grant.'

George's pen hovers above the paper. 'The one who married into the Fairgrieve family? The one whose wedding—'

'Ended in a bloodbath? Yeah, her.'

Ah. She finally understands Zoe's hesitance – and wonders if her referring to Edith by her maiden name was a slip, or another method of erasing the Fairgrieves from Kirkcree's lore that's been handed down through the generations. 'Your brother thought he saw a ghost?'

'He's not the only one,' she replies, her tone a little defensive. 'Even though the road is supposed to be off-limits, there's loads of stories about people seeing her out there. Apparently she haunts the border between the two families, trapped by her grief ... or by her guilt at being the reason they came together that day.'

'Well, it wasn't her fault,' George argues, before remembering that they're talking about *ghosts*. As much as she enjoys a spooky tale, it doesn't extend to taking a report like this seriously – regardless of what she *thinks* she saw this morning. 'I can understand why your brother quit. Seeing ... whatever he saw must have given him a fright.'

Zoe nods eagerly, happy to speak now that she knows George isn't ridiculing her. 'Enough that he didn't go back for his last paycheque. It was the final straw – he was already freaked out by all the crying.'

George groans. 'The *what*?'

'From what we've heard, ever since they killed the Grants, Fairgrieve boys die young – usually only one or two make it all the way to adulthood in each generation, but even the ones who survive have something off with them. Sometimes, when my brother was working in the gardens of the lodge, he swore he heard cries on the wind, coming from the direction of Murtair Beag.' She waggles her eyebrows, enjoying the dramatic retelling. 'People say that the cries are the ghosts of dead kids ... or the wails of the mothers who couldn't handle the grief and threw themselves off the roof.'

Despite a new tightness in her stomach, George works to keep the scepticism from her expression – there are three Fairgrieve sons there now, and all adults. Although Gerald mentioned dead brothers, and he's not in good health himself; Hamish has apparently inherited the same condition. And Gerald *does* believe they're cursed.

Could this be part of that curse? That when they manage to marry and conceive, the males of their line are doomed to suffer, or die?

Is that so hard to believe? a snide voice in her mind whispers. *Don't you think you're cursed with bad luck?*

George brushes the thought away – *that's* a conversation for her next session with Dr Kassab.

The rumble of an approaching engine drags her from her musing. A weather-beaten van pulls into the driveway, the sides splattered with mud all the way up to the curtained windows. A young couple get out, then retrieve two massive travel backpacks from the back.

Zoe waves and calls out a greeting.

'You know the Fairgrieves aren't monsters, right?' George asks, rising.

Zoe rolls her eyes. 'We know that. The youngest Fairgrieve went to school here, and still comes into town a few times a month to get groceries. He seems nice enough, and pretty normal. Pretty cute, too,' she adds casually, not meeting George's eye. 'But if you grow up in Kirkcree, you're spoon-fed the story with your Weetabix. Some of the older folks look at him funny, and whisper when he walks by, but it's not like anyone spits on him.'

They step aside to let the couple walk up the stairs.

'Honestly,' Zoe continues, gathering her gardening tools, 'the only reason anyone still talks about what happened back then is because they keep themselves holed up in that dingy castle like *bodachs*.'

George doesn't need a translation for that one; she's sat around enough campfires to know the Gaelic word for 'bogeymen'.

'Maybe if they stopped acting like outcasts,' Zoe goes on, 'we wouldn't treat them as such.'

With a final, proud glance at the devastation she's caused in the flowerbeds, Zoe climbs the stairs. But before she heads inside, George calls out to her.

'Hey.' When she turns, George asks, 'What did she look like? The woman your brother saw?'

'He didn't see her clearly.'

'Then why does he think it was Edith Fairgrieve?'

'Oh, she was wearing a wedding dress.' Then she cocks her head, a sly smile on her lips. 'Did you see her, too, Inspector Lennox?'

The portrait of Edith flashes into George's mind, specifically that pale yellow dress.

She climbs the stairs, sidestepping Zoe. 'No,' she says lightly, slipping through the front door. 'I didn't see a thing.'

Richie opens the door on the second knock; she can tell he's about to say something grouchy until she lifts a pastry-laden plate into view.

'Neither of us ate breakfast,' George says through a mouthful of croissant.

He waves her in wordlessly, and she sets the plate down on the desk. The coverlet on the bed is rumpled on one side, an open laptop sitting atop one of the pillows with papers spread out around it. He's been resting, then. *Good.*

'Did the ice help?' she asks, settling on the corner of the mattress.

He sinks into the chair slowly, then grabs a pastry. 'A little. It's just tender. No permanent damage.'

'Only to your dignity.'

'Yes, well, I said goodbye to that long ago.'

She lets him eat as she pulls some of the documents towards her. They're a mix of case notes, pathology reports, witness statements and other sparse information he's collected about both Bambi and Cara.

'Looking for anything specific?' she asks, flicking from Cara's high school report to the inventory of Bambi's clothes.

'Wanted to see if any similarities jumped out. It was either that or beat my head against the wall.'

'I've tried that before. Doesn't work.'

'What does?'

She looks up, ready to laugh, but his expression is genuine. 'You're asking *me* for advice?'

'You've always had good instincts, Lennox. You know what people *aren't* saying.' He points to the papers. 'What are those not saying?'

She picks up a few more to flick through. 'I mean, they're not saying much at all. That's the problem, right?'

He grunts, frowning down at the plate. She thinks he's considering his next pastry carefully, but then he looks at her sideways. 'And when we were out there today … talking to the Selbys, and the Fairgrieves … didn't you get a *feeling*?'

Oh. That's what he'd meant by 'instincts'.

She makes a *so-so* gesture. 'I did when I found the badge … and there was *maybe* a moment at the lodge, standing out by that garage.' Wary of getting his hopes up, she adds, 'But I think I was just cold. Regular pins and needles, you know?'

He seems a bit disappointed with her admission, but then he clears his throat. 'You were good today, with the Selbys. I should have told you earlier, but I—'

'Fell through a bridge,' she finishes, trying to distract him from the way the unexpected praise is making her cheeks warm. 'I feel sorry for the Fairgrieves.'

'Me too. That young one in particular. Not a nice place to grow up.'

'Especially since it's cursed,' she says, only half joking. She's not joking when she adds in a mutter, 'Like me.'

He smirks at her over the top of a Danish. 'Like you?'

'Laugh all you want, but you haven't been around to see the pit of despair that my life has become.'

'You seem fine to me.'

She barks a laugh. *'Really?'*

'Yes,' he says, completely earnest. It kills the next laugh in her throat.

Richie senses the shift in mood; he doesn't meet her eye, staring far too intently at the half-eaten pastry in his hand. 'I don't know *how* you're doing it, because I'm not ...'

He trails off, and she waits, hoping that if she stays quiet he'll finally say *something*.

And eventually, he does.

'We have more doorknocks to do in the village,' he says, his tone brusque. 'Wait for me downstairs?'

She's at the door when Richie calls her name softly. He's still in the chair, looking down at his injured leg. 'Can you do something for me?' he continues.

'Whatever you need,' she says too quickly.

'If you speak to Cole again' – he gestures towards his knee – 'don't tell her about this.'

She frowns. 'You've never let me keep an injury off the books.'

'This is different.'

'How?'

'It just *is*.'

She snorts. 'Bullshit—'

'*George*—'

'No,' she snaps, anger searing through her chest, 'you can't keep doing that.'

He blinks. 'Doing what?'

'Calling me George when you need something from me, and then icing me out the rest of the time – like we haven't been best friends for years, like what happened on Eadar undid everything we've been through together!'

His lips open, close. 'I ... I didn't realise I was doing that.'

'Well, I fucking did!' She exhales sharply. 'You want me to lie about your injury? Fine – but if you start taking painkillers for it, and develop an addiction, and sink to your absolute fucking lowest, I *will* have to report it. They'll put you on administrative leave, you'll get assigned to cases a toddler could solve, and a few of your colleagues will pretend you don't exist for months, but, hey – I hope you'll understand that I'm just *following procedure.*'

The door is swinging closed behind her when she hears his quiet 'Thanks'.

CHAPTER 16

The afternoon passes much as yesterday did; except this time, the people who open their doors are surprised, then annoyed, to find her back with the same two photos.

'I'm sorry, but I told you yesterday, and the other guy just before,' a harried man says, trying to prevent a large and very excited dog from charging out the door at George. 'I have no idea who— Trapper, no! Trapper, get down!'

The other guy? Shit – she and Richie must be overlapping. She apologises for the interruption and walks back out to the street. Looking around, she's struck again by the grim beauty of this place – the shabby façades of the houses and shopfronts cradled in the palm of the mountains, their snow-dusted faces stark against bright blue sky. She knows the national park is a major tourist attraction, but that feeling of being stranded on an alien planet lingers – Kirkcree is a tiny village, and with only the one road in and out, she wonders what would happen to the people here if that main artery was severed.

She can't see Richie, so she shoots him a text to check his progress, and holds her breath as the *sending* bar pauses right before the end. The reception is a little weaker out here – down to two bars – and she fires off two more texts as if to force them through a digital barrier. A few seconds later, all three send. She exhales.

As she heads down the next street, a man steps out of a car that's parked in a driveway. She looks him over, adopting her standard practice of logging face, height, body type and skin tone, then does a double take when she spies the familiar coat.

'Are you fucking *kidding* me?'

Hendry Shaw jumps upon hearing this exclamation, but when he sees her, his expression morphs from fearful to delighted.

'Georgie!' he crows, kicking his door closed. 'I *knew* I was onto something big!'

When she reaches him, she jabs a finger into his chest. He winces, but then his smile widens.

'You cannot be here,' she snaps, only refraining from poking him again because he seemed to enjoy it the first time. 'Get back in your car and go home.'

'Wish I could, G. But I'm on an assignment.'

'An assignment that will definitely interfere with mine.' Then she remembers what the man with the dog said. 'Have you been speaking to people?'

'My job does require me to speak to people every now and again. And I'm not the only journalist sniffing around.'

'Like mangy dogs?'

He groans. 'Look, can we call a truce? I won't bother you, you won't threaten to dismantle my career.'

'*You* threatened to do the exact same thing—'

'Anyway,' he continues loudly, making his way around the car; she follows him doggedly. 'I didn't even know you'd be here. But I'm glad I get to tell the public that *you're* investigating.' He looks at the door he's parked in front of, then back at her. His expression is speculating. 'Want to trade information?'

'Excuse me?'

'You know people tell reporters things they don't say to police. They don't think it's important enough because it's gossip, or a rumour. I'll tell you what I hear if you give me a little tidbit from your official interviews in return.'

Her outraged expression is answer enough, and he shrugs. 'Not sure that's your smartest move, Georgie. We could really help each other out.'

She's going to need a mouthguard to cope with all this grinding; her jaw already aches. 'Go fuck yourself, Hendry.'

He grins, walking backwards up the driveway. 'First name basis? I told you we were friends.'

'Stay out of my way, *Shaw*,' she calls.

'Make it worth my while, and I will. You've got my number.'

She doesn't hang around long enough to hear him knock and wheedle his way into an interview; instead, she marches to the next house over and bangs on the door with a clenched fist.

'What was this meant to say?'

Richie's question draws her attention away from staring unseeingly, still seething, out the front window of The Kirk. She didn't bump into Hendry again, but she saw his car in different streets over the next couple of hours before she came to meet Richie. His mood is a little lighter; a shop owner thought they recognised Bambi, and agreed to send over their single camera's surveillance footage for the past week.

Now he's holding his phone towards her, open to their text conversation.

Nearly done. You?
Getting hungry. Meet at Kirk.

And then:

Hisorsdoui

'It's Gaelic for "Send, you piece of shit",' she grunts. 'It wouldn't go through and I ... I don't like not being able to reach people.'

He hums. 'Neither do I. Especially after Eadar.'

George's mouth drops open in surprise; this is the first time he's mentioned the island.

As if also aware of that fact, Richie takes a steadying breath. 'I drove the girls insane with check-ins for a while. Still do, if I'm honest. They try to be understanding, but … I showed up at Poppy's work once. She hadn't answered a few texts and nobody picked up the salon phone when I called. She'd told me they were understaffed, but I just couldn't shake this terrible feeling that something was wrong. So I drove past the salon. Six times.' He shakes his head, mortified. 'She saw me. Gave me hell for it.'

A waiter arrives and places a large pizza between them; she nudges it a little closer to him and is pleased when he immediately tears a slice free and starts to eat.

'If it makes you feel better,' she says, taking her own slice, 'my parents tried to bully me into turning on my location on my phone.'

'You said no?'

'I don't know many nearly-thirty-year-olds who want their parents watching their every move.'

'So I've been told by my daughters, repeatedly.' He pauses to swallow, then adds, 'I've been keeping tabs on you, though.' Her perturbed expression makes him snort. 'I haven't bloody microchipped you – I just keep an eye out. After we got back from Eadar and I was writing out my statement, I realised how many times I'd lost sight of you. I don't want to let that happen again.' He shrugs, aiming for nonchalance, but from the way his eyes cast around the restaurant she can tell that he's going to quickly change the subject.

'I notice everything now,' she says before he can. 'People's faces, their clothes, where their hands are. How many cars go past, the number of windows in a room – there are eight in here, if you're interested. There are also two knives and three forks on our table, and the man sitting behind you has had mustard on his chin since we sat down. His friend hasn't told him.' She laughs at his stunned expression. 'You might have lost sight of me, but I didn't see what was right in front of my face. I think that's even worse.'

The front doors open; a man in a blue coat enters. It's not Hendry, but Richie notices George stiffen. 'What is it?'

'Hendry Shaw is in Kirkcree.'

'The journalist? Is he here for our victim?'

'That's what he said, but he has a really annoying habit of showing up everywhere I am.'

'He's been following you?'

'Apparently you can do that if you hold a press pass.' She looks out the window, almost expecting to see Hendry pressing his nose up against it, waving at her. 'He says there are other reporters in town, too.'

'He doesn't know about the Cara connection yet?'

'If he does, he didn't say anything about it.'

Richie grunts. 'Let's stick together for the rest of the day, then. If he or any of the others come near you, I'll happily send them on their way.'

This is quite a shift in sentiment from two days ago when he told her to look busy for the cameras. Her chest warms.

Richie checks his watch. 'I called Fiadhain Lodge to let them know we're coming tonight. We're to arrive at six-thirty sharp. You finished your streets?'

She confirms and he rises, pulling on his jacket. She doesn't miss the pained twist of his lips when he puts weight on his injured leg, but his voice sounds normal when he says, 'Let's finish off mine, then.'

The air outside has cooled a little; the sudden contrast in temperature makes her nose start to run. Patting her pockets for a tissue, George pauses when she hears a familiar giggle behind her.

Zoe has her back to George, a cigarette held loosely between her fingers. She's talking to a man leaning against the wall of

The Kirk, a cigarette drooping from his lips. George inhales sharply – it's the man from last night, the one who stared her down from across the street. His pale eyes are trained on Zoe, his gaze is warm, lips curved in a lazy smile. He plucks the cigarette from his mouth to say something quietly, smoke-dressed words that make Zoe laugh again, and she aims a playful kick towards his shin.

'Who's he?' Richie has noticed her preoccupation.

'Don't know,' she murmurs, watching Zoe wave at the man in farewell before walking off towards Ivy House. The man watches Zoe leave; then, as if feeling their eyes on him, his chin swings around.

Being on the receiving end of his focus now is starkly different from last night; the residual warmth from his interaction with Zoe has transformed his face into one that George might look twice at if they passed each other on the street, had she not already experienced the chill of his stare. He seems to know it, too – his eyes dart towards Richie then away dismissively before sweeping over George from head to toes.

'Looking for something, gorgeous?' he asks, his voice deep and edged with smoker's gravel. 'Ditch your da there and I'll, uh' – he slides one hand towards the waistband of his jeans, resting his thumb on the button – 'help you find it.'

She swallows a shocked laugh – less at the crude proposition, more at his audacity to do it in front of Richie. The man either has outrageous confidence or no impulse control.

'I'll pass,' she says, then gestures to his cigarette. 'This time, put that in the bin when you're finished.'

The man's eyebrows lift, as if he's surprised that she didn't immediately tear her clothes off. But he rallies fast; he knocks two fingers to his head in a salute, the cigarette clamped between them.

She turns her back on him and walks up the street, Richie at her side.

'What a piece of work,' Richie mutters.

'Are you more offended at his proposition, or that he thought you were my dad?'

'The latter, obviously.' He purses his lips and glances over his shoulder. 'He looked familiar.'

'From a door knock?'

'Maybe.' He points over to the right, to a small house with a dark green door. 'Let's start there.'

As they cross the street, a prickling sensation on her neck makes George look back down the street to The Kirk.

The man is watching them still – watching *her*, specifically. And as soon as she meets his eye, he wiggles his fingers at her in a mocking wave.

CHAPTER 17

Though Richie seems to be trying to shift his attitude, his mood sours as door after door is closed in their faces without any new information. He is particularly peeved when a woman asks, 'Didn't I just speak to one of your guys? Good-looking fella in a blue coat?' and George has to explain Hendry's sartorial fixation to him.

They head back to Ivy House with no new additions to their notebooks.

'I'm going to call Jenny before we head to the lodge,' he says as they arrive at their doors. After a full afternoon on his injured leg, he's basically hopping as he fumbles for his key.

She chews the inside of her cheek, choosing her words carefully. 'You know ... it might be good if one of us stayed here tonight and did a bit more research into the lodge's history with trespassers. Observing a hunt doesn't seem like a two-person job, and that's an interesting avenue to pursue.'

He narrows his eyes, onto her immediately. 'I'm not staying behind, Lennox.'

She gives up the pretence. 'You're clearly hurt. If you're still adamant about not seeing a doctor, you should at least keep your weight off it for the night.'

He stomps – kind of – towards her, using his key to point at her accusingly. 'When you came back after your accident last year you asked me – *ordered me* – not to sideline you. Didn't want to feel like you were being babied, that I was getting in the way of you doing your job. And what did I do?'

She groans. 'You got out of my way.'

He smiles, a tight grin of vindication. 'See you shortly.'

She doesn't wait for his door to be fully closed before she hisses, 'Stubborn idiot,' and then wonders how many times Richie has whispered the exact same thing about her.

She upends the contents of her bag, considering her options. She's not entirely sure what one wears on a stalk, and considering that she only packed for one night, it's either going to be jeans or pyjama pants – and neither seems particularly suitable for an evening traipse through muddy fields. An idea occurs to her.

As George descends the stairs, Zoe awkwardly smiles around a mouthful of food. There are a few suitcases stacked beside the desk, and George can hear music and voices coming from the sitting room.

Zoe places a half-finished burger down on its shiny paper wrapping – from The Kirk, George assumes – beside her computer. 'Sorry, got distracted during my lunch break and didn't have time to eat.' She clears her throat. 'What can I do for you?'

'Bit of a weird request – I was wondering if you have any outdoorsy clothes I could borrow.' She gestures down at her jeans and leather boots. 'I don't fancy chasing a deer across the countryside in this get-up.'

'You're going hunting? At the lodge?'

'It's part of our investigation,' George rushes to explain. 'Trust me, I wouldn't be doing it if I had any say in the matter.'

Zoe doesn't look convinced. 'Yeah, I've got some things you can wear – I'll bring them to your room. Actually,' she says, tapping the laptop awake, 'I was going to come up anyway and ask if you two were planning to stay tomorrow night, as well? We've had a couple of bookings come through today, and I'm guessing there'll be more because of the market tomorrow night.

The organisers have been dropping flyers in all the nearby towns for weeks, trying to get tourists to come along, and it seems to be working.'

'That's good news for you guys,' George says. 'We'll just be here tonight, I think.'

'Great – oh, also, I saw Rory Fairgrieve earlier.'

George smiles – he must have taken her advice. 'He's a nice kid. Single, too,' she adds, 'just in case you were interested.'

'I'm not,' Zoe says, but her pink cheeks betray her. 'I did say hi, though, and I told him he should come to the market if he's free. And that he should bring his brothers.'

'That's really kind of you, Zoe.'

Zoe shrugs, but she's clearly pleased with herself. 'Well, I figure if they start coming to events and stuff, eventually new memories will record over the old ones. Besides, it's hard to look like a *bodach* when you're drinking a giant hot chocolate.'

George is still pondering Zoe's words as she gets into the shower a few minutes later. Once upon a time, she would have said it was impossible for someone – or in this case, an entire community – to truly forget such a significant event. But after the Villo incident, she knows all too well how easily memories can be distorted – or, in her case, wiped entirely.

She touches the raised scar behind her ear, an action that, despite its violent origin, has surprisingly become one of comfort. A permanent reminder, one like the little phrases that she falls back on when everything else gets too loud and confusing and frightening, that she's still here.

I can think, I can move, I'm all right.

In-in-in, out-out-out.

Ironically, her breath catches.

A permanent reminder.

She stumbles out of the shower, hurrying to the bed and opening her laptop. She clicks through the tabs until she finds the article about the trespassing activists and scrolls down to the image. Then she grabs her phone and pulls up Bambi's autopsy photos. Her breath catches, but she's not there yet; the final step is opening another tab and pulling up the Fearless for Fauna website.

'Oh boy,' she breathes.

Seeing the pictures side by side, she wants to smack herself for not making the connection earlier. She's sure Richie will agree, and very much looks forward to showing him that the Fearless for Fauna logo bears a striking resemblance to the tattoo inked on Bambi's right ankle.

The connection between the logo and Bambi's tattoo brings a gleam to Richie's eyes. As George drives out of Kirkcree, he sends the images to Cole, then spends the next ten minutes combing through Fearless for Fauna's website and social media pages.

'They barely post about their members,' he complains, thumbs skating across the screen. 'And they're all wearing masks.'

'Considering they are routinely accused of trespassing and property damage, I assume anonymity is encouraged.'

Regardless, he sends an enquiry to their website with Bambi's description. Given their commitment to secrecy, George doubts he'll have much luck, but it does feel good to have a lead – as tentative as it is.

'What if our victim is a member of this group?' Richie asks, looking up from his phone. 'They lost the court case, but they still want to keep fighting. And so our victim is sent out to Fiadhain Lodge to do … *something*. Tamper with the vehicles. Take photos or videos of dodgy practices, or animal cruelty. Whatever it is, our victim sneaks onto the property to see it for herself, and she's caught.'

She glances at him doubtfully. 'And they kill her?'

'They said it themselves – they'll do whatever it takes to protect their reputation. You don't think it's possible?'

She considers what they've learnt about the Selbys so far. 'Anything's possible. There's no denying that the Selbys are pieces of work, but murdering a young woman?' Before Richie can protest, she adds, 'I could believe it was an accident – they were shooting deer out near the road and they clipped her.'

'That still leaves us with the question of how Cara is connected.'

'Your theory does, too,' she points out, then taps her fingers on the steering wheel as a thought occurs to her. 'The activists are wearing badges in that picture, aren't they?'

'They certainly are,' he says, trying and failing to keep the excitement from his voice. 'If only the one we found wasn't missing the face – that might have been enough to lean harder on the Selbys. But hopefully the blood tests will connect the pin to our victim, and we'll be able to go after them with that.'

Thinking of Dr Bùi, she recalls his parting words yesterday, his concern that whoever killed Bambi was trying to send a message. 'Any chance Cara was an animal lover?'

Richie contemplates this for a moment. 'Ben's never mentioned it, but there's a lot about her life that even he didn't know.' He fires off another email to the activists with Cara's description.

After he hits send, they fall silent for a minute.

'If the Selbys feel like we're looking too hard in their direction, they'll disappear behind their army of lawyers,' George says, 'and we'll have to fight for every question and answer. We need to keep handling this carefully.'

'We *need* to get answers.'

'We need to stay cool,' George says firmly. 'And more importantly, stay out of sightlines.'

Their journey along *An Rathad Damainte* seems to go faster tonight. The sun is well below the western horizon, but the sky is clear and the moon casts a particularly bright glow across the hills. She's still white-knuckling the steering wheel for most of the drive, wincing as the car plunges into dips, and as they pass the shadowy spot that marks the top of the driveway to Fairgrieve Castle, she can't stop herself from glancing out the side windows for someone walking among the trees.

'Apparently, night shooting is a controversial practice,' she says to distract herself. 'Hunters accidentally shoot females with young fawns, or the fawns themselves. I assume most hunters want the males, right? For the antlers?'

'Trophy hunters, certainly.' He twists towards her. 'Did you notice that the deer in Fairgrieve Castle were all female?'

'I was trying not to look at anything in that room too closely. Why would they do that?'

'I assume it's because they hunted for resources – meat and pelts – instead of for vanity. On that note, I asked Gerald whether any of his rifles took a .270 calibre, and they do, but he said they don't use them anymore now that they only go after small game around their property. A .270 would turn a squirrel into a Jackson Pollock painting.'

'Thanks for that image,' she says, disgruntled.

The turn for Fiadhain Lodge appears ahead. George doesn't realise how stiffly she is holding herself until they pull into the driveway and she relaxes back into her seat, easing her grip on the wheel. She can blame her tension on the treacherous road, but she'd be lying if she wasn't also a little relieved that the ghost of Edith Fairgrieve didn't decide to pop out of the shadows.

Even from a distance, the house looks gorgeous: every window alight, exterior sconces angled down to illuminate the perfect gardens, the whole residence bathed in a golden glow. Smoke puffs lazily from the chimneys to thicken the evening air, a grey blur against the deepening navy sky. She parks their car beside one of the SUVs and they walk around the side of the house, their boots crunching on the gravel until they hit grass. The garage door is already rolled up, that sterile white light flooding the lawn and battling for dominance with the warmer light spilling out from the dining room and over the deck. The sounds of mellow jazz music float across the deck, curling around the guests who are standing in a loose circle over a blazing firepit, with sparks shooting up high over their heads.

'Inspectors!'

Appearing at the mouth of the garage, a pack in either hand, Patrick strides towards them. The guests look over curiously but don't seem surprised by their presence. They must have been informed that George and Richie would be observing tonight – although judging by their guarded expressions, which George can interpret despite the flickering light and shadows across their faces, they don't know *why*.

'Francina and I are so happy you decided to join us,' Patrick says as he comes to stand before them, placing the packs at their feet. 'Have either of you been on a stalk before?'

Richie explains his experience, and George happily details her lack of.

'After tonight, you'll be itching to try it yourself. There's nothing like lining up a beast in your sights, knowing you're a heartbeat away from the perfect shot.'

George smiles. 'I doubt it.'

Patrick's smile slips for a second, but he rallies. 'Tonight, you'll be bringing up the rear with Belle. Obviously, you won't be carrying a rifle, but you'll both have a pack of emergency supplies, just in case someone rolls an ankle.'

She can almost hear him adding: *Which is the worst possible thing that could ever happen here!*

He calls over to Belle, a young woman with braided pigtails tucked into the high collar of her jacket. She says a cheery hello, radiating the energy and enthusiasm of a Scout leader, and gets straight into the briefing. She drops to one knee and pulls everything out of one pack – first-aid kits, a folding knife, a large water bottle, rope, a powerful torch and headlamp, and a tightly rolled rain cover 'for under you or over you, depending on where's wetter'.

There are also snacks stuffed into a side pocket – nuts and protein bars and dried fruit. 'But Finlay and Rab will be bringing supper to the first rest point,' Belle says as she efficiently repacks everything, 'so only tuck into those if your guts are growling loud enough to scare off the deer.'

Once the guests have their packs on, Patrick takes his position at the front of the group and the stalk begins. George notes – and she sees Richie glance back at the house with confusion – that Francina doesn't seem to be joining them.

There's low chatter among the guests as they head off. The sun and its tail of pink and red streaks are gone, the sky succumbing to a blue so dark it's almost black. But the darkness allows for an abundance of stars, bright pinpricks in black velvet. The moon is rising, too, its reflection a silvery ripple against the midnight blue water of the loch. As they draw closer to the bank, they're met with the mild scent of cool water and wet earth.

Patrick leads them around the loch to the left, the ground becoming less even underfoot. Sometimes, the only warning George gets that someone ahead has discovered an unexpected clod or divot is the heavy trip of a boot or a startled exclamation. After the third person stumbles, Patrick instructs everyone to switch on their headlamps. George tightens hers over her beanie, then helps Richie when he grumbles about his gloves getting in the way of the buckles.

With their lights trained on the uneven ground, they move surprisingly fast, staying in single file as they leave the loch behind. George doesn't know what she expected from the guests, but it isn't this efficient, practised pace; they barely slow even when the grass gives way to patches of deep, sucking mud and catchments of rainwater that must never fully dry out. Bringing up the rear, George, Richie and Belle cop the worst of it, the ground turned to sludge by the time they pass through. George hisses when she sinks up to her ankles in a muddy puddle, and makes a mental promise to thoroughly scrub these boots before returning them to Zoe. Behind her, she can hear Richie let out an occasional hiss of pain. She wishes she'd tried harder to talk him out of coming tonight, though she knows it would have been a waste of breath.

The rich smell of earth rising up from their feet is now tainted with manure; evidence of wildlife passing this way. The moonlight is strong enough to illuminate their surroundings, and George has spent so much of this walk with her eyes on the ground that she didn't realise how far they've come. The house is a beacon in the distance now, a comforting reminder that they're not totally alone in this vast landscape – and vast it is, because, aside from the lodge, there isn't a single sign of other habitation in any direction. The moonlight traces the snowy tops of the mountain range, gets caught in shimmering puddles, dances along the tips of the grass when the wind blows. Though George's blood is hot, pounding in the pulse points in her underarms and her throat, the breeze is too icy to be a welcome relief.

As she'd hoped, Zoe supplied a far more appropriate wardrobe. The pants are thick and water-resistant, the inside lining of the boots is spongey and insulated, and the waterproof jacket brushes the middle of her thighs. Her gratitude morphs into a fresh wave of sadness. She's in all this gear and still cold; Bambi was wearing far less, and most of it the wrong size. The harsh wind would have found every gap in her loose armour. She must have been freezing.

Sliding her hands into the pockets, she discovers a handful of plastic-wrapped lollies in one side. An idea occurs to her, and she unwraps one and pops it in her mouth, then offers another to Belle.

Belle is surprised. 'Oh, thanks.'

'You're welcome.' George makes a show of glancing around. 'No Francina tonight?'

Ahead of her, Richie slows his pace and angles an ear towards them.

'Yeah, she wasn't feeling too well.' Belle's tone is neutral, no hint of a lie – but George and Richie discussed the reality of the staff being coached to dodge questions.

'That's a shame,' she says lightly. 'I was hoping to see her in action. She's got a big reputation, I hear.'

Belle's expression shifts – she must have been expecting a more accusatory line of questioning. 'She's a legend. She holds shooting records in four countries, *and* she's the second woman in history to get the Big Five with a bow. That's a lion, leopard, elephant, buffalo *and* a rhino. And she comes from a pedigree bloodline, and her family have hunting lodges all over the world.' Belle jerks her thumb back towards the house, now just a shining dot in the dark. 'This place is the *least* luxurious, if you can imagine that.'

George attempts a polite sound of interest, but she already knew most of that information from her research. Francina's personal kill count was enough to make her nose wrinkle – including *thirty-five* lions – but it was the pictures that really turned George's stomach.

Though she's seen many human bodies in various states of death and decomposition, there was something about looking at the striking Francina crouching next to a dead rhino, with the broadest smile on her face, that felt especially sickening. There was another of an antelope, with Francina gripping one of its curved horns and foamy blood crusting at the corners of its lax mouth; another with a leopard, its golden fur matted and soaked red, draped across her shoulders like a stole. And in each photo, Francina was clutching a different weapon: a high-powered bow, a sleek black rifle with a long scope, a vintage-looking bolt-action rifle with plain iron sights.

'And you're a trained hunter too, right?'

'That's right,' Belle says, her tone neutral again. 'Fourteen years of experience.'

'You must have started young.'

'I was ten when I brought down my first buck. My dad still has the antlers up in the den at home.'

'How ... sweet. How long have you worked here?'

'Six years.'

'That's a long time. You must like it here.'

'I do,' she says. 'The Selbys are great bosses, and I like creating safe and enjoyable experiences for our guests.'

A rehearsed answer if ever George has heard one. 'What about your colleagues? Do they feel the same way?'

'Yep, everyone's very happy here. People only leave if they get other job opportunities, or if the Selbys need them at other lodges.'

Well, she knows that's not true – Zoe's brother quit because he was scared of the things he saw and heard out here. But she doubts Belle is going to indulge questions about potential supernatural sightings, so George decides to change tack.

'Have you ever had issues with guests? Patrick told us that they're not always the most qualified to be out here.'

Her use of Patrick's words stumps Belle for a moment. 'Er ... yeah, those people might need a little extra help.' Then she rallies, firmly adding, 'But we keep those people on a short lead. They're never out of our sight.'

George sighs. This is going exactly how she thought it would. On a whim, she asks, 'What do your friends think of you working here?'

Again, it's surprise that breaks Belle's curated neutrality. 'My best friend hates it – she thinks this place is horrible. But she's a vegan, so her opinion counts for shit.'

Ah – *a new angle*. 'Kind of like that animal welfare group.'

Under the beam of George's headlamp, there's nowhere for Belle to hide her nervous expression. 'Uh ... yeah, I-I guess.'

George has to bite her tongue again – she hopes Richie is hearing this. 'I read about the court case. Sounds like they were planning on causing a lot of damage – I'm glad to hear that justice was served.'

Belle makes a noncommittal sound. 'Yeah, our lawyers know how to do their job.'

They certainly do. 'I'm sure Fearless for Fauna got the message. Unless you've seen other members hanging around your property since the court case?'

'Um,' Belle begins, her voice notching up an octave, 'not that I know of. But,' she continues in her normal pitch, 'it's so funny you ask, because we've noticed things going missing from our supply sheds for a little while now – tools, medicine, even an entire box of toilet paper. It's really strange – we're not sure who it could be, but we're pretty sure that whoever is sneaking around our property probably isn't coming from the road – they must have another way in.' She looks at George sideways, then her eyes drift over to a darkened landmass that George assumes is Murtair Beag. In an unconvincingly casual voice, Belle asks, 'Have you heard of the Fairgrieves?'

George is impressed; she didn't expect the Selbys to be pushing this narrative so hard. Before Belle can keep delivering her lines, a radio crackles from within her vest, followed by a man's gravelly voice.

'Wait here,' Belle says, her face awash with relief. As she passes the main group, she says, 'Let's keep our voices down for the next few minutes, folks. Our ghillie says the deer are close.'

The guests fall out of the single-file line as Belle and Patrick talk, the radio crackling every now and again as the ghillie contributes to the discussion.

'Having fun yet?' Richie murmurs, settling onto a large rock. She eyes his leg. 'Are you?'

'I'll survive.' He cocks his head. 'Nice work with her.'

'Thanks. I just did what you normally do – talk absolute shite until they start talking back.' Handing him a drink bottle, she continues, 'And it went exactly as we expected. She might as well have been reading from a script.'

'They're giving the appearance of cooperation *and* handing us alternative suspects.' He sounds annoyed, but also a tiny bit impressed. 'The lawyers are certainly earning their paycheques.' He's about to continue, but then his eyes flick over her shoulder. A second later, George hears footsteps approaching.

'You're the cops?'

George knows who the voice belongs to before she turns around. The square-jawed American is standing with one foot propped on a rock, gripping the strap of his pack in one hand. It looks like he's posing for the cover of a stalking magazine.

'So, which one of us did it?' he continues, throwing a smirk over his shoulder. The blonde titters; the others are all watching with varying levels of amusement.

'Did what, exactly?' Richie asks.

'You know …' he teases, forming his fingers into the shape of a gun. 'Had a little' – he makes a *pop* sound, jerking his hand in faux recoil – 'accident.'

Richie crosses his arms over his chest. 'You tell me. Should we be looking at any of you in particular?'

The man barks a laugh. 'I'm kidding. Come on, lighten up, man.' He thrusts out his hand to Richie. 'David Kyle, of KWM Financial.'

'I'm DI Richard Stewart, and this is my colleague—'

'Nice to meet you, Rick,' David says brusquely, turning to his group. 'That's José, Rupert, Trish – José and Trish work for me at KWM, Rupert is an old college buddy from Oxford – that's my sister, Sookie, and this' – he snaps his fingers and the young blonde approaches, leaving a trail of giggles in her wake – 'is my baby doll, Kendall.'

'Oh my God, Davey, they don't care who I am.' Her accent is caught halfway between English and American, and George can't tell which one she's putting on.

'Of course they do, everyone does. And if they don't, they're about to.' He smiles smugly. 'She's just landed a TV show. Pilot shoots in Germany next month.'

Kendall raises her hand, a self-deprecating gesture. 'A recurring character, not a lead.'

'Is this research for the role?' George asks drily, gesturing around them.

'Oh God, no,' Kendall says emphatically. 'I haven't even touched my gun. I don't want to kill anything.'

David laughs raucously, and Belle throws a scowl his way but doesn't rebuke him. Apparently, paying guests get to be as rowdy as they want, despite the order for silence.

'Isn't she a sweetheart? I've shot all over the world,' he says loftily. 'Rupert, too, Sookie a bit. We're all addicted to the feeling: knowing that you're in control of the beast's life, that so many things have to sync up in order for you to take that shot. And that just for one second, you're God.'

'You already think you're God,' Kendall says, and behind her the others laugh.

'That's right,' he growls, tugging her back into his chest. 'So I know there's a killer in you somewhere.'

George fails to stop a snort, and David looks at her sharply.

'Don't you tell your secretaries to be seen, not heard?' he asks Richie, and then scowls when George openly laughs. He looks George up and down like she's something he found on his very expensive shoe, before allowing Kendall to tow him away.

'What a dick,' George murmurs. 'Laughing was a bit unprofessional. Sorry.'

'It's fine ... secretary,' Richie says with a chuckle. 'I suppose you did use to fetch my coffees in the morning.'

'Only because you used to moan about the morning traffic. Should have walked to work, like me.'

'Couldn't, sorry. I live in a much further-out, significantly wealthier area than you.'

She throws an elbow towards his ribs, which he isn't fast enough on his injured leg to dodge.

'Bad secretary,' he scolds, rubbing his side.

A low whistle gets their attention; Patrick beckons everyone closer.

'Okay, team. We were just having a wee chat with our ghillie, Liam, who has been tracking the deer west. He says they're on the move again, but if we put our heads down and motor along, we should be able to catch them before they disappear into the trees. It means we'll have to push supper back an hour or so, but at least we'll get a good crack at bringing something down.'

He waits for a moment as if for a reply; when none comes, he gives the group a double thumbs up. 'Let's do it, then.'

'Motor along' is the correct phrase for the speed they move at now. Richie puts as much weight on his leg as he can, but George accidentally kicks his lagging heel a few times, resulting in muttered curses from him and whispered apologies from her. After about twenty minutes, Patrick throws up a hand and they all come to a sudden stop.

There's a low rise ahead of them that overlooks a shallow basin and Murtair Beag just beyond. Patrick flicks his headlamp off and makes his way up the rise on his hands and knees, finally dropping to his stomach beside a long, dark shadow. For a second, nothing happens. Then the shadow shifts, and George realises that it's actually a *person* – Liam, she assumes.

'One by one,' Belle whispers, waving them forward, 'and lamps off.'

At Patrick's instruction, they all wriggle forward on their bellies until they can see into the basin. It's mostly flat and grassy along the bottom, with a few deep shadows that indicate divots in the earth. On the far side, trees line the base of Murtair Beag, dense and dark. When she squints, she can see the break in the trees where the dirt track begins; and she realises with a shiver that this could very well be the same path the doomed Grants walked on the day of the wedding. Was the wind rustling through the trees like it is now, the sound like overlapping whispers, warnings?

Get out of here, it seems to say, and George hates her imagination for punctuating the order with a thin cry. *Get out, get out, get out!*

'There,' Belle breathes into George's ear, making her jump. 'At your ten.'

About eighty yards away, fifteen dark shapes are dotted across the plain.

'We're only going to get one shot off here before they all make a break for the trees,' Patrick murmurs. 'There's a buck right up front on a really good angle – who'd like the honours?'

It's no surprise that David is the one to line up his shot. George wonders if Patrick's fussing over David's retrieval of his gun from the pack, his loading it – with a .243 Winchester, he risks raising his voice to announce – and then talking him through the steps before firing is for David's benefit, or theirs.

David shifts his weight on his elbows, swaps the scope from one eye to the other, scratches his cheek. 'Something is digging into my ribs,' he murmurs, fidgeting once more.

'Just breathe,' Patrick says encouragingly, 'then squeeze.'

'I *know*.'

'You can do it.'

'If you shut up, I will.'

Patrick falls silent.

The *crack* is louder than George expected; for a few seconds her hearing is muffled, then there are panicked barks and snorts, thundering hooves. She can't see a body, so she counts the fleeing shapes as fast as she can.

Fifteen shapes streaking across the moonlit grass. Fifteen deer reaching the safety of the trees.

David handles the failure as well as George expects.

'There was a fucking rock under me,' he shouts, pushing himself to his feet, rifle dangling from his left hand so he can rub his sternum with the right. 'How the fuck am I meant to hit anything when I'm in fucking agony?'

The next few minutes are an exercise in second-hand embarrassment; George and Richie settle onto a low, flat rock to watch Patrick, Belle and Kendall fawn over David. Patrick says he swears David clipped the deer and directs Liam, who George finally sees is a stout older man with a thick moustache, to slip away into the darkness to try to confirm it.

'This is a fucking joke,' David hisses. 'We could have gone to South Africa instead and had a whole goddamn pride of lions in our lap by now! So what's it tell you that none of us can pick off a fucking deer?'

It certainly tells George something – and Richie, too, by the way he's trying to suppress a smile. Even David's friends look unimpressed with his tantrum, though Patrick jumps to soothe David's wounded ego – probably the only thing that will be wounded on this stalk.

Eventually, Patrick suggests they break for supper, and he radios Finlay to bring over the supplies. About fifteen minutes later, the rumble of the engine reaches them, and the headlights sweep over the fields they've just come through. Two figures dismount, Finlay and another man, and Belle helps them unload.

When the other man switches on a few powerful lanterns, George kicks Richie's uninjured foot. 'It's *him*. The guy from The Kirk.'

Richie squints across the circle. 'The one who tried to sweep you off your feet?'

David, now sulkily allowing Kendall to run her fingers through his hair, spots the man, too. 'Rab,' he barks, 'you need to look at my gun – I think the sight is off.'

Rab starts to lower a table he's setting up, but Patrick approaches. 'I'll check that out, David. Rab is getting your supper ready.'

It's only because she's watching him that George sees Rab shoot Patrick a resentful glance before stomping back to the quad bike.

'The name as familiar as his face?' George murmurs to Richie, who shakes his head.

Soon there's an impressive spread of drinks, thermoses of soup, chunks of toasted focaccia glistening with butter, and some other fancy finger foods that would look more at home in a five-star restaurant than on a rugged hillside in the Scottish Highlands. The guests dig in, but George and Richie aren't invited to participate; Kendall is the only one who shoots George a sympathetic smile before David reclaims her attention.

Beside the quad, Belle is whispering rapidly to Rab and Finlay, and George guesses she's filling them in on David's failure. Finlay is listening intently, but Rab seems to only have one ear on the conversation – he's watching Kendall, who is now feeding David bits of bread from her own plate.

George turns to Richie. 'Feel like we've seen enough?'

'More than.'

She tugs him to his feet, and the action catches Rab's attention. The only indication that he's surprised to see George and Richie is a small crease between his eyebrows, though she assumes he was informed about the presence of strangers tonight – he likely just didn't expect it to be people he's already spoken to.

Richie notices, too. 'Yes, it's us,' he murmurs loud enough for only George to hear, 'me and my troubled daughter.'

George snorts. 'I think he's just figured out who we really are.'

'I saw one!'

It's José, pointing down towards the trees at the foot of Murtair Beag. The others rush over, peering into the dark. 'If David did hit it, he should go finish the thing off,' he continues excitedly.

Patrick hesitates, and George swears his eyes dart towards her and Richie. 'No can do, I'm afraid. That ridge marks a boundary line.'

'A boundary,' David echoes as if he's never heard the term. 'But ... my stag is right there. I want it.'

Patrick looks at Belle, and then more overtly towards George and Richie. When nobody offers him any solutions – George wonders if he'd hoped they'd step in to referee this debate – he grabs his radio.

'Liam, Liam, this is Patrick.'

A crackle, then: *'Aye?'*

'Potential sighting at the base of Murtair. Confirm?'

'Thought I saw it, too. Might have crossed the boundary.'

David huffs. 'What the hell is up your asses?'

Patrick chews his lip – then, with another glance towards George and Richie, says into his radio, 'We're heading down.'

There are some muttered complaints among the group, and eventually it's only Patrick, Belle, David and the detectives marching down the slope, leaving everyone else to continue eating supper. The energy from the beginning of the stalk has dissipated into the air like the fog from their heavy breaths, but at least David isn't pretending to be in pain anymore.

They come to a stop around eighty yards from the treeline. Patrick chews his lip as his eyes sweep from side to side, the thin beam of his headlamp barely penetrating the shadows. Behind him, David makes an impatient sound.

'Just a little closer,' Patrick says reluctantly. 'But we'll have to stop at the trees – that's the edge of our property, you understand.'

This statement isn't acknowledged by anyone in the group, except for Belle, who gives Patrick a nervous sideways glance.

They're close enough now that George can make out each individual tree trunk on the frontline of Murtair Beag. The ground beneath them is layered with years – decades, probably – of detritus, compressed over time into a thick mat. The air down here smells musky, sweet with decay and stagnant water, thick and unshifting.

They're about fifty yards away when there's the distinct sound of a throat clearing – but it didn't come from their group.

Patrick groans quietly, then lifts his radio.

'They're here,' he mutters. Then he raises a hand in greeting towards the trees. 'Evening, boys.'

The darkness replies. 'Bit close, Pat.'

'We're still on our side,' Patrick argues.

Suddenly, light explodes from the trees and everyone yelps, shielding their eyes. George reaches blindly for Richie's shoulder, making sure he's still next to her, then squints into the brightness.

The light is coming from a spotlight mounted on what looks like a beefed-up golf cart – all black, two seats, no windows, with a cargo bed on the back for transporting larger items – parked at the base of the track. A shadow peels away from the cabin, eventually solidifying into a man.

'You're only a few steps away from being on ours,' he says. 'Any closer, and you'd be pulling out your chequebook again.'

Patrick makes a show of holding up his palms, the image of diplomacy. 'We were just tracking a buck we think was clipped. Did you see it go past you, Angus?'

George nudges Richie, who nods without taking his eyes off the interaction. *The middle Fairgrieve brother.* Now that her eyes have adjusted, she can see that he shares his father's nose, but his hair is curly like Rory's and pulled back into a low bun.

Angus's eyes run over the group, taking in the new faces. Then he twists slightly to jerk his thumb towards the ridge – the movement revealing a bulky double-barrel shotgun strapped to his back. 'They headed up. None of them looked injured.'

There's a gravelly burst of static – this time coming from Angus's waist.

'Did they cross the boundary?'

Angus wiggles the radio – an older, clunkier model than the ones the lodge staff are using – from his waistband and brings it to his lips. 'No, Father. A few yards shy.'

No reply comes, and after a few seconds, Angus lowers the radio.

Patrick clears his throat. 'Well, we'll be on our way, Angus.'

'But my deer went that way,' David whines.

Angus looks at him, taking in every expensive stitch and button. 'So?'

'So?' David splutters. 'I fucking paid for it.'

'Did you? How much?'

'More than you make in a year, pal.' David looks Angus up and down, sneering. 'Maybe even a decade.'

Surprisingly, Angus laughs. 'Seems like that money would have been better spent on learning how to shoot so you wouldn't make such a fool of yourself.'

David swells with anger. Sensing this, Patrick hurries to his side. 'The deer are gone, David, but they never stay over there long. They'll head back to the good grazing land in the morning, on *our* side of the line.'

David glares at Patrick, then Angus. 'A waste of fucking money,' he spits, storming back up the rise with Patrick and Belle hot on his heels. Angus watches them, amusement curling his lips – but George can see that his jaw is tight. David's comments about money must have stung.

'Sorry about him,' she offers. 'That wasn't nice.'

Angus looks at her, and his voice is a little softer when he says, 'You two better get back to your group. Wouldn't want to get lost out here.'

George is more than happy to heed the warning, pushing Richie ahead of her. When they reach the top of the rise, she turns back to look at Angus.

It seems he was waiting for them to make their way safely up, because as soon as she clears the top, Angus raises a hand in farewell; then his hand becomes a fist, and the spotlight goes out.

CHAPTER 18

When they enter the foyer of Ivy House, George sends Richie straight upstairs.

'Leg up,' she orders, shooing him away. 'I'll ask for some more ice.'

She looks for Zoe in the dining room, then the sitting room, before the sounds of metal clanging and water running beckon her to the kitchen.

There's a compelling – and perplexing – blend of architecture and design in here. The low ceilings with dark timber beams, a wide stone oven dusty with disuse, and crooked doorframes suggest that builders called 'tools down' several centuries ago. Renovations have been made since then, for better or worse: the walls are an attempt at baby pink and falling short, cracked black and white tiles form a rough chessboard pattern on the floor, and the upper and lower cabinets that wrap around the room are covered in peeling white laminate.

The counters are clean but cluttered with stacks of plastic-sealed bread, an overflowing fruit bowl, and plastic tubs filled with different pastries. There are two fridges – one full-sized, dented in the lower door, the other half its size with a padlocked chain twisted around the handle. The latter has a handwritten sign stuck to the door: *STAFF ONLY*.

Disappointingly, Zoe isn't the source of the sound. George almost succeeds in backing out silently before Dean turns from where he's washing dishes at the sink.

'Oh, hello lass,' he says brightly. 'Can't sleep?'

She glances at her watch – it's already after eleven pm. 'Haven't tried yet,' she says wearily. 'My partner and I only just got back from the lodge.'

He frowns. 'Are you staying there?'

She hesitates. 'No, sir. We're staying here, at Ivy House.'

His frown lingers for a few more seconds, then dissolves into a smile. 'If you've been out all evening, you'll need a hot drink.'

'I'm all right, sir. I'll just make one in my room.'

But he tuts, turning the kettle on. 'Caring for guests of Ivy House is one of my great privileges. Even if young Zoe would prefer I left you all alone.' He follows this with a wink, unbothered by Zoe's wishes.

'Zoe's been very helpful,' she says, taking Dean's place at the sink. There's still a few dirty dishes to be washed, and the water is steaming and bubbly – she may as well make herself useful while Dean is making her drink. The hot water makes her fingers ache at first; she grits her teeth until the warmth becomes pleasant, then starts scrubbing.

'Aye, she's a good girl. Runs this place well, runs herself into the ground doing it.' His liver-spotted hands find cups, saucers, teabags. 'A godsend.'

'She warned me and my partner to be careful out on the Cursed – er, *An Rathad Damainte*.'

'As she should. That land is soaked with the blood of the betrayed. Stepping on it doesn't come without consequences. Sugar?'

'Jesus. Er, one, thanks.'

She rinses the final dish then dries her hands off. Dean hands her a mug, the steam curling gently upwards, and sets another in front of himself. She takes a deep sip, the warmth lovely in her cold chest. Dean ignores his own cup, turning to fuss with the kettle again.

'I spoke with the Fairgrieves,' she says lightly, unsure if Dean's generation shares Zoe's more modern views. 'Have you interacted with them much over the years?'

'Not with the lads, no. I've spoken with Gerald once or twice, but he seems to prefer the company of his family.'

That's a nice way of saying he hates the village and everyone living in it, she thinks. 'Did you know Gerald's wife?'

Dean takes the kettle back to the sink and starts refilling it. 'I never spoke with her, but I remember her. She was a pretty wee thing, dark hair all down her back.'

'Was she from Kirkcree?'

'No.' He ponders for a second, and George wonders if she's lost him already. But then he smiles. 'Louise. That was her name.'

'Louise,' she repeats, committing the name to memory. 'What was she like?'

'Haven't the foggiest,' he says, replacing the kettle on its base and setting it to boil. 'Nobody knew Gerald had taken a wife until he brought her and their first baby into the village one day. She was painfully shy, a homebody – she made Gerald take the bairn with him to go into all the shops while she sat in their truck and watched.' He pulls down two new mugs and drops a teabag into each. 'Come to think of it, I haven't seen her in a while.'

George sighs – she's definitely losing him. 'She passed away a few years ago. I was going to ask if you knew what happened, but—'

'Well, I assume she went the same way as the rest of them.'

George blinks. 'Excuse me?'

'Into the crypt,' Dean says, spooning out sugar. 'It's their tender hearts. They just can't handle the sadness.'

George feels her stomach sink a little. 'Er, right.' Deciding to end this before Dean spirals any further, she gestures towards the fridges. 'Do you mind if I take an ice pack to my partner? He banged up his leg earlier today.'

He gets it for her, fusses over wrapping it in a hand towel and making sure her fingers won't touch the freezing plastic.

'Thank you, sir,' George says, taking her tea and heading for the door. 'Good night.'

'Don't forget your tea.'

She turns, confused. 'I've got it right—'

But Dean is holding out one of the fresh cups he just finished making, his expression expectant. 'You asked for a drink, didn't you?' Then his face falls. 'Or ... have I done something silly again?'

'No,' George replies swiftly, tucking the ice under her arm and extending her free hand, 'no, that's perfect. Thank you.'

His eyes crinkle again, but this time George sees the mist in them, the cloud that Dean has disappeared into. 'Sweet dreams, lass. And protect your tender heart. I wouldn't want someone to take advantage of it.'

Three heavy footsteps are her only warning. Then there's a hand clawing in her hair and she's being dragged bodily from the bed. Her breath leaves her chest in a *whoosh*, strangled by pain and shock as she hits the floor – but instead of thin carpet it's dirt beneath her, and instead of dust and carpet cleaner, the smell of damp earth fills her nostrils. Her assailant – she *knows* his name, she recognises the grunts, the whimpered apologies – starts to pull her across the ground.

She tries to scream, but the freezing air catches in her throat; she tries to reach up, to claw at the hand that is ripping her hair out at the roots, but her hands are numb and heavy.

'I'm sorry,' the man says and his voice is the pounding of water against rock and the screech of a gull, 'I'm sorry, I'm sorry, I'm—'

There's a flash of colour in the corner of her eye.

Her throat constricts on another scream. This isn't what happened. Nobody else was with her that night on Eadar – nobody was moving through the trees alongside her, mirroring her ill-fated path, the train of their pale yellow gown keeping pace as she's dragged towards—

The sudden freefall turns her stomach, makes her dead muscles awaken only to clutch uselessly at the wind that whips around her. Falling, falling, falling ... *too* far, *too* long – a new fear seizes her because this isn't right, this isn't how this nightmare normally goes, these aren't the fused memories of being dragged through Eadar's woods and tumbling over Margaret Villo's balcony, this is *new*—

She lands somewhere pitch black and bitterly cold. The air is still, and thick with an earthy smell. She's on her feet, and the ground is firm beneath her – stone, rather than earth. Raising her hand in front of her face, she can only *just* make out her fingers – she swipes that hand in an arc around her but feels nothing but icy air.

Where the fuck am I?

She takes one tentative step, then another, moving with the caution of the blind; she keeps her hands extended until she finally feels rough stone beneath her fingers. A wall, grit coming loose beneath her fingers as she uses the rough surface to guide her progress around the room – which is far more expansive than she expected – until a sound makes her freeze: the scuff of a footstep.

George stops breathing. She can feel how wide her eyes are, her head is starting to ache with the strain of trying to see in the darkness. But she's still denied sight, vulnerable to whatever – *whoever* – is moving towards her with soft, purposeful steps. Relying only on her ears, George flattens herself against the wall and tries to keep her heart from leaping out of her chest.

And then the footsteps stop.

Heart battering at her ribs, George has half a second to contemplate her next move when a sudden flare of fire makes her gasp.

A flickering candle casts only a shallow circle of light, but it's enough to illuminate the silhouette of a woman standing in the centre of the room. She's in a dress, but it's not a gown – this is a thin, white shift. Her feet are bare, the skin of her arms and chest marbled with purple streaks from the cold. She's facing away, a mess of tangled hair tumbling down her back and ending at the top of her buttocks, the colour shifting from blonde to brown then black as shadows compete with the flicker of the light. Based on the bend of her elbows, George thinks the woman is holding the candle that is casting such unreliable light.

George tries to speak, fails. In her mind, she whispers, *Who are you?*

The woman doesn't move – in fact, it's almost as if she doesn't hear George at all.

Edith?

A hoarse murmur.

What? George begs. *What did you say?* There's a beat, a long second for bile to start churning in George's stomach. *What did you say?*

A strained breath, lungs rattling. 'I … said …'

The candle flares; George blinks in the sudden brightness. And when her eyes adjust, the woman is right in front of her, the candle directly between them, the flame so suddenly large and bright that George can't make out her face.

'Get out.'

And George discovers that her voice has returned when she screams, terror racing through her like wildfire, but she still can't move, her body a mere passenger in this story. As her scream trails off into a childlike cry, the woman draws in another long, rattling breath, draws the candle closer to her face, and blows.

*

For the second time, George feels like she's falling.

Only this time she really *has* – her upper body is sprawled beside the bed, legs still twisted up in the sheets. For a second she thinks the nightmare is responsible for tearing her so aggressively from sleep; but then a loud *thud* comes through the wall directly above the bedhead.

'What the fuck?' she hisses, detangling her legs from the sheets and fumbling in the dark for the bedside lamp. The thudding continues while she finds the switch; three sharp knocks, then three more. In the soft light, she looks at the door, groggy and confused, then back at the wall. The thuds really are coming from there – and then her phone screen lights up.

It's 4.13 am and she has four missed calls and eight texts. All from Richie.

Her body moves before her brain catches up – she snatches her room key from the desk and is out the door within seconds, hammering on his door in just a few more.

'Rich? Rich, I'm here. Open up!'

The door flies open; her relief at seeing him whole and unharmed is short-lived when he grabs her arm and hauls her inside, muttering, '*Finally.*'

All of the lights are on in Richie's room – overhead, the lamps, the bathroom. She blinks in the sudden brightness. 'Why were you banging on the wall?'

'You weren't answering your phone,' he says, releasing her at the bed.

She sinks onto it, rubbing at her eyes. 'You could have knocked on my *door.*'

He ignores her, and now that she's used to the light, she can finally take in the room. What she sees gives her a tiny pulse of alarm.

'Jesus, Rich,' she says, taking in the chaos around her. 'You been working on this all night?'

It's not clear when he started building the wall, but it's obvious that he hasn't slept since they got back. The art has been taken down, the desk shoved almost all the way into the bathroom. The papers that had been on the bed earlier are now stuck up on the wall, plus about a hundred other documents, images, maps of the area and of the Fairgrieve property, even a printout of David Kyle's photo and career profile from what must be his company's website. She wouldn't put it past Richie to have packed a printer in his enormous suitcase, but she suspects he must have hijacked the one at reception.

As well as these, there's a close-up photo of the writing on Bambi's arm, a line drawn from that floating F to the words *Fearless for Fauna? Francina/Fiadhain Lodge? Fairgrieve?* And then there are full pages of handwritten notes and tiny scraps with questions and ideas that he must have thought of on the go – they're torn out of notebooks, written on the back of receipts, even on a branded serviette from The Kirk. Thumbtacks and brown strings zigzag across the papers, the tacks stuck directly into the wall, heedless of the damage.

'Just needed to see it all out in front of me,' he says, and George now turns her attention to him. He's wearing a grey sweatshirt and a faded pair of football shorts. His hair is ruffled, as if he's run his hands through it over and over again, and his eyes are bloodshot with fatigue. 'And I'm glad I did, because' – he turns to George, his mouth tugging into a triumphant smile – 'I found him.'

But George isn't listening – her eyes have zeroed in on his leg. 'Holy shit. Your knee is *purple*.'

Richie scoffs, but she's not exaggerating – the skin on either side of his knee is deeply bruised, and there's still a lot of swelling.

'You've definitely done some damage,' she says, dropping into a crouch to get a closer look. 'Soft tissue, for sure, but it could be worse. Can you bend it at all?'

He waves her away. 'It's fine, George. I'll trot off to the doctor as soon as we get home. But come, come – look at what I found.'

George rises, still perturbed, as Richie limps to the wall and jabs a finger at a photo she hasn't seen before. The man, no older than twenty-five, has a soft, fleshy face, a thick neck and doughy shoulders. She doesn't recognise him at first, but then she notices his eyes.

It's the man from The Kirk, from Fiadhain Lodge – Rab, he was called.

'Is this a mugshot?' she asks, recognising the familiar positioning, the plain background. 'Who the hell is he?'

'That,' Richie says, coming to stand beside her, 'is Robert McAllister.'

George's neck cracks with how quickly she looks at Richie. 'The man who raped Amy Buchanan?'

'The very same. I *knew* I recognised him. His face has thinned out, he's obviously much older now, but those eyes ... they haven't changed a bit.'

'But isn't he meant to still be in prison?'

'Paroled.'

'Fuck!' George stares at the photo. It's undoubtedly him: Robert 'Rab' McAllister, the man who attacked and assaulted the beautiful Amy Buchanan and launched her into the world of victim and survivor advocacy and himself into a prison cell. 'When was he released?'

Richie crosses his arms. 'Two months ago.'

'So he was out when—'

'Yes.'

'Then he could have—'

'*Yes.*'

George rubs her eyes, tiredness lingering despite this adrenaline spike. 'Well, this complicates things.'

'We need to speak with him right away,' Richie says, crossing to the tea station and flicking on the kettle. 'We'll see what he has to say for himself, and then take him back to Glasgow.'

As he lines up two mugs – one has a distinct coffee stain around the rim that suggests recent use – she looks back at Rab's photo, at the string connecting him to Bambi, to a press photo of Amy Buchanan, and then … to Cara.

'We can definitely start the conversation,' she says tentatively. 'We'll call Fiadhain Lodge in the morning to find out where he lives.'

Richie frowns. 'Morning?'

'Well, we're obviously not going to go banging on his door *now*. It's four am.'

'So?'

'*So?*'

Richie gestures out the window. 'He knows we're here, and he probably knows we're digging around. He could already be on the road.'

'Then he's already got a good head start, and going after him would be useless – not to mention dangerous, speeding along all these winding roads. Come on, Rich. He'll still be wherever he is in' – she checks her phone – 'four hours, when it's a far safer time for us to show up on his doorstep. Ideally, after we've *both* slept.'

The kettle clicks and falls silent. Richie holds a coffee sachet in one hand, a spoon in the other.

'How many of those have you had?'

One shoulder jerks, dismissive. 'Do you think this wall built itself?'

You could have asked me to help, she thinks grudgingly, but strives for patience instead. 'Okay, well, you've done it, and you figured out something huge. Congratulations – time for bed.'

Richie's jaw clenches. 'Don't baby me, George.'

'I'm looking out for you.'

'Well, don't do that either,' he snaps, emptying the sachet into his mug.

Tiredness, leftover anxiety from her nightmare, and irritation combine. 'Hey, *no*. We're not doing this anymore, okay? We're actually going to talk to each other.'

'Well, I don't *feel* like talking.'

She laughs. 'Then *I'll* talk. You look terrible, your attitude is shit, your knee looks like a fucking balloon, and I don't feel safe confronting convicted rapist Robert McAllister with you half dead beside me.'

She pushes him towards the bed, again and again, until his knees buckle and he slumps back onto it. She feels bad for just a moment when he hisses with pain, but she gets over it as soon as she sees his disgruntled expression, mouth opening to protest.

'Nope,' she says, cutting him off, 'you said you don't feel like talking. So get your skinny arse into that bed, and close your damn eyes, and be ready to be my partner in a few hours. Got it?'

He glares up at her. 'I said don't baby me.'

'Don't act like a bloody baby, then.'

Grumbling something too softly for her to hear, he shuffles along the bed until he's up by the pillows, feet still on the floor. Then he pauses. 'Well, I'm not waiting for you to tuck me in.'

She rolls her eyes and goes to leave – but instead crosses to the tea station, unplugs the kettle, and carries it with her to the door.

'I'll see you at eight,' she says primly.

'Seven.'

'Seven-thirty, you stubborn bastard.'

He glowers. 'Fine, you nasty creature.'

She points at him warningly, flicks off the lights, and leaves.

CHAPTER 19

She's already dressed when the knock comes at seven fifteen.

'Good,' Richie says when she opens the door promptly, 'I thought I'd have to bang on your wall again.'

'You're already going to be in enough trouble for damaging their walls.'

He still looks tired and he hasn't shaved today; maybe didn't yesterday, or the day before either. She's not accustomed to the bristles across his cheeks, and she might be concerned if his eyes weren't so bright with the knowledge of their new lead. He practically vibrates as they head downstairs – but she sees that his limp has worsened.

'You two are up early!'

Zoe emerges from the kitchen hallway, holding a tray laden with clean cups and saucers. 'Harris is about to start serving breakfast.' She drops her voice. 'It's just a fry-up, but I'm bullying him into pancakes.'

'We didn't put an order in,' George says.

Zoe shrugs, then continues to the dining room, where a few people are already lounging around the long table. 'I won't tell anyone if you won't.'

George checks her phone, then glances at Richie. 'Quick cuppa, at least?'

Richie chews his lip, then nods. 'I have to call the lodge to get Robert's address,' he says, then looks towards the sitting room. It's empty aside from one occupied armchair; she can see a head of tight black curls over the high back. 'Grab a seat in there – I'll make the call then get us a cup.'

George eyes a cosy set-up by the window, a little round table between two low armchairs. She heads in, and is about to sink into a chair when she feels eyes on her. From this angle, she can now see the person sitting in that other chair.

Grinning like the Cheshire Cat, Hendry raises a teacup in greeting. 'Fancy seeing you here, Inspector.'

He must see the outrage ripple through her; he holds up a hand defensively. 'I swear to God, I didn't know this is where you were staying. Most of the other hotels are booked out for the night market.'

'Feels a bit fucking coincidental, Shaw.'

'I'm genuinely starting to think we're linked by fate. Have you ever heard of the red string theory?'

A dozen venomous retorts bubble on her tongue – she swallows them all back with a grimace and drops into her chair, planning to ignore Hendry's attempts to bait her into conversation.

A plan that falls apart as soon as Hendry clears his throat.

'So, how is Cara Reid connected to all this?'

She's moving before the last word is out of his mouth, three quick steps until she's towering over him.

'Forget that name,' she hisses, gripping the back of his chair to cage him between her arms. 'Delete it from your brain.'

His throat bobs, his eyes wide as he gazes up at her. 'Can't.'

'Won't.'

'*Can't*,' he reiterates, almost helplessly. 'My brain is a dog with a bone.'

George breathes through her nose. 'How did you get that name? Has there been another leak?'

He surprises her by snorting. 'Yeah – *you*, genius. You've been shoving her name and photo in the faces of everyone in

Kirkcree. About half of the people I talked to yesterday asked what *I* knew about her. Had to play it cool, pretend I knew what the hell they were on about.' He smirks at her. 'But you know how good I am at that.'

'Pretending you know what's going on?' she snaps, anger at him temporarily smothering the urge to berate herself.

'Good one. Anyway, if I didn't think there was something to pursue before, your reaction confirms that she's important.' Hendry waves her towards the opposite armchair. 'So, are you going to tell me about her, or will I have to get out my shovel and do some digging?'

'Is this you asking nicely? Or are you going to threaten me again?'

'If I actually thought you took a single one of my threats seriously, I'd stop making them.' He curls the fingers on his free hand to form a paw. 'I'm a kitten, Georgie. Not a vicious bone in my subtly muscular body.'

'Cats famously have claws.'

He grins. 'Some women like that. I reckon you're one of them.'

'Going from regular harassment to sexual harassment? I'm *so* going to enjoy testifying at your trial.'

'It's called flirting, G. I'm trying to make you fall in love with me.'

'Does this method usually work for you?'

'You tell me.'

'I've never felt less like giving a man my number.'

'Lucky I've already got it, then. But enough foreplay.' He straightens up, eyes sharpening. 'Tell me about Cara. Who is she? How is she connected to this?' As if predicting her immediate refusal, he quickly adds, 'Clearly, people tell me things.'

George bites her tongue against another batch of insults, looking over to the dining room. She can't see Richie, but she can make out his voice: a low rumble, polite back and forth with whoever else is lining up for tea. George knows from her own experience that she can't fix whatever is going on with him; she can't be his therapist, and there's a lot he needs to figure out on his own. But she can help shoulder *this*, even if the risk is losing whatever shreds of her reputation she's managed to stitch back together; because if Cole finds out what she's about to do, not even Hendry and his flood of pro–DI Lennox headlines will save her.

Hendry's eyes haven't left her face; when she turns back to him, they light up with anticipation – and surprise – as he guesses the decision she's come to.

She holds up a finger. 'I speak, you listen. Understood?'

'Yes.'

'You say yes and no when asked, but do not ask questions of your own unless it's about something I've already said. Understood?'

He doesn't hesitate. 'Yes.'

'You chase the leads I give you and report to *me* first. Not your editor, not your socials. And when you do, you do not name me, and you do not name DI Stewart. Understood?'

He nods, snatching his notebook up. 'Yes, yes.'

She rubs her eyes, already feeling the strain of a mostly sleepless night. She can't *believe* she's doing this – and from the look on Hendry's face, he can't either.

'Final thing – stay out of Richie's sight.'

At this, Hendry pauses. 'Permission to ask why?'

'Denied.'

'Why don't you want him to know we're working together?' he presses.

'Do you want the information or not?'

He groans, smoothing out a new page. 'Okay, hit me.'

With one more anxious glance towards the dining room, she falls into the chair opposite Hendry.

'Cara Reid went missing ten years ago at the age of twenty-two. Shuttled around the foster system with a younger brother.

History of sex work and drug use, but was in the process of getting sober. Last seen at a convenience store north of here – not close, but close enough to be of interest—'

'CCTV?'

'Blurry, but confirmed it was her. Don't know where she went next.'

'Don't know if she came here?' he asks to confirm, and she nods. He rolls his wrist; the joints crack. 'Right. What else?'

She doesn't go into details about the gruesome connection between Bambi and Cara, just hinting at 'something on the victim's person' that links the two. He acknowledges the evasion with a disapproving glance, but she distracts him with their theory about the link to Fearless for Fauna.

'I've heard of them,' he says. 'A friend of mine wrote an article a few years back after they were linked to the alleged arson of a dairy farm in Netherburn. Nearly drove her insane with their insistence on total anonymity, but she did eventually get through to someone.'

'Can you get me those contact details?'

He clicks his tongue. 'They *definitely* won't talk to police.'

'Not even if one of their ... colleagues, I guess, was killed?'

He shrugs. 'They call themselves vigilantes – even they acknowledge that they break some pretty serious laws. It makes sense that they'd protect their members' identities, even dead ones, especially if the Selbys have already taken them to court.'

George starts to rise. 'Then you're entirely useless to me.'

'Woah, woah,' he protests, 'I didn't say I wouldn't *try*. I'll talk to my friend, see if she still has a way in with them.' When she sinks back into the seat, he adds, 'If your victim *was* a member of this group ... are you implying that the Selbys murdered her because of that affiliation? Or do you think she found something big enough to bring them down?'

She exhales slowly, rubbing her eyes again. It's going to be a very long day, and it's barely started. 'I don't know,' she says wearily. 'There are also allegations that they like to throw money at their problems, and use their connections to grease a few wheels.'

He cocks his head. 'Bribery?'

'Allegedly,' she stresses, conscious of how many times he's broken her rule about asking questions, 'and that allegation comes from a source that has a very personal stake in the outcome, so I'm taking it with a grain of salt … but I also wouldn't be surprised if it was true, considering how difficult it's been to get an interview with them.'

He writes that all down. 'Right. What else have you got for me?'

When she explains the very recent discovery of Rab McAllister's presence back in Kirkcree, Hendry's mouth falls open.

'Why didn't you lead with that?' he demands, writing fast.

'Because we haven't spoken to him yet. And you're not to speak to him, not until we have,' she warns, and waits for his nod before continuing, 'but ask around about him. Feel free to make it known that he's back in town, too. See if there are any stories going around about other women he's harassed or attacked – now *and* back before he went to jail.'

'Wouldn't the prosecutor handling Amy's case have found that?'

'Not if the women back then didn't report the attacks. And since you're *so* good at getting people to tell you things …'

Hendry rolls his eyes, but ignores the jab as he continues writing. 'I think … yeah. I think I've got some people who might know some things.' He stares down at his notes. 'What's in this for me?'

She raises her eyebrows. 'Aside from the highly confidential information I just shared with you?'

He taps his notebook. 'Chasing these leads might take a while, and I have no idea if any of this will pan out. For all I know, you could be sending me on a wild goose chase to keep me out of your hair.'

She purses her lips; the thought *had* crossed her mind. 'So, what? You want to send me an invoice at the end of it, or something?'

Hendry leans forward, his eyes shining. 'I want the Eadar story.'

'No.'

'Thirty minutes,' he presses, 'an hour, max. Just to walk me through the case. Keep it as surface level as you need. Just the facts, no feelings.'

'I said *no*. I'm already risking my career looping you in on this.'

Hendry chews his lower lip, then taps the notebook again. 'How much is this information worth to you?' When he sees her hesitate, he jerks his chin towards the dining room, and she hates him for it, hates that she allowed herself to be read so easily. 'How much is it worth to *him*?'

He must also read the defeat in her expression, as his becomes benevolent in victory. 'We'll keep it casual – have you been to The Kirk? We can talk over dinner, maybe have a wine, or two.'

'It's not a fucking date.'

Hendry stands. 'Hey, I never said date. But I will say seven o'clock.' He snaps his notebook closed. 'See you tonight.'

He crosses to the stairs and starts to jog up them – *just* as Richie finally appears from the dining room. She observes the reason for his delay; he's precariously balancing two laden plates and two steaming mugs across his hands and forearms.

'No, don't touch,' he says as she rushes to help him, 'I have everything perfectly balanced.'

She does help him unload at the table, and he sinks into the armchair Hendry just vacated with an appreciative groan. 'Zoe strong-armed me into this,' he says, gesturing at the plates, 'so eat fast.'

Considering she pushed for an eight am start, George feels no need to be throwing herself out the door. The tension from the close call between Richie and Hendry, and from Hendry's final request, still has her feeling on edge – which is further complicated by her realisation that she and Richie are supposed to check out of the hotel today, though this does give her a good excuse to bail out of the dinner. Hendry can share his findings over the phone just as easily as in person; even better, this way she won't be forced to look at his smug face when it comes time to hold up her end of the deal.

She reaches for the coffee.

'I do love a free breakfast,' Richie admits, fork hovering over the fare – toast, scrambled eggs, a bit of charred meat, and a tiny pastry tossed atop like a garnish. 'I'll be offering that at the pub I open.'

'That still the retirement plan, then? Does Jenny know yet?'

'Oh, yes. Told her a few months back.'

'And she's on board?'

He makes a *so-so* gesture with his hand. 'Coming around.' He closes his eyes around the first bite, chewing in blissful silence. 'Heaven,' he says, before his eyes open again. 'I think Emma Fairgrieve is pregnant.'

'Oh, really? Who told you that?'

'Zoe said she saw Rory buying baby formula.'

She frowns. 'She can't be far along enough to be needing that.'

But Richie waves her doubt away. 'Ness was a formula baby. We ran out once and I went to six different supermarkets to get the right kind at two in the morning. Kirkcree may be a tourist village but it's remote, Fairgrieve Castle even more so. I assume they're stockpiling. It's smart.' He pauses before taking another bite. 'They have a *lot* of childproofing to do.'

She hums in agreement. *They should probably just seal off that room of weapons entirely – not to mention the crypt.*

'Did you get on to Fiadhain Lodge?'

'I did. Patrick was very interested in why I was calling about Robert McAllister – especially considering that he knows him as Rab Brown.'

'He's going by another name?'

'So it would seem.'

She leans forward to grab a slice of toast. 'We're supposed to believe that people who do their time deserve a chance to start over.'

When Richie goggles at her, she adds, 'I mean, he was in jail for years. Maybe he's remorseful.'

'The man was convicted of aggravated sexual assault, George. And there's no way Amy was his first offence, even if the prosecutors couldn't prove it.' He jerks his chin towards the dining room. 'Do you think it's a good idea for Zoe to be spending time with him alone?'

'I think we have to be open to the idea that Rab McAllister might be a criminal, but a criminal who has served his time. And one who maybe doesn't have any connection to Cara – who might not have even been in Kirkcree when she disappeared. I saw your wall, Rich,' she says, sensing his protest, 'I saw the string linking him to her.'

His eyes flash. 'He attacked Amy at around eleven-thirty pm, but he wasn't arrested until midday the next day. Plenty of time for him to do something to Cara.'

'On paper, sure.' Before he can protest, she holds up a hand. 'It's a theory, Rich, but can we agree that our unknown woman is our first priority in this interview?'

He looks frustrated, but he works to keep his tone even. 'Of course. But just keep in mind that despite *multiple* eyewitnesses seeing him watching Amy at the supermarket, Rab tried to claim he'd never laid eyes on her before. And then pleaded not guilty to all charges. He wasn't a good man, George – still isn't, I'd wager. Men like him don't change. Darkness is in their DNA.'

She exhales. 'Jesus. Noted.'

For a few minutes, they eat in silence. George's mind is racing — about Rab, about Cara and Bambi and Amy, about the deal she's made with Hendry. She wonders where he'll start, which route he'll venture down first. Despite Richie's new fixation on Rab, George's gut is pulling her towards the Selbys being responsible for Bambi's death. But, as always, that still leaves the question of Cara — how does she fit in to all this?

'Rich?'

'Mm?'

'You don't think there's a chance she's still alive, do you?'

He doesn't need to confirm which *she* George is referring to. 'No, I don't,' he says slowly. 'But Cara *is* out there, George. People don't just disappear, not entirely. Whatever is left of her is waiting to be found; whether she's six feet under, or on top of a mountain, or at the bottom of a loch.' He pauses, his voice thick. 'Cara is out there, and she's been waiting ten years for me to find her. And I'm going to.'

He catches the sympathetic twist of her lips. 'I know it's a long shot ... but I have *hope*, George. I have to. If I don't ... what else keeps us going?'

After a beat she nods, and Richie seems to accept that as a satisfactory response. But as he tucks back into his breakfast with an appetite she hasn't seen in him for a while, she wonders how long this hope can sustain him before he completely falls apart.

CHAPTER 20

George feels uncharacteristically apprehensive as they approach Rab McAllister's caravan. She's dealt with far more frightening offenders: she once rapped on the front door of a man who'd barricaded himself inside his house with a hatchet, threatening to swing it at the next person who walked through the door. She took his threat seriously since she could see his brother's body cooling in the foyer, but even then she felt steady, prepared for anything.

So finding herself jittery now, she wonders if the difference is the desperation she can feel radiating from the man beside her.

Patrick's directions have led them to an unexpected destination. The caravan she noticed in the back corner of the supermarket carpark is a 1980s model with a yellow band running around the sides. It's covered in scratches and dents, the towbar held on by layers of duct tape, and the windows are obscured by yellowing lace curtains.

Richie knocks on the door, and waits approximately five seconds before repeating, harder.

George takes a deep breath. So much for not going in swinging.

Footsteps approach, there's the sound of something being kicked along the ground, and then finally the click of the lock. The door swings open with a strong waft of cigarettes and body odour.

Robert McAllister – Rab Brown, nowadays – squints in the morning light.

'What the fuck?' he mumbles. He's clad only in a pair of black briefs, his barrel chest exposed to the crisp morning air. When he crosses his arms, his biceps bulge; though he's not overly tall, his mass is intimidating – and George suspects he knows it. The hard-bodied man in front of her is unrecognisable from the baby-faced boy who attacked Amy Buchanan; ten long years in prison have altered all but his eyes.

'Robert McAllister?'

Rab looks at Richie; after a beat, his eyes narrow with recognition. 'What the fuck do you want?'

George appraises what she can see of the interior. A light is on somewhere to the left, the faint yellow glow highlighting a tiny kitchenette with grease stains on the cabinets, a built-in table, and cardboard boxes stacked on the floor with clothes and shoes spilling out.

'We have a few questions for you,' Richie says tersely.

Rab glances back into the caravan, looking harried. 'Can wrap this up real fast for you – I don't know either of them, the dead girl or the one that went missing. Never saw them, spoke to them, played fucking hopscotch with them, *nothing*.'

There's a soft but distinct *thud* from inside the caravan. Rab makes a point of not reacting to it.

'What was that?' George asks, trying to see around him.

'None of your business.'

Ignoring that, George shifts so that she can see a little further past him. 'Is there someone else in there?'

Rab swears, then calls into the caravan, 'You don't have to come out. They haven't got a fucking warrant.'

'A *warrant*?' someone squeaks.

A woman around George's age hops into view behind Rab, hair mussed and clearly having dressed fast. One long boot pools around her ankle; she bends at the waist to grasp the zipper and draw it up her calf.

Rab turns his back on George and Richie, waiting for the woman to rise so he can grab her hips. 'They're about to leave,' he murmurs, his tone unexpectedly simpering. 'There's no need to run off.'

The woman's eyes flick to George over his shoulder; George shakes her head slightly.

'I, er ... have to go,' the woman says slowly. 'My group is heading to Edinburgh this morning ... but we might be coming back through here in a couple of days. Maybe I'll see you then?'

Rab's fingers tighten on the woman's hips for a moment, then he slides one hand up to her neck and pulls her into a protracted kiss. Her cheeks are flushed when she pulls away, and she murmurs an embarrassed 'Excuse me' as she walks down the steps past George and Richie.

Rab stares after her, but as soon as she's out of sight behind a row of cars, his gaze drags to George. His simpering expression curls into something more lecherous. 'You wish that had been you, gorgeous? I suppose I could look past the badge if it ended up on my bedroom floor.'

Richie sucks in a breath, but before he can defend her honour – and get himself into more trouble – she says, 'I didn't think these things came with a bedroom.'

Rab's eyes flash, steel caught in the light. But his voice is a crafted purr when he says, 'Come see for yourself.'

'Enough,' Richie says, his lip curled with disgust. 'We need to talk.'

'Already told you, I haven't seen either of them. And even if I did, I don't remember. I like girls with big eyes.' He smirks at George. 'I like to see my reflection in them.'

She works to maintain an unaffected expression. Though there was no official diagnosis in the reports she read about Rab before heading down to meet Richie this morning, he is displaying some textbook narcissistic traits. She knows better than to feed his desire for a reaction.

Dissatisfied with her lack of response, Rab leans against the doorframe. 'Come on – I've been out for eight weeks. Do you seriously think I'd fuck that up by shooting some random woman? No way,' he continues before George or Richie has time to answer. 'I did my time, I'm out, and I just want to be left alone.'

Richie tilts his head. 'Is that what Amy Buchanan said when you followed her back to her campsite, pinned her down and raped her?'

A shocked gasp catches in George's throat.

'Fuck you,' Rab hisses, lurching down a step. 'Don't say that lying bitch's name around me ever again.'

'Lying?' Richie echoes harshly. 'Evidence doesn't lie, Robert. You were found guilty.'

'Because her rich daddy set me up.'

Richie laughs – a sarcastic chuckle. He might as well have waved a red rag at a bull; Rab bristles.

'Where were you Monday night?' George asks quickly, coaxing his baleful stare towards her. It works, and she steels herself to weather his cold fury.

'I was at work,' he spits. 'Punched my little card in and out, right on time.'

But Richie isn't done. 'How did someone like you get a job at a place like that?'

'Why, think it's too good for me?'

'Without a doubt.'

George says a string of bad words in her head; she looks forward to saying them out loud to Richie in a few minutes' time.

'My great-uncle is the ghillie there,' Rab says. 'They needed someone to manage the equipment, and he brought me in.'

'Was it his idea to give your employers a fake name?' Richie asks.

'It's not fake – Rab is a nickname, and Brown was my mam's maiden name.'

Richie writes that down. 'I'm guessing you didn't explain the gap in your résumé. Do you handle the guns?'

'I clean them and store them. I don't take them out for target practice.'

'But do you know how to shoot?' Richie presses.

Rab stares at Richie for a second. Then he chuckles roughly. 'Oh, no. No, thank you. Unless you've got a warrant to wave at me, we're done here.'

He starts to retreat inside, but Richie's hand shoots out to block the door from closing.

'One last thing,' he says quickly. 'Fiadhain Lodge has had some things go missing: tools, medical supplies … and hygiene items.' He looks over the caravan in the same manner George did earlier. 'You wouldn't know anything about that, would you?'

George acts on instinct – she senses Rab's weight shift and throws herself between him and Richie. It's just in the nick of time; Rab leaps to the ground, hurling himself against her raised palms.

'Cool it,' she orders, and with her eyes locked on Rab's thunderous face, she adds, 'Take a walk, Richie.'

For a long moment, she thinks he's going to argue. But then she hears the twist of his heel on the asphalt, followed by receding footsteps. Once she's confident he's far enough away, she drops her hands. 'Thank you for your time, Mr Mc— er, Mr Brown. We'll follow up with you if needed.'

His glare slides to her, and his temper fizzles fast – so fast that part of her wonders if the outburst was just for show, a posturing attempt to look like some red-pill alpha.

'He'd be real dumb to show his face here again,' he says, 'but you?' He brushes a hand over his chest, right where her palms were just pressing. '*You're* welcome anytime.'

And before she can respond, he stomps back up into the caravan and slams the door closed.

Despite Richie's bad leg, George has to jog to catch up with him as he storms down the street. There are a lot more people out and about than George has previously seen – then she remembers the market is on tonight, tourists arriving in unexpected droves.

'Richie, wait,' she calls, weaving through a group of coffee-toting Australians.

'He knows something,' Richie barks. 'We should have asked if he's ever taken women back to the lodge.'

She catches up, panting slightly. 'So he can romance them in a garage instead of his caravan?'

'It can't be a coincidence that he works up where this woman was found.'

'Yes, it can,' she says, 'and if it's not, and we need to talk to him again, then you've got to pull yourself together. He's either going to hit you *or* file a complaint against you, and that's exactly the kind of thing Cole is looking for.'

Richie lurches to a stop. 'Excuse me?'

Her heart jumps to her throat. '*Oh*. I just … I meant …' She exhales sharply. *Fuck it*. 'Cole is concerned about you.'

Richie's mouth drops open. 'What?'

She doesn't insult him by playing dumb. 'She told me that there have been complaints. And she ordered me to let her know if you do something stupid – like, I don't know, refusing to report an injury, or antagonising a man who has a violent criminal history.' She jabs a finger at him. 'Until now, I haven't told her anything, but I will if you're going to keep pulling shit like you did back there.'

A flurry of emotion contorts Richie's face. 'That's rich coming from *you*.'

'Yeah, yeah – the irony isn't lost on me, either. But Rich …' She runs her fingers through her hair, searching for the right words, desperately wishing they weren't having this conversation in the middle of a busy street.

'I thought you reported the drugs because you were following the rules,' she starts slowly, struggling to meet his eyes, 'but after watching you these past couple of days, I wonder if maybe you just didn't know how else to help me – because as much as I want to protect you, Rich, I'd rather lose your friendship than watch you lose yourself.'

Richie's expression twists. 'I don't need anyone's help.'

George shakes her head again. 'Just think about it. And *talk* to me – you know I won't judge. Like you said, it would be rich coming from me.'

His reply seems to get stuck in his throat – he just stares at her, frozen with whatever emotional storm has got him into this state. She knows the feeling well, remembers her chest constricting so hard that it felt as if her words were encased in ice. So she gives him an out.

'What is it with these people demanding warrants?' she asks, gesturing for them to continue walking. 'First Emma Fairgrieve, now Rab McAllister. Has the village been doing Friday night screenings of *Shetland* or something?'

It takes a few seconds for Richie to get out of his head, to come back to her.

'Emma just seems angry at the world,' he says, his voice subdued. 'And Rab knows how the system works. He was doing his best to get under your skin.'

'He certainly tried. That woman has no idea who she just spent the night with.'

'She has no idea how close she might have come to being his next victim – if he's lying about not knowing the woman from the road.'

It's more than possible, given his history. And despite her gut telling her that the Selbys are hiding something huge, Robert McAllister is certainly a person of interest.

She picks up her pace. 'Let's go find out if he is.'

Settled comfortably on the desk chair back in his room, Richie guides George through his wall of notes in more depth. He's done a fairly decent job considering there really isn't that much information on either of the women, and that it was made by a sleep-deprived fifty-seven-year-old man.

They dive deep into Rab's rap sheet, finding a slew of other offences: a B&E at age fourteen, aggravated theft of a bicycle at sixteen, and a pub fight at eighteen that ended with both Rab and the other party taken to hospital and charged with property damage. At twenty-one, there's documentation for a protective order filed against him by an ex-girlfriend who alleged that Rab locked her in his car and coerced her into performing a sex act.

'The severity of his attacks escalated,' Richie notes grimly.

Cross-legged on the bed, a cup of tea balanced on her knee, George nods. 'Incredibly fast. But if Cara *is* one of his victims, he escalated to rape and murder within a matter of hours. That's a hell of a leap.'

'It's possible.'

'Of course it's *possible*, but is he arrogant enough that he's free for only a couple of months before he snatches another woman off the street and shoots her?'

'Yes.'

'And then writes Cara's name on Bambi's arm ... why? To brag? To taunt us?'

When the silence lasts a little too long, George finds Richie looking at her with a strange expression. 'What?'

'You called her Bambi.'

Her stomach drops. 'Fuck, I ... Hendry called her that, and after seeing her in person, it just started to feel like her name.

A placeholder,' she corrects, 'until we find out who she really is, of course.'

'I see.' He cocks his head. 'You talked to Hendry about the case?'

'He wrote an article about her on the day she was found, and he caught me heading into work to press for more information. That was before I was assigned to her case, so I didn't have anything to tell him,' she says, clutching at the technicality.

Richie pulls a face. 'I hope you wouldn't, even if you did. I don't think either of us is foolish enough to get into bed with a journalist and expect to leave it satisfied.'

She laughs, a high sound. 'Right. No way.'

He looks back at the wall – at the photo of Bambi specifically. 'I see what you mean, I suppose. I don't think I need to tell you not to refer to her as Bambi in the official paperwork.'

'You don't, and of course, I won't. It just felt more personal. We have Cara's name – I didn't want to just keep calling this woman our "victim".'

He nods, then yawns and stretches his arms over his head. 'I need to call Dr Bùi to chase the test results.'

'Er, leave Bùi to me. You should follow up on the CCTV.'

Richie looks confused, then sheepish. 'I didn't handle that one well, did I?'

'Not your best work. But your current attitude is doing wonders for my reputation – everyone thinks that *I'm* the nice one.' She looks back at her laptop, navigating to one of her newer tabs. 'Did you know there are seventy-six active missing persons cases across the UK right now?' She presses her fingertips into her forehead, staring at her screen in distress. 'And *hundreds* of long-term cases.'

'Cara is one of the long-terms,' Richie says gravely. 'When the working hypothesis is "presumed dead", they get bumped from the active list.'

'Some of these are decades old, and less than half of them have photos. What if our victim is one of these? Look – Nancy

Tate, disappeared eight years ago at age fifteen. Tatiana Harvey, eighteen when she vanished, missing for four years.' She turns the screen around so that Richie can see the greyed-out boxes where their photos should be. 'Either of these could be our unidentified woman, but we'll never know because whoever reported them missing didn't have a single photo of them. Or whoever took the report didn't bother to ask for one.'

'Frustrating, isn't it?'

She exhales roughly. 'Sorry. You know all this.'

'I do, but it's nice to have someone else be angry *with* me. Cara needs another person on her team. She'd be glad it's you. I know I am.' When George waves his compliment away, he shifts in his seat to face her. 'I mean it, George. I know I haven't made this easy on you, but I wouldn't want to be working on Cara's case with anyone else.'

She pushes her laptop away. 'Honestly, Rich, I thought I'd be doing you a favour by *not* taking it. I think I'm bad luck.'

He tuts. 'Don't be ridiculous.'

She starts listing off on her fingers. 'On this trip alone, we almost hit a deer, I put my head into a spider nest, and you fell through a bridge. Not to mention all the things happening to me back home – furniture breaking, plants dying, a coffee cup literally falling apart in my hands and making it look like I peed myself.'

He does his best to repress a smile. 'And when did all this misfortune start?'

'Two years ago, I guess, but it seems to have ramped up since ...' She hesitates. 'You'll think it's stupid.'

'Undoubtedly, but I'd still like to know.'

'Well ... do you remember, back on Eadar—'

'I remember everything about Eadar.'

'Then you remember that someone planted an honest-to-God bad luck charm on us. And I absolutely thought it was rubbish at the time, but ... I'm scared that it might have actually worked. That I'm actually cursed.'

He snorts. 'I don't think you're scared of anything.'

'Then you have no idea how many times a day I make sure my phone is nearby, in case I need to call for help.' She slumps back on the bed, staring up at the ceiling. 'How am I meant to do my job, to help people, when I'm constantly hoping that someone will be around to save *me*?'

'That might be my fault.'

She tilts her head to frown at him. 'What?'

'I told you that you needed to let your guard down, and it got you hurt. Got *both* of us hurt.' He chews his lip, looking to the window. 'You said yesterday that you see everything? Some days, I feel like I don't see anything at all. It's all a blur, just shapes and noise and people talking at me. I get home and I can't even tell Jenny where I've been, or what I did. It's all gone, or it just never stuck.'

There's a moment of silence, both of them a little cowed by their respective confessions.

'Jesus,' she eventually mutters. 'I'm cursed, you're losing the plot. No wonder Cole paired us up again – she can't let this shit spread to the rest of the force.'

Her hyperbole works; he laughs, and the mood in the room lightens.

'Okay, enough commiserating – let's make some calls.' He grabs his phone, but pauses before tapping in a number. 'Knowing what we know now, with Rab McAllister being back in the area—'

She pre-empts the end. 'We should stay another night.'

'Oh. Thought that was going to be harder.'

It's a decision she grudgingly came to earlier. She knows that they have more to do here, and need more time to do it; but now she has no reason not to meet Hendry for dinner. She shuffles off the bed and stretches her arms over her head, the joints popping. 'I want to drive back down *An Rathad Damainte*, walk around a bit more.'

'Why?'

'Because Fiadhain Lodge still has a lot to answer for. We found the bloody badge on their land – maybe something else was missed.'

'With the level of competence PC Bear has already demonstrated, you'll probably stumble across a signed confession from the Selbys. Or Rab.'

George laughs. She thought the same thing after meeting Bear. It's nice to see that their thoughts are synching up again.

He looks down at his knee, his brow furrowing. 'I think … I might stay put for a little while longer. And if I ask something silly, will you forgive me?'

'Depends on what it is.'

Raising his phone, he says, 'Will you share your location with me? Just while you're gone,' he adds quickly, seeing her expression twist.

She rolls her eyes, but pulls out her own phone. It takes a second to do so, but then his phone pings with the notification. 'Just for a few hours,' she warns, 'then I'm turning it off. Don't need you knowing which shady parts of town I stray into in my personal time.'

She expects some sassy reply, or for him to frown at her; instead, Richie's expression is soft, unguarded.

'Thank you, George. I'll keep an eye on you.'

She nods, swallowing around the new lump in her throat. 'Thanks, Rich. I know you will.'

CHAPTER 21

George is surprised by the amount of noise that greets her when she goes downstairs. The sitting room is lively with conversation, and in the dining room some kids are playing an energetic card game around the table. She catches Zoe coming out of the kitchen, looking a little flustered – likely due to the influx of guests. That expression deepens when George asks if they can stay one more night.

'Er ... possibly,' she says, chewing her lower lip. 'How close are you and DI Stewart?'

'Not close enough to share a bed,' she says, guessing the direction of Zoe's thoughts.

'What about an air mattress on the floor?'

George shrugs; she's slept in less comfortable conditions. 'Fine by me.'

'Sure. I'll get things set up for you this afternoon.' Zoe's eyes light up. 'You can come to the market! Dean gave me and Harris the night off for it, since we figure all the guests will be going. The mulled wine is *so* good, but crazy strong.' She lowers her voice conspiratorially. 'I drank two last year and woke up in the flowerbed.'

'Maybe avoid it this year, then?'

Zoe cackles. 'I'll try!'

George sends Richie a text to update him on the room plans as she walks out to the carpark. It's very full – a few drivers have parked on the grassy verge beside the road, and she can see other hotels along the street have the same problem. *A good problem,* George thinks as she heads for their car, *when there isn't a killer on the loose.*

It's a relatively mild day, but the thin layer of clouds glow almost painfully from the afternoon sun just behind them. She's digging through the glove compartment for Richie's sunglasses when her phone rings.

Dr Bùi sounds even more badgered than Zoe. 'I received a phone call *very* early this morning from your superintendent, instructing me to expedite your victim's tests. We're still waiting on a few things to come back, but I can confirm that her fingerprints aren't in any UK databases. There was evidence of recent sexual activity, but we're still waiting on results from the swabs.'

'Can you tell if it was consensual?'

'Undetermined right now. I've identified a potential internal injury that might indicate assault, but I'm seeking a second opinion from a colleague.'

Her stomach sinks. 'Jesus. Right. Did you test the pin?'

'Not as simple as I'd hoped, unfortunately.'

'It never is. Why?'

'Because there are different blood types on the pin.'

'Hers and her killer's?'

'Possibly, but considering how mixed the sample is, it's going to be quite difficult to work with.' Before George can sink too far into despair, he continues: 'I do have something interesting for you regarding her blood work. I did a toxicology screen, and none of the usual suspects showed up – but have you ever heard of xylazine?' When she answers in the negative, he says, 'It's become a real problem in the States and is making its way here. You might know it as "tranq".'

'As in tranquilliser?'

'Exactly that. It's a common veterinary drug used to sedate livestock – cows, horses – for medical treatment. But street drug makers are terribly creative; they're mixing xylazine into opioids, fentanyl most commonly. The first UK fatality was recorded in 2022.'

'Jesus,' she mutters again. 'What effects does it have on people?'

'Well, it's a muscle relaxant first and foremost, which is the appeal for drug makers. The other, not-so-pretty effects are drowsiness, dry mouth, irregular heartbeat and low blood pressure.'

'And you found tranq in our victim's blood?'

'Yes, but I couldn't find evidence of fresh track marks, so if this woman was using or given xylazine it was orally, and it was undiluted.'

George's stomach turns, but she thanks him for the update and hangs up. For a few seconds, she can't summon the energy to start the car; the growing tally of abuses perpetrated upon Bambi's body is sitting heavily on her shoulders.

If they're unable to squeeze answers out of the Selbys, and if the Rab angle falls through, and nobody makes a missing person report, and all of the other leads they chase turn into dead ends … what then? Is Bambi fated to become *her* Cara? Will she spend her entire career wondering what happened to this poor, forever unidentified woman, torturing herself over all the details and red flags she likely missed, another stroke in the growing tally of people she failed to help?

That unsettling panic spikes within her again. George opens the window, inhaling deep lungfuls of fresh, damp air, trying to smother the feeling with other sensations the way Dr Kassab taught her.

In-in-in.

She cannot let Bambi's death go unsolved. There are answers here, buried somewhere out in that troubled land, and she's going to find them.

Out-out-out.

Starting by asking the Selbys – hunters of large, warm-blooded mammals – if the stock of medicines that Belle mentioned they keep onsite happens to contain a common sedative for large, warm-blooded mammals. She'll call Richie on the way – she knows he'd demand to come with her if she went back inside to tell him now, but his leg is not getting any better and clearly he's only making bad choices for himself at the moment.

Her phone buzzes. Glancing at the sender, she grimaces. Speaking of bad choices …

Can we meet earlier? Hendry asks. *Got something for you.*

She checks the time, thinking about how long it will take her to get out to the lodge and back. *5.00?* she writes.

His reply comes almost immediately. *Sharp.*

She rolls her eyes and shoves her phone into her pocket. Then she starts the car.

As with her first visit to Fiadhain Lodge, nobody comes to greet her when she knocks on the front door. George finds it unlocked when she tests the handle, but Richie was clear when she called him before: under no circumstances is she to go inside the house without him there, not even if she's invited. So she walks around the side to see if anyone is out the back.

But it's a ghost town out here, too – the French doors are sealed against the cool, petrichor-heavy breeze, the firepit overturned as if anticipating rain. The garage door is closed, too; everyone must be out for today's hunt. She scans the landscape, squinting against the overcast glare, but can't see any shapes moving through the wild land.

A squeal of metal makes her jump; a smaller door on the side of the garage is slowly swinging open, pushed by the breeze, hinges protesting the creeping pace. It's dark within, devoid of those awful flickering lights, but she can just make out the shelves, some storage boxes … and, like last night, she feels that same urge to approach.

She shouldn't – for so many reasons, the least of which is Richie's order. But she *knows* this feeling, this compulsion, a magnetic tug that beckons her in the direction she *needs* to go.

There's something inside she needs to see.

It's cold in the garage; she shivers as she moves into the space, stepping lightly, using only the light from outside to guide her way. It smells like petrol in here, and she can see scuffs on the floor that indicate where the quad bike usually sits; beside it are two muddy dirt bikes, resting on their stands. The shelving is more extensive than she guessed – it takes up most of the back part of the garage. She weaves between the rows, scanning the boxes labelled *Spare Parts, First-aid Kits, Backpacks, Torches*. Against one wall is a padlocked cabinet that interests her; she assumes medicine would be locked away, especially if Belle was telling the truth about supplies being stolen, but it could also be home to the Selbys' arsenal of rifles; however, the magnet pulls her further, along another row until she arrives in the back corner.

She's surprised by what she finds. This small square of space is … well, empty. A folding chair leans against the wall, one of the kinds that has retractable arms built in. It's the same kind as the ones Rab and Finlay brought for the guests on the stalk last night. George looks closer and sees why this one was left behind; one of the legs has been knocked loose.

It's because she's looking so closely that she notices the cable ties. Two of them: one caught in the hinge of the retractable arm, the other looped through the base of the unbroken leg. They've both been cut, releasing whatever they were holding – but the tie on the arm didn't fully let go. On the inside of the plastic is a dark smear, so brown it almost looks black.

Blood, she identifies immediately, and the images of Bambi's wrists springs to mind – the angry welts around that delicate skin.

'Shit,' she mutters, fishing out her phone. 'Shit, shit, shit.'

She can't just walk out of here with evidence – Jesus, she's breaking so many rules just by *being* in here. But there's something she *can* do. Despite her heart kicking into gear, her hands are steady as she snaps a few photos – the evidence she'll need to show Richie, the evidence they will never be able to submit at a trial. But hopefully it's enough to get them a warrant that will enable them to batter through the Selbys' legal fortress in order to *officially* search this place.

Hurrying from the garage, she glances around nervously before nudging the door closed with her foot.

'Hello?'

She feels like she's been electrocuted.

'Oh,' she says, making her tone light, 'hi. You're Finlay, right?'

The boy – he really does look like a child, perhaps seventeen at most – frowns, confused. 'Yeah ... and you're the detective.'

'That's me,' she says cheerily, edging away from the garage door. 'I'm actually here to speak to your' – she does a double-take, notices the striking eyes, the high cheekbones – 'parents?'

Finlay's eyes shift from her to the garage. 'They're out,' he says flatly, his confusion morphing into suspicion. 'You know, you shouldn't be back here.'

'I was just looking for someone to help me,' she says, taking more purposeful steps towards the side of the house. 'I knocked on the front door, and remembered these back doors were open last time. Thought I'd check.'

Finlay trails behind, but his eyes are locked on to her; he might be young, but he seems to already possess his mother's intensity.

'You can tell your parents that I stopped by to follow up about' – she scrambles, then finishes – 'that staff member my partner enquired about this morning. Your dad will understand.'

She's at her car now – she throws Finlay a wave as she closes the door behind her and locks the doors. As she pulls away, trying not to spin the tyres in her haste, she glances in the rear-view mirror to see him staring after her, his radio already raised to his lips.

*

'He knew I was in the garage, Richie. There's no way Francina and Patrick haven't told him to pull everything out and burn it.' She thumps the steering wheel. '*Goddamn* it.'

'But you have the pictures,' Richie says, his voice loud through her car speakers.

'That we can't use! I went in there without permission.'

'Yes,' Richie says, surprisingly patient despite what she just told him, 'but at least we know that it's very, *very* possible that she was in there. Cole trusts our judgement, George – she'll get the warrant if we tell her there's something to find. I doubt it'll be all guns blazing tonight, but I'll impress upon her the urgency – so maybe first thing tomorrow.' He pauses, and George hears papers being shuffled. 'Of course, this brings us no closer to the Cara connection, but hopefully that will be revealed when we start applying pressure to Patrick and Francina. Are you on your way back here now?'

'Yeah, just about to pass the driveway to the Fairgrieve place.' George glances at the time and suppresses a groan. She's only just going to make it to her meeting with Hendry. 'Er, I'm going to head into the village and grab something to eat first. I'll get something for you, too.'

She hangs up and presses the accelerator down. Her mind is racing about this latest discovery. Of course, she can't know for sure that the blood on those cable ties belongs to Bambi – but she also doesn't feel like it's too much of a reach to connect those kinds of restraints and the fact that the woman found *beside* the Selbys' land had been tied up just before she died.

She eyes her phone again, wondering if she should cancel on Hendry. Richie's right that a warrant likely won't come in time to catch the Selbys disposing of evidence, but she could at least contain her restless pacing to the hotel room instead of letting Hendry see her sweat.

She's still debating the point when she sees the figure in the trees.

Her foot stomps on the brake so hard that the tyres lock up, and the car slides off to the left.

'Fuck, fuck, *fuck*,' she yelps. Her heart is beating a frantic tattoo in her pulse points – it aggravates the old twinge behind her eye, which she ignores as she climbs out of the car.

Striding towards the spot where she thinks she saw the figure, she calls out, 'Hello? Is someone out there?'

There's no response.

It would be shamefully easy to turn back to the car, to convince herself that she's imagining things, that the adrenaline rush after getting caught by Finlay is making her jumpy. But then there's a rustle in the trees behind her.

She spins back, her gaze darting between the trunks. There's still plenty of light to see by, but the source of the sound isn't immediately apparent.

'Hello?'

There's another rustle, the sound of a branch snapping and then—

A pale flash, gone as quickly as it appeared. Her heart launches into her throat and almost sends her rocketing towards her car.

'Who's there?' she calls, fear turning her tone into a demand. 'Come out, now!'

There's another rustle, followed by a high, thin wail.

'Shit,' she mutters, then raises her voice. 'Are you injured? Do you need help?'

The cry comes again, a bit further away, but it still scrapes along the knobs of George's spine – Zoe's brother was right. It does sound like a baby.

She immediately chides herself. *Don't be ridiculous*, she thinks, *it's probably an animal*. An animal that gives another pitiful cry, thin and wobbling and demanding to be acknowledged, to be helped.

She stares up at the sky and groans. 'Fuck it,' she mutters, then rolls her shoulders. 'All right, wait there. I'm coming.'

CHAPTER 22

It's not a comfortable feeling, being surrounded by trees – not after her last experience working a case that led to her life nearly ending in a dense patch of woods. Even though her phone holds strong with three bars of reception, George's anxiety manifests as nausea the further in she walks. It doesn't help her roiling stomach that this is Fairgrieve land, and with that comes an immediate and overwhelming scent of sweet decay, animal faeces and boggy earth.

There's no obvious path among the skeletal trees. The trunks and branches are covered in the same blue-green lichen that was around the Fairgrieves' front gate, though here it grows in spidery shapes, branching out like ventricles. She ponders what manner of eldritch creature these tiny lungs could be breathing *for* – and if it's the thing making those pained wails. She's just grateful that the trees are so skinny and barren that she can still see the overcast sky.

Despite the lack of a path, it's easy enough to follow the sounds – especially when whatever it is seems to be stumbling around like a drunk. Eventually, she comes across a shallow gully that stretches off further than she can see in both directions. There's a thin but steady stream running along the base, the water no more than ankle-deep. And standing at the base, long legs quivering, is a deer.

A doe, to be precise, her tawny flanks heaving with every

rapid breath. And as George watches, the doe lets out a long, thin cry.

Relief washes over her. 'You're certainly not Edith Fairgrieve,' she murmurs. She approaches the edge of the gully and looks the deer over for injury, then does a double take at the sight of dried blood on its white belly in roughly the same spot where she prised the barbed wire from the deer they came across yesterday.

'We meet again, hey? You and I must have the same bad luck.'

As if to confirm it, the doe suddenly staggers to one side, knobbly legs tangling. The movement reminds George of the kids she used to see stumbling between nightclubs and pubs in the city, up to their eyeballs with shots of Jäger, or buzzed on something they had swallowed or injected. The doe manages to keep her feet but the shaking continues, and her head sways from side to side as though she's dazed.

Like last time, George keeps her movements slow as she steps down into the gully, water lapping gently around the ankles of her boots. But unlike last time, the doe barely seems to notice her approach; in fact, George is almost within arm's reach before the doe even looks up.

'You're okay,' she croons, pausing until the doe decides how to react. 'I'm not going to hurt you. No guns here. Very anti-them, personally and professionally.'

The doe doesn't react to her approach at all; in comparison with yesterday, she almost seems tame. George hopes that means the doe will allow her to touch her, to guide her up and out of the gully and hopefully back towards the road, where she can call a vet or someone far more qualified to be handling wildlife.

'Please don't kick me, please don't bite me, please don't stomp me,' she chants, stretching her arm towards the deer's neck at a glacial pace, until she's close enough to feel the doe's warmth, maybe even the slightest brush of silken pelt under the tips of her fingers.

'I'm not going to hurt you,' she whispers. 'I'm just here to help—'

The bullet enters the doe's head a half-second before George hears the *crack*.

Shock turns George into a statue, and she remains frozen long after the doe's body has toppled to the ground. Its head flops heavily onto George's boots, and mucky water splashes up her trousers, icy pinpricks digging through the fabric and into her skin.

But George can barely feel it; nor can she make out the shouting that's getting louder and closer, not above the deafening squelch of blood in her ears. Even her breaths are drowned out, though she can feel the air whistling through her throat. She doesn't close her mouth, she *can't*, not when she can taste metal and feel a warmth that isn't her saliva on her tongue, coating her lips and cheeks, dripping down her forehead.

Then hands are grabbing at her, wrenching her around, and Belle is staring at her, absolutely aghast. Her mouth moves, and it takes George a few seconds to realise that she's asking a question: 'Are you okay?'

She brings her hand to her face, pulls it away red and slick and shiny, then blinks at Belle, who's panting, clearly having sprinted here. Belle speaks again, asking George if she's all right, if she's hurt, if she was *hit* – and George responds by hinging at her hips and allowing the thick mixture of saliva and doe blood to dribble out of her mouth.

'Was she hit?' a voice calls.

'I don't think so,' Belle replies, running her hands over George's head, shoulders, arms, checking for wounds.

'Lucky,' the voice says, much closer now, and then Francina is beside them. She stares at George, her face strained but her eyes wild. 'What the *hell* are you doing out here, you foolish girl?'

'I ... I was just—'

'Just setting yourself up for a bullet in the head,' Francina finishes with a snarl, glancing up and over George's shoulder. Her eyes tighten, and, a beat later, George understands why.

'I hit it!'

A group of hunters are making their way through the trees on the same side of the gully that George came from, though whereas she came from the south, they're approaching from the west. It's the lodge guests, with David in the lead. He steps down into the gully, his gaze fixed on the body at George's feet as he makes his way through the water. At first his expression is a twisted mix of triumph and hunger, but it soon crashes with disappointment.

'It's a *doe*,' he whines, crouching to prod at the animal's head with a gloved finger. 'I wanted a goddamn buck.'

The rest of the guests have stopped at the edge of the gully. Unlike David, they only have eyes for George — and their faces are a mix of shock and horror. Liam is up there too, slightly apart from the group and muttering into his radio. And behind him is Patrick. He's also staring at George, his eyes wide.

Clearly unhappy with being ignored, David looks around. 'What?'

'You ... almost hit her,' Kendall says, a hand covering her mouth.

'I didn't see her!' David looks up at his friends, and is confronted by their unchanging expressions. 'None of you saw her either, right?' His tone is a little wobbly when he looks past the group to Patrick. '*You* said I was clear. You said I could take the shot.'

'I— it looked clear to me,' Patrick says, and his tone takes on a frantic edge when his eyes dart to Francina. 'I wouldn't have approved the shot if I'd seen her.'

George turns in time to see Francina's eyes flash — with anger, or shock? George isn't sure, but her stomach tightens anyway. Is it possible that Patrick really didn't see her? It seems too coincidental that less than an hour after being caught sneaking around their property she's nearly been killed by one of their guests. But surely Patrick wouldn't risk their precious reputation by orchestrating the death of a police officer – unless that's exactly how far they're willing to go to protect it.

'You've got to be *fucking* joking.' Striding between the trees on the northern side of the gully, Angus Fairgrieve takes in the scene with a thunderous expression. 'You're out of bounds by a hundred yards!'

Francina mutters something to Belle. The younger woman climbs out of the gully and starts ushering the guests back through the trees in the direction they came from. David reluctantly follows, and though Kendall glances back, she doesn't slow for him.

'It wasn't intentional,' Patrick calls to Angus, looking a little relieved to have the gully between them. 'We were tracking a deer and didn't realise we'd crossed the line.'

'That's the same excuse you use every time!'

'Oh, shut up,' Francina barks, moving to stand beside her husband. 'We'll send over another bloody cheque in the morning, Angus. Would you like a gift basket, too? We can send some lovely chocolates, flowers – maybe even a bar of soap and some toilet paper for you and your filthy brothers to share so you don't have to keep looting our supplies.'

Angus's face flushes with anger, humiliation; George thinks his hand twitches towards the shotgun on his back.

Not wanting to be accidentally caught in his sights, she edges downstream a little and then climbs out on the side she entered from. Nobody glances her way, as they're all too caught up in the argument, but even with some distance between her and them she can hear every furious word.

'You know, we've got the right to protect our property from trespassers,' Angus says.

Francina just laughs. 'You sound like a little doggy when you make threats, boy. Yip-yip-yip, all bark and no bite.'

This seems to incense Angus even further; he tugs at his

shotgun strap until the muzzle points towards the Selbys' feet. Despite the less-than-subtle threat, Francina stays cool, perhaps because she has withdrawn her own rifle from her pack and holds it loosely in her hands, the barrel aimed in the airspace beside Angus's hip.

Fuck. George really doesn't want to get in the middle of a shoot-out, but she has to do *something*. She pushes her hair back from her face, cringing when she feels how sticky some of the strands are, and tries to remember everything she knows about de-escalating a situation involving firearms. Maybe she ought to call for backup—

'Boo.'

George gasps, spinning on the spot.

Emma Fairgrieve emerges from the trees behind her. 'Jumpy little thing, aren't you?' she quips, coming to stand beside George. 'Doesn't seem like a good thing for a cop to be.'

George looks around. 'Where did you come from?'

She points across the gully to a spot behind Angus. 'We heard the shot, and then shouting. Angus told me to circle around and cut across the gully to make sure we caught you all.' Then she looks her up and down. 'What happened to you?'

'That deer down there. I was trying to help it.'

Predictably, Emma scoffs. 'You ran out here on your own, no backup or gun, and almost got your head blown off – all for a *deer*? You really are stupid.'

George stares at her. 'Do you hate police in general, or is it just me and my partner you've taken a particular dislike to?'

'You didn't leave a card.'

She's thrown by the topic change. 'Excuse me?'

'You said to get in touch if I remembered anything, but you didn't leave a card. Are all police this bad at their jobs?'

'Jesus,' George mutters. 'Did you remember something?'

Emma sucks her teeth. 'Wouldn't matter anyway. No phone at the house.'

George blinks. 'Surely, you have a mobile.'

'Don't need a phone if nobody wants to talk to you.'

'Oh. Er, what about your husband? Your in-laws?'

'None of them, either. They just talk to each other over the radios.'

Getting ahead of being called stupid again, George rips a corner from her notebook and writes down her number. 'Take this anyway. Someone in the village will let you borrow a phone.'

Emma stares at George, then takes the paper and tucks it away. 'Proper genius, you are.'

The argument is intensifying between Angus, Francina and Patrick, but the guns have been put away at least. She's reassured by the fact that Emma doesn't seem concerned; George supposes this kind of situation is relatively common between the neighbours.

Remembering what Richie told her earlier, she appraises Emma's stomach from the corner of her eye. There's no obvious swell beneath the oversized coat, though Emma likely isn't that far into her pregnancy. If they're proceeding with it, she must not be worried about the alleged curse on the Fairgrieve line – and Gerald must be delighted that the next generation of Fairgrieves is on the way.

She looks over at the doe again. It appears much smaller with its thin legs crumpled beside it. The stream is dammed at her torso and runs in thin ribbons around her rib cage. Fresh blood continues to ooze from the wound, tinting the water.

Suddenly a hand darts towards George's face.

She reacts automatically, catching Emma's forearm in a tight grip – a beat too late she sees the fraying, mostly clean handkerchief in her hand.

Emma scowls, tugging her arm free. 'Your face is disgusting. Just ... trying to help.'

George blinks. 'Oh. I— Sorry.'

There's nothing gentle about Emma's ministrations, but George holds still as Emma drags the cloth across her cheeks and forehead.

'Does this happen a lot?' she asks, gesturing towards the argument.

'The Selbys are cunts,' Emma says bluntly. 'Never met a problem they couldn't make disappear with money, or by pointing a gun at it.'

Having just experienced that firsthand – she suspects, anyway – George believes her.

The shouting suddenly quietens. It's probably because Francina is storming away, leaving Patrick and Angus in a tense but far less aggressive conversation.

'Does your mam know this is what you get up to at work?' Emma asks, recapturing her attention. 'She must be *so* proud of you. Bet she brags about you to all her friends.'

Her tone fans George's irritation again, and she blames the shock from her near-death experience when she lashes back with, 'Is your mother proud of what *you're* up to?'

Emma's expression shifts so dramatically from bitter to wounded that George is immediately guilt-stricken.

'Wouldn't know,' Emma mutters. 'We fought a lot when I was a teenager. Never put hands on each other, but the arguments were bad enough that she didn't stop me when I walked out the door.' Emma stares down at the handkerchief, threading the bloody fabric through her fingers. 'Probably hasn't even noticed that I didn't come back.'

'Em? What are you doing?' Angus has crossed the gully and is walking towards them. Patrick is looking down at the deer with an expression of dismay.

'Hosting a dinner party, obviously,' Emma says flatly.

Despite his lingering anger, Angus snorts a laugh. He wraps an arm around Emma's shoulder and presses a kiss above her ear. It's this gesture that makes George remember that *this* is the brother Emma is married to.

'We can leave now,' he murmurs into her hair.

Emma glances at Patrick. 'What's he still doing here?'

Angus shrugs, but there's a forced innocence to his expression. 'We signed that hunting contract. They pay for it — the deer belongs to them.'

She narrows her eyes. 'Shouldn't we get to keep it if they trespassed? We could use the meat.'

'We could,' he says lightly, then his innocent expression gives way to a devilish smirk. 'But I want him to drag all fifty kilos of it out of here by himself. I think he'll remember the boundary line a bit better after some blood, sweat and tears.'

Then he looks at George, and his expression softens. 'I remember you — are you all right? Do you want some water? You look like you've been standing beside a meat grinder.' He jostles Emma. 'Did you bring that bottle?'

George waves the offer away. 'I'm fine, thanks.'

He clucks his tongue. 'You sure? It's a long way back to the lodge from here, and your friends seem to have left you behind.'

'Trust me — they're not my friends,' she says emphatically.

'It doesn't seem like it,' he says with a sympathetic smile, and she realises that after seeing her on the stalk last night and again today, he must assume she's one of the guests. She expects Emma to jump in with a scathing correction, another opportunity to bluntly critique both George and the police force, but Emma's expression is a study in boredom as she gazes off into the trees. She's probably decided that introducing George by her title risks implying that she has respect for it.

Before George can correct him herself, he continues. 'At least come to the house to clean up a bit. It's just through the trees — see there?'

He points to a thin trail of smoke rising above the trees; just above the canopy, she can make out the crooked top of a chimney. George tries to orient herself on the property — she thinks she's looking at the south-west side of Fairgrieve Castle, whereas she and Richie entered from the east yesterday.

'I'm sure Em won't mind letting you borrow some of her clothes,' Angus continues. 'Yours are covered in ... well, bits of deer.'

From the look on Emma's face, she'd *very much* mind that. And even though George is suppressing the urge to vomit at the smells coming off her jacket, she shakes her head. 'It's fine.'

'If you're sure,' Angus says, then jerks his chin towards Patrick. 'Don't help him, even if he offers to refund your stay. Then again,' he adds, gesturing to her clothes, 'he should refund you anyway.' With that, he nods a farewell and leads Emma back across the gully.

'I want you – and *that* – gone by sunset,' he calls to Patrick. 'Better get going.'

The pair walk off in the direction of the house. It's only once they're out of earshot that George wonders if she should have asked Angus and Emma to walk her back to her car. Remaining alone with the man who may have just attempted to have her killed probably isn't the wisest decision.

As if hearing her thoughts, Patrick looks up at her. 'That was a close call. You're lucky.'

'I'm lucky that David is a good shot.'

He hesitates, then looks at Emma's and Angus's retreating figures. In a casual tone, he says, 'Finlay radioed earlier. Said you stopped by.'

She swallows, revolted by the metallic tang in her saliva. 'I was there to ask you about Rab Brown.'

'You mean Robert McAllister?' When she nods, he says, 'As of this morning he's no longer employed by us. And his great-uncle Liam is on notice.' He heaves a sigh. 'Finlay is coming on the quad to help me. If you'd like to wait, I can take you back to your hotel after we drop this off at the lodge.'

Recalling the chair in the garage, the snipped cable ties – neither of which will still be there now – she is quick to say, 'My car is close,' and starts to walk in the direction of *An Rathad*

Damainte. But then she stops, and without turning asks, 'Have you ever heard of xylazine?'

He doesn't answer right away; when she finally faces him, he's wearing a quizzical expression. 'I believe it's medicine.'

'A sedative,' she specifies. 'Do you use it at Fiadhain Lodge?'

'Well, when a deer requires medical attention, tranquillising it is the only way to treat it safely.'

'So you only use it for medical reasons?'

His Adam's apple bobs. 'Of course.'

'And not to make it easier for a well-paying guest who has grossly overstated their skills to finally hit a target?' She inclines her head towards the doe. 'I understand that bucks are the preferred prize, but you'd increase the guests' odds of finally bringing something down if multiple targets were moving a little slower, right?'

Despite the distance between them, she hears his sharp inhale.

'I read that's a controversial practice among hunters,' she says, keeping her tone conversational even as she watches the flush rising in Patrick's face. 'So I imagine it wouldn't be great for someone's reputation if someone – say, a member of a very vocal animal activist group – found out this was happening and was going to report it?'

He takes a step towards her. 'You don't know what you're—'

'And if I were to tell you that the victim – the one found right *beside* your property – had been tied up before she died, *and* had xylazine in her system? What do you think I should make of that combination of things?'

Patrick doesn't seem capable of a response at this point; he just stares at her with wide eyes, his lips slack.

She smiles. 'We'll be in touch, Mr Selby.'

With that, George turns on her heel and starts jogging ... but not before she catches Patrick's stunned expression shift into something closer to fear.

CHAPTER 23

As soon as she pulls up in the Ivy House carpark, she moves at triple speed — scaring the life out of Zoe, who takes in her gory appearance with horror, before handing George the spare key to Richie's room.

By a stroke of luck, Zoe informs her that Richie has been waylaid by Dean in the back garden — George spent most of the drive home agonising over how she was going to manage Richie's reaction to the blood. She has the quickest shower of her life, dumping her bloody clothes in the bin, then shimmies into her pyjama pants and steals one of Richie's jumpers before running out the door.

The set-up for the night market is well underway. The high street is now blocked off in both directions with orange barriers, and marquees are going up along both sides of the road. Though the sun is already below the western horizon, the market isn't meant to officially start for another hour or so. Tall lights have been erected at a few points along the road, firepits are being wheeled around on trolleys and deposited at both entrances to the market and a few spots along the street, and some of the stallholders are stringing up fairy lights and festoons along their marquees. The aroma of hot oil and something sugary wafts towards her as food vendors fire up their barbecues and appliances in anticipation of what might be a fairly decent crowd.

A large section of the carpark has been roped off to make room for a stage. A couple of technicians are walking across it, setting up speakers and lights, and there's a dark tent set up at the rear; as George watches, a woman exits, uncoiling a long cable as she climbs up onto the stage. She can't see Rab's caravan behind it.

The Kirk is crowded this evening, the sound of cutlery scraping around either very late lunches or very early dinners. She spots Hendry tucked away in a corner, his laptop and notebook both open on the table with a half-finished pint beside them. His blue coat is draped over the back of his seat.

He looks up as she drops into the chair opposite him, and his expression is immediately annoyed. 'I know I asked to meet earlier, but you *did* confirm that five pm was fine and it's now five-forty, and I told you I had something important, and— *Is that blood*?'

She swears, then licks her finger and scrubs at the spot on her neck he's gaping at. She must have missed it during her rushed shower.

'Calm down,' she hisses. 'It's not mine.'

This answer seems to alarm him more. 'Whose is it?' he asks, aghast.

'It's not important. Tell me what you've found.'

'George—'

She narrows her eyes. 'If you want the Eadar story, you have to keep your end of the—'

'Oh, fuck the Eadar story – where did that blood come from?'

'I was standing next to a deer and someone shot it.'

'*What?*'

'It's *fine*,' she growls, scrubbing at her neck even harder. But she's not sure that's true, actually; now that she's finally stopped moving, the emotions of the day – though she'll never be able to prove if Patrick knew she was in harm's way – are catching up with her.

Their whispered argument has drawn the attention of onlookers. George closes her eyes and hunches in on herself. She hears Hendry scoot his chair around to the space adjacent to hers so that she's blocked from prying eyes.

'Deep breaths.'

'I know how to breathe, Shaw.'

'Then stop talking and do it. Here's some water.'

She feels a glass pressed to her hand; Hendry leaves his hand on hers until it stops trembling. She keeps her eyes closed for the first sip and coaches herself: *In-in-in, out-out-out.*

His expression is still concerned when she opens her eyes; in an attempt to wipe it off his face, she gulps the rest of her water and clears her throat. 'Okay. Right. Tell me what you've got.'

'I think we can park that for a second,' Hendry says, refilling her glass. 'Let's just … let's just sit for a bit. Have you eaten?'

'A deal's a deal, Shaw.'

'Georgie, I'll tell you anything you want to know. But that can wait until you've got some food in you.'

He flags down a waitress and gestures for George to order. She isn't hungry, but knows that's probably the last lingering effects of the shock. She settles for a bowl of chips 'and a latte, if you're still doing coffees'.

Hendry raises an eyebrow at this. 'Surely, you'd want something a little stronger.'

She just shakes her head, bringing the water to her lips again.

He stares at her for a second, then smiles up at the waitress. 'Make that two lattes, thanks – actually, could you take this away?' he asks, handing her the half-finished pint. 'I'm done with it.'

George watches the waitress walk away. 'You didn't have to do that.'

'Eh, I needed a pick-me-up, anyway. I've got a long night ahead.'

They sit quietly for a couple of minutes until George feels the panicky buzz finally leave her fingers – just in time for the shame to set in. 'Sorry about that.'

'You don't need to be. Sounds like you've had a hell of an afternoon.'

'You'd better not be pitying me.'

'Of course I am. You have deer blood in your hair.'

'Jesus,' she mutters with a wince. 'Come on, what's so important that we needed to meet early?'

Hendry swipes a hand across his face; he looks as tired as she feels. 'Right,' he says, pulling his notebook towards him. 'My friend still had a phone number for her contact inside Fearless for Fauna. She was pretty reluctant to hand it over to me, but I said I'd owe her a favour, so she eventually agreed. I called and texted a few times, told them exactly what I wanted, but there was no reply – until this afternoon.'

'You spoke with someone?'

'Firstly, let's just acknowledge that there is no way to verify that the person I spoke to is actually a member of Fearless for Fauna, and that their commitment to anonymity will be a major problem if you press charges against the Selbys.'

George gestures for him to continue, having already thought about this – and also filing away the fact that Hendry indebted himself to a colleague to get this information.

'The person I spoke to was very nervous, was convinced I was a cop. And after a lot of charming on my part' – he ignores George's scoff – 'they finally admitted that the woman matches the description of one of their newer members. And before you ask, no, they wouldn't give her name. In fact, they said they didn't know it. Anonymity and all.'

George's heart kicks up a gear. *I knew it.* 'Did you ask if they sent her out there?'

'They declined to comment. I guess if your group has a history of breaking into private properties to destroy equipment and set animals loose, you'd be zipping your lips about current or future targets. Even if one of their members was killed, the anonymity prevents them from doing anything about it. However, they did say that, and I quote' – he raises his notebook – '"No legal ruling could ever stop us from going after the villains who maim and slaughter defenceless animals." That's all they gave me before they hung up.'

She presses her thumb to her right eyebrow, digging into the bone to relieve the tension headache that's building. 'Okay. Well, that's definitely something we can work with.'

Hendry rolls his eyes. 'Don't spoil me with praise.'

'If you wanted me to clap after every sentence, you should have made it part of our deal.'

He tries to look annoyed, but his amusement wins out. 'To the next item on your agenda – my contact in the Scottish Gamekeepers Association was a dead end. She said she hasn't heard anything about the Selbys and any dodgy dealings, but from the way she was talking, I suspect she has a personal connection to protect.' He pauses to take a sip of water. 'I also knocked on doors, but not much to report. There was something about being asked the same questions four times in two days that really irked people. A few people who went to school with Robert remember him getting in trouble a lot. Someone said he was pulled out of class by the police a couple of times.'

'He was picked up for a few things as a teen, and the charges only got worse as he got older.'

'Until he was put away for the Buchanan assault,' Hendry says, nodding. 'Ten years is a pretty remarkable length of time for a sexual assault, though I know the Buchanans had public outrage – and a lot of influence – on their side.'

Their coffees arrive. Hendry clinks his cup against hers. 'Cheers, partner.'

'We're not working together. We're working … parallel.'

'Semantics,' he says, taking a sip.

She pauses as the waitress reappears and slides their plates in front of them. Hendry bypasses his own plate of roasted vegetables and slightly overcooked salmon to steal a chip from her plate. 'So, it sounds like it's between the Selbys and this McAllister guy.'

She shrugs, picking a chip for herself. 'After nearly getting my head blown off this afternoon by one of their guests, I know which lead I want to pursue first.'

Hendry stops chewing, his eyes back on her neck. 'You know, if you told me why you think these women are connected, I could help even more.'

'Nice try.'

'I'm going to find out eventually,' he says, wagging another pinched chip at her. 'And you're going to have less-ethical journalists than me digging around.'

'Maybe if I promise them the Eadar story, they'll behave.'

He looks outraged. 'We have a deal. We shook on it.'

'I don't recall a handshake.'

'It was a gentlemen's agreement.'

She laughs grudgingly. 'Which tell-all do you want first, Shaw? I'll be trusting you with my reputation either way.'

'That's why I want you to tell me the story, in your own words,' he says, suddenly earnest. 'So people understand what was happening in your head at the time.'

She runs her finger around the top of her water glass. 'What if there are parts I can't talk about?'

'Then we don't talk about them.'

The glass emits a high-pitched whine.

'What if there are parts I need to *lie* about?'

She doesn't look up, even when his pause stretches on a little too long.

'I'll print what you tell me,' he says finally, 'but if something comes out later … something that goes against what you've told me … I'll have to cover my own arse.'

'You'll turn on me?' She's not mad; the question is one of curiosity.

'I won't have to if you're honest with me from the outset. I'm kind of the go-to guy when it comes to the public's perception of DI Georgina Lennox. Neither of us is stupid enough to think that there won't be people who try to dig up your skeletons, but I know I can be the loudest voice. If you let me.'

She doesn't know if it's the leftover adrenaline from almost getting shot, or the mounting frustration with the twists and turns in this case; either way, there's a recklessness brewing in her.

Fuck it.

'When the inquiry begins, I'm going to have to testify in front of an official panel. And when I do, it's going to come out that the whole time I was on Eadar – and for about five months before it – I was illegally acquiring and abusing prescription medication. The hero in your articles, the "brave and beautiful DI Lennox", was an addict.' She forces a grin, digging her fingernails into her knees. 'How are you going to control *that* narrative, Shaw?'

Hendry sucks his teeth. 'Probably the same way I have been already?'

'What?'

He sighs, and there's a slight twist of shame to his lips. 'Ten days after you left the hospital, your parents hired an addiction counsellor to come to your flat.'

A new crackle of panic stings her ribs. 'How do you know that? Did *she* tell you?'

'No, of course not. But she obviously wasn't family, and she stayed at your place for three days straight. I was curious. Got her licence plates, then her name ... then her occupation.'

'That is ... disgusting.'

'That is my job.'

'Then your job is disgusting.' When he just shrugs, she glares at him suspiciously. 'Why didn't you use it to blackmail the story out of me earlier?'

'Blackmail is such an ugly word,' he says loftily, an attempt at humour. When she doesn't crack, he sighs again. 'Don't get me wrong, I thought about … *leveraging* what I knew. Would have been huge for me, especially if I waited for the hero story to cool off and then dropped that.'

'So why didn't you?'

'Because it's nobody's business,' he says, trying for nonchalance and failing. 'Because you did something absolutely incredible out there, and I didn't want to be the one to throw mud at it. Believe it or not, *not* printing it was me being selfish – I didn't want to be the guy who took down Goliath.'

'David is the hero in that story,' she says through stiff lips.

'Not in this one.' He watches her for a long moment; she has no idea what he's seeing on her face. The confusion is still there, largely because she now has to revise her opinion of Hendry from an overall terrible person to a *mostly* terrible person.

'You've got a plan, then?' she finally asks, pushing the last few chips towards him. 'For how you're going to frame a drug habit into something the public can stomach?'

Hendry chuckles, the sound coloured with relief – he clearly expected her to be angry for longer. 'I've got a few ideas. I'll bounce them off you when you've told me the full story. Maybe when we get back to Glasgow.' He hesitates, staring down at her plate. 'Maybe I won't dance around calling it a date.'

Her fingers dig into her knees again. 'I'm *really* not sure about the ethics on that one.'

'Clearly, neither of us is a completely ethical person. What's one more bent rule?'

For a few seconds, they just look at each other; as the moment stretches, the buzz in George's stomach morphs into something else. She leans back, putting some distance between them. 'Let's close this case first.'

Hendry rolls his eyes, but he seems a little relieved at the break in the tension, too. 'It's always work, work, work with you, Georgie,' he grumbles, plucking the last few chips from her plate. 'I can already imagine all the missed dinners, anniversaries. Me sitting at the table alone, sad and gorgeous, the candles melted down to stubs.'

'Jesus,' she mutters, then gets to her feet. 'I'm going to the bathroom.'

'I'll practise my sad face while you're gone.'

She shoots him a warning glare over her shoulder before turning the corner and heading for the door beside the bar. Then she comes to an abrupt halt.

It's a different woman, but the set-up is the same: Robert McAllister stands against the bar beside a girl around Zoe's age. He's wearing a thick wool-lined denim jacket, one elbow resting on the bar top as he leans towards her ... Only this time, the woman seems to be enjoying his company; he says something that makes her throw her head back with a laugh.

Gritting her teeth, George keeps walking ... but as she passes, she hears the woman speak.

'I've gotta get back to my friends, but I'll see you at the market?'

Rab's reply is a purr. 'I'll be looking for you.'

George's chin swings to the side like there's a fish hook in her lip. She can't see Rab's face, can't decide whether those words are swimming on an ominous undercurrent. Regardless, they've stirred up a sense of unease like sediment within her, a feeling that has only intensified by the time she returns and sees that both Rab and the young woman are gone.

Back at the table, Hendry is typing on his laptop.

'Thought you'd dined and ditched,' he says without looking up.

She slides into her seat. 'It crossed my mind, but then I realised you'd probably just write an article about it.'

'I'd never make our personal life public, Georgie. That's between you, me and our marriage counsellor.'

When she doesn't immediately hit back with a snappy retort, he looks up with mild concern. 'What's wrong?' he asks. 'Your frown is particularly frowny right now.'

She recounts what she saw and overheard.

Concern settles deeper into the lines of his face. 'Robert McAllister is prowling for women?'

She lets her forehead fall into her hands. 'Apparently.'

'Why didn't you stop him?'

'He's allowed to talk to women, and he's allowed to take them home if they want to go.'

'And if they don't? I know he's served his time, but come on – do you really think he's the kind of guy who takes no for an answer? Are we willing to take that chance?'

George notes his use of 'we' – it seems that Hendry has decided to make this his problem, too. The dinner has caused a seismic shift in their dynamic; she doesn't quite know how to feel about this new, but strangely solid ground.

'What are we supposed to do? Follow him around for the rest of his life?'

'At least tonight,' Hendry presses. 'Just to make sure. Just to keep girls like her safe.'

They sit in silence for a moment. Then she pushes up to her feet with an exhausted groan. 'Come on.'

'Where are we going?'

'To my hotel room.' Before he can make the obvious joke, she holds up a finger. 'Trust me, we aren't going to enjoy ourselves.'

'Why?'

She sighs. 'Because Richie is going to be so pissed off.'

CHAPTER 24

He is *so* pissed off.

'You're working with a *journalist*?'

From his perch on the desk, Hendry laughs nervously. 'You say that like it means something else.'

Under Richie's glare, Hendry wilts.

'And not just a journalist,' Richie continues, jabbing a finger towards him, 'but the one who's been making your life miserable for months?'

'Yes, a horrible choice, I know. But it was for a good cause,' George says from her position beside the door – she made Hendry go in first, a distraction, while she chose the best place to escape from. 'And as I just explained, he's handed over some very helpful information – now we know that our victim was likely a member of Fearless for Fauna, and that they still consider Fiadhain Lodge fair game. This is the information we can take to Cole to push that warrant through.' She pauses. 'And while we're waiting for that, we have another thing to take care of.'

Richie crosses his arms. 'Is it regarding the dinner you promised to bring me? Because I did notice that you walked in with empty hands.'

Though she does feel bad about forgetting to get him something to eat, she ignores the tart comment. 'We were at The Kirk tonight. To talk about the case,' she stresses in response to Richie's raised eyebrow, 'and I saw Rab chatting up a woman.

When I walked past, I overheard her saying that she and her friends were going to the market, and he responded that he would be *looking* for her.'

Richie grimaces. 'How old was she?'

'Zoe's age. Amy's age.' *Cara's age*, she mentally tacks on.

'And you want to keep an eye on *him*.' He breathes out slowly, then turns to look out the window. They can't see the market from here, but the music has started. 'Which is the right decision, of course. The only right one you seem to have made tonight,' he adds, glowering at Hendry. 'Do we have to take him?'

'Unfortunately. But if it makes you feel better, I'll still buy you dinner.'

Richie grunts, then scans her from head to toe. 'Do we all have to wear our pyjamas, or have you just let yourself go entirely?'

She shoots him a withering look. 'Get out, both of you.' Then she looks towards her bag. 'I'm about to perform a miracle.'

She certainly doesn't feel like a miracle-worker when they walk towards the high street twenty minutes later. But after scrubbing vigorously with hand soap at the bloody trousers – which she'd had no other option but to fish out of the bin – and drying the damp spots with a hair dryer so weak she may as well have just blown on them herself, then stealing one of Richie's long-sleeved shirts and another jumper, she is at least no longer in pyjamas.

They're greeted by the smells of frying meats and onion, woodfire smoke and candy-like sweetness long before the marquees come into sight. Traditional folk music blares from the direction of the stage: lively strings, a lilting flute and the steady heartbeat of a bodhrán. The speakers must be right on the ground – even from a hundred feet away, she can feel the vibration under her feet, then shimmering up her shins, her knees, her thighs. She's not sure if it's that strange sensation or the crisp night air that makes her shiver; thankfully, the firepits are already ablaze, shooting sparks and white smoke up into the navy night sky.

Cars are packed tightly into every available space right up to the orange barriers. Some have even mounted the footpath outside the shops, risking a fine in order to get as close as possible to either entrance of the market. Many of the shops seem to have bowed to pressure and closed early, assuming all their customers would be attending the market.

If so, it was a correct assumption – there must be a few hundred people here already, red cheeked and merry, their laughter and loud voices ringing out across the street. Many are gathered around the blazing firepits, gloved hands holding paper plates of greasy food and steaming Styrofoam cups, but most of the teeming throng are moving between the stalls, jumping into long queues, poring over handmade trinkets and pieces of junk sellers have rebranded as antiques.

Hendry whistles. 'It's bigger than I expected. And *way* more people than I thought.'

Richie's lips are a thin line. 'Let's get eyes on him fast.'

Against the spirited backdrop of Celtic music, stallholders beckon the three of them over to sample homemade shortbread and crumbly tablet; hand over plastic tumblers of whisky in shades of amber, tawny, burnt umber; and coax them into trying on silver thistle rings, Tree of Life earrings, and chunky pendants emblazoned with the Lion Rampant.

As they slowly make their way along, George's chin moves on a swivel. Seeing so many young women flitting between stalls, laughing and bringing cups to their lips over and over, is making her nervous. She spots the woman and her friends from The Kirk crowding around a large firepit, watching a whole pig rotate on a spit over the flames with horror and fascination. George, too, is temporarily hypnotised by the sight; she winces when the flames lick up the pig's taut skin, the shiny fat bubbling before it chars.

'He has to be here,' Richie mutters, breaking her distraction.

'We'll find him,' she reassures him. She offered to buy him whatever was piled on those greasy plates earlier, but he turned it down; the situation seems to have killed his appetite.

A crowd has gathered around the stage to watch the latest performers, a quartet arranged around a middle-aged woman with an enormous accordion balanced on her knee. George spots Rory among the crowd, his dark curls poking out from under a blue beanie. He's speaking with a group of men around his age and seems relaxed, breaking into laughter at someone's joke – she assumes the steaming cup he keeps raising to his lips doesn't contain hot chocolate.

'Inspector! You made it!'

Zoe has emerged from the crowd, her eyes glassy, lips slack in a broad smile. She's holding a similar takeaway cup to Rory; the steam wafting from the surface smells like Christmas, warm and spiced.

'I thought you were avoiding the mulled wine this year,' George says wryly.

'I did try,' Zoe says, 'but the smell called to me, and it's my first night off in, like, *a year*. I fucking *love* that job,' she adds, her words slurring, 'but sometimes, man. *Sometimes.* Y'know?'

She tips her head back to drain the last of the wine; her equilibrium is already off, so this imbalance sends her staggering towards a middle-aged couple perched on a bench seat. Luckily, Hendry seizes her arm before she can crash into them.

'Maybe it's time to call it a night,' he says, easing Zoe back.

'Are you on your own?' George asks.

'Na, I came with Harris.' She squints over Richie's shoulder. 'I think he's at the stage.'

'Well, go and find him and tell him to walk you home.

But if you can't find him, I want you to come and find me. Understood?'

Zoe presses her warm hands to George's cheeks. 'You're *so* nice.'

'Allegedly,' she mutters, twisting out of Zoe's hold. 'Now *go.*'

George watches her until she's swallowed by the crowd. Then she rounds on Richie.

'Did you hear what she said? I'm *nice.*'

He nods. 'I think I felt the earth shake in protest.'

Hendry looks between the two of them, nonplussed. 'Am I missing a joke?'

'You're missing quite a few things, I suspect,' Richie says primly. 'Let's get back to the task.'

A few minutes later, Hendry bumps her shoulder.

'He's there.'

Rab is at the tail end of a large group that's approaching the crowd around the stage. His head is inclined towards a woman as she speaks in his ear, and George is relieved when another man turns to join their conversation.

New musicians are setting up on the stage now, and they seem to have a bit of a following; Rab's group is part of a new swell of audience members, and they soon disappear among it. It becomes difficult for George, Richie and Hendry to stay together when the crowd starts to move, swaying and shuffling around as a young man starts to sing.

'Can you still see him?' she asks Richie, raising her voice as a drum kicks in.

He shakes his head, and Hendry gives her a thumbs down. 'Maybe we need to split up?' he shouts.

George doesn't love the idea, but they're clearly not going to make much headway as a trio. She cups her hands around her mouth and presses them to Hendry's ear. 'If you see Rab, you let us know – do not approach him.'

Hendry pulls back and salutes. 'Yes, ma'am.'

To Richie, she shouts, 'Let's circle this area, okay? Meet back at the wine stall in fifteen minutes.'

Richie and Hendry split off in opposite directions. For a couple of minutes, George lets herself sway with the crowd, softening her gaze as she searches the faces of the people around her. The musicians are quite good, switching between traditional songs and covers of classic rock music that have the crowd enthusiastically joining in. She starts easing her way through gaps, trying to avoid catching swinging elbows or spilt drinks. The conversations she overhears are giggly, loud, slurred. Her gaze jumps between the faces of the men she passes, but she recognises none of them until a flash of blue catches her eye, and she spots Rory in his blue beanie chatting to a girl up ahead, the pair swapping shy smiles.

Whoever placed the speakers is clearly unbothered by the fact that anyone within five yards of the stage will lose their hearing; the drone of the double bass is making her bones rattle as she scans the people in this section. Her pulse jumps when she recognises the group Rab arrived with, but the man himself seems to have detached from them.

Frustrated, she catches sight of a waving hand. It's Richie, over on the left side of the stage. He holds up his phone, then points at her. Getting the hint, she slips her phone from her pocket.

His text reads: *Circling around again. Thought I saw him heading to the rear.*

The trill of a tin whistle makes her clap her hands over her ears. Apparently, the volume is actually a problem, because she watches a man run into the tent that's set up behind the stage. Thick cables run between it and the audio equipment, so George assumes it must be some kind of tech station; her theory is confirmed when a few seconds later the volume lowers slightly.

But her relief ends there – two more people are heading around the side of the tech station. The woman is stumbling, leaning heavily into her companion, a man who is wearing a wool-lined denim jacket.

'Shit,' she mutters, simultaneously trying to weave through the crowd and pull out her phone.

Behind stage NOW— she quickly texts to Richie.

Finally free of the crowd, she hurries towards the tent. Compared with the front of the stage, this area is jarringly dark; the carpark has only one central pole with a weak white light at the top, and the moon is smothered behind thick clouds. The music is duller here, too, with the speakers aimed the other way.

As she rounds the first corner of the tent, she hears voices. The woman is speaking, her words slurred. 'I don't ... I just wanna—'

'You're fine, gorgeous. Just relax.'

'No, I don't feel—'

'Shh, shh, you're all right. My place is just over here.'

'I don't wanna ... I wanna go *home*.'

Panic and anger flood George's veins – because she knows the woman's voice. And when the next sound is a thump, followed by a cry of pain, George doesn't hesitate to throw herself around that final corner.

The scene is exactly as she feared.

Zoe is sprawled on the ground behind the tent, her head on a concrete block that's weighing one of the tent legs down. Her puffer jacket is open and tugged down off one shoulder, and she presses a shaking hand to the back of her head.

Rab is standing over her, fists clenched, but when he clocks George, he takes a few steps back. 'I didn't do anything,' he says immediately, holding up his hands for emphasis.

'Inspector?' Zoe says tremulously, blinking up at her with an expression of fear and confusion that makes her look like a child.

'I'm here, Zoe. Are you hurt?'

Zoe pulls her hand away from her head and squints at it. Even in the low light, George can see the streak of blood on her palm.

'She fell,' Rab says, crouching down and giving Zoe a perfectly friendly smile. 'Poor thing's drunk.'

'I didn't fall,' Zoe protests weakly, 'you pushed—'

'You tripped over your own feet. I was helping you, remember?' He looks up at George. 'We're friends. I saw her staggering around and thought I should look after her.'

George's heart is hammering against her rib cage, as if the drummer from the stage has set up in her chest. She hopes Richie isn't far behind. 'Back up, Mr McAllister,' she orders.

'I didn't do anything to her,' he repeats, then returns to staring at Zoe. 'You asked me to bring you back to mine, right?'

'I said *back up*,' George snaps, putting herself between them.

'Tell her, Zoe,' Rab insists, the friendliness fading from his voice as he rises to his full height. 'Tell her you wanted it. Tell her it was your idea.'

Zoe sniffles. 'I didn't ... It wasn't—'

'Don't lie,' Rab hisses, the friendly façade slipping entirely.

George has had enough; she plants her palms on Rab's chest and sends him staggering back a few steps. 'Don't make me put you on the fucking ground, okay? When my partner gets here, you'll have a chance to tell your side—'

'I didn't *do* anything,' he explodes, and for the first time George hears panic in his voice. 'She *wanted* me, she fucking *begged* me to take her back to mine.'

'George!'

She breathes a massive sigh of relief as Richie appears, his cheeks flushed. He takes in the scene quickly, and his expression becomes thunderous.

'Hands where I can see them, Mr McAllister,' he orders.

Rab takes a step back – towards the stage. 'No, no way – I'm not going back to prison because of another lying bitch.'

Richie points at him warningly. 'Robert, don't even think about—'

But the instruction falls on deaf ears – and before Richie or George can reach for him, Rab turns tail and flees back towards the market.

For the length of a heartbeat, George and Richie stare at one another. Then his eyes cut to Zoe, now sobbing and clutching at her head, and his lips twist.

'Go,' he says to George.

And she does.

CHAPTER 25

Rab hasn't got too much of a head start on her, and as soon as he plunges back into the crowded market, George steadily closes the distance. His bulk slows him down, but it also makes him more desperate – when shouting at people to get out of the way doesn't work, he starts shoving them aside. George has to jump over the thin legs of an elderly man Rab aggressively shouldered, as passers-by drop to their knees beside him.

She's almost grateful when Rab exits through the far end of the market, minimising the risk of more people getting injured, even though she's leaving the safety of the crowd behind. She's made up enough ground that Rab must hear her right on his heels. She can hear him, too – his rasping breaths, sucking in air like a dying beast.

She shouts at him to stop; he doesn't, of course, but he does change direction abruptly to head down one of the residential streets lined with neat cottages. It's easy enough for her to follow him, and even easier to launch herself onto his back and bring him crashing down on someone's front lawn.

'Give me your hands,' she barks, shifting her knee to press into the centre of his spine. 'Now, *now.*'

'Bitch,' he spits, and she wrenches his arms back one at a time, drawing more pained sounds from him. He keeps up a stream of insults, despite her weight on his back.

'You're going to run out of air if you keep that up,' she tells him, wiping her nose on her shoulder – the cold temperature and her overheated body are contradicting each other.

'You'd fuckin' like that, wouldn't you?' he snarls. 'Bet you wish you could just put a fuckin' bullet in me.'

She lets the silence answer for her as she looks over her shoulder. She hopes Richie will come as soon as he gets help for Zoe, but she knows he isn't going to be sprinting after them on his injured leg. She really doesn't like the idea of waiting out here alone, but she prefers it over trying to wrangle Rab back through the crowded market herself, without handcuffs or anything to secure him with.

'I don't understand,' she says, panting. 'You got out early. Why would you fuck this all up for yourself?'

'I didn't do anything—'

'That cut on Zoe's head says otherwise. And more importantly, *she* says otherwise. If you have any decency in you, you won't pull the same shit you did with Amy—'

He jerks his hips to the side suddenly, causing her knee to slip. In the second it takes for her to readjust, Rab wrenches a hand free and uses it to shove himself up and flip George onto her back.

'Help—' she manages to shout before Rab's forearm presses down on her throat like an iron bar. The sensation of suffocation is immediate, panic-inducing. Her eyes feel like they're bulging out of her head, her cheeks are immediately hot, and it's as if someone is tapping their fingertips against the pulse points in her temples and neck. The world shrinks until the only thing she can see is Rab's face, his eyes blue fire, sweat dripping down his temples and landing on her cheeks. Her heartbeat drowns out almost every other sound, loud and urgent in her ears; but over the frantic tattoo she hears heavy footsteps approaching at a run, and then a dull *thud*.

As if he's a marionette whose strings have been cut by an enormous pair of scissors, Rab slumps over her. Though the pressure is gone from her throat, his bulk is now compressing her chest; she struggles to get air back into her lungs.

Large hands grasp her shoulders and slide her out from under Rab.

'Jesus Christ — are you okay, love? Breathe, just breathe.'

She does, sucking in huge lungfuls of air, blinking hard as tears stream from her eyes and her vision swims back into focus.

Kneeling beside her, Angus Fairgrieve's face is creased with shock.

'Are you okay?' he asks again, and she tries to answer but her words come out as a cough.

She presses her hand to her neck gingerly and finds the skin there hot and tender. It feels awful, but she doesn't think there's any real damage. She's just going to have a hell of a sore throat.

Seeing that she's back in control of herself, Angus helps her to sit up. Beside her, Rab is lying on his back, mouth agape, eyelids fluttering. A bloody rock sits on the ground beside him.

'You did that?' she asks.

'Sure did. It looked like he was trying to turn your lights off. A few more minutes and he probably would have. Are you out here by yourself?' When she nods, he clicks his tongue. 'Lucky we were here then. Do you think you can stand?'

She does, with his assistance, and her legs quiver like those of a newborn fawn. He keeps an arm around her waist. 'Steady, steady — you're all right. Em,' he calls, 'bring that water over, will you?'

George looks around. Emma is standing a few yards away. She's wearing the same outfit as earlier, but now with a small backpack slung over one shoulder.

'Emma,' Angus says again. 'Water.'

Emma withdraws a plastic bottle from the backpack and passes it to George. She unscrews it and takes a long sip, the water wonderfully cool in her swollen throat. She has no idea how long Richie will take to find her down this street. She pats her pockets, feeling for her phone, and her heart clenches when the search comes up empty. Wobbling in a circle, she searches the ground intently.

Fuck. It must have fallen out during the chase.

'You don't look so good, love,' Angus says, watching her closely. 'The Ranger is just around the corner. You can sit in it until you feel better.'

She shakes her head with a wince. 'Help is coming.'

'I'll wait here,' he promises. 'My phone is in the Ranger – you can use it to call the police.'

George shakes her head, preparing to argue, but the sudden movement makes the world sway. Jesus, Rab must have squeezed her harder than she thought. Considering that, and the need to give Richie her exact location, she reluctantly gives in. As Emma leads the way, George glances back and sees Angus prod at Rab's thigh with his foot. She turns away and swallows another few mouthfuls of water. It's none of her business if Rab has one or two more bruises by the time Richie shows up.

'Did you see a phone on the ground?' she asks Emma.

Emma doesn't look at her when she curtly replies, 'No.'

George groans, then brings the bottle to her lips again. They're starting to feel a little numb; shock must be setting in.

Now back on the high street, George squints towards the market. The music is still pumping, the lights glaringly bright. She takes a few steps that way, but Emma grabs her arm. George's foot skids off the gutter and she stumbles into the road.

'Hey, careful,' she says – she *tries* to say. But the words catch on her tongue as if it's made of flypaper.

'The Ranger's over here,' Emma says, tugging her. 'Hurry up.'

She's telling the truth – the off-road vehicle George saw Angus climb out of the other night is parked in the shadows between two streetlights.

'Wait,' she says, her tongue heavy, 'sl … slow down.'

But Emma just tows her along, and it's all George can do to keep her feet under her. Distantly, a voice says that *something's wrong*, that this isn't just exhaustion from the chase, or the shock of Rab's attack that's making her clumsy.

Something's wrong, something's wrong, wrong, wrong.

A thought swims slowly back to her. Didn't Emma tell her something about the Fairgrieve men and phones earlier today?

Emma steers her to the passenger seat. 'Up,' she instructs, tapping George's knee.

Her shin knocks sharply against the metal frame of the door. The pain is dull, just like the alarm bells blaring in the back of her mind. With Emma's help – a shove, really – George flops onto the seat.

'Ph … phone …' George takes a breath. She feels drunk, her head spinning like an off-kilter carousel, nausea swirling in her stomach. 'You said … they don't … have phones.'

Emma is looking back down the street; when she turns to George, her eyebrows draw into her signature scowl. 'You said help is coming. Who? Just your partner, or more police?'

George opens her mouth to reply, but her head falls back against the headrest and her eyes slide closed.

Emma swears. 'No, no – open your eyes! Who is coming? How many?'

But George can't peel her eyelids back, and words are completely beyond her. Every thought is slow, like it's trudging through deep mud. Emma releases her with a frustrated growl, and then George hears footsteps approach.

'She out?'

'Almost.'

The footsteps get close, and then George feels warm breath on her face, thick fingers tapping her cheeks. She can only groan, and her neck muscles are like syrup.

Angus gives a little laugh. 'Did you see her phone?'

'No, must be back there on the ground somewhere.'

'Damn. Let's move then.'

Large hands grip her arms and she's tipped forward until a broad shoulder is wedged into her stomach, and then she's lifted. Angus doesn't take her far, but each step is a jolt that forces air from her diaphragm that she struggles to draw back in, and within seconds she's tipping backwards again. Cold metal bites her cheek, digs painfully into her arm and hip. She's in the cargo bed of the Ranger, she thinks dully; that's confirmed when Angus forces her legs up against her chest in order to close the tailgate.

The last thing she's aware of, before slipping into a forever kind of darkness, is the crinkle of a tarp settling over her face.

CHAPTER 26

Something is on top of her.

A heavy blanket, a person, a layer of concrete – whatever it is, it's pushing down on every surface of her body with firm, unyielding pressure. Even her ribs strain with the effort of expanding.

In … in … in …

She tries to wriggle out from under it, can't. Tries to roll over to shift it, but that's even harder. Despite the weight, whatever is on her offers no heat. She's freezing, and yet her mouth feels like a desert, her tongue hot and rasping against her teeth and cheeks.

Where am I?

What happened?

What's that smell?

Musty, cut with the bitterness of stale urine, sharp body odour. Damp fabric, mould, earth and dust. It smells vaguely familiar. She tries to open her eyes, but the mysterious weight is on them too, keeping the lids glued shut.

Help, she begs, her lips unmoving. *Help me, help me, help me.*

The only thing that comes out is a whimper.

But it works. Someone comes.

A hand slips under her head, tips it up a little so that one arm, then the other can slide under her armpits. George is hauled into a sitting position, her helper grunting with the effort, and then leant back against what feels like a set of vertical bars.

Then there's the crinkling of plastic, the sound of a top being unscrewed, and the lip of a bottle pressed to her slack lips.

She manages to turn her head away, letting it flop to one side.

'It's just water this time,' an irritated voice says. 'Come on, I know you're thirsty.'

George resists again, and her helper – *helper?* – digs her fingers into the hollows of George's cheeks hard enough that her lips open. The first dribble of water makes her choke, but the next few mouthfuls go down smoothly, before the bottle is wrenched away all too soon.

'More,' she rasps, and is taken aback by the gravelly sound of her own voice, the realisation that she *can* speak.

'Shh. I'll get you more soon.'

In the subsequent silence – that might last a few seconds or a few hours – George's mind drifts. Then the hand on her face returns, delivering two brisk slaps against her cheeks.

'Wakey-wakey. Come on, open your eyes.'

Her helper is unsympathetic as she repeats the order until George peels her eyes open. Her focus swims, the figure crouched in front of her just a pale smudge in a midnight void. A glow in the corner is the only source of light.

'There you are,' Emma says, a tiny hint of relief in her voice. 'Was touch and go for a minute. I have no idea how much he put in the water.' She uses her thumb to pull George's right eyelid back further, then the left. 'You stopped breathing for twenty-one seconds. I counted.'

George swallows thickly, unable to make sense of Emma's words just yet, then looks around. Her eyes have adjusted enough to see that they're in a high-ceilinged stone room lit only by an upturned torch on the floor. It's too shadowy to make out the dimensions of the room, but there's a slight echo to Emma's voice and their movements, which suggests the room goes far further than she can see. Some kind of curved cellar? There are no windows, so it definitely feels subterranean. She tilts her head, looking around her. She's sprawled on a stained mattress that's slightly too small for the iron bedframe it's placed upon, which has been shoved against one of the rough walls; when her eyes drag upwards, she sees the tails of snipped cable ties hanging from the corner rungs at the head and foot.

The first pulse of panic shoots down her body, dulled by whatever weight is still on her; but her toes twitch in a pathetic attempt to get *up*, get *out*.

'Where ... am ... I?'

Emma looks around, her lips thin with distaste. 'Where we all start. And end.' Then she looks back at George, and her eyes are as cold as the air. 'This is the crypt.'

Though already freezing, George feels a different kind of chill trickle through her veins. The Fairgrieve crypt, the final resting place of centuries of men, women, children. There isn't enough light for her to see whether there are markings on the walls or floor that might indicate where bodies are interred; for all she knows, she could be lying right on top of somebody.

Autonomy is returning to her; her feet – bare, her toes numb – slide against the mattress on command now, and it's not so much of an effort to speak.

'What happened?'

Emma snorts. 'Yeah, it's a bitch, isn't it? You'll twist yourself up in knots trying to remember, but those blackouts are blacked out for good.' She rises and brushes powdery stone off her pants. Her hair is loose now, more brunette than blonde in the dim light, the straggly ends brushing the middle of her back. 'Sometimes, that's for the best.'

George's expression must reflect her dawning horror, and Emma makes no attempt to calm her – not even when George hears the distant *clunk* of a lock turning, and then the creak of ancient hinges. A fresh spill of yellow light illuminates a curved staircase inside a stone arch.

Emma looks down at George impassively. 'Keep your mouth shut,' she whispers.

The horror doesn't lessen, and the fear doubles when footsteps descend.

Angus enters, looking first at Emma, then at George.

'She's up?' he asks, coming to stand beside his wife. 'Talking?'

'Still groggy.'

'I bet.' He looks George up and down, then his face splits into an enormous smile. It's a jarring contrast to Emma's detached expression – George feels as if she's a stray dog that they have very different opinions about bringing home.

'You'll be right soon enough,' Angus says, his tone earnest and soothing. 'And you'll stay all right, as long as you're a good girl.'

He crouches down and brushes a few strands of hair away from George's cheek. Frozen in both terror and the lingering effects of whatever the hell they gave her, she remains completely still as his fingers tuck the strands behind her ear, then linger on the spot where her jaw meets her neck. 'I told Rory I found him a sweet one,' he adds, his eyes crinkling with a genuine smile. 'They're coming now.'

Emma stiffens. 'It's too soon. They'll scare her.'

Angus rises. 'Well, that's what you're here for.'

'She doesn't trust me.'

He wraps his fingers around Emma's bicep and draws her closer. She goes to him, allows him to tuck her into his chest. 'You handled Mathilde well,' he says, running his hand over her hair. 'It's not your fault that she couldn't see how good she had it here. You don't need to keep blaming yourself for what happened.'

He looks like he's about to continue, but his head jerks up. George hears a sound a second later – voices, faint but getting closer.

Angus releases Emma and walks towards the torch. 'Did she tell you her name yet?'

'No,' Emma says – and as dazed as George still feels, she's with it enough to realise that Emma just *lied* ... and that Angus – who wasn't at home when she and Richie came to call and who has only seen George among the guests from Fiadhain Lodge or in the company of Francina and Patrick – has *no idea* that she's a police officer.

The voices grow louder, and heavy footsteps descend the stairs. Rory tumbles in first, his cheeks and nose ruddy from the cold – and alcohol, probably. Hamish is just behind.

Angus grins. 'There he is – are you ready to meet her, Rory?'

Rory shuffles closer, stumbling a little. 'Er ... yeah, sure.'

'Now, she's a little older than the one you were chatting up, but I think this one is even prettier.' Angus directs the torch right at George's face. She flinches back, smacking her head against the bars, and tries to block the light from her face.

There's a beat of silence, then—

'Oh, my God.' It's Rory, aghast. 'Oh, my *God*.'

Angus misinterprets it. 'Those bruises aren't from me – she was almost killed by Robert McAllister. She needed help, and me and Em *saved* her.'

But then Hamish's voice whips through the dark.

'You fucking *idiot*.'

Angus jumps; the torch does, too, and he turns it on his brother. George's eyes are slow to adjust to the change in lighting, so Hamish's face is a little blurry. Even still, she can tell his expression is one of fury – it completely warps his narrow face, turns his eyes black.

'You've fucked us,' Hamish continues, then there's a sudden flurry of movement as he seizes Angus's collar and shakes him. 'You've *fucked* us, you fucking moron!'

Though confused, Angus defends himself nonetheless – he drives his weight back into Hamish, charging forward until he slams his older brother into a wall. The torch is knocked to the ground, the light bouncing around erratically. It's not a fair fight; Angus is probably twice Hamish's weight, and the only grunts of pain that ricochet off the walls and ceiling belong to the eldest Fairgrieve son. Rory quickly intercedes, wrestling Angus away.

'What the fuck is your problem?' Angus roars.

There must have been a punch thrown, because Hamish's bottom lip is trickling blood. He points at George with a shaking hand. 'Don't you know who she is?'

'I know, a guest from the lodge,' Angus replies angrily, 'but I saw those rich fuckers take off in the helicopter hours ago – and they left her all on her own. She's the one who almost got shot in the gully today. I tried to bring her up to the house then, but Patrick was hanging around.'

Rory is staring at George again, desperately trying to focus his glassy eyes. 'And what about tonight? She wasn't with an old man?'

'No, I told you – she was on her own! She needed help. I saved her life!'

'*Saved* her?' Hamish's voice drips with sarcasm. 'We're the ones who are going to need saving, brother – because she isn't some rich bitch on holiday. You've gone ahead and caught us a *cop*.'

Even in the dim light, George can see the blood leave Angus's face. He whips around to look at George.

'The one who came to the house?' Then he turns to his brothers again, his expression pleading. 'She and the bloke had left by the time I was done with the boiler – how was I meant to know?'

'You were meant to get Rory to help you,' Hamish hisses.

'I *had* help,' Angus protests, gesturing towards Emma. 'I thought – like we did with Mathilde, using Emma to lure them in.'

Hamish tilts his head and stares at Emma. 'You've met her. You know who she is.'

'It was dark,' she protests, 'and she was rolling around with that McAllister guy. I couldn't see her face properly.'

Hamish's suspicion doesn't wane. 'You're seriously trying to tell me that you didn't recognise one of the only two fucking police officers to ever come to our door?'

'We saw her earlier, too, in the gully,' Angus adds, though he sounds more confused than suspicious when he looks at Emma. 'Why didn't you tell me then?'

'Because we were dealing with the fucking Selbys trespassing on our land, yet again! And' – she links fingers with Angus, gazing up at him with a stricken expression that sits strangely on her face – 'Francina pulled her gun on you, Angus. Forgive me for not making introductions right after I thought I was about to watch my husband bleed to death.'

Perhaps thrown by Emma's uncharacteristic show of emotion, Angus's expression softens. But when she sees that Hamish seems unaffected, Emma's simper morphs into a snarl.

'Jesus Christ, Hamish,' she says, her tone caustic. 'You really think I *want* her here? When we have so much to lose? After everything I did to stop Mathilde from getting away?' Her ire swells; she drops her husband's hand and points at each of the brothers in a sweeping gesture. 'You fuckers had no idea she'd even escaped! *I* fixed your mistake then, and now' – she sucks in a wild, indignant breath – 'you're *doubting* me?'

For a second, none of the Fairgrieves seem to know how to respond.

'It *is* dark out there tonight, Hame,' Rory offers, his voice thin. 'If she says she didn't realise who they found, then I believe her.'

Hamish still doesn't look completely convinced, but he's smart enough to see that he's outnumbered. He turns his glare on Angus instead. 'You better be coming up with a plan, brother.'

Angus claws his hands through his hair and looks down at George, his expression wounded – as if it's her fault for not announcing her job title before he drugged her. 'We can fix this,' he mutters, almost to himself. 'She was on her own. Nobody saw us. And Robert isn't going to be an issue with how I left him.'

'She has a partner,' Hamish points out. 'And he'll bring the entire Scottish police force down on Kirkcree—'

'Exactly – they'll swarm *Kirkcree*,' Angus interrupts, then repeats, '*Nobody saw us*. They'll have no reason to think she's all the way out here.'

'They'll want to talk to us – they'll go to all the places she's been.'

Angus shrugs, and even in her foggy state, George can see how forced his composure is. 'It's not the first time we've had to hide someone. This will blow over – it always does.'

Silence falls as Hamish considers Angus's plan. For a few seconds, George genuinely doesn't know which way things are going to go.

'You'd better be right,' Hamish says darkly. 'I'm going to talk to Father. Make sure she stays put. Emma, with me.' With that, he shuffles back up the stairs, Emma hurrying behind.

George yelps when her legs are suddenly yanked down the bed. Angus drops his knees onto the mattress, straddling her hips, and pins one of her wrists under his knee as if expecting her to resist. He needn't have bothered; she can still barely move her limbs, but she tenses her other arm as much as she can while he secures her free wrist to the iron rungs with a cable tie he pulls from his pocket – the same kind she saw in the Selbys' garage. He repeats the action with her other hand, both now locked to the bars on either side of her head.

'This doesn't need to get ugly, you hear?' he says, his voice strained with the effort of manoeuvring her. 'We don't want to hurt you.' Her hair fell over her face during the struggle; he gently brushes the strands away again, then runs his thumb across her quivering bottom lip. 'But if you cause any more trouble,' he continues softly, 'I'll knock your fucking teeth out. Understand?'

He waits until she nods before he gets up. Then he reaches into a pocket and withdraws a set of keys; tossing them to Rory, he barks, 'Don't take your eyes off her.'

Then he's gone, too; a few seconds later, the yellow light cuts off with the slam of a creaking door.

For a minute, she closes her eyes and concentrates on breathing, the action a conscious effort. When she finally looks up, she finds Rory staring at her. His expression is hard to read in the torchlight, but she holds his gaze, her chest heaving.

'Rory. You have to help me.'

His throat bobs; his eyes fix on a point somewhere above her head. 'Please be quiet.'

'You're not like them, Rory,' she persists, tugging fruitlessly at the cable ties despite Angus's threat. 'You know this isn't right.'

He turns his back on her, his shoulders taut. 'I … Angus said he saved you. Just like Em, she had nowhere to go. And Mathilde was hurt and lost, and—'

'That's good, Rory,' she breaks in, letting him hear her desperation, 'that's good that you all like to help. But Rory, I need *your* help now. Please, *please* get me out of here.'

Rory exhales shakily, almost a whimper, and for a second she thinks she's broken through to him.

But her hopes are dashed when he hurries to the stairs and steps into the bubble of yellow light. It disappears with a squeal of metal, and then the lock turns. She guesses he's right outside the door, though; he wouldn't defy his brother's orders that far. But still, even this disobedience tells her that their anger is easier for him to face than listening to her beg for her life.

CHAPTER 27

Perhaps it's a sign that whatever Angus spiked the water with is still very much in her system, because rather than try to pull together a plan of escape as she tugs uselessly at her restraints, George can think only of how disappointed Dr Kassab is going to be with her: the next time he asks if she's used drugs since their last session, she's going to have to say yes. And despite her complaint about eating a cake to mark every thirty days of sobriety, she had her eye on a white chocolate monstrosity from the bakery near her house to celebrate eleven months.

Her appetite is non-existent now, though; even more so when she sees the cockroaches. The torch was knocked from Angus's hand during the scuffle, and the beam crosses the grimy floor, illuminating centuries of dirt and dust.

The panic is still there, muted under that heavy blanket of drugs, but the longer she's left alone in this dismal crypt, watching cockroaches scuttle across the filthy floor, the more the horror of her situation sinks in.

She's been *kidnapped*. Stolen off the street in the night, within shouting distance of hundreds of people. Tricked, drugged and whisked away in a matter of minutes.

The tears come then, hot and relentless. Without a free hand to wipe them away, they slide down her neck and into the neckband of her jumper – *Richie's* jumper.

There's no indication of how much time has passed since she was dumped into the Ranger. Is it possible he's still looking for her in Kirkcree, sweeping the streets with however many other officers have arrived? Is Rab still sprawled on someone's front lawn, left alone to endure the repercussions of that inevitable concussion? Or did Angus bring that rock down again and again on Rab's skull after she walked away, leaving no witnesses to her abduction?

She's so lost in these thoughts that it takes some time for her to notice that something is digging into her thigh. She awkwardly pushes herself back into a sitting position and peers down at the mattress. Her eyes land on something jutting out of a tear in the mattress – a concave disc a little smaller than her palm.

Her fingers start to tingle – though that may be due to the position her hands are trapped in.

It's the hard plastic face off a campaign badge. The design shows a blood-red pig on a white background – the logo of the Fearless for Fauna activists, the tattoo on Bambi's ankle.

'Oh, my God,' she murmurs. If this is the missing piece of the badge she found on the outcrop, then the magnetic tug that pulled her towards the Selbys' garage was wrong. Instead of confirming the Selbys' involvement in her death, finding it *here* only creates more questions.

Bits of conversation are coming back to her now. Angus said Emma wasn't to blame for what happened to someone called Mathilde ... was he talking about *Bambi*? Are *they* responsible for her death? Clearly they can shoot, based on the decomposing taxidermy in Gerald's trophy room, the line-up of doe busts representing years of skilled hunting, distastefully adorned with jewels, ribbon, glasses, a delicate glove ... which, now that she is pulling her syrupy thoughts together, she realises are all women's personal items.

Her body flushes hot, then cold, racked with shakes she can't even begin to control. She feels like she's trapped in the worst hour of an overnight flu.

'It's a tradition in our family to begin marriages with a successful hunt,' Gerald said in that room, gazing up at the row of heads. She remembers Richie noting that the Fairgrieves seemed to prioritise resources over trophies, considering they seemed to hunt only female deer ... but what if, in the years following the Grant massacre, when women in the village were rejecting proposals from Fairgrieve men, they started hunting females of other species – resources *and* trophies, at the same time?

'*We only want what's been denied us – what's* owed *to us.*'

Have the men of this family been stealing women off the road in order to forcibly replenish their dwindling numbers?

The cocktail of revelations sends her spinning, and for a moment she sits locked in dizzying silence. The cold presses in on her, adding to the weight of her mistakes.

Jesus. She feels so, *so* sick.

Half an hour passes before she's able to work one of her wrists free of the cable tie. Tensing up while Angus secured her was a deliberate move – it resulted in a small gap being left between the tie and her wrist. Still, it's a painful process; tears flow freely as the skin of her right wrist and hand twists, burns, *rips* with every millimetre she gains towards freedom. Her hand is swollen and tender and stinging in places where the skin broke, but she wastes no time before she grabs Bambi's – Mathilde's – badge.

Wedging it between two close-set bars on the bed frame, she applies pressure until it snaps into two uneven pieces, and uses one of the sharp edges to saw through the tie encircling her other wrist. Pins and needles radiate from her hips down to her bare feet when she stands; she presses her palm to the rough wall for a few moments before she feels brave enough to take a step.

She has to get out of here fast – that much is certain. The household must be in absolute chaos with the realisation of who Angus has brought home, and she knows there can only be two outcomes – they'll either keep her here until the heat dies down, before inducting her into whatever horrors await stolen Fairgrieve brides, or …

She has no idea if they would bury her down here, among the bones of their ancestors, and possibly those of women they've stolen over the years – but, either way, she's not going to make things any easier for them by still being in this crypt when they come for her.

She slides the two halves of the badge into her pocket, stoops to pick up the torch, then shines it around to get a clearer picture of the space. The walls and ceiling are curved, giving the impression that she's crawled into some enormous creature's burrow. The stones are chipped and slick with green algae, and when she swipes her finger against a crack in the wall, it comes away covered in gritty dust. Her heart leaps when she finds another archway set in the opposite wall to the stairs, this doorway barred by an iron gate; her momentary excitement flickers and dies when she sees the thick padlock and solid hinges.

Determined still, George shines the torch through the bars. The passage beyond the gate is much longer and narrower than the one she's currently in, and it occurs to her – with great relief – that her current prison seems to be an antechamber to the crypt proper. The torchlight sweeps across pillars and arches bearing intricate carvings and symbols, to low stone benches on either side of the passage that disappear into a void the light can't penetrate. She guesses it's back there that the crypt – and the final resting places of generations of interred Fairgrieves – actually begins. She thinks she's imagining the breeze that caresses her hot cheeks, cools the sweat at her hairline and the back of her neck. It's stale, cold; perhaps only ever disturbed by death and the living who bear it through the gate.

She presses her forehead to the bars, staring into that void, and wonders how many women before her have done the same thing. The bars are like icicles against George's skin, but she doesn't pull back, her imagination running wild. Did Mathilde manage to slip her ties, too? Did Louise, Gerald's wife, pace this room, desperately searching for a way out? Perhaps, like George, Edith the painter stared through these bars and wondered if freedom lay at the other end of this passage; if, like Eurydice, she might travel through the underworld in an attempt to return to the land of the living. Though everyone knows how that story ended.

Get out.

The words seem to come from the void; the same ones spoken by the terrifying woman in George's nightmare, whose hair shifted from blonde to brown to black as if she were an amalgamation of however many women have fallen victim to the Fairgrieves over the last two hundred years.

She wishes she could follow those instructions now, but with a locked gate between her and that hypothetical freedom, the void only represents despair – and though it's tempting to sink into it, George knows she can't. Just like Richie said, she needs to have *hope* – it's the thing that will keep her going. But she also needs a plan.

Getting upstairs is the priority; from there, her goal is the road. But considering her boots and socks have been taken, and the driveway is around a mile long, she knows that attempting this escape on foot would be foolish ... which means she needs to steal a car, and the only vehicle she's seen the Fairgrieves use is the Ranger. There must be another if Angus and Emma were able to bring her back here while Rory remained at the market, but she's not going to plan for a vehicle she's never seen before.

She presses her hand to her forehead, tapping it roughly to beat back the panic. *Take a breath,* she orders herself, *then think. Strip back the plan, keep it simple.* It has to be – she hasn't got the capacity for complex.

She grounds herself, gripping the bars.

In-in-in.

Out-out-out.

With this gate sealed shut, it just leaves the door at the top of the stairs as her way out – though she has to assume that Rory is still on the other side of it. In a fair fight – one where she's not still feeling the effects of the drugs – she could take on Rory without issue. But nothing about her situation is fair, which means she doesn't have to play fair, either.

One of the rungs on the bed is a little loose; she spends a few minutes working it free, pausing every few seconds to listen for movement at the door. The rung's not as heavy as she hoped, but it does feel good in her hands as she tiptoes to stand beside the stairs. Then she takes a deep breath, raises the rung, and screams.

As expected, the lock turns and the door bursts open. Rory charges down the stairs in a tumble of footsteps, fear and tipsiness making him clumsy. He looks straight towards the torch that she's deliberately left beside the bed, which means he only catches sight of the rung swinging towards him right before it cracks across his cheekbone.

He shouts in pain, dropping the keys and staggering to the right – but George follows him, the next blow landing on his shoulder, the one after that in his stomach. It's a final blow across the back of his neck that sends him to his knees, gasping for the air she just knocked out of him. She doesn't give him the chance to recover it – the yellow light tells her that the door is still open, so she can't let him make another sound. Tossing the rung to the side, she tucks Rory's neck into the crook of her elbow, grips her wrist with the other hand, and squeezes.

She barely feels the tear of his fingernails down her cheek, angling her head back so he can't reach her loosened hair. His panic works to her advantage; he can't think about anything other than getting air – it's easier then to bring him thudding to the hard floor.

Her arms are burning by the time his arms go slack. She lowers his torso carefully, then presses two shaking fingers to the pulse point in his neck. There's a steady beat there, and she feels his slow breaths against the back of her hand when she brings it to his nose.

It's an even greater feat to drag him onto the mattress, and she has to take several breaks to let dizzy spells pass. She uses his own belt to secure his wrists against the bars of the headboard, then removes his boots and socks. They're too big for her, but at least she won't be making a run for it with no shoes on. Or just one boot, like Mathilde.

Her small success deflates like a balloon. Is she just following in Mathilde's doomed footsteps?

Escape first, answers second. That's the plan.

Unfortunately, she's never been very good at sticking to one.

CHAPTER 28

The door at the top of the stairs opens onto the stone-flagged courtyard. The yellow light comes from an iron sconce mounted on the wall beside the door, the glass frosted with the chill. The sky is still inky black, but George's internal clock suggests that the stroke of midnight passed while she was unconscious; based on the position of the pale moon and stars, she guesses it's the very early hours of the morning.

There are lights on throughout the ground floor, but she can't see any movement within. All she can hear is the breeze rustling the dead leaves in the overgrown garden beds, and the distant screech of some poor creature disturbed by a night-time predator.

Her legs almost give out when her gaze passes over the curtain wall – the Ranger is parked just beyond the entrance. She wondered if the keys Rory dropped would include one for the Ranger, but as soon as she picked them up, she knew that they were forged long before the invention of the modern automobile. All four keys are unique, but are similar in that they're thick, blunt and encrusted with rust. Only one looks as if it's used with any kind of regularity, which she assumes belongs to the exterior crypt door.

It seems too much to hope for that they would have left the Ranger keys with the vehicle, but she knows she has to check. Dropping this useless set to the ground, she gives herself a silent countdown, then launches from the doorway.

Shadows protect her as long as she hugs the curtain wall, but she cringes at every crunchy leaf and scrape of loose stone under her feet. Being out in the open makes her body feel like an exposed nerve, and she doesn't breathe until she's through the archway and in the driver's seat of the Ranger. She's too scared to turn the torch on, so she blindly feels around the ignition, the compartments along the dash, sliding her fingers into the gaps between the seats. The tension in her chest builds as the seconds pass without hearing the tell-tale jingle of keys.

'Come on,' she whispers, patting above the doors, the roof. 'Where the fuck are you?'

The longer she fumbles around, the more her stomach sinks. The keys are either still with Angus, or they're somewhere in the house. She rubs her arms, seeking warmth through friction, debating whether it would be a safer choice to find a good hiding place in some gully or up a tall tree until help arrives, but the idea falls to pieces almost as soon as it forms – as does the brief idea to run to the lodge. These men know the land intimately and infinitely better than she does, and even though Mathilde made it to the road, one of the Fairgrieves still clocked her through the scope of a rifle.

Which presents another confusing question – why did they leave her there to be found, and put themselves at such risk of being caught?

Answers come after escape, she reminds herself. She has to keep moving, keep feeding the hope – which, at this precise moment, is that she'll find a set of car keys in a house of horrors. She's already lingered too long, and someone will surely check in with Rory soon.

The torch is a reassuring weight in her hand as she runs as quietly as she can in the oversized boots, up to the front doors. She tries the handle and is only partly surprised to find it unlocked. It's hardly warmer inside; in fact, George feels even colder than she did in the crypt as she slowly lets the door close behind her. It's far too much to ask for the Fairgrieves to have a key dish, or a jaunty set of hooks beside the door. She looks around the hall, sweeping over the minimal furniture; the weak light of a lamp draws her eye to a side table, and she rushes to search the drawers. Desperation creeps in upon finding them empty of all but dust bunnies, and she has the odd sensation of other eyes boring into her; she looks up at Edith's portrait and feels the woman's silent judgement.

Get out, she insists again.

'I'm trying,' George hisses. She blames the drugs for the fact that she's arguing with a portrait – it must also be why she can barely feel the sting in her cheeks from where Rory's nails raked her. She touches her forefinger to the tender skin; it comes away red with sticky blood.

Movement catches her eye down that long hallway, the one with the flickering bulb. Her heart leaps into her throat when she realises that it's Hamish. She's grateful for the weak lamplight; he doesn't seem to have spotted her, so she slips silently to the base of the stairs.

Go into the sitting room, she begs, listening to Hamish's stilted steps get closer, *or go out the front door—*

But regardless of his destination, he will see her as soon as he exits the hallway. She has no other option – she hurries up the stairs, losing herself in the dark.

Despite her efforts, several of the stairs creak under her weight; one of them is missing entirely, and her foot plunges into the cavity about halfway up. Rory's boots are so big that for two frantic seconds her foot becomes wedged; she yanks once, twice, almost pitching forward when she finally gets free.

At the first landing she presses herself against a wall and peers between the banister rungs into the front hall. Hamish has stopped at the base of the stairs; George jerks back as he cranes his neck, staring up into the void.

'Emma?'

It's totally dark up here; he shouldn't be able to see her, but she doesn't take the risk of looking back through the railings. Instead, she looks around. The landing stretches off in opposite directions into two darkened hallways; the next flight of stairs up to the top floor begins just to the right. As undesirable as the prospect is, she could go up there – Hamish told her that the entire floor was closed off because of the birds getting in through the roof. It might be a good place to lay low for a while until she can strategise her next move; she doubts that Hamish, whose strained breathing she can definitely hear getting closer, will push himself up that final flight if he's just looking for Emma.

She's about to make a break for it when she hears it. Not a cry of discovery ... but it *is* a cry.

A buzz starts at the crown of her head and crackles down her neck, across her shoulders, down her torso and legs; even her toes scrunch in Rory's too-big boots. And then they seem to act of their own accord – not taking her up the stairs, but down the hallway to the right, passing the first door, the second, until she comes to a stop outside the third.

She didn't realise at first glance, but now she sees that a faint light is leaking under this door. And while a tiny voice in the back of her head is screeching that *this could be a brother's bedroom, an occupied bathroom, a door to your death,* a louder voice orders her to *grip the handle, open the door, slip inside.*

It is a bedroom.

There's a window against the far wall, with splintering boards nailed over the glass. Beneath the sill is a small wardrobe, two of the drawers missing handles. There's a fireplace – a low flame the source of the weak light – a straight-backed wooden chair at the hearth, a flat cushion on the seat. A wicker basket beside the door is filled nearly to the top with soiled clothes and blankets, with more draped over the back of the chair. The floor is dirty, streaked with something that looks sticky, and in the corner is a stack of baby formula tins. Against the far wall, a metal bucket sits beside a double bed, brass feet glowing in the firelight.

And propped up on three thin pillows, squinting at George first with confusion, then with outright fear, is a woman.

George can only describe the feeling that hits her as a lightning strike; all her muscles seize and her fingers spasm before she claps them over her lips to smother a gasp.

The woman shifts slightly, the firelight bouncing off the sheen of sweat across her forehead, accentuating the shadows under her eyes and cheekbones. Her curly hair tumbles down an oversized white shirt, the unkempt ends grazing the blankets pooling around her hips. It's grown so much longer than it was in the photo; her face has changed so much, too, as the years – all ten of them – have passed.

George's hands slide down from her lips; words leave her mouth in a trembling whisper.

'You're Cara Reid.'

CHAPTER 29

They stare at each other for what seems like an eternity. George couldn't form another sentence even if she tried; her thoughts are elbowing one another out of the way as they rush to her lips.

Cara collects herself faster. 'You know me?' Her voice is soft, thin.

A shocked laugh catches in George's throat. 'Yeah, I ... I *know* you. I can't—' She breaks off, threading her fingers through her hair and gripping the strands tight. 'I'm not hallucinating this, am I?'

Cara shakes her head, her eyes wide.

'I can't believe it,' George breathes. 'This is incredible, this is just ... Richie is going to lose his fucking *mind* when he—'

Uneven footsteps thud down the hallway.

George has two seconds to press a silencing finger to her lips before she dives under the bed. There are more tins of baby formula under here, cardboard boxes, tumbleweeds of dust. One of the metal slats scrapes the back of her head as she turns to the side; through a gap between two tins she can see the door when it opens.

For a few long seconds, there's silence. Then—

'Did Emma come in here?' Hamish asks.

The mattress shifts above George's head. 'I don't know. I just woke up.'

There's another moment of silence.

'Are you feeling better?' he asks.

'A little.'

Hamish hums. 'I'll send Rory out for medicine as soon as ... as soon as we know it's safe.'

'Is something wrong?'

George watches his feet approach the bed. 'Nothing for you to concern yourself about, my love. You just need to rest.'

The bed depresses as he sinks a knee into the mattress. There's a sound of lips smacking on skin, then—

'So bonnie,' Hamish breathes, before turning for the door.

George waits only a few seconds after it closes before wriggling out.

'Who are you?' Cara demands. Her terror is palpable, and George rushes to reassure her.

'My name is Georgina Lennox. I'm with Police Scotland.'

Cara's lips part with a gasp. 'The one who was here the other day? Emma told me someone was asking about me and Mathilde.'

The confirmation of their victim's name feels like a rush of warmth; George almost sags with it. She sits on the bed before her legs give out. 'Yes,' she says thickly, 'that was me.'

Cara leans forward, her sad eyes suddenly bright with hope. One hand comes to rest on a rolled-up blanket beside her thigh. 'Have you come to save us?'

George hesitates. Looking over Cara again – taking in the prominent bones of her face, her sternum, her shiny skin and non-stop trembling – the only word on her lips is *shit*.

Cara is in a bad way. How long has she been holed up in this room? For the first time, George takes in the stale, cloying scent: the bitterness of sweat, vomit, ammonia, and something metallic that George instinctively wants to cringe away from. She looks at the sheets around Cara, at the ones piled beside the door. The sheet on top was once white, is now yellowing, and stained with rust-coloured patches.

George allows herself the space of one deep breath to suppress the horror, then reaches for Cara's thin hand.

'I have,' she says firmly. 'Can you stand? Once I find the keys to the Ranger, we'll need to get you down the stairs.'

Cara looks down at her body, the shape of her thin legs beneath the sheets. 'I–I've been sick. I haven't got up in a while.'

George keeps her expression smooth, though Cara's answer has sent a spike of anxiety through her. On any other day, she'd feel up to the challenge of carrying Cara down herself; today, however …

'That's all right,' she says bracingly, 'we'll figure that out later, then.' She looks around the room. 'Have you eaten anything today?'

'I've been trying,' Cara says, her voice small. She places a hand lightly on her abdomen. 'I think something is wrong in here.'

Shit, shit, shit. 'We'll get you to a hospital. They'll sort you out.'

'He'll need a doctor, too,' she says.

'He?'

Cara's fingers flex on the rolled-up blanket beside her leg. George watches, nonplussed, as her forefinger curls around the top fold and carefully draws it back so that George has a clear view of a tiny baby's face. But even that minute movement has disturbed his sleep; his eyes scrunch and his lips part to release a thin cry.

It's the sound George heard earlier – the one she heard when she first visited Fairgrieve Castle … *Jesus, was that only yesterday?* If she'd only believed her ears instead of letting Hamish convince her it was just the birds.

Cara shushes him, running a finger across his cheek, and he settles almost immediately. 'This is Benny,' she whispers.

George's first attempt to speak comes out as a croak. 'How old is he?' she manages to ask.

'Five days.' She pauses. 'I think. I know he was born right after midnight on Monday, but I've been kind of ... out of it since.'

George crunches the numbers in her head. If Cara is right, then Benny was born just hours before Mathilde died. 'And he's yours?'

'Mm. My third.'

George's heart stops. *Third?* She's already panicking about trying to get just this one baby out, as well as his poorly mother – how the hell is she meant to manage two more?

But Cara continues, and George immediately regrets the direction of her thoughts.

'The first one died inside me,' she says, stroking Benny's nose, 'and the second only lived a few minutes. But you,' she says, gazing at her son's serene face, *'you're* still here. And you're *strong.*' Her voice becomes a fierce whisper. 'And I'm getting you out of this place.'

She looks up at George. 'We said that if he lived longer than an hour, then we'd make a run for it ... but I was bleeding too much, and I could barely move. So Mathilde said she'd take him. She promised that if they made it, she'd find my brother, and make sure Benny was with his uncle. Uncle Ben,' she says, her smile growing.

Every sentence has felt like a punch to the gut. Struck dumb, winded, all George can respond with is, 'I met your brother.'

Cara's jaw drops. 'You did? Is he— How is he?'

'He's good, really good ... he's got a job, a wife. Two little girls.' She nods down at Benny. 'Cousins.'

'Ben is *married*? And has ...?' Cara's lower lip starts to tremble. 'I never pictured him ... but of course he has – why wouldn't he, he's *amazing*, he's, he's ...' She swallows. 'He must be so angry with me.'

'What? *No*, of course not.' George squeezes her hand. 'Ben has missed you every single day you've been gone.'

The trembling turns into a sob. 'I was looking for somewhere I could bring him once he turned eighteen. Kirkcree was just a random stop.' Her expression twists. 'I was asking for work at the supermarket when Hamish saw me. He waited until I came outside and told me he had a big house and his mam needed help cleaning it. The supermarket didn't need staff, and by that point I was so low on money that I didn't think twice – I just got in his truck.'

George blows a breath out slowly. She thought Hamish's illness was preventing him from seeking a wife – as it turns out, he already had one locked up inside his nightmarish home. She can't blame Cara at all for the decision she made, one born from desperation and need – after all, didn't she herself fall into the same trap? The Fairgrieves know what they're doing.

It's the same story, you understand? Dean said to her back at Ivy House. *Young women like them go off on their own and the night swallows them whole. You see it on the news every day.*

How many women have the Fairgrieves abducted over the past two hundred years? It seems so impossible that someone wouldn't have noticed ... yet, she was just scrolling through a list of missing women that numbered in the hundreds – and that's only from the last few decades, and made up of women who had people in their lives who cared enough to report their disappearance.

Could any of these women – or perhaps women who didn't have someone to report them missing – also be victims of the Fairgrieves? She isn't sure yet, though one thing is certain: she isn't the first woman to fall into their trap. But she is determined to be the last.

'Was Mathilde next?' she asks, trying to wrap her head around the timeline.

Cara shakes her head. 'Emma was next, then Mathilde just a couple of months ago. They didn't plan that one – she'd just escaped from the Selbys, and she was—'

'Sorry – what do you mean *escaped* from the Selbys?' She thought finding the badge in the crypt meant that the Selbys were in the clear, but apparently not.

Cara looks guilty. 'Oh, er ... Mathilde was part of this group—'

'Fearless for Fauna.'

Her eyes light up. 'You know about it? Well, yeah, in September the group sent her out to investigate the Selbys, and they caught her sneaking around their sheds. She told them she was just a tourist who got lost, but they went through her phone and found photos of their equipment and guns and medicine.'

'Medicine?' George repeats, the word raising a flag in her mind.

'Yeah, her group suspected that the Selbys were drugging deer to make them easier to hunt. Mathilde said they freaked out when they saw the photos of the medicine, so she figured their suspicions were true.'

'Did they tie her up?' George asks, thinking of that folding chair, those cable ties. The buzz she felt in the garage *was* right – just like her hunch about the drugged deer was right, too.

'For a few hours. Said it was a citizen's arrest. But they seemed to realise that could get them in trouble, too, because they cut her loose, threw her in a truck, and dumped her out by the road. She was making her way back to where she'd stashed her bike when Gerald saw her.' She takes a breath, her thin finger moving to stroke Benny's button nose. 'Mathilde was in the crypt for a few weeks. They kept sending me and Emma down there to be with her, to try to ... to explain how things are here. They knew – they *know* – that we're the key to this working.'

'What do you mean?'

Cara's lips turn down, and her gaze shifts to the window. 'Isolation only makes you more desperate to escape,' she says slowly. 'You have nothing to lose except your life, and after a while, even that's worth the risk.' Then she looks back at George, and there's something in her eyes that begs for understanding – as if she expects George to judge her. 'There are more ways to control a person than just a locked door, okay? Letting us love one another is more effective. They made sure we had something to lose if we tried to run ... or if we told anyone what was going on here.'

Judgement is the furthest thing from George's mind – she recalls Dean's story about Gerald bringing infant Hamish into town, Louise watching from the truck. He attributed it to shyness, but George considers it in a whole new light now. Wielding children as weapons is common in cases of intimate partner violence. She has seen it often, and spent a lot of time learning about coercive control and how abuse encompasses so much more than the physical. Emotional shackles can be far harder to break.

'Did you know Gerald's wife? Louise?'

Cara's expression darkens. 'No. That was the first lie Hamish told me. He thought I'd be more willing to come back to the house if I believed there was another woman there, but then I found out she died a few months before I got here. Nobody would say how she died ... but Rory was just a kid, so I pushed him to tell me. He said she fell out a window.' Cara looks back at the window again. 'But I don't think it was a window. And I don't think she *fell*.'

The cries are the ghosts of dead kids, Zoe said, *or the wails of the mothers who couldn't handle the grief and threw themselves off the roof.*

Cara takes a shuddering breath. 'Mathilde shouldn't have been anywhere near this place. She moved from Berlin just last year to work with those activists. The Fairgrieves had been talking about finding someone for Rory for a while, but they hadn't had any luck with solo travellers passing through the village. They never take local girls,' she adds, 'and normally they only take one in each generation, since there's usually only one Fairgrieve man. But this is the first time that three have lived past eighteen. Gerald was – is – *so* excited. He thinks this is the turning point – that Hamish and Angus and Rory are the ones to restore the Fairgrieve name.' Her full lips curve down. 'They just need to keep making more Fairgrieves. So they got me, then Emma. And when Gerald saw Mathilde all alone and almost already on his land, he thought it was fate. He radioed Angus and Emma to get there, fast.'

George rubs her forehead roughly, trying to keep her composure. 'And what did Rory think when they brought her here?'

'He seemed ... unsure. I think he was scared of her. He didn't visit her in the crypt much.' Cara surprises George by smiling. 'She was so beautifully angry – she *burned* with it. She was so alive and real, and to me and Emma, it was like she had the whole universe inside her. She was the biggest, brightest thing Em and I had known in so long. A reminder that the world still exists outside the boundary, and that there are people waiting for us out there.' She motions to Benny. 'He has *cousins*.' Then, as if it just occurs to her, she adds, 'I have *nieces*.'

'And Hamish is his father?'

'Benny is mine,' she corrects. 'Mine, and Emma's, and Mathilde's. *Ours*, not theirs.'

George nods, but stress is pressing on her now; in her shock, she's allowed too much time to pass up here. Rory could be already stirring, screaming through that locked door. The Fairgrieves could already be combing the castle grounds and halls, hunting her.

'I am going to get you out of here, Cara,' she says, hoping she's projecting more confidence than she feels. 'Do you know where they keep the keys to the Ranger?'

'In the kitchen, usually. You can hide here until Emma comes – she'll show you.'

'Emma is the reason I was thrown in the crypt tonight,' George says, acid leaking into her tone. 'I understand that you have both been through so, so much ... but it might be possible that Emma has chosen a different way to survive this, and that means I can't trust her to help.'

'No, Emma is good,' Cara says fiercely. 'She just ... she doesn't understand. She doesn't believe.'

'Doesn't believe what?'

'That she deserves better.'

A creak in the corridor; the quick steps of someone approaching.

'Hide,' Cara hisses, gesturing under the bed.

But it's too late; whoever is approaching now is much faster than Hamish, their pace light and quick. And George is still too sluggish, stuck staring at the door as it swings open.

'I got the ratio perfect this time,' Emma says, looking at the baby bottle she's swirling in the air, 'and the temperature is good to go—'

She breaks off with a gasp, goggling at George.

'Em, it's all right,' Cara says, struggling to push herself upright. 'She's going to help us.'

But Emma is not calmed by Cara's words; in fact, they seem to have the opposite effect, because the glare she turns on George could melt glaciers.

'She *was* going to help by staying put,' she snarls. 'But now she's fucked us all.'

CHAPTER 30

'Em?'

Emma ignores Cara's confusion, kicking the door closed and crossing to the bed in a rageful silence. She thrusts the bottle into Cara's hand.

'Feed him,' she orders, before retreating back to the foot of the bed. 'They're already all worked up down there, and you know they hate hearing him scream.' To George, she spits, 'What the fuck are you doing in here? You were meant to stay in the crypt.'

The anger George thought she'd be able to repress for another few hours, days, weeks, comes hurtling out of her. 'Where *you* put me after you drugged me and helped Angus *kidnap* me.'

Emma looks at George as if she's watching a puppy bare its teeth. 'And why do you think that is, stupid? You and your partner weren't taking the hints, and I didn't trust you to figure it out in time.'

'So letting me rot in the crypt was your plan?'

Emma's face twists with the condescension in George's tone, but she doesn't reply right away; instead, she crosses to the basket of soiled laundry and starts to toss out items, one by one, until finally she straightens.

'The *plan* was for you to sit tight and wait for your people to see through their bullshit and tear this shithole apart,' she says, holding out her hand, 'which is going to be a lot harder once those cunts figure out that you've escaped.'

George stares at the object in Emma's hand. 'That's my phone.'

Emma glances over at Cara. 'I told you she was a genius. Now I understand why we've both been here so long.'

But George barely hears the insult. She has no idea if Emma realises the absolute firecracker of hope she just set off in George's chest – *she never turned off location sharing with Richie.*

'You told me you hadn't seen it,' she says, snatching the phone and tapping the screen. The charge symbol flashes once. It's dead now, but surely Richie would have checked it as soon as he couldn't find her on the street.

'Obviously, I had. It was going crazy in my pocket on the drive here.'

'With calls? Why didn't you answer?'

'While Angus was right next to me? Brilliant idea.' Emma leans back against the door, her arms crossed. 'While he was taking you into the crypt, I told him I needed to check on the baby and stashed it. Then I went back down to make sure you didn't die.' Her eyes zero in on George's cheek, examining the shallow scratches there. 'Where's Rory?'

The fiery rage has been turned down to a simmer; she feels a little hollow without it. 'Still down there. I knocked him out.'

'You should have caved his fucking head in.' Emma nods towards the phone. 'How long?'

'What?'

'Until your lot come. Cara needs a doctor.'

Cara smiles weakly. 'I'm okay, Em.'

'You're fucking not,' Emma snaps. 'Neither of us has any clue what's wrong with you, and you're getting worse every day.' She looks at George. 'So? When?'

George licks her lips; they're dry, cracked. 'Mobilising a rescue like this takes time. Richie would have told them that the Fairgrieves have firearms, which means they'll need the Special Ops guys, and they have to come all the way from Glasgow.' She glances at the window, the boards too closely laid to reveal the state of the sky outside. 'What time is it?'

'Almost three.'

'Okay ... then maybe it's dawn by the time they're fully assembled,' she muses. 'But then they need to plan their entry – the Fairgrieves are going to be hypervigilant now, so it's not safe for a rescue team to just barge in here, not with the weapons the Fairgrieves have access to. There's too high a risk of casualties – to them, and to us.'

'I bet your lot would still come for your body. Even *dead* they would have given more of a fuck about you than they ever did about us.'

'Em,' Cara chides gently. 'That's not helping.'

A tiny cough comes from the bed. Cara pats Benny's back as he coughs again, and George notes that the movement is clumsy. There's a fresh sheen of sweat across Cara's forehead and chest – her energy is draining right before their eyes.

'Angus kept saying that, down in the crypt,' George says. 'That he helped me. That he *saved* me.'

'It's important to them,' Emma says bitterly. 'They want to believe that we need them just as much as they need us.'

'It makes them feel less guilty, we think,' Cara adds. 'And they do care about us ...' That nervous look returns, waiting for George to judge. 'Gerald talks about taking women like it's a right, but sometimes ... it sounds like he's just repeating what he was taught as a child.'

'You don't think he believes it?' George asks doubtfully; Emma also looks unconvinced.

'No, I think he believes exactly what the first Fairgrieves did when they started taking women – I think he has to, or else they'll have to face what they've done. And I think maybe the guilt is already there, a bit.' She looks at Emma. 'They've tried to make us happy. And it's made things easier for us, over the years, to ...'

'Try to be happy?' George finishes.

A tear slips down Cara's cheek, but her hands are occupied; with a low grumble, Emma reaches over to wipe it away, showing far more tenderness than she did scrubbing the blood off George's face. Her expression is tightly controlled, but her eyes are shiny.

'We've done what we had to do,' Cara continues, her voice wavering. 'But then Mathilde came, and she made us believe that we could make it out. I couldn't run, but Mathilde and Emma waited until the boys were asleep—'

George looks at Emma, surprised. 'You were out there that night, too?'

Emma makes a reluctant sound of affirmation. 'We were almost at the road when they spotted us. I didn't even realise Mathilde was hit.' She jerks her chin towards Benny. 'He was in her jacket — it's a miracle the bullet missed him. After she went down, I took Benny from her. I couldn't see well — the moon was back behind the clouds — but I could feel the blood, and heard her t-trying to breathe, and from the way it sounded ... I just knew that she — we — were done for.' Her gaze grows distant, caught in the memory. 'Her blood was so warm. Like all her fire was pouring out.'

'Why didn't you keep going?' George asks.

Her expression turns bitter. 'Because I was too weak. It was a long way to the village, and hardly anyone comes along the road. I knew at some point I'd be left behind — that's why Mathilde was carrying Benny. Her body was stronger. *She* was stronger. She had a better chance of finding help.' A muscle in her jaw jumps. 'So instead of trying to keep going, I did nothing.'

'That's not true, Em,' Cara murmurs. 'You sat with her. You made sure she wasn't alone when she—'

'She probably didn't even know I was there,' Emma growls. 'I wasted time holding her hand instead of making myself keep running, while you were in this bed getting sicker and sicker.

She probably couldn't even feel it.' She sucks in a shaky breath. 'After she ... well, I heard them shouting for us, and I realised that they didn't know exactly where we were now that it was dark again. So I—'

Emma looks away, her chest rising and falling fast. Cara reaches for her hand, runs her thumb over Emma's knuckles in a soothing gesture.

After a moment, she looks up. Her jaw is set, gaze defiant. 'I dragged her to the edge, and I pushed her onto the road.'

George's eyes flutter closed as she's struck by the familiar, stomach-turning sensation of falling. She swallows the nausea and asks, 'Why did you do that?'

'Because we needed her body to be found – just not by the Fairgrieves.'

Cara squeezes her hand. 'Show her.'

Emma hesitates, then rolls back one of her sleeves. 'It's been hard keeping this hidden from Angus. I told him I burnt my arm on the stove.' Blood-spotted fabric is wrapped tightly around her forearm; she unwinds it to reveal scabbed red lines that have been carved into the delicate skin.

CARA REID
MATHILDE BAUER

Emma's voice is oddly subdued when she speaks. 'It was Plan B, if neither of us made it out alive. A way to still be useful to the others.'

'But Mathilde only had Cara's name. And the letter F?' She'd wondered if it was the start of *Francina, Fiadhain Lodge, Fearless for Fauna*, even *Fairgrieve*—

'The start of an E, for Emma,' Cara murmurs. 'It should say Emma Begbie.'

'We ran out of time to finish,' Emma says gruffly, 'and their names were more important. They've actually got people who care about them.' She sniffs again, then forces a laugh. 'Surprised you could even read my writing. We used a pin off a badge Mathilde had in her pocket.'

George pulls the two halves of the badge out of her pocket. 'This one?'

Emma seems surprised. 'Yeah. We popped the face off so we could use the pin easier. It was her idea to leave it in the bed down there. Evidence, she said, in case police ever came. And you found it.' She looks down at her arm, finger drifting over the thin scabs. 'She was so much smarter than me.'

Her words feel layered with a deeper meaning; for a moment, George considers what other cries for help were hidden under that veil of acrimony: saying that Cara looked familiar, that she thought Mathilde wasn't from 'around here'. That she knew George and Richie were investigating a murder without them saying so; the insistence that they should return with a warrant that could have allowed them to search the castle.

'Did the men punish you?' George asks. 'You ran, too.'

'But I came back. After I pushed Mathilde, I walked to where I could hear them calling. They were raging at first, but I told them that Mathilde stole Benny and that I managed to get him back.'

'And they believed you?'

Emma's eyes are haunted. 'After all these years, they thought they'd beaten the defiance out of us. They almost did.'

'And they didn't go looking for Mathilde?'

'They tried for a while – but then, unbelievably, a car came along.'

A lump swells in George's throat. Those traumatised tourists who found Mathilde have no idea how important their grisly discovery was – not yet, anyway.

'The plan worked,' George manages to say, her voice tight. 'She was found. She brought me here.'

'Yeah, you're here,' Emma says heavily. 'Now what?'

The air in the room, already stale, feels burdened with the weight of Emma's despair, of George's own guilt at missing so many signs just because they were masked in hostility. She glances at Cara. Benny has finished the bottle, and Cara is struggling to raise him to her shoulder to burp him. Seeing this, Emma scoops him up and pats him briskly, her attention locked on George.

'We can't wait around for help to get here,' George says.

Emma's eyebrows flick upwards. 'You want to make a run for it? After what I just told you?'

'We won't be running. Cara and Benny will stay here while you show me where to find the keys to the Ranger. Then we'll come back for them, and drive over Murtair Beag to Fiadhain Lodge.' It's a more realistic plan, now that they won't be making the journey on foot. And as luck would have it, they already have a place for an air ambulance to land, and time is of the essence for Cara right now.

'No,' Cara says, 'take Benny with you now. If you have a chance to escape, don't waste it by coming back for me – I'll only slow you down.'

'We're not leaving you—' Emma begins.

Cara's eyes blaze. 'You promised to get him out, Em.'

Emma stares at her, her jaw tight. 'I'm surrounded by fucking idiots.'

Rather than bite back, Cara smiles. '*Get out*,' she says, more gently, then looks at George. 'Then *come back*.'

CHAPTER 31

George thought she knew fear: what it feels like in her chest and body, what it tastes like in her mouth, how it can be laced with anger, with curiosity, with revulsion. But standing in the inky stairwell of Fairgrieve Castle, a five-day-old baby swaddled against her chest, George knows that all those moments of fear were just the prelude to this.

This, she thinks as she nods at Emma and they begin to descend the stairs, *this is true terror.*

She doesn't let it show on her face, though, doesn't let Emma see anything except determination and control. It's a mask she cemented in place as soon as she lost the argument as to who should carry Benny during this escape attempt.

George insisted that she was still feeling the effects of the drug – which she assumes must be xylazine, one of the many things the Fairgrieves are accused of looting from Fiadhain Lodge – and that it would be easier for Emma to justify having the baby with her if she was caught. But Emma made a convincing argument: she said she'd be slower and less agile than George, so if the Ranger plan failed and they had to escape on foot, George would have a better chance of outrunning a pursuer – or a bullet.

So George grudgingly held her jumper up as Emma arranged Benny, his pink lips slack in sleep, over her shirt and against her sternum. Then she used some of those soiled clothes to craft a makeshift carrier, tying sleeves tight around George's waist and neck.

'They don't give us clothes unless we're going out with them,' Emma said as she double-checked the knots. 'I had to steal their coats and boots when we ran with Benny last time. At least you've got boots, but you're going to be cold.'

It wasn't totally true. Benny was already providing a nice warmth; it was like holding a hot water bottle against her chest. As if hearing her thoughts, Cara smiled at George and beckoned her closer. Understanding the request, George pulled the neck of her jumper down far enough for Cara to place a soft kiss on Benny's head.

'See you soon,' she whispered, and raised her eyes to Emma. 'Both of you.'

Now, as they reach the bottom of the stairs, Emma goes ahead to check that the hallway is clear while George lingers on the last step. Once Emma waves her over, they repeat the process – Emma pads down to the end and peeks around the corner towards the study. Then she waves again. Every step, every scuff of their feet against the thin carpets, every time Benny's head bounces against her collarbone, makes George feel light-headed with anxiety. He could wake up at any moment and let out a cry that will signal her location to every Fairgrieve within earshot.

Emma cracks open the door to the study and looks inside. George can see a very weak light coming from within, and when Emma opens the door wider to admit the three of them, George identifies the source as dying embers in the fireplace.

Emma goes straight to the far door, then peers out into the next hallway. 'I hear voices in the kitchen.'

'Who? How many?'

'I don't know.' She looks back into the hallway. 'I can't hear Gerald. Maybe he went to watch the road for your lot.'

'We need to know where everyone is or we could drive

straight into them. We're already going to be making a lot of noise.'

George thinks Emma didn't hear her, or is ignoring her. But after a few seconds, Emma takes a deep breath and George realises she was bracing herself. 'I'll be back.'

George looks around. Aside from the desk, there's nowhere for her to hide. 'I can't stay here.'

Emma bites her lip, thinking, then pulls George into the hallway. So deep in the belly of the house, and now able to hear those rumbling voices herself, George can't even protest when she understands Emma's plan; she can only shake her head vehemently as Emma pushes her into Gerald's room of bloody heirlooms.

Emma follows her in, pulling the door closed behind her. 'Don't be a coward,' she hisses.

'But—'

'I've been in this house for six years — you can wait in this room for five minutes.'

Emma steps back out into the hallway and starts to close the door — but George stops it with a hand.

'Wait — do you have children here, too?'

Emma's face goes blank. 'None that made it this far.'

The door clicks shut, and George is left in complete darkness.

The tidal wave of shame following Emma's statement — the clanging horror of the extent of these women's losses — is almost enough to distract George from her surroundings.

Almost.

But as soon as the door closes, the atmosphere of this room — drenched in blood and violence — presses in on her. The sensation invades her nose, pushes down on her tongue, brushes against her legs like a black cat.

This last thought makes her swallow thickly, staring in the approximate direction of the cabinet of taxidermy. She doesn't remember seeing a cat among the zoo of creatures the Fairgrieves have hunted down and kept behind glass. And then there are the deer on the walls, and their horrific accessories ... George feels their eyes on her now, imagines the empty sockets of the skulls, and she shivers despite Benny's reassuring warmth on her sternum. She considers rummaging through the shelves of weapons, trying to find one that she might use to defend herself and Benny, but the thought of her bare fingertips catching on the sharp, grimy edge of an axe or a dirk is a good deterrent. And even if those ancient rifles are loaded, she has no idea how to use any of them.

She shivers again; this time, it's from the cold air that is sinking down from the hole in the ceiling. And, as if carried on that draught, a whisper curls towards her through the dark.

Get out.

George doesn't flinch, and she doesn't feel judged now. She can hear the desperation, the plea. Maybe the words are her own this time.

An instinct she's never felt compels her to kiss the top of Benny's head, mentally apologising to him for how chilly her lips are. But he doesn't stir; so, seeking the comfort of another living thing in this room drenched in death and despair, she keeps her lips pressed to his warm skin as she waits for Emma to return.

The minutes creep by like hours as George crouches against the wall, murmuring song lyrics into the fuzz atop Benny's head to distract herself, until finally Emma comes.

She doesn't bother knocking; the door simply creaks open. It's hard to see her face with the dim light behind her, but George doesn't need to ask if her mission was a success – the faint jingling of keys is enough. But she's confused when Emma closes the door again, sealing them both inside.

'What are you—'

Emma presses a hand to her lips. A few seconds later, George hears Hamish's uneven gait as he walks down the hall. She holds her breath, her heart pounding so hard that she's certain it will wake Benny and bring this whole plan crashing down – but then the footsteps fade, and Emma's hand drops.

'Gerald and Angus have split up to patrol the boundary on foot,' she whispers, tentatively opening the door and peering out. 'They've got guns,' she adds, and now George can see her grim expression. 'Angus is still confident that nobody saw us take you, but they're being cautious. Gerald told Hamish to go to the top floor to watch out the windows for cars or lights, and to be ready to get Cara, Benny and me into the crypt in case someone comes.' She holds up a radio in her other hand. 'He was about to take this out to Rory, but I told him I'd do it.'

'Brilliant,' George breathes, taking the radio. 'Well done, Emma.'

Emma blinks. 'It's ... I ...' Then she scowls. 'Hurry up.'

But George gestures for her to wait. 'Here,' she says, bending awkwardly over Benny's bulk to remove Rory's boots and one of the socks. 'Put this sock on one foot and a boot on the other,' she instructs as she pulls a boot onto her bare foot. 'Now at least we'll both have a bit of protection from the ground.'

Emma complies, and makes a sound that approximates a thank you.

With their feet somewhat covered, the keys clenched in Emma's hand, and the radio clipped to the band of George's jeans, she treats herself to a fresh glimmer of hope.

We're going to make it, she thinks, almost giddy as they rush back through the study, down the flickering hallway, heading back towards Cara. *Benny won't cry, the Ranger will turn on first go, we'll be all—*

They're halfway across the front hall when Emma yelps; a split second later, a hand claps over George's mouth and she's being towed backwards into the sitting room. Muffled whimpers and the desperate scuff of feet against the ground are the only indications that Emma has been dragged inside already. It's impossible to fight back and protect Benny at the same time; she shoves her assailant's arm down to keep it off Benny's back, dread flooding her when they use their foot to push the door closed.

In the darkness, at first only filled with Emma's whimpers and the exerted breaths of their captors, a voice growls, 'Stop resisting.'

George freezes – then whips her head from side to side. Whoever owns the hand over her mouth seems to understand what she wants; it withdraws willingly, and she's able to whisper, 'Richie?'

A phone light comes on.

Richie has one arm wrapped around Emma's torso, locking her arms to her sides, the other covering her mouth. When his eyes find George in the dim light, he makes a quiet, strangled sound.

Then Emma is sliding to the carpet, suddenly released from Richie's grip as he limps towards George. She manages to wrap a protective arm around Benny just before he hauls her tightly to his chest.

'Are you all right?' he demands, one hand smoothing down her hair, the other squeezing her waist. 'Are you hurt?'

She shakes her head, close to tears with relief. 'I–I'm okay.'

He pulls back to look her up and down, to verify her answer for himself; and that's when George notices Richie's stand-in partner.

Panting a little from the effort of towing George into the room, Hendry is watching Emma, one hand outstretched as if to grab her while she gets to her feet.

'Put a finger on me and I will bite it off,' Emma says, her voice wobbling.

George holds out a calming hand. 'She's all right, Hendry. She's with me.'

Emma glares at her, but George doesn't take it to heart; she has bigger fish to fry. 'What took you so fucking long?' she snaps at Richie.

Richie's voice is hoarse when he replies. 'I wanted to come as soon as I saw your location, but I was ordered to wait. There are units from Inverness and Glasgow already in Kirkcree, and a tactical response team gathering at Fiadhain Lodge. Francina is being a surprisingly accommodating host,' he admits grudgingly, 'but I suspect she's trying to win favour before we tell them what you saw in the garage. I had to describe the layout of the house and outbuildings to about fifteen different people, then name everyone who might be inside, and make lists of all the potential threats and weapons the Fairgrieves have access to. A helicopter is on its way to provide aerial support, but I wasn't bloody waiting any longer.'

The fierceness in his voice, and the way he's obviously favouring his bad leg, raises a lump in her throat. She was so desperate for Richie to get here, so mired by her muddled thoughts, that she didn't consider that he might be given orders to stay away. If she had, there's no way she would have expected him to storm Fairgrieve Castle without the full weight of Police Scotland behind him; she's watched him shelve his own opinions, beliefs, *friendships* in order to comply with rules and procedure. So to not only defy orders tonight, but to bring Hendry – a civilian, a *journalist* – along with him for the charge …

She can't speak for a second, overwhelmed by the scale of his disobedience. 'Cole is going to kill you.'

He shrugs, seemingly already resigned to that fate. 'She'll have to get in line behind Jenny.'

George looks at Hendry. 'And what are you doing here?'

'Couldn't let him come alone,' he says brashly. 'And, you know … this will be a hell of a story.'

'A story none of us will get to tell if we don't get out of here,' Richie says, then looks at George. 'Do you know where the Fairgrieves are right now?'

She briefs him, finishing with 'And Rory is locked in the crypt.' When Richie cocks his head, she shakes hers. There's not enough time to tell that part of the story, because it will only crack open the *whole* story – and they *really* don't have enough time for that.

'We have the keys for the Ranger,' she says. 'We were planning to gun it to the lodge.'

Richie pulls out his phone. 'I'll tell the team to meet us halfway.'

'We won't all fit in the Ranger,' Emma says.

Richie looks around. 'There's only four of us.'

'Five,' Emma says tersely, 'and a half.' To George, she says, 'Fuck the promise.'

Her expression is needlessly defensive; she's prepared to argue her point, anticipating that George will remind her of Cara's final order. But George now has two extra pairs of hands at her disposal.

'Fuck the promise,' she echoes firmly. 'We're not leaving without her.'

Richie looks between the two of them, nonplussed. 'Without *who?*'

Before either of them can answer, the clock runs out.

Benny's wail doesn't last long, but the sound is high and loud. George and Emma jump; Hendry almost topples over the back of a low loveseat. But Richie handles the shock best; his eyes widen, then narrow, and then he tracks the source of the sound with his phone torch. For the first time he properly takes in George's outfit, the way her – *his* – jumper bulges out over her chest.

'What was *that?*' Hendry demands.

Carefully, George pulls the neck of her jumper down. Benny reacts to the fresh air; tiny fingernails scrape against her shirt as he nuzzles into her chest hungrily, squeaking.

Richie's eyes flicker to George's, surprised, then he looks to Emma. 'Yours?'

Emma shakes her head, her lips a thin line of tension.

'Rich.' George takes his hands, feels the warmth of them transfer into hers. 'His name is Benny Reid. His mother is Cara Reid.'

She watches the ground fall out from beneath Richie's feet; she squeezes his hands tighter, tethering him here, to her, to the incredible truth.

'Cara's here, Rich. She's been here this whole time. *She's still alive.*'

CHAPTER 32

It's a heroic effort for Richie to not go to pieces entirely; his hands are like clamps around hers. He opens his mouth to speak, to ask one of what she guesses will be about a thousand questions, when a burst of static interrupts. George tugs her hands free from Richie's grip to unclip the radio from her belt.

'Angus, head up Murtair,' Gerald instructs, *'see if anything is happening at the lodge. I'm circling back towards the house.'* There's a pause, then he adds, *'I can hear a helicopter.'*

Hamish breaks in. *'Rory, still got eyes on her?'*

Emma looks at George, wide-eyed. But before George can offer a solution, she snatches the radio from George's hand and presses the speak button.

'Cara needed my help with the baby,' she says, her voice thin. 'I'm taking this to Rory now.'

Another pause, then *'Hurry.'*

Emma hands the radio back, and George feels her trembling as their fingers brush.

'That was good, Emma,' George reassures her. 'Quick thinking.'

'Good news is, we know where they are,' Hendry says.

'Bad news is that Hamish could come down from the top floor at any moment,' George continues, 'Angus is between us and the lodge, and Gerald is heading back this way. And they're both armed.'

Richie looks down at Benny again. 'It makes more sense now why they've protected their borders so fiercely.'

An ache is making itself known behind George's right eye, the radiating pain reminiscent of the migraines she used to get. At home, she'd head it off by crawling into her bed with a bottle of water. In lieu of both of those things, she presses her thumb to the brow bone and blows out a long breath. Then she points at Hendry.

'You and I are going upstairs to get Cara. She's conscious, but she's in bad shape. You'll have to carry her.'

Hendry looks terrified but nods.

As she expected, Richie isn't happy with this. 'You and I can get her,' he protests.

'How's your leg?' she asks bluntly. 'Feel up to carrying someone down a flight of stairs?'

Richie's mouth snaps closed. Feeling only a hint of remorse, she starts to ease her jumper up and over Benny. 'You're taking this guy and the keys to the Ranger. If you're spotted, or something goes awry in here, you head for the lodge.'

He's sullen, but he helps her extricate Benny without further complaint. Once the baby is wrapped within Richie's coat and he has the Ranger keys in his hand, George turns to Emma.

'Do you remember where you found me with that deer yesterday, to the east?' When Emma nods, George hands her the radio again. 'You're going to take the radio to Rory, and you're going to tell him that you saw me running in that direction. And you're going to get him to radio the others and say that not only am *I* escaping, but I've also got Benny. Once he leaves to chase me, go straight to the Ranger and wait with Richie. Hendry and I should have Cara out by then.'

Hendry looks understandably panicked. 'That's the plan?'

'Yep,' she says, the image – and image *only* – of confidence again. 'We all know what we're doing?'

Three nods, each varying in levels of reluctance and trepidation. She adds her own.

'Then let's do it.'

For the next thirty seconds, George considers all the ways this plan could fail; and in every scenario, failure always comes down to timing.

From their position just inside the sitting room, George and Hendry watch Emma and Richie slip out the front door, Emma's face bloodless, Richie's grim but determined.

She jumps when a weight presses on her shoulders; it's Hendry, draping his blue coat over her.

'You're shivering,' he murmurs.

She stares at him for a beat, then pushes her arms through the sleeves. 'Let's go,' she whispers.

He is her shadow as they hurry along the first floor hallway.

Cara barely lifts her head from the pillow when they enter. 'You came back,' she says weakly.

'Told you I would,' George says, hurrying to the bed. 'This is Hendry.'

Cara squints at him, her eyes glassy. The hair at her temples is damp with sweat. 'You're police, too?'

'I am tonight,' Hendry says with a nervous chuckle, then quietly asks George, 'Has she got warmer clothes?'

'We'll wrap her in the blanket. Cara,' she says, slipping an arm behind Cara's back, 'it's time to go.'

Her shirt is soaked, and far too warm. 'Benny?' she murmurs. 'Em?'

'They're with my partner, they're safe. Is it all right if Hendry picks you up?'

Cara's eyes flutter as if she's on the precipice of passing out, but she does manage to make a sound of assent.

Hendry is quite well built, but even he looks alarmed at how easy Cara is to lift. Now that she's free of the sweat-stained bedsheets, George is able to take stock of just how wasted her body is. The evidence of her recent pregnancy is there in the soft swell of her stomach, but her bare legs look like toothpicks, and the bones of her elbows and wrists jut out of her waxy skin. Something passes between George and Hendry in a quick glance – the knowledge that if they don't move fast, they'll be rescuing a corpse.

It's this thought that makes her too hasty – she and Hendry move too fast back down the hallway, and though George cringes at every creak of the ancient floorboards, slowing down is the furthest thing from her mind. Her body feels as taut as a piano string by the time they're halfway down the stairs – a string that snaps when a shout rings out.

George whips around, eyes following the source to the top of the stairs where Hamish now stands. His mouth drops open at the sight of George; and when his eyes slide to Hendry, Cara cradled in his arms, George knows what he's going to do before his hand even moves.

She doesn't think – she launches herself back up the stairs, reaching him just as he brings the radio to his mouth. He doesn't get a chance to use it; she barrels into him, bringing them both crashing onto the landing. The radio skitters across the floor – as it thuds against the far wall, it emits a burst of static before Rory's frantic voice comes through.

'*She's out, she's out,*' he shouts, '*she's cutting across the gully to the road! She's got the baby!*'

'*How did she get out?*' Gerald thunders, the end of his sentence nearly lost in a cough.

'I ... she got—' Rory stutters. '*I'm going after her now.*'

Hamish draws a breath to shout – George drives her elbow into his gut, hears his shout fizzle out as a gasp. Hendry looks on nervously, but he's powerless to help her with Cara in his arms.

'*Angus, where are you?*' Gerald barks.

'*I just got to the base of the fucking ridge! I'm running back now, but there's no way I'll get to the road before she—*'

'I'm almost at the house,' Gerald interrupts, coughing again. 'I'll take the Ranger and cut her off at the road.'

'What if she gets away?' It's Rory again, breathless.

Gerald doesn't reply right away. 'Hamish, get the girls into the crypt, then get the rest of the guns out.'

George doesn't need to tell Hendry what to do next – he's already curling Cara closer to his chest and running down the stairs.

Hamish struggles weakly beneath her, torn between trying to push her off and reaching for the radio. Both are doomed efforts; she doesn't hesitate as she drives her knee between his legs, and while he's choking for air, she gets to her feet and stomps down as hard as she can on the radio until she feels it splinter beneath Rory's boot.

'You – can't – take – them,' Hamish wheezes. 'They – belong – to—'

He cuts off with a wail when she plants the boot on his brittle rib cage.

'They don't belong to anyone,' she snarls, 'least of all you and your disgusting family.'

Hamish blinks up at her, eyes watering. 'We – saved – them.'

In lieu of a response, she simply rocks her weight onto her foot. Something quietly cracks; Hamish howls with pain.

She catches up with Hendry just as he's passing through the curtain wall. The Ranger roars to life, headlights blazing. Richie climbs out to help Hendry buckle Cara into the passenger seat.

'Where's my baby?' she murmurs, and Richie – who, to his credit, only freezes for a moment when he claps eyes on Cara for the first time – opens his coat enough for her to see her son as Hendry leaps into the driver's seat. He revs the engine once, twice.

'Get in,' he barks at George and Richie, eyeing the darkness around them.

Richie climbs into the cargo bed with difficulty, letting out a low groan as his injured leg bends. He shifts over as far as he can to make room for her — but George looks around frantically.

'Where's Emma?'

'We'll come back for her, George, but we have to move.'

She squints into the darkness towards the driveway, then back to the house. Could she still be in the crypt? What if Rory hurt her?

'George,' Richie says, 'don't even—'

'There's no time to argue,' she snaps. 'We'll go on foot to the driveway — send a team to meet us at the gate.'

When he opens his mouth to protest, she cuts him off again. 'You can't have eyes on me all the time, not in this job. Not if we're going to do it right.' She nods towards Cara, then pats the spot where Benny rests against his chest. 'And they need you more.'

Hendry whips around. 'What's going on?'

She ignores the question and points to the west. Moonlight illuminates Murtair Beag, the outline clear against the navy sky. 'Head that way and you'll see a dirt track that runs up to the crest. It looks steep, but the Ranger can handle the terrain. Just don't fall out.' She reaches out to grip the collar of Hendry's shirt. 'And *do not stop* — for anything.'

His distress is palpable, but he nods once, then shifts the Ranger into first gear. She releases him and steps back.

'George?'

She looks at Richie, her jaw clenched against whatever protest he's come up with.

But it doesn't come; Richie just stretches out a hand, and she steps into it, letting him softly palm her cheek. 'You'll be the death of me,' he says hoarsely.

'Probably. But not tonight.'

She sees Richie speak once more, but his words are lost under the spin of tyres on the gravel, and then the Ranger is shooting off into the night. With no small effort, she turns her back on her most promising avenue of escape to face Fairgrieve Castle. She might have just made the worst decision of her life ... or the *last* decision of her life, if this goes as badly as it could.

She hardens herself against the fear, the regret, that last look on Richie's face, and ducks back through the archway.

George's stomach sinks as she approaches the crypt. Now feeling the sting of Rory's nails along her cheek, she realises how foolish she was to plead with him to help her. There was never any chance of her breaking through to him, not when he's been raised to view women as objects that his family is owed. How many desperate pleas must he have heard? How many did he turn his back on?

She steps into the alcove and is unnerved to find the heavy door wide open. Straining her ears for sounds from within, George tiptoes down the stairs. It takes a second for her eyes to adjust to the dim light, but she soon spots Emma sitting cross-legged on the mattress, her chin in her hand. She looks up, startled, when George emerges from the stairwell.

'What are you doing here?' she demands, rocking up to her knees. 'Where's Cara and Benny?'

'Hendry and Richie took them in the Ranger. They're on their way to the lodge.'

'They're gone, *definitely* gone? You promise?'

'I promise. They're safe.'

'That's – that's *good*. Good.' She frowns. 'Then ... then what the hell are you still doing here?'

'You weren't in the Ranger.'

Emma grunts, a frustrated sound. 'So? Gerald is coming!'

George beckons, starting back to the stairs. 'Then we'd better get a move on.'

But Emma just stares at her, and the longer the moment drags out, Cara's words from earlier come to mind. Looking at the woman kneeling in front of her, who has spent the past few days snapping and snarling at George – who seems to have no further need for her teeth now that Cara and Benny are gone – George finally sees the damage, how deep that self-loathing and shame run. She recognises it; she knows that bitter taste.

So she sinks to her knees before the mattress. 'Let's go, Emma.'

Emma's expression ripples. 'I-I'm too slow.'

'You aren't. And I'm going to be with you the whole time. So, let's get you up, and—'

'No, someone has to stay back, to distract them, to m-make sure they don't go after Cara or Benny—'

'It's not your job, Emma. Not anymore. It's time to go home.'

'You don't ... I can't just—' Her breath hitches; her shining eyes can't seem to find a spot to settle on. 'I don't know ... where do I go, what do I say ?'

'We don't need to worry about any of that right now.'

But this just seems to make Emma even more frustrated.

'Didn't you hear what we told you at the house?' she asks, her voice high and strained like something's pressing against her throat. '*I'm* the reason Mathilde was here – I told her that it was safe. And because she believed me, *I'm* the reason she was killed. And then I pushed her onto the road like she was a piece of meat, and told the Fairgrieves that she was a thief in order to save my own skin. A-and now Cara is dying, and Benny, Benny will probably die, too, so' – she chokes on a sob – 'so why don't you understand that I deserve this, that it's all my fault, mine, mine, *mine*—'

George grabs her heaving shoulders; slides her hands up to cradle Emma's face, just as Richie did to her only minutes ago.

'Listen to me – *listen*,' she says, her voice harsh to cut through Emma's cries. 'It is *not* your fault. You didn't *deserve* any of this. You were forced to make horrific decisions to keep yourself alive – to keep your friend and her baby alive, and to try and get them rescued. You were hurt, over and over again, by men who have been hurting women for far too long. Who stole your body, your freedom, your youth, and your time. *That* is what you didn't deserve, Emma. And from now on, every single good thing that happens to you is what you're *owed*.'

Tears trickle down George's fingers. 'My mum will be so disappointed in me when she finds out what I've done.'

'She won't.'

'She didn't even look for me,' Emma sobs, her head heavy in George's hands. 'Why, *why* didn't she notice I was missing? Why didn't she tell anyone that I was gone?'

George can't stop her own tears from spilling over.

'She might have told someone,' she says, stroking Emma's lank hair behind her ears, 'and she probably did notice. But you know who *definitely* will notice if you don't come with us now? Cara. She's your family, and so is Benny, and they're both going to need you out there.' She tilts Emma's chin up, forces her to meet her eye. 'And *I* noticed. I was looking for you. I came to find you. And I'm not leaving without you.'

With some effort, she releases Emma's face and pushes herself back to her feet. And then she holds out her hand.

For a second, she thinks Emma won't take it. And she wonders if she even has enough strength to wrestle Emma out of this shed and towards the road, if the other woman really intends on resisting.

But then she feels Emma's cold, shaky hand in hers, and George maintains a firm grip on her long after she pulls Emma to her feet – afraid that if Emma floats away for even a moment, she'll retreat to the only familiarity she knows. Even if it's behind a door that locks from the outside.

'Ready to run?' she asks Emma.

Emma swallows, then nods. 'I won't be very fast.'

'As long as we stick together, we'll be fine.' She manages to sound confident enough that Emma seems to believe it.

Convincing herself is a different story.

CHAPTER 33

'Gerald will be here any minute,' she says, towing Emma up the stairs. 'He wasn't sounding too good on the radio – I think we can outrun him.'

'How are we going to outrun a bullet?'

George bites her lip, bringing them to a stop just inside the door. She has no way of knowing if Gerald's poor health has affected his aim, but they have no other choice than to run across the property and hopefully find enough cover in the trees to avoid giving Gerald a clear shot.

She stiffens, then squints into the shadows at the base of the door. Maybe there *is* another option – not to run *across* the property, but to run *under* it.

'What are you doing?' Emma hisses as George crouches, feeling around on the ground until she comes across a ring of rusted metal – the ancient keys she dropped there earlier. She grabs them, then drags Emma back down the stairs.

'Get the torch' is all she says in response, and Emma grumbles as she scoops the torch off the floor with her free hand. George doesn't release Emma until they reach the iron gate on the opposite wall, where she urges her to train the light on her hands.

'You've got to be joking,' Emma says, watching George wiggle the first three keys into the hole without success. Bits of rust flake away as she desperately forces the last one in, and nothing happens when she attempts the first turn. But then, after enough effort to leave her sweating, there's finally a deep *clunk*.

Panting a little, George nudges the gate. The sound the hinges make as they move – possibly for the first time in decades, if not longer – is otherworldly. Like something waking up, or something *complaining* about being woken up. But nothing comes rushing at them from the dark, radiating ancient fury, so George takes a deep breath of stale air and turns to Emma.

'Let's go.'

Predictably, Emma backs up a step. 'There's no way I'm going in there.'

'There'll be another door,' she says confidently, praying that Richie's niche knowledge of crypts is accurate. 'We can get out that way.'

When Emma seems set to argue, George seizes her wrist. 'I've got you, okay? I'm going to get you out. Trust me.'

Emma looks as if she's regained enough of her usual attitude to keep arguing, but a sound makes them both freeze. Not the bellow of a crypt dweller, or the screams of disturbed ghosts, but a boot scuffing a stone step. And then another. And then—

'Well, well,' Gerald says, emerging from the stairwell with his rifle raised, a lantern dangling from his elbow. 'This makes things nice and easy. You were going to end up in there anyway.'

George doesn't hesitate – she rips the key from the lock and drags Emma through the gate and into the passage beyond, just as Gerald fires the first shot. A section of a stone pillar explodes over their heads, and Emma shrieks as shards land on them, but George simply urges her along. Emma is still holding the torch, but she's running so erratically that the light is bouncing off the carved arches and curved walls, and, increasingly, on writing carved into the walls in evenly spaced blocks – names and dates that they're moving past too quickly to read. George wonders if even *thinking* the names of the dead is enough to make them stir, if their pounding steps aren't already an alarm clock.

The passage curves to the left, then sharply back to the right; Emma doesn't see the second turn coming, and lags against George's hold enough that she's forced to slow down. Emma's breathing is already harsh, punctuated with little gasps.

'Come on,' George urges. 'You're doing so well—'

Her words are silenced as the air splits with a *whoosh* and stone bursts from the wall. Emma screams again, covering her head.

'Emma!' Gerald bellows, his voice echoing off the stone so much that it sounds like ten Geralds are pursuing them. 'Get back here now!'

George chances a glance over her shoulder. She can't see him in the dark, can't tell how far behind he is until—

A chunk of the wall explodes beside her. She yelps as a piece of stone grazes her temple, then feels fresh blood start to trickle.

'Are you okay?' Emma squeaks.

'I'm fine,' she says through gritted teeth, 'just keep moving.'

A burst of deep coughs precedes another shout. *'Emma!'*

Time stretches, condenses. George's heart is beating impossibly fast. The air gets trapped in the shell of her ears; it muffles their pounding footsteps, is swallowed by the deathly silence surrounding them.

She keeps Emma in front of her. If one of Gerald's bullets is going to find them in the darkness, let it find her first. The next two shots are close enough that she senses the air shift; with the second one, a pillar in line with her head bursts into powder. Gerald roars Emma's name again and again. Emma tries to look over her shoulder, but George just shoves her forward.

'Keep going,' she orders, her throat painfully dry. Two more shots come, and Gerald's rattling cough reaches for them around every corner, until—

'I see it,' Emma rasps. 'A gate.'

If George had the energy to weep, she would be blubbering right now. Instead, she follows Emma up a short flight of very steep steps and fumbles through the keys until she finds the one she thinks she used earlier, hoping it works for every gate in the crypt system.

'Quickly,' Emma urges, and George responds by jamming it into the lock and heaving her weight into the twist. When it judders open, she pushes Emma out ahead of her, then slams it closed behind them. The keys are still in the lock on the other side, but at least it will put a few more seconds between them and Gerald's gun.

This crypt exit rises from the earth as a humped stack of stones barely taller than George. Snarled weeds and thorny vines have crept up and over the stones, turning the whole thing into a misshapen lump in the middle of a small clearing. She looks around, trying to establish where they've come out on the property. Everything looks the same to her – trees, hills, shadows that could be hiding any matter of monster.

Then Emma gasps. 'There's the driveway,' she says, pointing through the trees ahead. And beyond that …

The bridge.

'Holy shit,' George breathes. 'Go, *go*.'

Despite freedom being so very close, George knows they've both slowed. Emma is wheezing harshly, and George has to loop an arm around her waist to keep her from tripping over her own exhausted feet. Wearing one heavy boot each is also impacting their balance, and George can already feel the damp earth soaking into her exposed sock.

They're only halfway across the bridge when the voice in her head sighs, *We're not going to make it.*

A split-second decision is made: she stops.

Emma looks up at her blearily, chest heaving.

'Keep going,' George orders. 'All the way to the end – someone will be waiting for you.'

'But—'

'You've done *so* well, Emma. Just a little bit further, now.'

Emma's next breath catches in her throat, but then she's staggering across the rest of the bridge, melting into the darkness on the other side.

It's only seconds later that George hears the footsteps coming.

She inhales deeply, trying to calm her heart. It doesn't work – especially when the darkness parts to reveal Gerald Fairgrieve, the lantern light giving off a pale white glow. His breathing is ragged, sallow skin dripping with sweat. He looks terrible – the exertion of chasing after them has aggravated whatever medical condition is causing him to waste away at the same rate as his cursed castle. If it wasn't for the gun in his unsteady hands, now angled at George's knees, she would run, confident that he'd never catch up; in fact, he looks like he's about to collapse.

'Where is she?' Gerald rasps, his thin chest heaving.

'Gone. They're all gone, Gerald. They're safe.'

His lips part for another hacking cough that rolls out before words do. 'Safe?' he repeats, wiping spittle with his sleeve. 'From who? Their husbands? Their family?'

'Don't you dare,' she snarls, unable to temper her rage despite the threat of the gun. 'You might have convinced yourself and your foul sons that what you've done is right, is what you *deserve*, but that won't work with me – or the rest of the world.'

He lurches forward, 'The Grants—'

'Were murdered in cold blood by Clyde Fairgrieve. If only Douglas Grant had managed to strike back, then maybe none of you would have been born, and Cara and Emma – and Louise, Edith and all the other women the men of your family have helped themselves to since then – would have lived their own lives, far away from this miserable place.'

Even in the dim light, she can see Gerald's fury, but he reins it in enough to ask, 'They're all gone, then?'

'Yes.'

'Even the bairn?'

'All of them,' she says, unable to stop a victorious grin.

Gerald cocks his head. 'So … you haven't got him tucked up in your coat there.'

He doesn't wait for her to reply – she can't; his words have popped her bravado like a pin in a balloon with the realisation that she no longer has her tiny, squeaking shield – just brings the gun up to point at her chest.

'More police are coming,' she says in a rush. 'If you shoot me, they will raze this place to the ground. Everything you hold dear – your family pride, your ancestral home, your *treasures*,' she spits, 'all of it will be destroyed, burnt, scattered to the wind. It'll be like the Fairgrieves never existed. And you didn't hide in this rotting castle for your entire life because you liked the view. You wouldn't have done what you did if you didn't care what happens after you're gone.'

For a beat, she thinks she's getting through to him – a tiny spark of hope flares in her chest. But then he cocks the rifle.

However, the shot – which would go cleanly through her torso, with no chance of survival even if there was an ambulance at the top of the driveway – doesn't come.

Instead, she watches Gerald stiffen, his eyes widening. They both turn as footsteps crunch through the undergrowth, and Rory steps out from behind a tree. He's breathing hard, his trousers hanging loose around his hips, and barefoot, but he holds his own rifle with steady hands … and he's aiming it right at his father.

Gerald stares at Rory, mouth agog. 'What are you doing, son?'

Rory doesn't answer him – though his aim is true, his eyes are wild when he glances at George. 'I didn't want her,' he says, his voice shaking with unshed tears. 'I never asked them to – to get me one.'

'Rory,' Gerald says, shocked. 'What are you saying, son? Put that down and talk to me.'

'No,' Rory says through his teeth. 'You've talked enough. All you do is *talk*.'

Gerald splutters around another cough. 'You know why we have to ... do this. You know how ... we were *wronged*—'

Rory shakes his head violently. 'Enough! I can't hear this story again – you can't keep telling it over and over and suddenly make it true. The Grants were already rich and well liked and successful. The only people who had something to gain from a massacre were the Fairgrieves.' His chin rises, defiant despite his fear. 'I think the Fairgrieves murdered the Grants because they wanted what they had, and then Clyde lied to the villagers, and lied to his children, and made them pass that lie all the way down to us, like one of those fucking heirlooms you love so much. And look where it's left us – four grown men scraping around in the dirt in a house that's falling down around us, no money, stealing anything we can get our bloody hands on. *Enough.*' He takes a deep breath. 'No more words, no more lies. Just let her go, Father. Let them all go.'

Gerald shakes his head, but it's less out of refusal and more in disbelief. 'Son—'

Rory's only reply is to slide his finger onto the trigger.

Gerald doesn't move – more importantly, his gun stays trained on George. But after a few seconds pass without someone pulling a trigger, she backs up a step. And another. And even when Gerald turns to watch her, his whole body shuddering with the effort of breathing, Rory's unwavering stance gives her just enough confidence to turn her back on them and keep moving. It's probably the bravest thing she's ever done, even though her chin trembles, even as she braces for the searing shock of a bullet.

Then she's around the first bend, back among the trees, and the shot has still not come. She doesn't hesitate – she pushes herself into a sprint, feet pounding along the driveway now, and by the time she sees the gates, sees Emma's exhausted face illuminated by the flash of blue and red lights, she's honestly not sure if she's still alive or if she's become just another one of Fairgrieve Castle's ghosts.

CHAPTER 34

For three hours, the A&E is in a state of chaos.

Nurses and doctors flit between bays, their shoes squeaking on the shiny floors. Curtain hooks scrape back and forth on their railings. People talk to each other, at each other, crying, shouting. And pulsing through it all are the sounds of beeps, the trill of machines, muffled announcements over the PA system, and static bursts from the radios clipped to the chests of the constables stationed outside three of the curtained bays.

Inside these bays are three of the six escapees from Fairgrieve Castle: Emma, Richie and George. Somewhere nearby, Cara and Benny have been admitted to a ward for specialist care.

Triage nurses rushed towards George after spotting the blood on her face, but she redirected them to Emma, who was staring around the room with wide, blank eyes. It was the right call; as soon as a nurse asked Emma for her name, Emma's eyes rolled back and her legs gave out. Within seconds she, too, was whisked away.

Which just left George, standing in the waiting area for a full minute before one of the nurses noted her full-body tremors and gently guided her into a bay.

Two constables have been assigned to each of them – through a gap in the curtains surrounding her bed, George spots PC Bear marching beside Emma's gurney as she's wheeled off for a scan, his expression flushed with self-importance. As she waits to be seen by doctors, George receives periodic updates from the two minding her. Apparently, Gerald, Angus and Hamish Fairgrieve have barricaded themselves inside the house and are refusing to come out, or to respond to negotiators. And a few minutes after George and Emma went speeding off in the back of a patrol car, a third figure appeared at the gate to Fairgrieve Castle.

'He didn't struggle,' the constable tells George. 'Just said he was the youngest Fairgrieve, and told them he'd talk if they got him out of there.'

It's not until the fourth hour of being at the hospital, when George quietly slips from her bed under the guise of using the bathroom, that she feels able to take a full, deep breath. She wishes there was somewhere she could go to escape the bright lights, the vigilance, but she knows that neither will be possible for a long while yet. She finds a corridor with less foot traffic and loiters near a drinking fountain, nodding tightly at the staff who glance at her. Wearing a hospital gown over her trousers and hospital-issued socks, and with scratches on her cheek, a bandage around her torn-up wrist, and dirt and blood under her nails and caked into the grooves of her skin, she must look like a wreck. She feels like one, but was relieved when all of her expedited tests came back clear – bar the blood results, which confirmed that it was indeed xylazine in the water. The doctors debated what kind of treatment to give her, but since she's walking and talking they've opted to just keep monitoring her breathing and blood pressure instead.

A TV is playing somewhere; she looks around the next corner and sees a smaller waiting area with plastic chairs lining the walls, magazines stacked on a tiny central table. Hendry is in one of those chairs, his laptop open on his knee. He's got his phone wedged between his ear and shoulder, and is engaged in a rapid-fire conversation as his fingers fly across the keys. Already plotting out the article he's going to write about the events of tonight, she guesses.

There's no bitterness attached to the thought, surprisingly; Hendry demonstrated a bravery and moral compass that she never expected from him. This revelation has shifted something quite … fundamental in her opinion of him. As long as he writes the truth, and handles all of the women's stories with great care, then he can write what he likes.

She drifts away.

The sun has risen, and she observes a staff handover from night shift to day. On the other side of the nurses' station, two unfamiliar constables are standing guard outside an open door. George nods at them as she approaches, but her eyes are quickly drawn to the scene within.

Cara is propped up in a bed, her hair pulled into a loose braid, her face flushed – but the glow in her skin doesn't look feverish now, probably a result of the cocktail of fluids trickling down from the IV bags hanging over her head. And she doesn't look frightened; in fact, there's a tired smile on her face as she watches Richie lean over Benny's crib, gazing down at him with wonder. One pant leg is rolled above his heavily bandaged knee; with a groan, he sinks into a seat beside Cara's bed and takes her hand.

George turns away, her chest tight.

As she returns to the A&E, a nurse waves her over to the desk.

'I just got a call,' she says, tapping a short fingernail on a phone. 'She has a visitor.'

That was fast. 'Right. Christ.' George looks around. 'Is there somewhere more private we can do this?'

'There's a family room just over there.'

She thanks her, then says, 'Could you give us a minute alone first?'

The nurse nods kindly. 'Just tell me when she's ready.'

*

Emma's fingers pluck at the gown over her thighs, bunching and smoothing the material on an anxious loop. 'You're sure?' she asks, not looking up from her hands.

'I'm sure. But there's no rush. We can sit here as long as you want.'

The family room smells mildly of takeaway food and body odour, which should be an unpleasant combination but somehow isn't. It feels human, and warm, unlike the cool, disinfectant smell of the wards. There are posters along the walls, the messages alternating between maintaining hope and preparing for the worst. Two couches take up the majority of the space; George and Emma sit side by side on one, the cushions shabby but soft. A table in the corner has a very basic tea and coffee set-up: foam cups stacked far too high and leaning to the left, low-fat milk in skinny sachets, a cardboard box of individually wrapped sweet and savoury biscuits.

There's a weak tea on the coffee table in front of Emma; she hasn't looked at it once since George set it down.

'You don't have to see her at all, if you don't want to,' George reminds her again. 'It's your choice.'

'Is it?'

George reaches for Emma's hand and gives it a firm squeeze. 'I won't let anyone in here unless you say the word.'

Emma looks up at this. Her eyes are red and glassy with unshed tears. There's an IV in her right hand, attached to the unit she wheeled in with her. She swallows, her gaze darting to the closed door. 'Will you stay?'

'As long as you need.'

She looks back at George as if trying to assess her sincerity. Then her thin shoulders lift with a bracing breath. 'Let's just … get it over with.'

George rises silently and crosses to the door. Leaning out in the corridor, she signals to the nurse. Then she steps back into the room, leaving the door open.

'Hey,' she calls gently.

Emma's attention was back on her gown, fingers fisted into the material. But she looks up, scowling again, nerves radiating off her.

'You're in control of this,' George says firmly. 'Say the word, and I'll clear the room. All right?'

Emma opens her mouth to reply, but then an agitated voice rings out from the hallway.

'Where? Which door – this one? Here?'

Shoes thump against the polished floor, getting closer, and then suddenly there's a woman standing in the doorway. She's wearing trackpants, Wellingtons, a sleep shirt stretched across her large chest, and a black jacket with a subtle leopard print – the precise outfit you'd throw together if you received a phone call in the early hours of the morning. Her hair – the same colour as Emma's at the roots, though professionally streaked with blonde highlights, is piled on her head with a claw clip, and she wears chunky black glasses.

Liz Begbie looks at George first, scanning her face. Then she looks around the room, and George hears the air whoosh out of her lungs as her eyes land on Emma.

On trembling legs, Emma rises. 'Hi, Mammy. It's me. It's … it's me.'

George doesn't think Liz has taken a breath yet.

'I'm, er. I'm so …' Emma looks down at her hands. 'I'm so sorry, Mammy. I-I know we were fighting when I left, and … and I've done some – so many bad things since then, but I really didn't want to, and I-I tried to come home but—'

The rest of her confession is smothered as Liz crosses the room and throws her arms around her daughter.

'I didn't know,' Liz says, voice hitching. 'I didn't— I thought you were done with me, Em. I thought you didn't want to be found. Oh, my baby. My girl. I'm so, *so* sorry.'

Emma gasps, and for a second her eyes are panicked as she looks at George over her mother's shoulder. George takes a step forward, ready to intervene, but then Emma's eyes close, her chin drops, and she begins to cry.

Quietly, George steps into the hallway and closes the door behind her. Her body is a tapestry of aches, her cheek still stings. But she ignores that, planting herself in the hallway, straightening her spine.

She can stand guard as long as she has to. For as long as she's needed.

CHAPTER 35

The pub is busier than she'd expect for a weekday; but it is a Friday, and it's the only place within fifteen minutes of the station that has a decent lunch menu. More importantly, the staff don't raise an eyebrow when you order a beer before noon.

She chose a small table against a wall, the wood scuffed and glossy. A few of the tables around her are filled: a pair in suits attempting bites into overstuffed burgers, a booth filled with men in orange work shirts. She assumes the other parties are tourists, based on the backpacks slung over the back of their seats, the coats that are a little too light for the winter day outside. Christmas music plays faintly from the speakers in the corners, competing with the football match on the television mounted above the bar. Two young men are behind the bar, one watching the game, the other wiping down the already spotless counter. The smiles they keep hiding from each other are more telling than the ones they share. She almost felt bad interrupting them to place her order, and took her pint without lingering.

George observes it all quietly, legs crossed at the knee. For a while, this kind of noise would have activated her fight or flight response, but in the fortnight since returning from Kirkcree, she's found herself feeling comforted by the sounds of life going on around her. Dr Kassab was impressed when she walked into his office on Wednesday. He was clearly expecting the shell of a woman she had been when she first started seeing him; there was an extra box of tissues on the side table.

She's surprised by her composure, too. Every morning that she wakes up after a decent, mostly nightmare-free sleep makes her feel as if one half of her mind is gaslighting the other. Perhaps it's all still too fresh, as if what happened out there is a spore she inhaled when she was running for her life down that driveway, and it's germinating inside her lungs and she won't know the roots are wrapping around her organs until they start to squeeze.

The alternative seems just as unlikely – that she's just become better at handling this kind of trauma. It is her job, after all … though she didn't argue with Dr Kassab when he suggested twice-weekly sessions for the next couple of months.

Unlike the last time she was swept up in the storm of a very public criminal case, this time she feels like she's on a steadier boat. Cold water still licks up her legs every now and again when she sees her face on the TV or news websites, but she no longer feels like drowning is an imminent threat.

As much as she hates to admit it, Hendry's reporting has been a major factor in that. Most outlets have centred on the men in their articles – sensationalist pieces on Gerald, Hamish and Angus, who surrendered to the police after Gerald started coughing up blood in the front hall and joined Rory in custody, a situation shared by Robert McAllister who, after a few days in hospital recovering from the beating Angus gave him, was taken in for the assault on Zoe.

Even the Fiadhain Lodge lawyers are having a hard time keeping their clients out of the press. Under their instruction, Francina and Patrick eventually admitted to holding Mathilde in their garage for several hours – stressing the fact that she was trespassing, that they'd been 'terrorised by activists like her before' – and explained that they denied knowing her out of fear of being linked to her death.

George was in that interview; she took grim satisfaction in telling them that, if they weren't so desperate to protect their reputation and had revealed that they'd last seen Mathilde walking in the direction of the Fairgrieve property, then Cara, Emma and Benny might have been rescued days sooner. And in the photos George saw online later that captured Francina and Patrick running between the station and a waiting black SUV, she felt even more satisfaction upon seeing the line-up of Fearless for Fauna activists waiting outside the doors. She suspects that Cara or Emma somehow managed to pass on Mathilde's discovery of the sedatives – the message on their posters seems to focus largely on the barbaric practice of drugging deer for hunts.

But Hendry's coverage is different. His stories are about the women – who they are, who they *were* before they were ripped from their lives. He has diligently traced family trees and combed long-forgotten missing persons reports, and has unearthed the names of more potential victims. So far, he has a list of names dating back a hundred years.

And in Hendry's version of events, DI Georgina Lennox is just a player in *their* story, not the main character.

She hears the door open, then the familiar uneven tread towards the bar. But she doesn't look up until Richie approaches her table. There's a pint in his hand, and a brown giftbag looped over his elbow. She pushes his chair out with her foot, and he sits with a grunt.

'That's new,' she says by way of greeting, indicating the complicated brace on his knee.

He scowls. 'There's more damage than they thought. Have to wear this thing for six weeks, and Cole wants me working lighter duties until it's healed.'

'But then you'll be back?'

'I ... don't know.'

She hums, crossing her hands over her stomach. 'Go on.'

His eyes flick up to hers. 'Six weeks is a long time to live a different way. Slower days. More time with Jenny, with the girls.'

'Less time with me.'

'Already on the list of benefits.'

She smiles; he does, too. 'And what are you going to do?' he asks.

'What do you mean?'

'I know your face. Come on. What is it?'

For a second, she considers brushing him off. But then—

'I guess ... I don't know, either. I'm not quitting,' she says quickly. 'I know I still want to do this job. I love it, even when it hurts.' She blows out a breath. 'That has to mean something, right?'

She hadn't intended for the question to come out tinged with desperation; but because Richie is who he is, he just gazes at her thoughtfully, then out the window.

'I think ... it can be admirable to love something despite the pain it causes,' he says, watching the world pass by outside, 'but there has to be a cap on the hurt. And I've been doing this so long that I can feel that ceiling – my head is brushing it. But if you've still got room, and this is still something you *want* to do, then ...' He lifts his shoulder in a shrug. 'Just remember to reach up every so often.'

Then he smiles, an impish glint in his eyes. 'As much as I've tried to mould you in my image, George, in this scenario, I do *not* want you to grow up like me.'

'Christ, I don't want that either. I don't think I can pull off your haircut. You barely can.'

He laughs loudly, enough that the pair in suits look over curiously, then he nods at her untouched pint. 'You going to drink that?'

'Thought about it. *Really* thought about it.' She runs her forefinger down the curved glass, collecting the condensation. 'It's what we usually do, isn't it? A drink to close a case? And you've closed two – you should be drinking from the barrel.' She stares at the amber liquid. 'But …'

'But,' he echoes, 'the tradition doesn't feel right anymore, does it?'

She shakes her head. 'Guess I'll have to come up with something new. Besides, I'm back on the wagon. My therapist said I don't have to count being drugged as a slip, but I've restarted the clock anyway. I'm already dreading Lennox Christmas – usually, Mam and I would knock back a couple of whiskies to cope with the stress of having Dad and Jane under the same roof for two weeks. Now, I have to endure that completely sober.'

Richie's eyes brighten. 'That reminds me.' He slides the giftbag across the table. 'An early Christmas present.'

She examines the bag suspiciously, but the opening is taped shut. 'What is it?'

'The thing with presents, George, is that you have to *open* them to find out. But,' he says quickly, ignoring her withering look, 'open this one when you get home.'

'Is it a bomb? Is it a vibrator?'

His cheeks darken. 'Retirement is sounding better and better every second we're together, *Lennox*.' Then he raises his glass. 'Once more, for the end of the tradition?'

She picks up her own, meeting his in the middle of the table.

'Job well done, George,' he says quietly.

She smiles again. 'Job well done, Rich.'

And then, without drinking, they place their glasses down and rise.

In her flat, she takes the bag to her living room. Sitting on the floor beside the coffee table, she pulls out the box within. There's a logo on it, the silhouette of a black cat with its tail curled into the shape of a crescent moon. She decides to treat it as a bomb, and tentatively opens the lid.

A sheaf of paper rests on top of several loose items.

'You absolute bastard,' she mutters.

But extracting the paper, which informs her that the box contains a *Spell Kit for Curse Breaking*, she can't help laughing. Richie must have been cackling when he bought this: the box contains eight vials of crushed herbs and powders, three black candles, a glassy black rock, and something in an organza bag that smells strongly of rosemary. The paper has instructions, but it takes her three reads to understand the complicated combination and timing of each ingredient.

First and foremost, it says she needs a cauldron.

Her deepest saucepan will have to do.

She's fairly confident that Richie didn't expect her to actually do this, probably thought she'd just appreciate the laugh; even now, back on the floor with her pot and all of the vials laid out on the table in front of her, she feels silly. But she follows each step to the letter, double-checking before she proceeds to the next, lighting candles when she's told, adding powders and what she suspects are actually pizza toppings to the pot.

And then she's at the final step. With three puffs, she extinguishes the candles. Thin trails of smoke spiral up towards the ceiling, but if something else is meant to happen at the conclusion of the ritual – a flicker of lights, an eerie sound, a mystical breeze – she's disappointed. All she's left with are three goth candles and a pot full of watery Italian seasoning.

Perhaps it's more of an internal thing; maybe something tiny has shifted within her. Maybe whatever bad luck has been stalking her for the past … two years, really, has been snuffed out with the flames. She carries all of the items to the kitchen and tips the candles into the bin and the contents of the pot down the sink.

Her phone vibrates. Dumping the pot on the draining board, she opens the message.

You still owe me a story. And my coat.

Another vibration.

x

She smirks, and decides to let Hendry sweat for a while before she replies. And she will reply — a deal is a deal, after all.

Sliding her phone away, George leans her elbows on the counter and stares at the lily — now housed in a plastic ice cream container that she's poked holes into the bottom of. The plant was still looking pretty miserable when she got back from Kirkcree, and she tossed up whether it would be more of a kindness to just throw it in the bin. But instead she finally did what she should have done months ago.

The instructions she found online for caring for an indoor plant, much like the curse-breaking kit, were overly complex, with suggestions for different fertilisers and humidifiers and something called a grow lamp. But step one was simple enough.

Water it.

So every couple of days or so since then, while she waits for her coffee to brew, she pours a small cup of water into the ice cream container. It's a new ritual for her, and she's probably overdoing it … but now, looking at the glossy, perked-up leaves of the peace lily, it occurs to her what her new case-closing tradition should be — one of *beginning*, rather than *ending*. It's far more conducive to her sobriety — but probably far more damaging to her wallet, based on how much those grow lamps were selling for. She'll just have to locate the nearest nursery. And buy some better quality shelves.

Because she knows Richie is right: when the day comes when she can sense that ceiling of hurt brushing against her head, she should be prepared to call it quits.

But she's not there yet.

Not even close.

ACKNOWLEDGEMENTS

I considered kicking these acknowledgements off with something profound, but all that comes to mind is, 'Holy shit, I wrote a second book.' So, with that done, now I can get on to the thank yous – because publishing a book is an enormous team effort.

First (and always) to my sister, Olivia. You sit through story pitches and read first drafts (and seconds, and thirds) and are the final word on whether something is good or bad. You would also raze the Earth if I ever went missing, as I would for you.

Next up, thanks forevermore to my agent Tom Gilliatt of a4 Literary for your brilliant insights and unwavering faith. I'm also incredibly grateful to my UK agents, Rosie Pierce and Felicity Blunt of Curtis Brown, for securing this Scottish series a UK home.

Immense love to the HarperCollins Australia team: Anna Valdinger, Scott Forbes, Fiona Daniels, Pam Dunne, Darren Holt, and everyone who hustles so hard to get books into readers' hands. Much love also to the Hemlock Press team, Julia Wisdom, Lizz Burrell and Sean Garrehy, for your fantastic notes and outstanding work.

To my family and friends – as in *The Wolf Tree,* I sprinkled a few of your names in this book, but everyone else needs to hope I keep getting published if they want a turn. Thank you for supporting me through this whirlwind and letting me dip out of events because I have a deadline. I love you so, so much.

And finally, to you, the reader – thank you for following George and Richie into yet another storm. We'll see you in the next one.

If you enjoyed *The Cursed Road*, don't miss Laura McCluskey's gripping debut crime thriller...

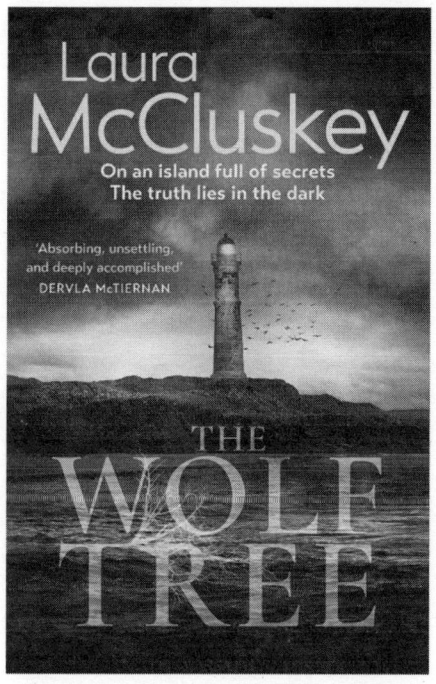

A mysterious death

On a small island off the coast of Scotland, an isolated community is grieving. Eighteen-year-old Alan Ferguson was found at the foot of the lighthouse – an apparent suicide.

Two detectives trapped on an island

DIs Georgina Lennox and Richard Stewart are sent to investigate. But a raging storm keeps them trapped on the island for four days. And the locals don't take kindly to mainlanders.

A village full of suspects

As George and Richie question the island's inhabitants, they discover a village filled with superstition and shrouded in secrets.